ONE

Private detective Claire Morgan has come home from the Keys, just in time for Christmas at Lake of the Ozarks. And for the sheriff's department, laid low with flu, to hand her a case guaranteed to chill her to the bone.

ONE CHANCE TO DIE

One of the homes in the local Christmas On the Lake House tour—the mansion of an aging rock star trying to turn his life around—has been "decorated" with the body of a young woman, arranged as a bloody angel on the balcony above his Christmas tree. There's a piece from a board game, gift wrapped and left under the tree, a hint that connects this murder to other deaths. With evidence of a gruesome pattern appearing, Claire suspects she's on the hunt for a serial killer.

IN A GAME WITH NO RULES

But the closer she comes, the more certain she is that the killer is playing his game with her, just waiting his turn. The next move might be on Claire herself—or worse, the people she loves . . .

FATAL GAME

Claire Morgan Investigations

Linda Ladd

LYRICAL PRESS
Kensington Publishing Corp.
www.kensingtonbooks.com

Lyrical Press books are published by
Kensington Publishing Corp. 119 West 40th Street New York, NY 10018

All Kensington titles, imprints, and distributed lines are available at special quantity discounts for bulk purchases for sales promotion, premiums, fund-raising, and educational or institutional use.

Special book excerpts or customized printings can also be created to fit specific needs. For details, write or phone the office of the Kensington Special Sales Manager:
Kensington Publishing Corp.
119 West 40th Street
New York, NY 10018
Attn. Special Sales Department. Phone: 1-800-221-2647.

Kensington and the K logo Reg. U.S. Pat. & TM Off.
LYRICAL PRESS Reg. U.S. Pat. & TM Off.
Lyrical Press and the L logo are trademarks of Kensington Publishing Corp.

First Electronic Edition: December 2017
eISBN-13: 978-1-60183-860-5
eISBN-10: 1-60183-860-3

First Print Edition: December 2017
ISBN-13: 978-1-60183-861-2
ISBN-10: 1-60183-861-1

Printed in the United States of America

Books by Linda Ladd

Claire Morgan Homicide Thrillers
Head to Head
Dark Places
Die Smiling
Enter Evil
Remember Murder
Mostly Murder
Bad Bones

Claire Morgan Investigations Series
Devil Dead
Gone Black
Fatal Game

Will Novak Novels
Bad Road to Nowhere
Say Your Goodbyes

Published by Kensington Publishing Corp.

Prologue

Play Time

The weather was absolute perfection. The sun blazed high in the sky, a bright fiery disk in an otherwise vast, cloudless blue dome that stretched up and down the coast from Malibu to Santa Barbara. California—the land of plenty, the land of movie stars, the land of milk and honey. Unfortunately for Junior, it was also the land of hell. Heaving a gigantic sigh, he dropped his head back against the red cushion of the double chaise longue and stared at his swimming pool. The azure water looked like a super clear blue mirror. After that, he shut his eyes so he wouldn't have to see the woman who was floating in the shallow end. Living the good life in Beverly Hills wasn't all that good, of course. At least, not for him. Other than his mom, Junior loved almost everything about it. She scored at the low end of his things-to-enjoy ladder; in fact, she dropped off the bottom rung into his very own black pool of abject hatred.

Even worse, she was planning to stay home all day, no doubt in order to enjoy making his life super-duper miserable. He supposed that her endless charity affairs were not being offered today, ritzy venues in which she could show off her five-million-plus Botox injections, annual face-lifts, and liposuction procedures. When he heard water sloshing, he opened his eyes and lifted his new Dolce & Gabbana sunglasses. Mommy dearest was splashing water over her bare legs, immersed in her usual despicable display of female vanity. She had turned over onto her back now, naked but for the itty-bitty bikini bottom, just out there displaying her reconstructed body on a blue raft. No ugly tan lines to mar her ultra-short, low-cut dresses. She was topless, and boozing it up big time. You name it, she slurped it down: beer, whiskey, vodka, gin, vermouth. Anything and everything. But her poison of choice had always been a martini on the rocks, with a twist of lemon and three olives speared onto one of her designer toothpicks, the ones she ordered out of Monaco that sported a tiny yellow tassel on the end. That's what she was guzzling today. A whole pitcher full so far, in fact. She was pretty much as lit as a Hollywood marquee, but she could hold her booze with the best of them. Junior would give her that much credit.

Good old mom had a cocktail glass in her hand right now. She considered the olives her brunch, lunch, and dinner and the lemon her vitamin C. Yep, Mom was now in her mid-fifties, a freakin' lush, for damn sure, but she didn't look near that old. Basically, she was a carbon copy of all the other divorced Beverly Hills first wives, whose husbands had left them for twenty-something lovers or more beautiful and conniving gold-digging second wives. Mom took good care of her body, yes she did, which was her only ambition of late, and her whiz-bang plastic surgeon made lots of money turning her into a fake and forever thirty-something. Her skin was every bit as smooth as the Chinese silk in her movie premiere gowns, glistening with sunblock that smelled like coconuts and lime. Another deep desire of mommy: acquire the best spray-on tan in her exclusive country club and tennis club and book club and French cuisine class and pseudo charity, aka look-at-me-everybody L.A. havens of big money.

While she bobbed around for useless hours in the pool, she hummed and sang along with her favorite music, which she listened to through white earbuds. It was turned up loud enough for Junior to hear faint strains of Maroon 5 singing "She Will Be Loved." But that was a laugh. She wasn't loved. Not by anybody, not even him, and he was her only child. Her money was loved, though, that was for damn sure, and there was plenty of it to covet, mainly by Junior and all the young, buff lovers she picked up in bars and brought home for one-night stands. Nope, not only did Junior not love her, he had graduated to sheer abhorrence. She just looked so utterly content out there on that float, well into drunken oblivion. There was just a little bit of booze left in the pitcher that sat on the round, glass-topped table shaded by three towering palm trees.

Okay, now the sun was really broiling. Junior loved the burn of it on his bare skin. He had dark skin, anyway, and had always tanned easily. Now eighteen, he could drink legally at home, and his mom sure as hell didn't care if he imbibed or not. But he didn't. Well, not much, anyway. He was too intelligent to turn himself into some kind of stinking sot. He didn't like feeling out of control of his mind, unsure of what he did or didn't do. He watched his mother drain her glass, then pull the olives off the toothpick with her teeth. After that, she carelessly tossed the stemmed Waterford glass out into the water, lemon twist, toothpick, and all. No telling how much of that crap his mom's pool boy/lover had to fish out at the end of the day. Probably enough to clog the drain. Then her phone buzzed, yet again, and she quickly jerked out the earbuds and picked up the phone off her flat belly. God, he really did despise her. More anger built up inside him every day, each time he saw her floating around out there, completely ignoring him, as she'd done since he was a little kid.

Disgusted by her, Junior took off his sunglasses, grabbed a towel, and scrubbed sweat off his face and chest, getting pretty riled up inside, pulse racing, but trying not to let his mom see his inner turmoil. If she detected how much he resented her power over him, she'd cut off his allowance again. Sometimes she did it just for spite. No reason. Just to teach him a lesson about nothing. Now she was getting one phone call after another. All probably about some stupid Hollywood gossip that didn't amount to a hill of beans to anybody except her rich, shallow, and self-centered girlfriends.

Junior closed his eyes again. She had to be the biggest bitch in a town full of selfish bitches. She treated him, her only son, her only child, like dog crap on the bottoms of her Christian Louboutin heels, which she even wore at the pool with her bikini. Hell, she treated the damn pool boy ten times better than him. But that was because he was the fabled L.A. pool boy with benefits, and he followed her around like a puppy, besotted with her cash and an easy lay.

Shielding his eyes with the flat of his hand, Junior searched the shady depths of the patio for the pool kid. For obvious reasons, he didn't particularly like the guy. Yep, old Lucky was a real jerk. Junior supposed he did get lucky, at least with Junior's mom, and nearly every day. Junior and Lucky were seniors at the same private school, but they rarely ran into each other. They moved in totally different cliques. Junior was the smartest kid in the school, a real nerd. He was proud of that. He wore the egghead badge with honor, because he was intelligent enough to see how stupid all the other kids were, and that knowledge came in handy in a myriad of ways.

Most of the other teenagers had little clue about anything, other than how to screw each other and screw each other over. He liked to study their habits, as if they were his lab specimens that belonged to a lower and rather ignorant species. That way, he knew pretty much everything about everybody, including what made them tick. That gave him leverage if he should ever want or need it, and Junior did like to wield power over the other kids at school. Didn't matter who. Anybody, really.

On the other hand, Lucky was the best jock in school, a total chick magnet. His tuition was paid with a walk-on football scholarship. Nobody knew much about him, other than the fact that his parents were dead. Brains didn't make an appearance much where he was concerned, but that was to be expected. He was a moronic jock. They had never spoken a single word to each other, not even when they passed each other in the hall outside his mom's bedroom. Distaste, disrespect, and a mutual disgust. They were not two peas in a pod.

Today, Lucky, aka Mom's gigolo, had pulled off his T-shirt, a move most likely designed to titillate good old, sex-starved Momma. It didn't take much, especially when she was soused. Lucky had on long red surfer shorts, the kind that hung just below his knees, and a pair of ridiculous brown leather Jesus sandals. He was really tall, well over six feet, super athletic, and tanned to a beautiful bronze. Strong as a bull, or so it appeared. He had penetrating eyes, a sculpted, muscular body, and a molded six-pack that Junior envied. Junior was in fairly good shape himself, but he was shorter and certainly didn't look like a Greek god when he took off his shirt. Not that he was jealous of anything else about Lucky. The other guy might be a sports star and a lover boy, but Junior didn't give a rip about that. It was rather astonishing, though, that Lucky really was so lucky.

Yes, sir, when said Superman played basketball, he racked up the most points and looked great doing it. Graceful, even. Probably didn't even sweat. When he ran track or jumped hurdles, he won all the medals and ribbons. No problemo, simply observe featured game and proceed to conquer. Like when he wanted the most gorgeous, sexiest girl in school; well, shit, easy pickings for a guy like Lucky. All the girls fell at his feet and kissed his dumbass sandals he wore everywhere. Lucky was the high school cock of the walk, all right. Junior pretty much ignored him as a mental peon until he walked right into Junior's house and had sex with Junior's drunken mother.

Alas, Junior had no such good fortune in Lucky's areas of expertise. But he still came out on top of their dual equation, because he had an absolutely brilliant mind. His strengths were cerebral logic, ingenuity, and photographic memory. In fact, he was a damn near genius. His teachers and counselors praised him regularly and acted all awestruck and impressed by his superb intellect, especially with math and physics. And well they should. They were all a bit on the stupid side, truth be told. He had tons of trivia and scholastic team trophies down in the basement, where he lived inside his own personal and giant domain, a spectacular bedroom/library/game room. His mom allowed him lone access down there, his private area that opened up with his one key, but she didn't fool him, not one bit. She didn't want him upstairs, where she entertained her influx of lovers.

More likely, they entertained her for the wad of cash she stuck down their pants on their way out of her bedroom.

Lucky the Unlucky Lover was how Junior liked to think of the pool boy. He was busy flirting with Junior's mom at the moment, and was she ever lapping up his cloying and clumsy amorous attentions. Almost as much as she lapped up her pitchers of martinis. She made no secret of the fact that she preferred Lucky's company to Junior's, and she was doing the same thing now, laughing and flirting with him as he cleaned the pool, one tiny scrap from naked, with no shame. She usually tipped him big time for pulling a palm frond out of the water, and then invited him for dinner as if he wasn't a servant. On those nights, Junior retreated to his basement sanctuary and left them to their romantic tryst, or whatever the hell they liked to call it. Blind animal copulation was what Junior called it. Sickening, but run of the mill for mom. She slept with every Tom, Dick, and tennis instructor in L.A. County. It was a mental illness with her, or a million-man march.

Lucky stood over in the shade of a palm tree and pretended to dip debris out of the pool with a long-handled net. What he really was doing was lusting after Junior's mom. His eyes lingered on her body the entire time. He was salivating. Man, get a room already. Jerk. Mom knew what he was doing, too. She bent her knees and opened her legs so he could better see what he wanted. Typical slut behavior. Might as well walk the stroll down on Hollywood Boulevard. Not that she needed money. When his famous dad had walked out on them when Junior was six, he gave her their huge estate and an ultra-generous divorce settlement. Sole custody of his son, too. Junior had never seen him again. Not on his birthdays, not on a single Christmas, never had laid eyes on the man again, and never had forgiven him for that. Oh yeah, Junior had hit the grand jackpot when it came to lousy parents.

Clamping his jaw, Junior poked his sunglasses back on and tried not to look at his mom and Lucky. Let them ogle each other. Do what they would. But he was going to stay right there so they couldn't get it on in the pool the way they wanted. He'd already caught Lucky inside his mom's bedroom a couple of times. The guy had just grinned at Junior and shut the door in his face.

Out in the pool, he heard one of his dad's songs come on his mom's earphones. She still played his music, probably because she knew half the royalties were trickling down to her. His dad was famous, a legendary rock star, but also a crazy, tattooed, womanizing, drug-addled disgrace of a human being. But those songs he wrote, the ones about death and destruction and doom, brought in tons of money, each and every day, just like clockwork. Junior assumed his mom's divorce lawyer had been better than his dad's back then, so there was a never-ending stream of cash to replenish his mom's bulging bank accounts.

Hell, his runaway dad was more famous than Ozzy Osbourne and Mick Jagger put together. Better singer, too. A wasted drug addict, for sure, but even he'd had the sense to see his first wife for a whoring gold digger. But hey, no problem. He had paid her off and then shrugged Junior off like a coat that was too small. All the hell Junior wanted now was a decent allowance like all the other kids at school got from their rich showbiz parents. But his mom eked out the dough as if they lived in a slum. He had to do chores to get his weekly money. Imagine that.

Man alive, he really did hate her guts.

Chapter 1

Beautiful snowflakes were fluttering down all around Detective Claire Morgan Black as she walked up the sidewalk toward the rear entrance of Cedar Bend Lodge. It still seemed strange to have tied the marital knot with Nicholas Black, something she'd sworn she'd never do. But the die was cast and turning out to be one of the best moves she'd ever made. So far, anyway. She walked slowly along, enjoying the magical winter wonderland into which Black had transformed his luxury resort on the Lake of the Ozarks. Her former partner, Bud Davis, had only just now dropped her off behind the hotel after they'd spent a long day working homicide together at the Canton County Sheriff's Department.

The flu bug had slammed the lake environs big time this year, and Claire had agreed to temporarily fill in at Homicide. Even Sheriff Charlie Ramsay had been laid low with the illness, along with a good portion of his staff. Schools had been shut down because of illness in some communities. Good thing Black had insisted on giving Claire her flu shot early. Although work today hadn't been particularly eventful, she felt tired. No homicides turned up, thank goodness, so they had mainly rifled through dusty cold cases from days gone by, murders committed long before either of them knew Canton County existed. Not many incoming calls, either. It appeared that most people at the lake were too busy Christmas shopping to whack anybody.

At the moment, she was cold, and more than ready to make it upstairs where Black and Rico were probably waiting for her. She swiped her card through the sensor and let herself into a downstairs corridor that would take her to the private penthouse elevator. Since her sweetie pie new husband owned the hotel and everything in it, she received many a perk, and there were plenty to enjoy. Claire supposed it was her hotel now, too, since he'd readily put all his holdings in both their names. Not that she wanted to be saddled with all his stuff. She still didn't feel comfortable with all that "what's mine is yours" crap—not yet, anyhow. Pulling off her departmental brown knit cap and scarf and gloves, she headed down the deserted hallway, leaving a trail of snowy footprints on the expensive red carpet. Oh well, snow would melt. When she reached Cedar Bend's rather lavish front lobby, she paused in the big archway and beheld enough Christmas cheer to knock one's boots off.

Cedar Bend Lodge had always been an unbelievably elegant, gorgeous five-star hotel, albeit in its own rustic sort of way. Today it was even more so. The row of giant crystal chandeliers fought off shadows cast by the heavy snow clouds building a gray shroud that hung low and threatening over the lake. At least a thousand crystal prisms sparkled bright pinpoints of light, and the bejeweled cut glass in the huge front doors reflected spots of color across the black and gold carpet. A wall of floor-to-ceiling windows presented Black's guests with a gorgeous view of Lake of the Ozarks, which at the moment looked dark and foreboding and restless—a black and white snow-frozen tableau. It was still beautiful, though not quite as much as its glittering blue sheen under the hot summer sun. Still a sight welcome to Claire's eyes, though, after their long Hawaiian honeymoon.

It was Christmas, after all, and did Claire ever love this time of year. Always had. Not as much as Black did, of course. Her guy had gone absolutely Christmas crazy this year. She stood back and beheld about fifty thousand blinking white and red and green and blue Christmas lights that covered just about everything not nailed down inside the lobby. It was a scene captured nearly everywhere else on the Cedar Bend grounds, too. Yep, nobody did Christmas like Nicholas Black. His holiday spirit made its appearance on nearly everything inside and outside of the hotel if he could find a way to attach it, and he usually did, by hell or high water.

Festoons of pine and pinecones and holly berries and shiny gold Christmas balls lit up the mantels, the bannisters, the tables, the reception desk, and up the bannisters and across the balconies, with pine wreaths everywhere, all of which gave off the most delicious evergreen scent that wafted around in the heater currents and made her feel as if she lived deep in the magical Black Forest. He had ordered Christmas trees put up, all pines, because he loved pine trees. So pine trees of every size and shape imaginable were carried in and decorated, crowned off, of course, by the majestic, towering thirty-foot super tree dead center in the front lobby. Lights had come on and the holidays were sparkling everywhere, and when Black was giving the orders, that really meant *everywhere.*

Claire stood a moment and smiled at the sheer joy of yonder old-fashioned and folksy Christmas, with all those lights and the twin giant rock fireplaces ablaze with huge logs and happy guests sitting around on leather couches and rocking chairs while sipping hot chocolate or warm apple cider, compliments of the hotel. Home sweet home it truly was, at least until her cabin on her own quiet cove across the lake was finished and ready for them to move back in. She missed the solitude of her place sometimes, no doubt about that, but it did not hold even a fraction of the Christmas cheer inside Cedar Bend Lodge, due to all those bottomless credit cards of her very own and dearly beloved.

Claire was super glad to be home, but it had been great to see all her former colleagues at the sheriff's office this past week. She had missed that kind of law enforcement camaraderie since she'd gone into private investigation with her partner Will Novak. The best part of this week was spending a ton of time with Bud Davis, one of her best friends in the world. Bud and Sheriff Ramsay both. Her badge was back in place, hanging around her neck on its chain. Her Glock 19 was snug in the shoulder holster under her brown winter parka, and her .38 snub nose was strapped in place on her right ankle. Just to be safe, of course. All of that felt familiar, and damn good, oh yes, sir, it did. The office had been so quiet, and nobody in Homicide was complaining. Zero murders or attempted murders were a pleasant thing in Claire's book.

Black should be upstairs, waiting for her, with all the fireplaces in the penthouse roaring. Yep, Black liked his real log fires as much as his Christmas trees. They had enjoyed a long and lovely leisurely honeymoon on the island of Kauai, but she loved the lake more, and just about everything that went with it, so she was in highly content at the moment. Couldn't possibly be happier, in fact. The lake was her true home now, her own private and peaceful haven, and its beautiful wooded hills protected her from the outside world and all the evils that she'd found there. So all was good and fine and beautiful, and she was definitely a happy camper on this lovely snowy day.

Claire took a moment to shrug off her parka and kick snow out of her boot treads. That's when she first espied the horror awaiting her at the other end of the lobby—a large throng of paparazzi. They congregated near the bar and the fancy Two Cedars restaurant. She quickly ducked back out of sight. The last thing she needed was for them to see her and give chase. Her high good cheer zoomed down to the floor and lay prostrate, groaning. Good grief, there were cameras everywhere, already attached to tripods, microphones tested and clutched tightly in grubby little annoying hands. Damnation. What the hell was going on?

Those bloodsuckers had not been at the hotel when Claire left that morning for work, but she guessed she shouldn't be surprised. Photographers had been dogging her and Black since their wedding day, due to the fact that he was *the* Nicholas Black, the handsome shrink to Hollywood stars and other rich and famous ilk, including philandering politicos. Not to mention the super big and life-threatening trouble he'd gotten himself into last summer. That had been the serious kind, which had delayed their wedding and whipped up the media into pure hysteria, a journalistic furor like you wouldn't believe.

The same creepy gaggle of photographers had trailed them out into the mid-Pacific and drifted around in boats off the private villa where she and Black had attempted to enjoy a nice, quiet time alone so they could lick their collective wounds. After the newlyweds spent a couple of weeks inside, off of their lovely private honeymoon beach, most of the reporters had given up and hightailed it home for their next celebrity stakeout, thanks be to God. Now, however, they were back in force, and she didn't like it. Hated it, in fact. Black was gonna like it even less. He'd had it up to his very sky-blue eyes with publicity and the way both of them had been hounded night and day.

Claire slipped into her parka again and flipped up the hood. She averted her face so the tabloid vultures wouldn't recognize her. There had to be at least fifty of them milling around. Yep, like the hyenas they were, circling a wounded gnu; Claire, of course, being that gnu. But why now? What the hell had happened? And this close to Christmas? Jeez, she loathed them all right, each and every one, no exceptions. Seemed as if they'd been chasing her forever for one reason or another, but her life had pretty much been a super terrible horror story from birth, so she could understand their macabre interest.

Still, she just wanted them to go away, disappear, never to return, and good riddance. They were disturbing Black's guests and the holiday magic he'd worked so hard to provide for them. Black wasn't going to like that much, either, and that was not good. He had been in one hell of a great mood since they'd gotten married, and he'd managed to push down the memories of the terrible things done to him last summer. In fact, since they'd recited their vows, he'd been as happy as a first-time kid at Disney World.

What's more, he had a trip to Disney World planned for New Year's Eve so that Rico could have some fun. Rico was a ten-year-old boy they'd rescued last summer during that horrendous fiasco with the Soquet family of criminal monsters, and he was the only good thing to come out of their Sicilian dark adventure from hell. Rico was living with them now, and Claire was happy he was. He had become an orphan last summer in one terrible moment, and they had brought him home with them. Black was trying to find any of the boy's remaining living relatives, but secretly both he and Claire hoped he could just stay with them. So far, so good on that count. Another thing that brought out lots of Black's big, happy, dimpled-up smiles, something that she did so like to see.

Right now, however, she wasn't so sure what the hell was going on. Something big must have happened to draw these creeps back into their lives. Lake of the Ozarks was not exactly a hot spot for paparazzi or celebrities preening for cameras, unless said celebrities had come to Cedar Bend for secret shrink attention at Black's clinic. Unfortunately, each and every reporter in the lobby looked way too agog and excited for something as simple as that. Never a good sign in Claire and Black-ville. She wasn't so sure she wanted to know what brought them running, either. Usually when the media showed up and created havoc it meant incoming big-time trouble for her and Black, and everybody associated with them. So now the trick was to escape upstairs before they caught sight of her. She kept her head down and walked swiftly toward the penthouse elevator.

One of Black's security people, a huge ex-Marine by the name of Isaac Ward, was standing in front of the elevator. He was as tough as hell and massive, with lots of hard muscles, and probably one of the nicest guys Claire had ever met. When he saw her coming, he pushed the button to open the doors, apparently also aware of the crowd of morons buzzing around in the lobby.

"Thanks, Isaac. What's with all the reporters out there? I thought we shook them off months ago."

Isaac grinned. He was a handsome man with ebony skin, and he was pretty damn intimidating whenever the occasion called for it. Truth be told, he was a real teddy bear under all that gruff, a guy who loved to play video games with Rico. But that sweetness only showed if he really liked somebody. Fortunately, he liked Claire. He said, "I take it you haven't talked to Nick yet."

"Well, I did have some delicious blueberry pancakes and whipped cream with him and Rico this morning. Everything was all good and dandy and smiley then. What happened?"

Isaac shook his head, smiling again, rather devilishly this time, as she entered the elevator. "Uh-uh. No way I'm gettin' caught up in this thing. You'll see. Word of warning, though. Nick is in one helluva foul mood."

"No way, Isaac. He's been in a fantastic mood, ever since we got back home."

"Like I said, I'm not sayin' nothin'. You ask him. Just beware the dragon." Claire had to smile. "Well, thanks for the warning. Maybe I ought to go hide at my cabin until he gets over his miff, whatever the hell it is."

Isaac kept his mysterious expression. All righty, now Claire's curiosity was indeed piqued. Black had been absolutely ecstatic and happy-go-lucky for months now, especially since they got home and he was seeing patients and ramrodding all his clinics and hotel properties around the country. And especially now that they were legally married, which was what Black had always wanted. The icing on the cake? A certain little Rico, who was running around the penthouse, always available for Black to dote on and shower with Star Wars junk. Things at the lake had finally gotten back to normal, if anything about their lives had ever been normal. News coverage had died down about their wedding, and about Black being held prisoner by those three maniacs. He was happy. She was happy. Rico was as happy as any child could be after having watched his parents gunned down. The boy still had nightmares, and so did Black because of a tiny bit of lingering PTSD, but it was rare now. He was good. They were both good. Black had even been in favor of her going back to work at Homicide, which he usually hated. Life was damn good. She wasn't gonna let anything get in the way of that. Not today. Not any day.

When the doors of their penthouse apartment slid open with a whisper of well-oiled efficiency, Claire stepped out and nearly collided with Black's longtime personal assistant, Miki Tudor. The young woman looked spooked, but somehow still managed to come off lovely and put together in a pink designer suit and matching high heels. Ms. Miki never had ruffled feathers. She was much too efficient and organized to let anything discombobulate her. Today, however, she was definitely rattled. There was even one loose lock hanging out of the smooth chignon coiled at her nape. Not a good sign, that.

"I'm calling it a day until Nick calms down," she told Claire breathlessly, pushing past her and stepping into the elevator. "I'll be back in the morning. I'm taking some comp time. I'm caught up, though, so don't worry about things getting behind."

Claire sure as hell wasn't worried about that. "What the devil, Miki? What's going on around here?"

"You don't know yet?"

"Well, I guess not. I've been holed up at the sheriff's office all day. Tell me."

"Oh no, I'm staying out of this. Ask your husband. But be forewarned: ask him gently."

Claire turned quickly when she heard somebody running down the hallway behind them, boots clacking loudly on the marble tiles. It was Rico, and he looked glad to see her. Their little white poodle, Jules Verne, was right on his heels, yapping like crazy, his claws clicking and sliding on the shiny floor as he tried to keep up. Boy and dog had become inseparable since Rico had come to live with them. Rico stopped long enough to give Claire a quick hug around the waist. He was tall for his age, with energy to burn. He was smart as could be, a handsome kid with an unruly mop of curly dark hair and big, expressive brown eyes.

"Nick's really mad, but not at me, so I'm going down to the sweet shop to get some candy canes to hang on our tree," he told her, but didn't elaborate further as he scooped up the dog and raced into the elevator with Miki. The door slid shut with no explanation.

Claire looked down the hall toward Black's office wing. Okay, enough was enough. Guess it was up to her to calm the raging beast. Great. And the day had been so peaceful thus far—except for the media hounds downstairs. But if Black was raising Cain over something, enough that Rico and Isaac and Miki were scattering like spooked chickens, then she was going to have to make him stop with the drama and take a couple of deep breaths. She headed toward his office, walking at a fast clip, now intrigued more than anything else.

Chapter 2

This kind of childish behavior from her newly designated husband was downright unheard of. Black rarely ever got angry. Or at least, he didn't show it openly. After all, he was a crack clinical and forensic psychiatrist. He didn't do furious or knock-down-drag-out much. Never, in fact. On the rare occasions he became livid, usually with her, he didn't show it outright, except for a mighty grinding of teeth and flexing of jaw. Other than that, he was pretty much Mr. Sangfroid of the Universe. Yep, he was all kinds of calm and studied reserve, no matter how angry he got, and that was a penchant that at times bugged the absolute hell out of Claire, especially when she was highly aggravated about something. He had been trained not to react to anything his psychologically challenged patients threw at him, but to remain calm, calm, and even more calm. It was irritating, really.

Even when they had their up-close-and-personal disagreements, which were few and far between, it was Claire who got all bent out of shape and lost her temper and yelled, not Black. Never him. It was infuriating how he could just sit and watch her pace and jump his case and fume without it getting under his skin. And he was overly generous to his staff, too, and they all loved him and were dedicated and loyal. So that meant whatever this thing was, it had to be quite a slam-bam, explode-in-your-face, awful kind of deal. Black was the most in control human being she'd ever met. Otherwise, he couldn't put up with her. Truth be told, she had never really seen him rage around, even when he was furious. When he was exasperated with her, he got real slow, his movements got deadly and his blue eyes glowed intense with anger, but he never let it loose on anyone. Especially over something business related. He just made a thoughtful decision and told somebody to make it happen.

So chances were this wasn't going to be a fun evening decorating the tree, smiling and smooching. Maybe the honeymoon was now over, and she was going to see his dark side that he had kept hidden until he put a ring on it. And if sweet little Rico, who was now the absolute apple of Black's eye, if that kid was heading for the hills with the family dog, something was definitely amiss in their happy little penthouse home.

Before she reached Black's office, Claire heard something crash to the ground. Great. Now what? Black was throwing things? Seriously? Come on. Get real. Black's office door was standing wide open, and Claire stopped in the threshold. Black was standing in front of the fireplace, his back to her, staring down into the dancing flames, completely motionless, the absolute picture of his usual unruffled self. Just like always. Serene and looking smokin' hot as hell, of course. He had on a black pinstriped business suit, a crisp white shirt, and, no doubt, a silk tie straight out of Hong Kong. She had snagged a sexy guy, all right. She looked around and found that the room was not destroyed. Black's weird Picasso was still hanging on the wall behind his desk, its one bulbous eye staring back at her. Lord have mercy, she hated that ugly thing. His lamp and blotter sat undisturbed atop his desk. Lots of magazines and newspapers were spread around on the desktop and coffee table, which was unusual but certainly no catastrophe. Black was a neat person, took care of his stuff. Maybe his crazy fit of anger had been exaggerated. Maybe he was waxing serene again. Then, while she watched, he suddenly turned around, leaned against the desk, and hit the desktop with both fists before swiping all the magazines and papers off with one swipe. They all landed on the floor, with pages rustling and fluttering, and Black let loose a string of low Cajun curses that would make a prison guard blush. Whoa. Okay, something was indeed amiss in paradise. Claire stepped inside the room and shut the door. She put her hands on her hips and stared at his back.

"What the hell's going on with you, Black?"

He spun around, still frowning massively, his face flushed with anger. Slightly shocked by that alone, she returned his glare. It appeared he was acting like a giant baby. As incomprehensible as that was, it was certainly something she'd never seen before. Nicholas Black? Petulant? Never in a million years. She could barely believe it was happening. Maybe she should just enjoy his childishness while she had the chance. Oh yes, he did so love to remind her that she should always resort to positive energy and self-control when she was furious and ranting about something. To quote the good doctor: "Remaining calm is the best way to handle one's problems. Anger never helps anybody right a wrong." Blah, blah, blah, and more stupid blah. She liked anger. It burned away the hard knots that had a tendency to lump up inside her chest. Better than holding everything inside. Yeah, right. Shrink platitudes. *Let's hear that from you today, my furious love,* she thought.

Black's face was forebodingly dark, probably from unbridled wrath. Or maybe it was embarrassment. He was pretty much perfect, but he could still feel humiliated at times, when Claire took it upon herself to point out a shortcoming. "Well, it's about time you got back," he snapped, narrowing his eyes. "I need to talk to you. Where have you been so long?"

Okay, now that just went all over Claire. She had never been one to let something stupid pass without comment. "Excuse me? Who the bloody hell do you think you're talking to here? Hey, I know what. I'm going to clear out of here and go back to the sheriff's office and let you be ignorant all by yourself. Just like everybody else has already done, including Rico."

Black's face immediately changed. *Uh oh, overplayed my ire,* he was no doubt thinking. It took a few seconds for him to get himself back in control. Wow, he really was super angry. He just stood there, staring at her, obviously working hard to calm his overheated engines. Claire watched and waited without comment. He was highly perturbed and didn't mind showing it. Now he displayed the usual telltale signs, gritting teeth and clenching jaw. He knew better than to jump her case any more than he already had, but his next words didn't sound all that conciliatory. "Okay, so I'm sorry, Claire, but you apparently don't know what's going on here."

"Yeah, you got that right, Black. That's what everybody I met told me, too. So how about you quit acting like a big jerk and fill me in. Nobody else wanted to tell me what has you so pissed. So go ahead, get it off your chest." Claire tossed her jacket over the back of the couch, not taking her eyes off his face. Then she sat down on the sofa, crossed her legs, and waited for him to spring whatever horrible news was making him go nutcase. It would be the first catastrophic thing that had happened to them in quite a while. Since last summer, in fact. Once Black had slipped that wedding ring on her finger and they'd both remained alive and well after their wedding, he had been the picture of masculine contentment. But not anymore, it appeared. This display of temper was pretty much "Nicholas Black and the Terrible, Horrible, No Good, Very Bad Day," or so it seemed. Claire crossed her arms and waited, now a trifle edgy herself.

Black took a minute to tamp down more rage, but his voice was still tight with anger. "Sweetheart, go ahead, sit there and look all calm and relaxed. But let's see if you stay that way after you get a load of these magazines. Then we'll see if I'm overreacting."

Scooping up a magazine off the floor, he strode quickly across the room and tossed it onto her lap. Presenting him with a withering stare so he would realize that he was really grating on her nerves, she picked it up. It was the latest edition of *People* magazine. The cover displayed a full-length body shot of Black. He stood on a beach, wearing white swim trucks, sporting a dark tan, hands on his hips, black hair slicked straight back, his six-pack as molded as steel coils. His bluer-than-blue eyes were gazing out to sea, and he had a smile on his face, all his killer dimples dug in deep and alive and sexy as hell. For a moment she just enjoyed the view, because he was her husband now, after all, and quite the catch. Then she realized the photo had been taken on their honeymoon beach in Kauai. Belatedly, the headline across the top of the page registered in her mind. *Psychiatrist Nicholas Black. Sexiest Man Alive.*

Claire was stunned. Didn't take long, though, for her to see the humor in the situation. She looked up at him and laughed, which turned out to be a trigger.

Black muttered a foul word under his breath but didn't throw anything or slap her. Lucky for him. "I cannot believe that you find this amusing, Claire." He shook his head and paced a few steps toward her. "How can you laugh? This is not only embarrassing for me, it's ridiculous. I'm a psychiatrist and a businessman. That picture makes me look like some kind of...some kind of...I don't know what. But I don't like it. And I don't like it being plastered out in public."

Claire tried but couldn't stop grinning. "C'mon, Black, get a grip here. It's not as if they are accusing you of murder—which has happened in the past, if you recall. This is an honor, I guess, sort of. Look at the bright side. If you are the sexiest man alive, thousands—I mean, millions of women will be panting after you."

"Ha, ha." Black leveled his intense gaze on her. "And you're telling me you like that idea? Women panting after me?"

Now that he brought it up, Claire decided she didn't like it so much. Huh uh. But, oh well. She tried not to crack a smile. It was hard not to. "It's done now. Nothing you can do about it. And you *are* the sexiest man alive. Oh, and by the way, the lobby is now full of impatient paparazzi wanting to talk to Mr. Sexpot, I presume. It's like they're having a convention down there. Why don't you put on those white swim trunks and go down and talk to them?"

Another string of low curse words that she luckily couldn't hear. "I can't believe you're okay with that ridiculous article. I do not want that stupid title, whatever the hell it even means. They did not ask my permission to publish my picture on their cover. My private life is just that: private. And you know why. That's the way I like it. That's the way I want it. We do not need this complication, Claire. I'm going to sue the hell out of them."

"No, you're not. You're going to ignore it and pretend it didn't happen. For Pete's sake, Black, you are really getting bent all out of shape over nothing. It's just the cover of a stupid magazine. You're not nude or anything. You do have on a swimsuit." Claire looked down at the magazine again and thought back to the honeymoon, how they did have some rather romantic fun in the surf a couple of times. She looked back at him, becoming a mite concerned herself. "Do you think they have one of us? You know, out in the water?"

"Oh my God, can this get any worse? I do not need to be the laughingstock of the AMA, of which I am now vice president, if you'll remember. You and I have both had enough publicity in the past, most all of it bad. Strike that—all of it was bad. Hell, they're still publicizing our wedding pictures, and they have to go and do this?"

"Yes, but we gave permission on the wedding photo thing, and donated the money to your mental health charities. We only gave them a couple, and we've got all our clothes on in them, so all's good on that front." Claire stopped, realizing that he really was über-upset and not getting over it. Time to be sweet and understanding. "Okay, listen, Black, I get it. I don't blame you for being furious about this. I wouldn't like it, either. Truthfully, I don't like it. But you know what? You are overreacting to this, big time, in a way that I've never seen you do before. Maybe you should take one of those little white anxiety pills that you prescribe to me when I get all crazy and bent out of shape. Not that I've ever taken them."

"Oh really? And I guess you're okay with the pictures of you, too?"

Claire stiffened. "What do you mean? What pictures of me?"

It was Black's turn to laugh, but he wasn't amused and he turned it off pretty damn fast. He walked back to the desk and picked a newspaper up off the floor. "Take a good look at this cover and see if you think that's nothing to be concerned about. Let's just see how you feel when it's you out there for everybody and their dog to see."

Alarmed, Claire jumped up and followed him. He turned around and held up a newspaper. "This, sweetheart, is the latest *National Enquirer*, and guess who made the cover? Know what else? *Sexy Lady Magazine* is offering you a million dollars to pose in the nude for them."

Claire was so shocked that for a moment she could only stare at him. Then she snatched the paper out of his hand. There she was all right, on that same beach in Hawaii, and apparently she was the person that Black was smiling at in his cover photo. She was wearing the tiny little yellow string bikini that he had bought her early on in their relationship. Claire's stomach did a forward roll. Mainly because she knew what she and Black had done on that beach a little bit later. "Do you think, do you think they could possibly..."

"Oh, yeah, I think they probably could. But if they dare publish anything like that, or anything else at all, I will rain hell down on them in litigation."

"Who took this? Oh my God. Look at me. I'm nearly naked!"

"Oh yeah. And you haven't even looked inside at the rest of their pictures, or read the article. There's a whole damn layout of you in there, all in that bikini I bought you. Every single one of them. Why the devil do you think I'm so upset? About me being on *People*? My God, every man in the country will see these pictures of you."

Claire quickly flipped the pages until she found the article, and then nearly died of humiliation when she saw the photos of them together, embracing, kissing, in the waves, lying on the beach. Luckily, that was the extent of what they'd done out in the open, thank God. How could they have been so stupid? But the whole estate was supposed to be private. They hadn't seen any boats out on the water that day. They'd looked. So where had the photographer been hiding? What else did he get? Her stomach lurched again, and she really did feel sick.

"Don't see you laughing now, sweetheart."

Finally Claire got mad. "Hell no, I'm not laughing. They had no right to print this, or offer me money to pose in the nude."

"Yeah, tell me about it. Damn them."

Then Claire realized that Black was probably jealous. He did that sometimes. But hell, this was pretty grim. She heaved in some deep cleansing breaths and tried to tamp down her agitation. Once the initial surprise faded some, she counted their blessings. She had her clothes on in the picture, and so did Black. "Okay. You know, Black, that's a lot of money they've offered me. There's a whole lot of good that I could do around here with a million dollars. You'd never have to pick up the tab at dinner again."

"Not funny, Claire. Not funny at all. This is serious. You need to treat it that way."

Truth was, though, Claire thought it was funny, because she was already over the anger. If somebody wanted to see them cavorting around on their honeymoon, so what? Who cared? They were happy. They had on bathing suits. "No, it's not funny, I guess, but don't worry. As soon as they pull in with a close-up and see all my bullet wounds and that big hatchet scar on my shoulder, they'll change their minds about wanting me in a centerfold."

"Oh God, what else can happen?" Black shook his head. He was not coming down quickly.

"Like I said, what's done is done. These magazines are already out on the shelves. Nothing we can do about it now. Best thing is to just ignore the whole thing. Think of it this way: you'll only have to be the sexiest man alive for three hundred and sixty-four more days, and then somebody else will take over."

"I don't like the fact that a sleazy magazine is publishing pictures of my wife and another one is offering to pay her to take off her clothes."

"Don't worry. You're the only guy who'll ever see my scars."

Black's face molded into what closely resembled a stone mask, so Claire moved up close, put her arms around his waist, and pressed herself against him. "Forget it, Black. It doesn't mean anything. Nothing's going to come of it. Who cares if people see us in our swimsuits? It's Christmas. Let's be happy."

Black's arms came around her and hugged her in closer. "I can't help it. I don't want those pictures of you out there. And Rico was there with us. He shows up in a couple of photos on the beach. I don't like that, either."

Time for the old change of subject tactic. "I know, but this'll all die down. We'll simply ignore it and it'll all go away. Besides, everything's going well otherwise. I'm enjoying working homicides again. It's good to partner up with Bud and see all the other deputies."

Black was coming down a little. "Well, that's good. So everything went okay again today?"

"Couldn't be better. Just like old times. Except there were no murders to investigate."

"Maybe I should just send somebody out to buy all the magazines around the lake."

Claire laughed at him. "Like I told you, who cares? We're home and we're together and it's Christmas. So let's decorate the tree tonight. Rico's dying to put it up."

Black finally smiled. "Okay. Rico and I went out to the cabin this morning after you left and cut down a couple more trees. I want to make Rico's first Christmas here special, so I got one for his bedroom, too."

"He'll like that. Along with the five hundred gifts you've got hidden in Miki's office closet."

"There's something for you there, too."

"Best news I've heard all day. Hope it's a new AR15. Why don't you quit with all the frowning and kiss me until I'm weak and helpless."

Black usually took her up on offers like that, whether he was mad as hell or not. He did this time, too. He pulled her up onto her toes and got the job done in high fashion, with plenty of panting and groping under her sweatshirt. But that's as far as they got before they heard Bud Davis calling out Claire's name from the hallway. A moment later, he walked into the room. They broke apart, still a bit breathless. Bud smiled and shook his head.

"Still the newlyweds, I see. Hey, have you two seen the *National Enquirer*?" Bud grinned, but his eyes were absolutely gleaming with his usual mischief. Her former partner was tall and nice-looking and pretty much slayed women with his big ash-gray eyes and sexy southern drawl. He was poking fun at them, but she wasn't sure Black was in the mood for that quite yet. She was right.

Black stiffened and then he frowned. "Yeah, I've seen it, and they're going to be sorry they printed it." Then, good for him, he attempted to shake the attitude off. "C'mon in, Bud. How are you? Claire was just telling me things have been pretty quiet."

"Not anymore. We just pulled in a homicide. Charlie wants us to take it. Thought I'd just drop back by and pick you up. I was still near here, anyway."

Black had settled down big time, had even harkened back to his rational self. On the other hand, every time Claire visualized those scantily clad pictures of her she cringed inside. But he didn't need to know that. His weren't so bad. He even got a good title. Hers just looked sleazy and nasty.

"What do you have on this murder?" she asked Bud.

"Not much yet, don't have any details, but it's not gonna be good. Never is."

Claire felt a tiny surge of excitement, just like she always did when a case came up. She wanted to go after the killer, bring him in. She couldn't wait to get him behind bars, no matter who he was. It was in her DNA. "Okay, let's go. See you later, Black."

Black didn't look thrilled. "Okay. We'll wait on you to decorate the trees. Have any new private cases come that I can help you with? Booker's available."

John Booker was Black's best friend and a highly capable private investigator. "We don't have cases pending right now. Will Novak's still down in Belize with his friend Jenn. By the way, the last time he called, he said she's doing much better. But he's staying on for a while until she gets back on her feet. So everything's under control."

"Okay, I'll just stay right here and burn all the magazines in town while you're gone."

Bud laughed. Black smiled, too, a little, and it appeared his Christmas spirit was creeping back in, slowly but surely. "Good deal. I'll probably be back in time for a late dinner. If it gets too late, you and Rico go ahead. Just keep my plate warm."

Black leaned down and kissed her on the cheek. "Be careful. Duck and weave, you know the drill."

"Will do. And you just keep on being the sexiest man alive, you hear? That's the important thing around here."

"Claire..." Black warned, narrowing his eyes.

Bud was laughing again; the dire mood had been broken. Black was back to himself, but still ready to call in his team of litigators, she suspected. All the frightened employees could slink back to work tomorrow and finish their day without getting their heads bitten off. Claire was on the job again and heading out to solve a murder. Screw those tabloids, she was excited. It had been too long since she'd worked homicide, and it made her feel as if she was home again and exactly where she belonged. Back in her comfort zone. She had missed Bud and Charlie and Joe McKay and all her other friends at the lake. This was going to be her Christmas present to herself: justice for the victim's family. She felt another spark of eagerness. Except for those *National Enquirer* photos, she felt unbelievably content. But she didn't have to think about that problem—Black would worry about it enough for the both of them.

Chapter 3

Claire and Bud took the back elevator down to the ground level. Outside, the temperature seemed to have dropped even lower. There was a brisk, wintry wind gusting in off the lakefront, but the snow had let up. The blanket of white covering the hotel grounds lay six inches deep, with drifts forming up against the walls and mounding over bushes. The outlying heliport looked slick with a thin layer of ice, and all the outdoor pools were covered for winter. It was still beautiful.

Inside the big glass windows of the lodge, Claire could see lots of guests using the heated indoor pools and hot tubs. The glass was partially steamed up, but everybody seemed to be having a good time, nice and warm despite the frigid weather outside. No reporters around, thank the Lord. Probably plenty of them still inside the lobby, though, busy making nuisances of themselves. Black would probably have to face them down eventually, and then he'd run them off. Truth be told, however, he was rather good at handling media types—as long as they didn't write for the *National Enquirer*, at least. They seemed to love the guy, no matter how many times he threatened to sue them into bankruptcy. Right now, though? She needed to concentrate on the case.

"The cops on scene tell you anything pertinent, Bud?"

"Some woman found the body and called 911. Dispatch said the victim is a young female."

"That's it?"

"Patrol officers had just showed up and were securing the scene when I got the call. I don't know much about the scene."

"Where's this place?"

"Some rich guy's pleasure palace, believe it or not. And get this, Claire: The house where they found her? Patrol said it's on the Christmas on the Lake house tour. And that it's still going on as we speak."

"Crap. Well, that's not good. But they're not letting anybody else inside the house, right?"

"I hope to hell not. A bunch of people went through the murder scene yesterday, though, as I understand it, and the day before, too."

"That's not going to help forensics much."

"The lady who found the victim got there late, and the people on the tour were waiting out front. Before she let them in, she went in to check out the house, light the candles, and junk like that, lucky for us. That's when she found the dead girl. Apparently, she screamed and ran out in a panic, and that freaked out the rest of them."

"Man, none of that sounds good."

"The newspapers are gonna love this. Not to mention all those media guys hanging around your lobby, trying to get snaps of you."

"Let's just try to keep a lid on this. Nothing more gets out, okay?"

"You are singin' my song. But you usually do." He looked down at her and grinned. Claire smiled back. She had really missed this guy. It half way made her want to partner up again.

After Claire had gone private, Bud bought himself a brand-new truck, a silver Toyota Tundra, no doubt aiming to match his eyes. He was inordinately proud of his new vehicle and had listed its glories to her at least fifty times since she'd come back. It was now sitting out in the driveway, right where the shoveled sidewalk ended, spotless and shiny and impressive. She suspected it had that new car scent, too. They walked swiftly toward the truck, heads down, not wanting to alert the vultures that Claire had ventured out of hiding and could be hunted down like a wild animal. She was glad for her brown leather snow boots because the weather had really gotten cold, and she wasn't used to low temperatures. Unfortunately, her body still had a Hawaii thermostat going on.

Claire swung open the door and stepped way up into the passenger seat. This was a big truck, all right. Bud took the driver's side, buckled himself in, and started the motor. Claire turned the heater on full blast. Just like old times. She felt so unbelievably comfortable about being back, exhilarated, excited, the whole nine yards. The cold, fresh lake air revived her. Now that Black had settled down to a combustible simmer, she could concentrate solely on the job. Make it her total focus. Her return to homicide felt good, as if she was doing the right thing at the right time.

Bud took off in a spray of salty slush and dirty snow. He had finally learned to drive on slick streets since he had come up from Georgia years ago. In the interim, she had become accustomed to his sliding sideways on ice and righting his car in the nick of time, sometimes even without hitting other vehicles. So today she rode just like old times: with one hand braced on the dash, just in case. Despite Christmas shoppers darting in every direction and cars crawling slowly in busy five o'clock traffic, the crowds somehow stayed out of their way, and thus remained alive.

"Temperature's supposed to drop below zero tonight," she told Bud, looking at the gauge behind the steering wheel. "It's already twenty degrees right now. Wind chill's even worse."

"Yeah, we're gonna have an arctic Christmas this year, so lucky you. I know how much you secretly pray for snowstorms."

"Yes, sir, I have missed the snow, and watching my breath smoke out into nice, crisp air. New Orleans and Hawaii are great places to visit, but this is home for me. This is where I belong. Snow banks and icicles and decorations everywhere. It's paradise on earth, and you know it."

"Well, I'm glad you're back. We need you. I need you. I've missed you like hell. Best partner I ever had."

"Thought you liked the new guy."

"I do. Brandon's okay. He's got a lot to learn. Luckily, we haven't had a homicide since you left."

"That's really good news."

"Good, but boring. I did get a domestic dispute upgraded to murder one about three months ago. Wife shot her husband while he slept in their bed. Pulled the covers up over his head and left him lying there rotting for two weeks. Pretty gross scene, let me tell you. Be glad you weren't here to work it. Open and shut, though. She admitted everything and pleaded guilty. Actually turned herself in. Yep, things have been quiet around here since you got married and left us to fend for ourselves."

"Well, here I am. Who knows? Maybe Black and I will stick around. I wouldn't mind that."

Bud jerked his attention to her. "No shit? You promise?"

"Rico really likes it here at the lake. We think it's a safe place for him to live. Schools are good. Black likes the privacy we've got out here, especially at my cabin. He likes that it's hard for the paparazzi to get down here. You know, plane, train, and automobile."

Bud laughed. "They'll go through barbed wire fences now that you two showed up on those magazine covers. Hey, you're the talk of the country now. The world, even."

"Trust me, we are going to lay low. Black's furious, but what good does that do? This, too, will pass. Just like our bad publicity always does. Then they'll go elsewhere and create havoc for other unfortunate people. Who cares what those media morons have to say? They lie about everything, anyway." Except truth was, her shrugging it off wasn't exactly the truth. She wanted the media out of their lives as much as Black did. Being hounded by obnoxious reporters sucked, all right, and they were getting more than their share today. She was damn lucky she'd gotten by them without being chased down. There ought to be a law against hounding people to death. The tragedy of the beautiful Princess Diana came to mind.

Bud's phone vibrated, and he pulled it out of his pocket. "Buckeye just texted. Says he and Shaggy and their team are loading their equipment and will meet us there."

"Good. I haven't seen those guys in a long time."

"They'll be bummed out about catching this case right before Christmas. There go any vacation days."

"Is Brianna gonna be here for Christmas?"

"Hopefully. She's still in Milan, for some kind of holiday fashion show. Not sure she'll get away in time to make it home for Christmas. Not sure she wants to."

Claire frowned. That didn't sound like Bud. "You guys having trouble?"

"It's not particularly good at the moment."

"Don't be too hard on her. Modeling is what she does for a living. Maybe she's got commitments she has to honor. Doesn't mean she wouldn't rather be with you."

"We don't seem to have a helluva lot in common anymore. Never did, I guess."

Claire hated it when Bud was unhappy. She loved the guy. "That hasn't seemed to bother either of you for the last couple of years."

"It's bothered me. But who knows? Maybe she'll make it back. I'm just not counting on it. Even if she does, you and I are gonna be tied up with this case. Sure as hell not going to have time to spend with her."

"Black's not gonna like me catching this case, either. But hey, don't worry. If she can't make it, you can spend Christmas with us. Black's got big plans for our first Christmas together. Harve's coming. And Black's going super overboard with Rico's presents." Harve was another of Claire's best friends.

"He's crazy about that kid. Harve's even worse. But it's the happiest I've seen Harve in ages. I just might take you up on that offer. Black doles out some pretty great gifts."

"That he does. And if Brianna gets here, she can come, too."

The drive around the lake took longer than expected, because Bud was forced to slow down as cars crawled and slid around fender benders blocking intersections. The snow started up again and made visibility worse. Sleet pelted the windshield and made little pecking sounds. More inclement weather was all they needed. She shivered and was glad the body had been discovered inside a warm house. Standing around in the snow and freezing precipitation for hours working a case did not appeal to her at the moment. The radio was predicting four or five more inches tonight. Not as bad as the last blizzard she lived through at Lake of the Ozarks, but the deep snow would slow down work on her new cabin.

Claire was eager to move back into her own place, or at least spend a lot of time out there. It was super private on its quiet inlet, completely surrounded by snowy woods. Even better, the cabin was wired with one hell of a security system, thanks again to her loving other half. No paparazzi would have a chance in hell of stepping foot anywhere near her place without her knowing, making it the place she wanted to be.

To Claire's relief, the murder scene was inside a gated community called Cliff Point. She'd been out there only once. It was fairly new and filled with plenty of personal surveillance cameras. All those precautions for the safety of the wealthy and famous residents were a good thing when looking for a murderer. Bad thing was the distance between residences. Not a neighbor in sight, most hidden within forested tracts and high brick walls, all owned by rich elitists who valued their ultra-expensive, private prime real estate. Not good for eyewitnesses to observe the comings and goings up and down all those long, private drives. Maybe she and Black should buy a house out there so they could fend off the jackals. Each home they passed boasted high and sturdy iron gates, all locked up tight with little lighted intercoms to announce who was good enough to step foot inside their hallowed halls. Actually, it was rather off-putting. Rich people usually sucked. Except for Black. He was one of the good ones.

As it turned out, the estate they were searching for had a glorious, elaborate entrance gate with white brick pillars hugging both sides. They stopped in front of it. It was white iron spiked with a big guitar and music notes all over it. Massive. Eight or nine feet tall. Huge green Christmas wreathes hung on both sides. An equally high wall ran down the length of the property, and Claire surmised it probably ran the entire length and breadth of the large acreage. Hell, an elite swat team would have trouble crashing this gate. An ornate sign atop the pine wreath read: *Christmas on the Lake Tour. Welcome, friends* was written atop the other wreath.

Lucky for Bud and Claire, however, the gate stood wide open, with no centurions guarding the royal portals. A mistake, that. Probably should have had a cop out there, blocking entrance to gawking rubberneckers. Maybe there were none available who weren't down with the flu. Bud drove onward, and they rolled up the winding tarmac drive, his wipers in a life-and-death struggle with some sloppy snowflakes that had begun to freeze themselves to death.

Claire had not been inside this particular property. It was an extremely ritzy enclave designed for reclusive celebrities, rich-as-Croesus folks, no doubt, who wished to put down roots in rural Missouri for reasons known only to them. That would be shallow roots, judging from the movie stars Claire had had the misfortune to meet—whom she could count on one hand, by the way. There were several B-listers and TV actors who had homes inside the development, but who they were, she couldn't recall. There were also a couple of state politicians, along with a few wealthy brain surgeons and other doctors who could, like Black, afford the good life. Except nobody had Black's kind of money.

Still, this gated community was the cat's meow to those requiring prestige and flashy layouts in *House Beautiful*. Like a lot of places on Lake of the Ozarks, it looked pretty much deserted at the moment, and would remain so all winter long. All these magnificent residences were summer vacation homes, elaborate and beautiful and expensive, with fancy boat docks and even fancier boats, but rarely occupied by the owners. It was a real waste of perfectly good lakefront real estate, all right.

Claire hoped to God that the victim wasn't a movie star or any other kind of celebrity. That's all they needed to engender a media frenzy. She and Bud had once worked the case of a TV soap opera star who had been murdered at Black's own Cedar Bend Lodge. That's how she'd met her husband, and the rest was history, especially since she'd vowed never to get married again. But she liked it fine. Better than fine, so far, at least. The publicity that soap opera murder victim had revved up had been god-awful. She would never be able to forget that case, no matter how hard she tried. She pushed thoughts of it out of her mind and locked it in a mental prison with the rest of her horrible memories. This was a new case, and very well could be open and shut. Anyway, it was Christmas, damn it. She was going to be merry and bright, even if it killed her.

Bud drove past snowy stands of pine trees, through a wooded tract that looked like a wintry-themed Christmas card, and then there were more trees, and even more trees, before the house finally appeared in its woodsy magnificence. Right in the middle of twenty acres or so, the home was absolutely beautiful. At first, neither of them could believe their eyes, and after the initial wonder at the magnitude of it all, they found that they didn't want to believe it. In the encroaching dusk, the whole place actually glowed, sent an aura of light up into the sky, like some monstrous radioactive house. It lit up the sky like a football arena. The residence itself looked gigantic, almost as long as a Marine barracks, perhaps. Beautiful. Modern. Rustic. *Expensive*. It was definitely a domicile owned by some complete idiot who just loved Christmas lights. This guy seriously left both Nicholas Black and Clark Griswold in the proverbial Christmas-decorating dust. Bud and Claire sat in the truck and beheld the over-the-top holiday décor that had ratcheted up to the crazy-as-a-loon degree. Of course, the house might possibly have had one single neglected, shadowy spot somewhere, maybe out back on a deck, but Claire sincerely doubted it. The dark, quiet woods had been switched up to the wattage of the portico of the Bellagio of Las Vegas. It verged on sacrilege to disrupt such a nice peaceful night in such a blinding way.

Bud had stopped the truck at the bottom of a long, bricked sidewalk that led up from a matching herringbone bricked driveway to the entrance. He turned off the ignition and they both climbed out, speechless under the fierce glare. Or maybe they just needed to slide on some sunglasses. They shut their doors and stood silently under five trillion lights, which outlined every eave and window and door and porch rail. It was breathtaking, but not in a good way. The December electricity bill would probably cost more than the house.

"Wow, just wow," Bud managed to get out. "We missed our turn and ended up in Vegas." Then he looked at her. They laughed together, just like old times.

"Tacky, tacky," Claire said.

"Tacky cubed." Bud shook his head. "Why the hell would somebody want to murder somebody in an electric plant?"

Claire didn't answer that question, but she considered it one hell of a good investigatory one. Two uniformed Canton County Sheriff deputies stood at the front steps. Six feet above those officers, she could see the all-glass, eight-foot front door etched with a huge J in the center. Lots of jagged lightning bolts were firing out of it at all angles. Probably personally designed by the owner while inside a particularly potent pipe dream and/or terrifying nightmare. The big, fancy wreath on the door was formed out of silver pine boughs and red Christmas balls. It was covered in lights, too, multicolored and dancing around like crazy. She was beginning to get dizzy.

It looked like the two patrol deputies were finishing up stringing yellow crime scene tape. Hell, it probably took five thousand yards of the stuff to encircle the house alone. The gargantuan size of the structure was not going to help their investigation. Neither were the dropping temperatures and the windblown snow. One of the men turned and waved at her. Claire smiled and waved back. She recognized her old friend immediately. Tim Corrigan had worked with her in Homicide. He was a nice guy. The other man, she had never seen before. The turnover at the sheriff's office had been surprisingly high since she'd gone private. Bud headed up the path, with Claire right behind him. The snow of the sidewalk was trampled by tons of footprints, most likely left by the Christmas tour. Her own boots left two-inch-deep prints in the new layer of white stuff.

"Hey, what do you have here?" Bud asked the two uniforms. Corrigan was smiling at Claire. He had been widowed recently, after nursing his wife through a long and horrific bout of stomach cancer. In his mid-fifties, he loved his job, and it was helping him through his wife's death. He had five grandkids and adored them more than anything else on the face of the earth. The other officer was new, young, tall, broad-shouldered, well-built, and nice-looking. Despite the biting wind and icy conditions, he was hatless, and his ears and nose had turned red in the biting wind. His hair was a bit strange, though: stark white and cut very close to his scalp. In fact, it looked like dark hair that had been bleached to the color of bones.

Claire decided that he looked like a guy who could take care of himself with just about anybody at any time. Nobody would want to mess with a guy like him, huh uh. Former military, she would bet on it. They always kept that air of strength and invincibility even after they got out. Bud was now introducing the new man to her as Colton Reid.

"Colt's just out of the academy," Bud was telling her. "Knows his stuff, too. Wants to join us in Homicide as soon as he can make the grade."

Colton Reid immediately jerked off his black leather gloves and grabbed Claire's gloved right hand. He gave her one of those hard, I-mean-it arm pumps, which was really more of a jerk than a handshake. She closed her fingers and increased her own grip to show him that she could hold her own, even with a strong guy like him. "I am distinctly honored to meet you in person, Detective Morgan," he was saying. "Your fame precedes you."

Claire smiled slightly but the praise surprised her. Other officers were not wont to heap accolades on detectives for doing their jobs, not much, anyway. He'd used her maiden name, too, but that was okay. Claire had decided early on to keep using her maiden name at work. On anything pertaining to legal documents or personal stuff, she was Mrs. Claire

Morgan Black, but here in her work world, with its murders and mayhem, she was still Claire Morgan.

"Nice to meet you, too. Sometimes that fame thing isn't so much fun."

Then the new guy messed up about as bad as he could on such short acquaintance. "Ah, you're talking about those *National Enquirer* photos, aren't you? Man, I saw them this morning." He started grinning, and oh yes, it was highly suggestive. Lascivious, even. Then he really stepped in it. "Tell you one thing, I felt like framing that cover of you and hanging it on my bedroom wall. That shrink you married? He's some lucky guy."

At first, Claire could not believe he actually said all that. Was he truly that much of an idiot? How did he make it through the academy? She was of a higher rank and he was a newbie. Even worse, she was a woman officer and he was a man. There was something called sexual harassment in the workplace. Something called good manners, too. What the hell was he thinking? And in front of two experienced officers, potential eyewitnesses to his stupidity? Nope, Reid did not appear to be the brightest bulb on any string of Christmas lights. He was the bum bulb that didn't light and ruined all the others. The one you had to throw away and replace. Colton Reid had a lot to learn, including good manners and office procedure and how not to talk to women. Bud and Corrigan were watching her, faces wary, no doubt with the expectation that she would double her fist and ram it into Colt's big, dumb kisser. She had doubled her fists, all right, but mainly from controllable irritation. She had slugged people for less, true. Not often, but they always deserved it.

But not today, no way, it was Christmastime. She was a happy camper, in a very good place, and fa la la la la, etcetera. Except for those stupid pictures that got Black all jealous. So, with some effort, she set her jaw and decided to let his ignorant remarks go by the wayside, with nary a physical or spiteful retort. *Be mellow, Claire. Go with the flow. Practice what you preached to Black. Merry Christmas. Colt Reid is probably just as dumb as a stump, or even less so.* She finally said, "Are you married, Officer Reid?"

"Oh no, ma'am. I'm still looking."

What he was looking at was her, up and down, as if she were most definitely a prospective wife. Talk about obtuse. Mellow was mellow, but rude was rude. She adopted her best withering glower and held it on him until he looked highly uncomfortable. Then she locked her eyes on his face for about a minute longer so she could watch his outspoken machismo dry up and die a horrible death in front of two male colleagues. After that, she turned to Corrigan. "Do we know who owns this bright and cheerful residence?"

Corrigan seemed glad at the change of subject. "No, but we're trying to reach the lady who sets up the tours. See if she can give us the owner's phone number. She hasn't been picking up. But she handles the Tinsel Town elites who want a place around here where they can hide from the paparazzi."

Claire gazed up at the blinding house. "I sure hope it's not some famous athlete or film star. They're known to slink and slither into this gated community from time to time, as you well know."

Bud said, "It's probably some jerk actor. Just look around. This guy is swimming in dough. This place is big enough to be a hotel."

Claire sighed. She just did not like celebrities. Not even when she tried. She detested them, in fact. Except for Black, but he was the down-to-earth sort. He was generous and kind and didn't act like he was some kind of a god. Even though he did look like one. Apollo, maybe. "Yes, Bud, there are rooms galore in this mighty edifice for a multitude of stoned, drunken Hollywood stars and hangers-on. Not a good scenario for us now, or in the immediate future."

Bud stomped his boots in the snow and clapped his gloved hands together. His breath vaporized and hung around awhile. Shivering inside his heavy winter clothing, Bud had never grown accustomed to the hardships of winter, being a born-and-bred Georgia boy and all. "This just gets worse and worse," he said. "Not gonna have fun tonight. Goodbye Merry Christmas."

Colt, aka "Dumb-as-Hell Dolt," as Claire now liked to think of Reid, was still watching her. Exclusively, too, as if he had x-ray vision and could see right through her bulky winter coat, all the way down to yellow bikini level. This guy was now on the verge of creeping her out. He just kept smiling and smiling, like he had this great big secret about her that he wasn't ever gonna tell. Man, he had a gigantic problem with the female sex. Bet on it. Then she wondered why Charlie would hire such a misogynist. That was a good question, and one she meant to ask the good sheriff if he ever got over the flu and came back to work—but only if he was in a good mood.

On the other hand, she wouldn't have to work with Reid after this brief and unpleasant encounter, so why should she give a damn? Somebody like him was a nonentity in her life, and thankfully so. What she wanted to do was to get started on the investigation. She still felt that little niggle of anxious anticipation, which told her she had missed her job as homicide detective more than she had thought. And she had missed living at the lake, too, a lot more than she had expected. All that stuff sobered her, and now she was second-guessing her decision to become a private detective. She missed the camaraderie in her department, Dolt being the exception, of course.

Corrigan was a guy who liked to joke around. So when he also brought up the article, she didn't mind quite as much. Didn't *like* it, mind you, but she knew he would never overstep his boundary. "Saw *People* magazine when I was in the Kroger checkout line, Claire. Guess you snagged the sexiest man alive. Congratulations."

"Shut up, Tim. Better not be a smartass and mention that to Black, or you might have to charge him with assaulting an officer."

He laughed. "No offense meant. I just hope the press gets you two out of their sights and gives you some breathing space."

"Amen to that." But enough about her and Black. "Okay, tell us what happened here. I take it the body's inside the house?"

"Yeah, back in the library. We're not sure who she is yet. They got her with what looks like blunt force trauma. Buckeye can determine if that's the official cause of death when he gets here."

Buckeye Boyd was the Canton County medical examiner, and the best one in the state of Missouri, that being Claire's humble opinion. "So he didn't leave the murder weapon?"

"No, but he left a wrapped Christmas gift in front of the tree addressed to us. Didn't touch it. Waited for you to open it."

"Are you shittin' me?" Bud said, shivering. Claire had bought him an entire set of L.L. Bean inner and outer wear for Christmas last year. This year, too, and it was wrapped and ready for the Christmas party that Black wanted to have. Maybe she should let him have it early. It seemed as if nothing ever kept him warm enough, though.

"To us. By name?" Claire asked Corrigan, half afraid to hear the answer.

"No, to the police. We've put in calls to all the necessary people. The realtor who takes care of this place, the tour director. Got their numbers off some business cards left on the kitchen island. Should be hearing back from somebody soon."

"Okay, let's go inside, Claire. This damn sleet is really coming down hard," Bud told her.

"Where exactly is the body?" she asked Corrigan.

"When you get inside the front foyer, you'll see a door at the back end of the hall. She's back there. You can't miss her, trust me. The body's posed. He went to a lot of trouble, too. We got ourselves a real dramatic killer here."

Claire grimaced, not liking the sound of that. Or anything else, so far. She turned her back to the wind-flung sleet hitting her in the face and bowed her head against the barrage. "Keep us posted if you hear anything else. We don't want the owner or any relatives showing up and blundering into the crime scene."

"Got it. We're stationed out here until you release us. Ben's inside. He'll show you the way. We checked out the house when we got here. Didn't find anybody else. Didn't find much sign of this place being lived in, either, but we'll do a more in-depth search after you give us the go."

"Good. Thanks."

Claire ignored the stupid guy and headed for the front porch. Colt just might not be a deputy very long if he didn't get his act together, and pretty damn fast.

Play Time

Still lazing around on her float, Junior's mom was going on and on about his dad to whoever was on the other end of the phone. As usual when she mentioned him, her voice was slurred and boozy and caustic. She talked on the phone incessantly, usually trying to manipulate party invites to celebrity homes. A few minutes later, she finally hung up. She rose up on one elbow and found his place on the chaise longue.

"Junior! Go fetch me a cold drink! Hurry it up, I'm dying of thirst out here!"

Oh, yeah. Junior wished. He sat up. She had turned over on her stomach now. He'd never seen anybody wear a bikini bottom that tiny, not even in the porn flicks he sometimes watched. His father had called her a slut the night he walked out for good. Junior had viewed their knock-down-drag-out fight through the upstairs bannisters. That had been the very moment she started on her way to being the richest divorcée in Los Angeles, and there were lots of wealthy women in that First Wives Club in southern California. All Junior liked about her anymore was her cash, so he had to remain docile and obedient until his twenty-fifth birthday, when his gigantic trust fund kicked in. That's the only thing his dad had ever done for him, but Junior should really send the thank-you note to his mom's greedy attorneys. He stood up and walked down the patio to the outside kitchen area. He pulled a frosted cocktail glass out of the fridge, poured booze all the way to the brim, and popped in the green olives and lemon twist, just the way she liked it. She hardly ate anything anymore, just drank, all day, every day. Her goal was to be the skinniest woman in her group of anorexic skeletons. She really was so unbelievably neurotic. Absolutely pathetic. She needed a shrink in the worst way possible.

Good old Lucky had disappeared now, probably inside the house, stealing their silverware or waiting naked in his mom's bed. Nauseating, all of it. Junior walked to the edge of the pool. "Here you go, Mom. I fixed it just the way you like it."

His mother didn't deign to open her eyes. "Well, bring it out here to me. You sure as the devil need to get some exercise. All you do is lounge around the pool or hide yourself down in that dark and gloomy game room. You act like you're some kind of creepy vampire or something. You better start swimming laps. You're getting pudgy."

Junior resented that. He was not getting pudgy. Not even close. She just said things like that to put him down. He had some weights downstairs that he lifted every day after school. He swam laps every morning while she slept till noon. Truth was, he was probably as strong as Lucky. He just didn't have those kinds of bulging muscles, but he was smart. He was going to be the valedictorian. He got off on knowing more than anyone else, understanding everything thrown at him. That's why he loved to play games. Especially brain games, board games, or video games. Any kind that made you have to think.

"Well, what are you waiting for, Junior? Get out here with that drink. I said I was thirsty. Can't you hear me? What the hell's the matter with you? You've been moping around for months."

Sometimes when Junior had to listen to her degradation and insults, he got this weird feeling twisting up inside his gut. It struck like lightning and burned, a rapid internal streak of tamped-down fury, red and lethal and hot. This time, too. His throat went dry and his palms got sweaty. He tried to shake off the murderous impulse sliding into his mind, but it wasn't easy. He'd been lying out there for hours internalizing his rage. Day after day after day.

Junior took a deep breath, then descended the steps in the shallow end and waded out to where his mom was floating. Her body looked hard and shiny, and the smell of the tropics enveloped him. He hated that smell now. He hated anything with lime or coconut in it, too. Even coconut cream pie. He held out her glass. "Here you go, Mom."

"Thank you, sweetie." She took off her sunglasses and actually smiled at him. "See, darling? You can be adorable when you want to. You were the most darling little boy. I really hate it that you grew up to be such a pain in my ass. Please try to do better."

"I will, I promise."

They shared a phony smile that had not one iota of true feelings. Sometimes she was okay. Not often, but right now, she was sort of, almost, okay. Well, not really. He still hated her guts and wished she were dead. Sometimes he just wanted to kill her, wring her scrawny neck and be done with it. He envisioned putting his hands around her throat and pressing his thumbs into her gullet until he heard bones crunch, then watching her face turn purple. Just the idea made him feel good inside. He often gazed at her and wondered if he could get away with it. Right now, even. Wouldn't that just be great? To just do it, end her, once and for all? That sounded downright sublime.

While Junior stood beside his mother's raft, she took a long drink of the martini he'd prepared. Then she turned over onto her back again. She relaxed and closed her eyes. That meant he was summarily dismissed, menial labor done, so get the hell away. Junior gritted his teeth. She was displaying her body for Lucky to see, as if she were up for sale, even right in front of him, her own son. More anger erupted inside his chest. Suddenly, and almost before he knew what he was doing, he grabbed her by the fat bun of bleached blond hair on top of her head and jerked her body off the raft. For the first few seconds, she seemed too shocked to fight back. Then she started screaming and struggling and cursing him. That's when he grabbed her oil-slick shoulders and pushed her head down under the water. Clamping his jaw, he exerted all his strength and held her under so she couldn't come up for air.

When his mom finally managed to jerk out of his brutal grip and make it up long enough to suck in a big lungful of air, her big brown eyes were bulging with anger and panic. After that, she fought against his tight hold for all she was worth. Probably because she was close to death now, and at the hands of her very own son. She knew that any minute could be her last on earth. She knew all that full well, and somehow Junior found that gratifying, that she would die knowing he hated her and wanted her dead. That he was ending her life with his own two hands and watching it happen, calmly and objectively, with no emotion whatsoever. Actually, that even surprised him a little bit. His mom had never been a quitter, though, and she fought harder and harder. Her legs came out of the water, kicking furiously as she jerked her body from side to side, splashing and roiling the water like a freakin' alligator, for God's sake. She was so oily and slick that Junior was afraid for a second that he wouldn't be able to hold her under long enough, not now that she was in this all-out, to-the-death fight. The actual act of murder wasn't turning out at all like those fantasies he'd enjoyed when he was in bed at night. Maybe he should have murdered her in her bed with a pillow.

Somewhere outside the roar filling his head, he heard someone shouting at him. The sound burned through his blood enough to make him look up. That's when he saw the pool boy. Lucky was standing on the side of the pool, yelling and gesturing, but Junior couldn't hear anything over the splashing and the noise in his ears and his own determination to put his mother down for good. He tightened his grip when he saw Lucky jump in the water and head out toward them. Junior continued to wrestle her under, yelling for Lucky to back off and mind his own business.

"Get outta here, Lucky! I mean it!"

Lucky was already to him, but he didn't do anything, just laughed and watched and didn't try to help Junior's mother at all. At first, Junior couldn't believe his eyes. Then the pool boy grabbed his mother's legs and trapped them under one arm. The violent kicking stopped. Then he grinned at Junior. "If you lay on top of her to hold her down, she's not gonna have bruises that'll look suspicious to the cops. Hold her head down by her hair. Then you won't leave marks around her neck, either."

Junior was more than happy to give Lucky's suggestions a whirl. As it turned out, Lucky's techniques worked rather well. Lucky held tightly to her legs while she bucked and tried to twist loose. After a minute, he started chuckling. "Your mom's such a freakin' bitch. I saw the way she bossed you around and called you names. But she's stronger than she looks. You better be glad I forgot my phone and came back to get it or she would've gotten loose and sicced the cops on you. You'd've spent the rest of your life in Folsom Prison."

Still holding his mother down, Junior stared at him, waiting for her to swallow enough water to drown. Grinning at each other, they both held on to her for dear life until she finally gave up the ghost. Then they kept her down a little longer after that, too, just to make sure. After a couple of minutes, Lucky let go of her legs. They both watched her sink slowly down to the bottom and then float back up to the surface. Then Junior let go, too. His mom's body bobbed slowly away, floating facedown in the water, her long blond hair loose now, and streaming out on top of the surface.

Lucky rubbed an open palm down the back of her naked thigh. "She was a good lay, I'll give her that. When she wasn't too drunk to give back."

"Ding dong, the witch is dead," Junior said, very serious. Lucky jerked a quick look at him, and then they both laughed together. Junior felt nothing but relief. No sadness, no guilt, no remorse, nothing at all. He was truly happy for the first time in ages.

"Yep, a witch she surely was. Congrats on a job well done." Lucky held out his hand, and Junior shook it. In that brief moment, they became partners in crime and inseparable friends.

"Thanks for the help," Junior said, really meaning it.

"Guess you'll get all her money now, huh? That's why you killed her, right? For your inheritance?"

"Yeah, I'll get every penny. But I killed her because I hate her guts."

"Don't blame you. I hated my mom, too, before I took off." He glanced back at the dead body and nodded, content. "All that money can buy us some big-time fun." Lucky started laughing again. "Bet she didn't expect you to just up and murder her. You do have some guts, I'll give you that. Very impressive, Junior. I wouldn't've thought you had it in you, man."

Lucky's high praise made Junior feel good. He was beginning to like this pool boy a lot. "How about we spend it together? Unless you intend to turn me in to the cops or blackmail me. Then I'd have to kill you, too. Don't think I won't. Because I will, Lucky, better believe it."

"Maybe you would. Or maybe I'll kill you first. But hey, know what? No need for us to talk tough like this. I won't tell anybody what we did. What? You think your mom's the first woman I've killed?"

Junior didn't know what to say to that. Surprised by Lucky admitting to committing murder, Junior just stared at him. But he was seeing the guy in a whole new light now.

Lucky grinned back, then turned and waded out toward the shallow end. He stopped at the steps and glanced back at Junior. "If I were you, man, I'd get the hell out of here right now and get yourself a damn good alibi. Looks open and shut to me. Your mom's been drinking like a lush all day, that's the good thing about all this. She's got to have a huge blood alcohol level. The cops'll think she passed out and rolled off that float and drowned. You might even get by with a few bruises on her, the way she works out at the gym every day. You're home free with the cops, trust me. But right now, we gotta get going before your cook shows up. She comes in at four to cook dinner, right? That doesn't give us much time to work out our alibis."

Junior sloshed out, too, and watched Lucky pick up a fluffy white towel and dry off. He was really curious about Lucky now. He grabbed a towel. "Hey, Lucky, you really mean you've actually killed somebody before?"

"What do you think? Don't know you well enough to start spilling my guts. This your first one?"

"Yes." Junior glanced back at the body. "Just my mom. Never really wanted to kill anybody else."

"No worries, you'll get used to it. And then you'll like it, trust me. I'm just glad I was here to help you hold her under or you might be headed off to the hoosegow right now. And know what would've happened then? They'd have thrown you inside a loony bin for the criminally insane. That's what they did to me when I was thirteen, but I escaped after a couple of months and took off. They never caught me. Thus, the name Lucky." He laughed some more.

"Who'd you kill?"

"I don't know their names. Didn't ask." He hesitated, and then he said, "I guess I can trust you after what we just did. Who're you gonna tell without me telling on you? Once, when I was driving my truck over to clean this lady's pool, about seven or eight months ago, I guess, I just ran this guy down who was crossing the street with his little dog. It was over in Glendale, and nobody was around. Street was completely deserted."

He shook his head and rubbed the towel over his hair. "It was crazy, bro. I just got this sudden, uncontrollable urge. Probably like you just did with your mom out there. That's what happened to you, right?"

"Yeah. I didn't plan to do it, not really. I got mad, and it just happened."

"Looks like we got a lot in common, huh? C'mon, let's get out of here. You got someplace to go, where they'll remember seeing you and can alibi you later?"

"I guess so. There's a big chess tournament at UCLA that started at noon. I'm sure it's still going on. Everybody's concentrating on their games and stuff, so nobody will probably notice when I come in. They'll just notice that I beat the crap out of them."

Lucky nodded. "That's right, you're the big brainiac at school, aren't you? Something tells me that we're gonna have some fun together, you and me. Just wait and see. I'll be the brawn and you'll be the brains."

Junior hoped so. He glanced back at his dead mother's corpse. She had floated over and bumped the top of her head against the side. Strange, but he felt exactly nothing. Just an overwhelming urge to smile and congratulate himself on a job well done. Right now, however, Lucky was right. Junior needed to get as far away from his house and his mom's dead body as humanly possible. Lucky had already disappeared around the side of the house, heading for his old Dodge truck. Junior ran down to his bedroom in the basement, threw on some clothes, and headed for the triple car garage.

His day was certainly looking up.

Chapter 4

The front porch of the estate was long and pillared, with an elegant style of rustic grandeur. It ran the entire length of the home's front. Although the designer used logs and rough-hewn wood on the exterior, somehow the house looked completely modern. Quite a trick to pull off. Lots of dark wood, lots of half logs, lots of river rock, lots of flagstones. It was designed to blend into the lake's granite cliffs and towering old trees. In Claire's opinion, the architect had gotten it exactly right. The blinking lights were giving her a headache, though, making her want to scream for mercy. Why couldn't the owner have been a Scrooge? Christmas overkill, and nothing less.

The house sat high on the bluff. She stopped on the porch and looked out over a lake that was obscured by the growing darkness and bad weather. You couldn't see the water at all, but in the quiet landscape you could hear the stiff winds pushing waves up onto the rocky beach far below. The wind up top had died down momentarily, and the sleet had miraculously turned back into large, intricate snowflakes floating softly to the ground in perfect straight lines. They looked like bits of torn lace dropping down all around them, but in this case each and every flake turned from white to red to green to blue and then to orange by the damned blinking and winking and twinkling tangle of lights. It was enough to make one dive for cover. Claire loved Christmas, especially now that she had Black and Rico to spend it with, an actual true-life family, which was a new concept for her heretofore bleak and lonely life. But this place? This was a sleazy L.A. overkill production with look-at-me syndrome. She could spot extreme narcissism anywhere. Especially here.

Way too much glitz and glamour, like everything else in L.A., which made that city her least favorite place on earth. Strike that—in the universe. She had worked LAPD when she'd first started out in law enforcement and had ended up the target of media sharks there, too. So she knew how celebrity Angelinos thought. If the owner of this place turned out to be an actor, or, heaven forbid, an A-list star, he or she would be an arrogant jerk and hard to work with. Count on it. It would be a miracle if said person wasn't self-centered, self-entitled, and self-righteous. In her experience, they all turned into pompous fools in accordance with their degree of fame, each and every single celebrity that she'd ever met.

Best scenario? There would be a heavy snowfall that would ground their deluxe private jets and keep them in warm and sunny southern California. Then she and Bud could conduct their celebrity interviews over the phone and not have to actually be near anyone. Now that would be a Christmas present worth its weight in gold. She wondered if Black could arrange it; he'd been able to arrange just about everything else she'd ever wanted. Bless his little darlin' heart.

After the cheerful glare outside, the interior of the home looked like an exploding supernova. What was wrong with these people? On the other hand, it was as warm as toast in there, which felt good to Claire's frozen nose. Bud already looked like a new man and was jerking off his brown sock hat. The interior was as woodsy as the exterior, but in a very "wow" and "whoopee" kind of way, and only if you disregarded the myriad of silver tinsel and endless evergreen swags from hell. The room itself was beautiful and smelled utterly delicious, like a fresh pine forest bedecked with cinnamon sticks and pumpkin pies and lots of other holiday things that Claire loved. Her stomach growled at the thought of pumpkin pie. With lots and lots of Cool Whip curled up high on top. She'd skipped dinner, and lunch, too. Her appetite would die off completely when they found the body, of course. It always did, so she definitely wouldn't have to suffer hunger pains long. They stopped just inside the big, bizarre, lightning-bolted front door. There, they tugged on protective paper booties and pulled on the obligatory disposable gloves.

Claire glanced around the central hallway. Giant and spacious and spread out, big time. It looked like there were two floors, both with matching hallways radiating out to either side and going on forever, all in the aforementioned rustic modern style. Somehow it was sort of elegant, too. A new and unusual concept. Cedar Bend Lodge was rustic, too, but with a homey kind of elegance that didn't sport the stark modern bent and modular furniture inside this house. She hadn't seen this décor anywhere else, lots of bare wood and black glass and marble and stainless steel, all very pricey by the looks of it. Everything reeked of Beverly Hills panache and exorbitant prices.

There was a black marble-topped table in the center of the foyer with a tall copper statue on its top that depicted Claire knew not what. Looked pretty damned peculiar to her, like an upside-down angel with barbwire sticking out everywhere. But, to each his own—even if their own was damn hideous. The walls were painted a warm, golden yellow, with fancy dark wood moldings just about everywhere you looked. Like something that would have its own spread in *Lake Living for L.A. Living Legends*. Black would probably love this place. Claire preferred small, cozy, old, and comfortable. Shabby chic floated her boat just fine.

The cop posted at the bottom of the main staircase was another young guy Claire didn't know. This one had the sense to be polite and respectful and not ignorant. He pointed at a door at the back of the hall, under a fabulous staircase that swept up into a wide spiral on both sides. "The victim is back there, Detectives. We checked out the room but didn't touch anything."

This new recruit was so young and fresh-faced that Claire suddenly felt decrepit. He had shaved off his hair, but she could tell by the shadows on his scalp that he'd had plenty of hair before he went crazy with that razor. His baldness looked out of place with his baby face, smooth skin, and innocent brown eyes. But he smiled at her, and it was a pleasant one. Better than that, he didn't mention *People* magazine or the *National Enquirer*, so she took to him right off the bat. His black name plate read Paul Wingate.

"Thank you, Wingate. Good job," she said to him.

Bud stood back and allowed her to precede him into the library. He was a veritable Rhett Butler, unless it came to foodstuffs. Then he'd eat all the pizza, except for her one piece. They stopped inside the door and observed the room. Unfortunately, more holiday decorations, stem to stern, top to bottom. A good Walmart aisle's worth of lights everywhere. Even Santa Claus's elves wouldn't subject some poor innocent family to this. Soft music played somewhere: Christmas carols. "Rockin' Around the Christmas Tree." Ironic, maybe, but not funny.

Bud was looking at a seventy-inch television screen right across from them. "How does anybody watch a football game with all these lights reflecting onto the screen? That would drive me up a wall."

"Maybe he hasn't moved in yet. My God, this is simply blinding. Wonder where we could pull the plug?"

Claire then looked down the long length of the room. One honking big Christmas tree took up most of the far wall, where it stood in front of a ton of built-in log bookcases, all empty of tomes. But her eyes latched solely onto the victim. The woman appeared to be dressed like an angel. She was wearing some kind of diaphanous, loose white garment, or maybe it was a flowing nightgown. There was a wide balcony running around the top of the room, lined on all four walls with more empty bookshelves. It looked as if the young woman had been posed to sit atop the balcony bannister right above the tree. Her arms seemed to be holding onto the rail, and her robe had been pulled out over the top of the tree.

"He made her look like an angel tree-topper," Claire said, feeling a bit sick.

"Good God," Bud breathed out from next to her.

Together, they walked slowly down the room toward the tree. Claire couldn't take her eyes off the victim high above them. "How did he get her to stay up there like that?"

"Dunno. Man, she looks like she's just a kid," Bud said.

At the bottom of the tree, they stopped and stared up at the victim. Her arms were outstretched at her sides, maybe tied somehow to the bannister railing, and the sleeves of her gown had been draped artistically, as if they were wings. The pose gave the impression that she was hovering up there on outstretched wings. But Claire could not take her eyes off the woman's face. Bud was right: She was young, really young. Her eyes were wide open, pale blue and staring straight down at them. She had been struck from behind. They couldn't see the damage done to her skull, but they could see the blood from the wound. It had run down over her face, weaving together in intersecting red rivulets. The blow that had killed her must have been brutal as hell.

Claire moved slightly to her right. That's when she saw the huge hole behind the girl's right ear. Long blond hair was matted with blood, making it look dark and sticky. More blood had soaked down into the front of the white gown, and the killer had wound a string of blinking white lights around her forehead to resemble a bright and glowing halo. Claire swallowed her revulsion. This young girl was dead and gone forever. A Christmas angel, no more.

"This guy is psycho, man," Bud muttered, angry. "What is she? Eighteen? Nineteen? Why would anybody wanna do this to some young teenager like her?"

Claire met his eyes. He had the most appalled look on his face—even after so many years in homicide, he was affected. So was she. She knelt down at the base of the tree and examined the small gift sitting just under the lowest tree limb. It looked like a ring box, maybe. She didn't touch it and wouldn't until the photographers had shot crime scene photos. But she could read the tag.

"What's it say?" Bud asked.

"It says: 'To my cop friends. Merry Christmas. May this angel light your way to me. I'll be waiting. Game on.'"

"Oh my God, this is gonna be brutal. Looks like he left us the murder weapon, too, Claire. See it back there, behind those presents?"

Claire hadn't seen it. "The killer's already playing games with us, Bud. Leaving the murder weapon behind is nothing but a taunt. He feels secure. And you can bet he wiped the thing clean, like everything else he touched."

"Killer could be a she. This is a staged scene like no other that I've ever seen."

"Highly imaginative, too." Claire hunkered down and studied what she could see of the weapon. It looked like some kind of a trophy. Another gift for them, this one unwrapped. It also looked heavy, and about a foot tall. "There's blood on it, and maybe some brain matter."

Bud squatted down beside her. "Yeah, I see that. Think he found that trophy somewhere in this house? What is that on top of it?"

"Looks like a bishop from a chess set, I think."

Bud turned his attention on her. "Chess? Really? Why would those guys get trophies? Trophies are for real sports. Contact sports, like football."

"Give me a break, Bud. Chess is a game. There are winners and losers. It's not like checkers. You've got to have brains to play it well. These guys pit themselves against each other in tournaments and get themselves a trophy to sit around and collect dust. Until they want to murder somebody with it. Like this guy."

"Trophies for chess?" Bud was still grousing around. "Man, that just does not seem kosher. Hell, Claire, they just sit there and stare at those little things on the board. No effort in that. So you're sayin' we got ourselves some kind of nerd killer?"

"I'm not saying that. And not all chess players are nerds. You have to be smart to play the game well. You know, lots of strategic moves and second-guessing what the other player's gonna do."

"How do you know all that? Don't tell me you play chess?"

"Well, no, of course not. Black does, but not with me. Too boring, and it takes forever. I tried once to play with him but I fell asleep waiting for him to make a move. Fast paced it's not."

Claire stood up and raised her gaze to the victim, who stared back down at her. "She's just a tiny little thing, isn't she? And she looks so young and innocent. I wonder who she is and why he picked her? Why her, out of all the girls in this county?"

"We'll find that out soon enough."

Claire nodded. The victim looked like the kind of kid who'd never hurt anyone in her entire life. Frail, skinny, pale skin that looked creamy and young and smooth. The loss of color might have been from all the blood, because there was plenty of it turning that filmy white gown to scarlet. Some of it had dripped down from her widespread arms onto the tree and its top ornaments. The whole scene was bathed in the glow of the lights strung around the balcony bannisters, all of them blinking on and off, on and off, coloring her face red, then green, then yellow, a bizarre kind of cheerful strobe, almost psychedelic in effect. Like some scenario out of a horror movie. It was horrible.

"How do you think he got her?"

"I don't know. She's so little that it wouldn't take much to subdue her. And that might be a nightgown. Maybe he came in the night, broke in somehow, and got her when she was asleep."

"So she must live here? Or maybe she's just a tour guide. Know what? Come to think of it, seems like I remember seeing a picture of the tour guides in the paper a few weeks ago. Some of them had on angel costumes."

"It could be a costume. Looks like a nightgown to me, though." Claire couldn't seem to drag her focus off the victim's little heart-shaped face. Her mouth was slightly open. Claire could see the tip of her tongue. The halo of lights was another of the killer's dramatic flourishes to set a shocking scene. He had been proud of his work and wanted to showcase it. Definitely. Claire felt slightly sick to her stomach.

"Look, there's a spiral staircase that goes up to the balcony. We need to go up and check her out," Bud said, heading quickly that way.

Claire followed him, and then rounded the wooden, winding steps. It was a two-story library without a single book. There were several rolling ladders for selecting books on the high shelves. Claire and Bud didn't touch anything. Hopefully they'd get some prints. This guy had gone to a hell of lot of trouble and might have gotten careless. There were a lot of dramatic flourishes that he'd had to have touched in order to arrange. Upstairs, they could see the damage done to the girl's skull, up close and way too personal. Half of the back of her head was gone, lying behind her on the floor in chunks. Claire looked away, nausea churning in the back of her throat. The blow had been brutal. Parts of her head had been crushed.

"Looks like he hit her twice."

"This guy's a friggin' monster," Bud was saying. "Look at this."

Claire leaned closer and realized what Bud was talking about. The killer had nailed the victim's hands to the bannister in order to get the effect of those outspread wings. "He's a psychopath, all right. She was still alive. Look at all the blood that dripped down the bannister onto the floor."

"What's that smell?"

Claire knew instantly what it was—singed human flesh. "The lights are burning into her forehead. He strung them over the wound, so he probably bludgeoned her first."

The whole scene was eerily horrendous, the young woman dead and bloody as all the lights around her blinked merrily. She looked like some kind of a scary mannequin in a Halloween haunted house. Claire's happy state of mind took a slow dive into dark oblivion. She stared at the back of the girl's head. "Who would have the stomach to do this to an innocent girl?"

Bud said, "Maybe she wasn't so innocent. Maybe she was a devil, disguised as an angel. Could be the killer's stab at murderous irony."

"Maybe."

"I've got a real bad feeling about this case."

"Me too. Too much theater. This guy has been practicing."

"He's a serial. I'd bet next week's pay on it."

Across the room, a new song came on, "Hark! The Herald Angels Sing." That did it; Claire had had enough. "Please, Bud, find that music and turn it off."

Bud descended to the ground floor and walked across the room. A moment later, the CD was turned off mid-stanza. Claire breathed a sigh of relief. Somehow the soft and melodious Christmas carols made everything seem worse. As if it could get any worse. She hadn't worked a murder like this in a while. Especially not a carefully staged one full of cruel clues left for them to puzzle over. This killer liked to play mind games, all right, so it was going to be complicated and messy. She had not forgotten the dread that processing the body at the scene brought up inside her. She steeled herself. They'd get him. They'd get him and he would pay for what he'd done to this poor girl.

Claire moved down the turn in the spiral stairs and met Bud at the bottom. They moved away from the tree; there was nothing they could or should do until forensics showed up. When they stopped at the other end of the library, Bud looked back. "I wish we could turn off those lights around her head. They're burning her skin, damn it."

"Well, we can't. Not until Buck gets here and we get our still shots and the video. I wish they'd hurry up. I want her down off that tree, too."

"I'm gonna look around and see if I can find her purse or something with ID. She could be a maid or housekeeper, something like that. She's got to be in this house for some reason."

"If it's an angel costume she could be a tour guide. But I still think he got her in her nightgown."

Bud nodded. They both sobered at once when the music suddenly kicked on again. Startled, Claire had her weapon out before she realized the music must be on a timed loop. For some reason, a chill rippled up her arms. "A Holly Jolly Christmas" was playing now. Huh uh, not with a well-lit bloody corpse in the room with them. "Guess you're gonna have to unplug it, Bud. I can't stand listening to any more cheerful music right now."

"Yeah, I hate this case already."

Claire did, too. Big time. Something terrible had gone down here, and the reason for it was not going to be a fun thing to investigate. "We've got to get an ID first. Somebody in this town really, really hated this girl's guts and wants us to know it in no uncertain terms. Who goes to this much trouble, for God's sake, and then spends time decorating the corpse with lights and tinsel? And then there's the trophy and gift left as clues. This guy definitely is a game player."

Games that left people dead. Games that Claire did not want to play. But she had to. They had to find this guy, and soon. She just hoped the clues he left panned out. Maybe he wasn't quite as brilliant as he thought he was—and maybe they were smarter than he thought.

Chapter 5

The Canton County Medical Examiner's name was Buckeye Boyd. He was an old friend of Claire's and as good as gold, through and through. Tall and lean and bearded, with dark hair streaked iron gray, the two of them had fished for bass countless times out on the lake. Buck usually beat her in the stringer count, maybe because he'd won so many bass tournaments that Claire couldn't keep up with them anymore. He was as smart as they came, and had gradually put together a crack team of criminalists, most of whom had stuck around and worked together amicably for years. They were a well-oiled machine, all the time, every time. Canton County was lucky to have them. They pulled up at the crime scene a bare fifteen minutes after Bud had placed his call.

Claire met them at the front door and gave tight hugs all around. She had missed the heck out of them, especially Johnny Becker. He was special to her, a crazy, goofy guy whom she adored like a little brother. The whole team had always called him Shaggy, Shag for short, because he looked so much like the character in the Scooby-Doo cartoons. He was probably the best criminologist the state of Missouri had ever seen, and he was the happiest of all to see her again. He locked her inside a great big bear hug, and then actually picked her up and swung her around. Not exactly professional, but it was Shaggy, so she let it go.

"Hell, Claire, I thought you'd gone off for good, never to be seen again," he fussed at her. Then he placed her down on her feet and gave her his usual and utterly contagious grin. Claire probably would've already slugged or arrested anybody else who dared do that to her, but Shag, well, he was a different sort of guy. Brilliant, quirky, irresistible. A nerd through and through, but Claire had a tendency to like nerds. And the nerdier the better.

He had worn dreadlocks for most of his life, but now they were gone. His blond hair was still fairly long, but this time straight and touching his shoulders, shorter than she'd seen it in years. He still had his multiple ear piercings, though, all eight of them. He was a southern California beach bum wannabe, but had never stepped foot on any Pacific sand. One could always tell his L.A. yearning by the way he dressed. It was the dead of winter, and he had on a yellow and black tropical shirt with surfboards printed all over it, ultra-long yellow surfer shorts, and snow boots. Luckily, he did have a heavy military overcoat that he'd bought at some army surplus store. Still, he never seemed to get cold. Crazy, but true.

Shag was absolutely brilliant at his job, found all kinds of things everyone else overlooked. Charlie even let him get by with wearing the surfer clothes in the lab because he was so good at his job. Shaggy and Claire had spent many a Friday night watching action movies at his house, eating pizza and drinking Mountain Dew. That was before she met Black, who tended to monopolize her time from that moment on.

"How you been, Shag? I missed the hell out of you. But a lot's been going on in my life the last year or so."

"Don't I know it. But it's cool. Newspapers just love you and Nick. Tabloids got a real romance going on with you guys."

Then it got quiet all around. They all knew how Claire felt about reporters and the media in general, so Claire knew full well what was coming next. She decided to just go with it. Get it over with. "Okay guys, go on, do it. Laugh about those damn pictures. I know you want to. Get it out of your system. But let me tell you: Black and I don't think it's so funny."

"Well, one thing is for damn sure," said Buckeye, his eyes glinting. "You look like a million bucks in that bathing suit. Don't tell my wife I said that."

They all laughed, but it was good-natured ribbing and Claire knew it. Buck had been married for almost thirty years, and he and his wife still enjoyed a true storybook romance. Claire shook her head, attempting to be a good sport, but the jokes about those stupid photos were already wearing a trifle thin. Maybe because she'd seen that poor bludgeoned angel in the next room. Not much sense of humor in Claire at the moment. The forensic guys wouldn't have much of one, either, not after they got a glimpse of the victim. "Okay, ha, ha. You got your laughs, so no more. Please." But she smiled when she said it. "By the way, just so you know, that was a private beach we were on that day. There weren't supposed to be photographers within miles. We had no idea anyone was around."

"Oh c'mon, we all know that. So, Claire, tell us, how's the sexiest man alive doin'?" That was Shaggy.

More amusement. "Stop already. Black's ready to throttle somebody as it is. Don't be the first to feel his rage."

After that, Buckeye took the hint and got down to business. "This's a bad one, I take it."

"Yeah." Bud nodded. "The victim's in the library, back there." He pointed.

"The perp used some kind of trophy to bludgeon the victim," Claire was telling Shaggy. "One that looks to weigh five pounds, at least. He left it behind for us to find. He also left a wrapped Christmas present for us."

"No shit." Shaggy said. "Wow, never had that happen before." Then he sobered. "What do you think is in it?"

"Let's find out." Claire led them back through the foyer to the library. "The victim's just a kid. Not twenty yet, is our guess. No idea yet who she is. C'mon, she's in here."

Claire stood back and allowed the forensic guys to carry their equipment cases into the library. Bud pointed down the length of the room to the Christmas tree. Everybody stared silently at the dead angel.

"Whoa," said Shaggy, very serious now. "This guy's got a bent for the theatrical, huh?" By the time they all climbed up to the balcony and stood around the body, nobody was saying anything.

Buckeye stepped up close and examined the back of the victim's head. "Good grief, he must've hit this woman with force like you wouldn't believe. God, half her skull is lying down there on the floor. I'd say she died instantly."

Nobody said a word, just stared at the brain matter and pieces of skull at their feet. Buck wasted no more time. "All right, let's get the still shots done first, and then we need to film every inch of this scene. Make it quick, but thorough. I want to get those lights off her head. I can smell her skin burning."

The woman who'd worked the cameras during Claire's tenure had left the department to concentrate on photographing weddings and graduations. Tired of blood and gore, probably. Ready for some rainbows and hearts and smiling faces. Claire couldn't say she blamed her. She hated going to weddings with a passion, her own included, truth be told, because of all the hoopla. But weddings were happier affairs than young girls with crushed skulls on top of Christmas trees. The new photographer stepped forward with his camera. Buck introduced him as Ryan Wright. He nodded to Bud and to her and then went right to work. Everybody else stood back and watched, waiting for the body to come down onto the floor so they could do their jobs and go home and wrap Christmas presents. Homicide work was a strange profession, to be sure. One had to be able to turn it off, but that was the problem. Most people couldn't, Claire included.

Nobody said a word while Ryan took photos from every conceivable angle. A young girl was dead before her time and now would be poked and prodded and cut on and photographed and put into a hole in the ground. It was not fair. A second victimization, to be sure, but necessary if they wanted to find her killer. When Ryan finished the still shots, he videotaped every inch of the murder scene up close, and then he moved around the room, recording every detail. He would document their every move, every word, and every decision as they continued to work the crime scene. Although new at his job, he seemed very thorough. Buck always hired the best personnel available.

"Okay Shag, shut down those lights and let's get her off that bannister."

"Her hands are nailed down," Claire told him. "The sleeves are covering them up."

"God Almighty. Then we'll have to pry them out. Somebody get the small hammer out of the kit. Ryan, tape us getting them out, okay?"

Ryan moved up close and turned on the camera. The end of the nail was left out of the skin a bit, so they used the claw of a hammer to pull it out. Shaggy got down on his hands and knees, found an electrical outlet behind the tree, and jerked out the plug. The lights around the victim's head went off, as did the lights on the tree, but the room still blinked and winked all around them. Claire grimaced, wanting to pull all the plugs. Hit the master switch, for God's sake. She never wanted to see Christmas lights again, not after this. Unfortunately, now every time Christmas rolled around, this grisly scene would appear inside her head and make her remember this poor dead girl dressed up as an angel. Yes, her lovely Christmas joy was on its last legs and staggering for the finish line. She just hoped she could get some cheerfulness back by the time she got back home.

Buckeye pulled on his gloves while Shaggy and Ryan lowered the body down onto a plastic tarp spread out on the floor. Buck stepped up to the body, knelt down, and turned the body over. The back of the girl's head was not a pleasant spectacle. Pretty much just an ugly, bloody mass of gray tissue and broken shards of skull. The attack had been tremendous, brutal, and deadly.

"Looks like one blow that killed her, maybe two, if he brought her upstairs to pose her body," Buck told them. "One so brutal that she couldn't survive it. Probably died instantly, or soon after she was struck. Let's get her on her back and see if what else we can find."

They obliged, and Claire thought the victim looked even tinier when stretched out beside Buck's large frame. She was so incredibly thin and white. This young girl had only just begun to live. Now her life was over for good. It was a tragedy, just like every homicide was a tragedy. Just a kid and gone forever. No more love or fun or goals or desires for her, all erased in a single second. All ended before she was old enough to vote.

Nobody said a word, which was what usually happened at this point at murder scenes. "Well, it looks like the perp surprised her, took her down with a quick, hard blow that killed her. From behind, I'd say. Then he could've bound her up here and hit her again, hard enough to shatter her skull and send this spatter and brain tissue down here on the floor. What a terrible way to end up. The terror she must have felt."

"Okay, let's go back down and open that gift he left us. It's probably a clue."

"Better be careful. It might be some kind of explosive," Shaggy told them as he and another technician struggled to get the body down the steps to the ground floor.

Once at the base of the tree, Claire touched the wrapped present with her finger to make sure there wasn't a wire leading out of it. The paper was covered with white angels. This guy was sick, all right. She slit the tape with her pocket knife and carefully folded back the paper. There was a small, blue velvet ring box inside. She picked it up and opened the top, fairly certain that it was going to be something awful.

"What in the hell is that?" Bud asked, leaning closer.

"Looks like some kind of game token. A miniature trophy."

Shaggy knelt down. "Let me see. Yep, I know exactly what that is. It's out of a game. It's from that Detection game. You know, the one when a murder goes down with a bunch of amateur detectives trapped inside a mountain ski lodge. They've got to figure out whodunit and how it was done. Or, it might be from the new version, because they've changed up the original one a bit, I think. I don't remember the motives or the weapons, but it's a fun game. "

Claire recalled playing Detection a couple of times in a foster home where she'd lived in her early teens. That family had been one of the okay ones. At least they treated her okay and not like a paycheck from Child Services. They had liked to eat meals together, too, and always had a family game night once a week. That's about all she remembered about that home, though. She had tried long ago to erase all memories of time spent in the Louisiana foster care system.

"That's exactly what it is," Bud agreed. "Brianna and I played Detection one night last fall. She likes guessing games."

Nobody commented.

Claire took out the token with her thumb and forefinger and examined it. "Well, he's left us another clue, I guess. One tied to a specific game. Guess the question now is: what's he trying to tell us?"

Nobody had an answer. Claire didn't, either.

"That he's a sick son of a bitch?" Bud finally guessed, and correctly.

Claire stared down at the victim's face as Ryan took close-up shots of the token and the small velvet box. This victim was getting to her. The young woman's face was so small and smooth and unlined and young and inexperienced. Waxy white and frozen in an expression that looked almost peaceful now. She turned to Bud. "Guess we need to find out who she is before we can do anything else."

"Yeah, and then we've got to notify her next of kin as soon as we find them. I guess she doesn't look familiar to any of you guys?" Nobody knew her. "Okay, Buck, let's see if she's got any identifying marks on her. Anything that we can use right now for possible ID. If you wouldn't mind to do just a quick cursory look-see before you bag her. Maybe she's got a birthmark or tattoo we could use."

As Buckeye started his examination, Claire stared at the blood-soaked angel robe. It was a nightgown. She wondered about that. Surely the killer didn't have time to dress her up like that. Most likely she was already wearing the gown when surprised and assaulted. So that meant this happened at night, last night, and maybe even in bed. She was barefoot, the skin of her ankles and feet dark now, as blood settled down into the lowest part of her body. Her eyes were the worse. Pretty eyes. Wide open, staring and empty. Claire tried not to look at her eyes again.

The gown was tied with several satin ribbons, and Buck loosened the knots and opened the front. Underneath she had on a pair of white cotton panties, but nothing else. No wounds anywhere else on the body and no signs of physical abuse, now or before. No bruises, no abrasions, no scars. When Buck turned her over, he found one large tattoo behind her left shoulder. A small skeleton holding a scythe: a grim reaper, inked in black and white. Claire leaned down for a closer look. The image seemed halfway familiar. "Okay, there's something we can work with. I doubt many people around here have that kind of tattoo."

Buck turned to Ryan. "We need to get a close-up shot of that, too, okay?"

"Yes, sir." Ryan shot several pictures.

Bud looked at Claire. "No shoes and the bottoms of her feet are clean. It either happened right here, or somebody carried her inside the house from somewhere else."

"Or from somewhere upstairs, maybe a bedroom, because I think this is her nightgown. I think she was attacked here. Let's get Corrigan and the other guy to check out the bedrooms and see if they can find any signs of a break-in."

Bud moved off to talk to the patrol officers waiting outside.

"But why here? This is a house on a Christmas tour, for God's sake. People coming through in groups. That doesn't make a bit of sense, and it's risky." Claire glanced around the room. "There's a French door over there that leads out to a screened-in back porch. We checked it out already. He didn't come in that way."

Buck nodded. "He staged her for shock value. He's got a flair for murder and likes to use it. He's a psychopath, if I had to guess."

"Yeah, I can tell you already that Black would think so. But I'll get his take on it."

Bud was back. "They're checking out the house now."

"The woods all around this estate are dense. It would've taken months for anyone to find her body out there if they hid her in the brush. That tells me he wanted us to find her right here and right now. Wanted to make us play his game on his terms. He didn't want to get away with this murder. He wanted to see if we can catch him."

"I hate the game players," Buck said.

"Are you done here?" Claire asked him.

"Yeah. Go ahead and bag her, Shaggy, and let's get her down to the morgue."

Shaggy and Ryan opened the black bag and carefully lifted the victim inside, zipped it up, and then set about getting her onto the gurney. Claire and Bud stood together and waited until they rolled her out of the library into the front foyer. "We need to find her family, and fast. My God, Bud, can you imagine them getting this call? Only days before Christmas. It's sad, it really is."

Bud sighed. "One thing for sure: She's too young to be on her own. Somebody's got to know her and miss her or recognize that tat. Which brings us to this question: Why the hell would a young girl like that have a tattoo of a grim reaper, of all things? That's weird in itself."

"Yeah, it is. But it will help identify her. Her parents are probably out looking for her right now."

"Let me call in to dispatch. See if any missing persons have turned up around the lake area. I don't remember hearing that. Do you?"

"Not since I've been here. We would've checked into it by now."

Bud moved off to call the office. Claire stood back and watched the rest of Buck's criminalists spread out around the room to do their jobs. Pure professionals. This had turned out to be a strange case with a murder scene she wouldn't forget anytime soon. The image was burned into her brain, all right, with all of her friends kneeling around a white angel with half a head, while twinkling lights blinked and the smell of pine boughs and burnt flesh mingled all around. Definitely a manger scene designed in hell.

"I'd sure as hell hate for you to have to alert the media to this one." Buck looked halfway angry. "I hear there's a ton of them out at Cedar Bend raisin' a ruckus about you and Nick."

"Yeah, the story of our lives lately. And they're reading the same tabloids as you are. Black and I are avoiding them like the plague, and we definitely don't intend to give any interviews. Never again, if Black has anything to say about it. In fact, we're pretty much hiding upstairs in the penthouse until they go away."

Buck smiled. "Fat chance of that. You and Nick are like nectar to them. You make them lots of money, you know."

"I just hope we don't have to go to the press to help with the identification. Or use her morgue photo. That would be awful."

They all turned as Corrigan and Reid showed up. Corrigan did all the talking. Fine with Claire. "We've finished searching the house, tossed every room, took our time doing it. Didn't find anything of much interest, except in one bedroom. Somebody was definitely staying in there. Bed messed up, cosmetics spread around on the bathroom counter. But no personal items, no address book, no family pictures, nothing in the medicine cabinets except some toothpaste and a toothbrush and some Excedrin. A couple of garments hanging in the closet. Looked like stuff the victim might wear and about her size. We found her purse but no ID in it. The killer might've taken it, though. No sign of a struggle in the bedroom. No food in the kitchen, except for a small pizza box and the leftover refreshments the tour provided. Nobody's been living here except for her, as far as we can tell."

"Where was the pizza from?"

"The box was plain white. No name of any restaurant."

"You've tossed every room? You're sure?" Claire asked. She looked at Corrigan and ignored the new guy. She just didn't care for him. Go figure.

"Yeah. Didn't take long because, like I said, there are no personal possessions to be found, except in that one room. A ton of bedrooms, but all with empty drawers, empty closets. The house is immaculate. Untouched. Probably cleaned up and sanitized for the visitors coming through. Looks brand new to me. Nearly all the furnished rooms have Christmas trees in them, each with different themes, like the Christmas tours usually do."

"Okay, we'll take a quick walk-through before we leave. Which bedroom was she staying in?"

"Master. It's right off the library's balcony, facing the back."

"Okay. First thing? We've gotta find out who owns this house."

"Could be just an empty house up for sale that they decided to use for the tour," said Bud, now back, his phone still in his hand. "No dice on a missing person. I'll call the realtor now. I found her card on the kitchen counter."

Bud turned and walked away again, his cell phone already up to his ear.

Shaggy was back. "I can't think of any reason the perp would leave us that game token. Or dress her up like an angel. Except that it's Christmas. What's he tryin' to tell you?"

Claire shrugged. "Maybe there isn't any reason. Maybe he's just a theatrical psycho freak and thought it would be fun to blow our minds and make us lose sleep trying to figure it all out. Or maybe this is his way of throwing us off the scent."

"Well, it worked. I sure can't figure out the trophy. I mean, I get the trophy was a murder weapon but it looks clean, too. Don't expect to get prints off it. Don't know why he left that token, but it's got to mean something."

"What it means is that he's playing games with us. He thinks he's clever. He thinks he can bait us and lead us around by our noses, but I'm not going to let that happen. I'm going to get him. He's not getting away with murdering that kid."

Bud walked back up, looking so grim that Claire hesitated to ask questions. "Brace yourself, Claire. You ain't gonna like this one bit. Guess who the realtor lady says owns this place?"

"Oh God, no. Who?"

"Wait for it…wait for it: Jonesy Jax."

Nobody said anything for a few seconds. Then Claire said, "Not Jonesy Jax, the whiskey-guzzling, drug-addled, sex-addicted hard rocker from hell."

"The one and only."

Claire muttered a couple of gross things under her breath, words that she rarely used out loud. Damn it. Jonesy Jax was a complete and utter moron loser jerk. "You're sure, Bud? Why the hell would he have a place down here? He's a big-time L.A. hell-raiser. Every day there are pictures of him in the tabloids, clubbing in some sleazy bar with women hanging all over him. He's constantly in the news for getting into some kind of trouble. Oh man alive, I bet he'll let his groupies stay here in this very house. I heard he buys places in the sticks just to give big, drunken raves with free booze and drugs."

Bud shrugged. "Well, we have celebs down here. You and Nick, for example. Nick Black's world famous. So are you since you married him. And now there's that Sexiest Man Alive thing goin' on."

Claire ignored every word of that. That was her new plan moving forward. If anybody mentioned *People* or the *National Enquirer*, she was gonna go nonresponsive and lapse into a stare down. "Is Jax in town now?"

"Nobody's been able to get ahold of him. His agent's not answering her phone. Her assistant said all she knows is that Jonesy wants to spend Christmas here at the lake. So, lucky us. We get to suffer the consequences. This house is brand new, she says, decorated by a top team from some elite Beverly Hills design firm, never lived in to date, but built to Jax's rather exhaustive specifications. He didn't ask to be part of the tour, apparently, but said yes when the realtor hit him up to use his place before he moves in. My guess? Jax is probably planning to have some drug-fueled New Year's Eve rave, with all his entourage stayin' right out here. More fun for us, huh?"

Grimacing and badly wanting to throw up, Claire still could not comprehend why a guy like Jonesy Jax would want to own a big house on a remote rural lake in the middle of Missouri, especially given his perverted brand of fun and games. Lake of the Ozarks was a beautiful place at any time of the year, true, but it was not riddled by high excitement twenty-four seven. That state of peaceful coexistence wasn't gonna last long once Jonesy Jax hit town, especially if he brought his own illicit brand of personal depravities into their fold. Good thing, though, now Jonesy Jax had come aboard as her prime candidate for this girl's death. She wondered if he and his scuzzy friends liked to play Detection and had grim reapers tattooed on their backs. Maybe that was something that she and Bud ought to find out.

Play Time

Every single thing about Junior's mother's inquest went off as smooth as a stream of melted milk chocolate. The cops' incompetence was truly a beautiful sight to behold. According to the LAPD reports, on the day of the drowning, a sweet little cook named Rosaria Fernandez let herself into Junior's kitchen around four o'clock in the afternoon on the day of the murder. Lucky for Junior, it took her almost an hour before she happened to notice Junior's extremely dead mother floating facedown in their swimming pool. Outright panicked, she became completely hysterical, and called 911 with all manner of garbled groans and screams for help.

By the time Junior got home that evening, around seven o'clock, the LAPD homicide detectives, forensic techs, and patrol officers were swarming the property. His chess tournament had gone well, of course, because he was such an excellent player, and he was able to concentrate on the matches, even after he'd murdered his mom only a few hours before. It was sort of funny, really, when you got to thinking about it. He'd won a bigger trophy than usual to join the others on his Shelf of Superiority in his game room. He beat six different players that afternoon, one right after another, with lots of spectators watching in hushed reverence. His alibi was as solid as it was false.

The black marble trophy he'd carried in with him that night and showed off to the cops was just icing on the verifiable alibi cake. That prize would always symbolize the reward he got for finally putting his mom out of her misery. Or maybe that should be out of Junior's misery. Not surprisingly, he felt absolutely nothing, zero, nada, zilch when the somber detectives broke the oh-so-sad news to him, but he did manage to cough up a suitable show of tears and cry like a slapped baby. Quite believably, too, if he said so himself. He was proud of that performance. He should've been in films. He'd always been able to cry on cue, and yes, those were pretty much tears of joy, because he was so damn relieved that that stupid bitch was finally dead. Plus the fact that he hadn't been caught, hadn't even come close to being caught. He had outsmarted the best of them, and it was freakin' gratifying.

Yeah, man, everything was just working out beautifully. Except that Lucky hadn't shown back up. Probably long gone and fleeing the scene of the crime until things cooled off. Junior was disappointed that he hadn't come around again. He sure did hope that Lucky would at least drop by so they could celebrate and have a beer together, or something. He wanted somebody around with whom he could share his joy about the murder and its delightful ramifications. Lucky was the only one he could safely talk to.

Three days after Junior had killed his mom, her funeral was held inside a cavernous Methodist church in downtown L.A. Junior's disgusting dad hadn't deigned to call and didn't even acknowledge his ex-wife's death or his son's new poor little orphan boy status. Surprise, surprise. The sanctuary was filled to the brim with some mighty pitiful sounds of phony sniffling and crying and whispering that rose up into the rafters and echoed back down in a muted murmur. All that dramatically expressed grief didn't fool Junior, not for a single second. Fake as hell, all of it. He knew full well that most of the mourners were no more grief stricken than he was. None of them gave a hot shit about Junior's mom. They just wanted everybody to see them in their super tight, short black dresses and their chic floppy-brimmed black funereal hats, all purchased on Rodeo Drive, no doubt. He felt even better when the first spade of dirt hit the top of the fancy white casket. Junior had faked some tears then, too, covered his face with his palms so it would look good to the pastor. He only had to keep the grief thing going a little bit longer, thank goodness. It was a real bore to pretend to mourn his mother.

Hell, he was good at it, though. He almost fooled himself. That's how well he carried off the weeping, rending-his-clothes crap. Truth be told, all he really wanted to do was laugh and sing and dance and count his new fortune, dollar bill by dollar bill. Millions and millions of dollar bills. All his for the taking. At last. Do not pass go. Do not wait until you are twenty-five. It was all his now, every single dime was his to spend, and his alone. He was going to be richer than anybody sitting in those folding chairs around that gravesite. Despite their teary eyes and kindly pats on his back, they were phony, false whiners, the whole lot a bunch of fools. All stupid as hell and greedy and self-absorbed, but they were all well-dressed and coiffed, of course. He bet he had fifty or sixty, or even seventy IQ points on all of them put together.

Best part of the service? The exact moment Junior caught a glimpse of Lucky where he stood a good distance off from the funeral tent. He caught sight of his newly minted friend the exact moment they started lowering poor Mom's coffin into the grave. Lucky was standing up on a knoll directly in front of the mourners gathered around the grave. He was leaning one shoulder against a big white monument under the spreading limbs of a giant oak tree. He was grinning from ear to ear. When he gave Junior a brief thumbs up, Junior almost laughed out loud.

After that, he had to restrain himself from smiling and giving everything away. Oh yeah, he and Lucky were going to be best buddies. They were going to have a ton of fun together. This was his first glimpse of Lucky since that sweet day in the swimming pool. And that's the last he'd probably see of him until after his mom's attorneys released the inheritance. But then, they would party hard. Man, did that sound great to Junior. God, he couldn't wait. He was so damn filthy rich now. He was free of his mom and his dad and anybody else who tried to tell him what to do. Junior couldn't really blame his dad for not showing up. He hadn't called, either, and certainly hadn't offered Junior a place in one of his many vacation homes, or even wanted the chance for them to get to know each other. That didn't matter to Junior. Junior didn't want a home with him. Not anymore.

Junior was as free as a bird for the first time in his life. Lucky knew his secret and hadn't told a soul about the murder. Now Junior finally had a friend who had helped him do what had been necessary that day, and without blinking an eye or casting a bunch of stupid guilt down on Junior's head. They would party and travel and do anything and everything they wanted, and they would do it to anybody they wanted. They might even kill again. Junior liked that idea. He liked it a lot.

Junior had lain in bed almost every night since he committed the murder, reliving the moment when Mom had stopped struggling and finally kicked the bucket. He enjoyed recalling in specific detail the way she released her last breath, the way it had come out of her throat and risen to the surface in that little narrow stream of tiny bubbles. Her last and final breathless goodbye, sonny boy. So long, never to see you again. Lucky had laughed when he'd seen those bubbles. That's the moment they had bonded and become murderers together. It was a fine moment, in a deadly, evil sort of way. But man, had it ever felt good to Junior. He was going to love being a multimillionaire. Maybe even a billionaire by now. He didn't know how much his mother had. But it was plenty. And he was going to enjoy having a blood brother who got off on killing people as much as he did. Life was going so well, and it was only going to get better.

Chapter 6

As the Canton County homicide team stood together at the scene and contemplated what evil the arrival of Jonesy Jax would bring to their law-abiding lake community, Shaggy was the only one who seemed delighted by the unwelcome new resident. Not surprising, really, with Shaggy being Shaggy. "Man oh man alive, this is so damn cool! I love that dude's music. He's awesome, people. More than awesome. He's spectacular. So's his band. I've got every single CD he ever made. Have you heard his theme song, 'Kill All the Women'?"

Claire gave him a look. "Shaggy, that's about as politically incorrect as you can get. If I were you, I wouldn't admit to anybody that you like that song. Especially to anyone of the female gender, of which I am, if you'll recall. What's more, a song like that sounds like he might be a prime candidate for this first-degree murder. Whoever did this doesn't have much respect for womanhood, believe you me."

"Nah, you're wrong about him. Listen to the lyrics, Claire. Jonesy doesn't say 'kill them all,' not really kill them, you know, like murder them, or anything. He means he kills them with his charm and sex appeal."

Claire could only scoff. "Well, good luck with that. He's the grossest, most arrogant human being that I've ever met. I'm already sick to my stomach just talking about him. Oh, and by the way, Jonesy Jax has a rap sheet three miles long. DUIs, drug busts, and last and most despicable, multiple counts of sex with underage girls. He has exactly zero redeeming qualities. Trust me on that, Shaggy. I had hoped that I'd never have to see him again, but it seems my luck is always bad where obnoxious morons are concerned."

"Again? You've met this guy?" That was Bud, and he looked shocked.

"No shit? You've actually met Jonesy Jax? In person?" That was Shaggy, all atwitter, with a bit of squeal in his voice.

"Oh yeah, I had the distinct displeasure of arresting him on Hollywood Boulevard when I was a street cop at LAPD. Long time ago, true, but I'll never forget that creep. He actually propositioned me for sex while I was frisking him. Tried to grab me, if you know what I mean. Then he had the gall to pull out a bunch of hundred-dollar bills to tempt me to oblige his needs. And yes, I was wearing my uniform. Trust me, guys: Jonesy Jax is a colossal dirtbag."

All three men grinned. Claire didn't particularly appreciate that. "Not funny, guys. I charged him with drug possession, drug paraphernalia, and having sex with the sixteen-year-old girl who was with him and half-dressed in the back seat of his limo. She admitted everything, and none of it was pretty. Last but not least, I added assault on a police officer to the charges."

That sobered them all pretty damn fast. "He serve time for that?" Bud asked.

"What do you think? He's almost as rich as Black. He assembled his team of fancy L.A. lawyers, who showed up within the hour and got him sprung from detention. They used every dirty, scummy trick in the book to get him off. But I'll never forget that guy and the way he treated me. And lucky me, now he's right here on our lake, in our jurisdiction. That means I'll probably have to deal with him again. The idea actually turns my stomach."

"What did you say this guy's name was?" That was Buckeye. He looked clueless about the rock star. He had finished up at the scene and was prepared to leave. The young woman's body was in the van, and his techs had already packed up and were waiting outside. Buck was good at his job. In and out, no mistakes, no wasted energy. Claire was not surprised that he was unfamiliar with Jonesy Jax's disreputable reputation. He listened to Johnny Cash and June Carter on the way to crime scenes, much to the chagrin of Shaggy and the other young CSI technicians.

"Jonesy Jax, you know, the hard rocker that wears all that black leather with silver chains and has a parrot on stage in a cage that shrieks out curses to the audience," Bud informed him. Buck frowned at that and still looked blank, and a bit skeptical. "Maybe you'll remember the time he threw pills out into the audience and then told everybody to take them on the count of three and they'd all trip out together. He got arrested for that, too, didn't he?"

Claire nodded. "Yes, sir, he sure did, but it turned out to be a publicity stunt. The pills were Tic Tacs. He got fined and got a ton of bad publicity, but he ended up smelling like a rose to all his fans. They thought it was a cool move. I just find it so distasteful that we are actually going to have to be in the same room with this guy, much less engage him in conversation. Or touch him, heaven forbid."

"I like some of his music." Bud looked sheepish at the admission.

"Me too. You're bein' too hard on old Jonesy," Shaggy told her. "I got his 'Hate Everybody' poster. Think he'll autograph it for me?"

They all collectively ignored him.

Claire turned to Bud. "Any way that you can get him on the phone?"

"Maybe. It's late, but I know a TV agent in Los Angeles who can get me to the right people, I think."

"Okay, then try to get hold of him ASAP and tell him we need to talk to Jonesy stat. Tell him it's urgent. You know the drill."

Bud moved off again, with his trusty phone in hand. Bud could work magic with that thing and get through to almost anybody, anywhere, Hollywood movers and shakers included. He used his southern charm like a weapon, plus a good bit of pure BS. Claire watched him walk off, and then she sighed, deflated. One of the biggest rock stars who ever lived was the last person on earth she needed to become involved in this girl's murder. Damn it, the paparazzi were already buzzing around and lying in wait for her and Black. This would jack up their feeding frenzy to bloodbath levels.

"Claire," Buckeye said, "I think we can count on blunt force trauma as cause of death. Not much else to go on yet, except for a small puncture wound on her abdomen and the minor burns on her head from the hot light bulbs. The victim bled out for a while before she stopped breathing, might even have regained consciousness for a few seconds, but I really doubt that. I'll know more and have a definitive cause after the autopsy. So I'm out of here. I'll do the cut first thing in the morning."

"Want us to be there?"

"Up to you guys. Our workload at the morgue is slow. That's why I thought I could dash off with the wife and fly down to the Bahamas for Christmas. Looks like that may be out now."

"Maybe we'll solve this case in record time. Bud and I are pretty good at this stuff when we work together, you know. And the sunny Bahamas are only a few hours away by plane."

"I suspect Jonesy Jax and all his crap is going to screw things up for our trip, take my word on that. Okay, I'm out of here. See you later, Claire."

Claire watched him walk away, but he was right. Jonesy Jax always screwed things up, wherever he was. It was embedded in his genes.

Within minutes, Bud was back beside Claire.

"Did you get hold of him?"

"Not yet. Left my number with the agent and asked him to return my call, told him it was urgent."

Claire glanced around. "Okay, there's not much else we can do out here right now. Let's shut down all these stupid lights and maybe we'll get hold of Jax in the morning. I'm fairly certain he's gonna know this girl, probably intimately."

"We do have the lady in charge of the Christmas tour outside. Corrigan's got her waiting in his patrol car. She's the one who found the body and showed up here earlier, thinking we might want to interview her."

"Well, she's right. Let's do it now."

By the time they wrapped things up inside and stepped out onto the front porch, the temperature had dropped even lower. It felt like ten degrees below zero, at the very least, and the wind chill even worse than that. Their breaths materialized, smoky in the cold air. Snow was falling again, harder now. It was a beautiful, snowy night on a dark and quiet cliff out in the middle of the deep woods. Peaceful, quiet, or at least, used to be. Too bad some unknown young girl had to die there in the midst of so much natural beauty.

Corrigan stood out in the driveway, leaning against the fender of his patrol car, stamping his feet and clapping his hands together. He looked pretty damn annoyed about having to stick around and wait for them to interview the witness. They thanked him, and then Bud invited the witness into his truck so Corrigan could go home to his family. Claire climbed into the back seat and sat beside the woman. Bud took the driver's seat, fired the engine, turned the heater up to full blast, and then swiveled slightly so that he could look back at them. He started the interview without delay.

"You are Mrs. Barbara Sherman, is that correct, ma'am?"

The woman nodded. She looked to be around sixty, maybe. Tall woman, five-nine or five-ten, around Claire's height. She had a pretty face that looked younger than she probably was, and long brown hair with lots of gray strands, which she wore pulled straight back in a tight, low ponytail. She seemed calm and unperturbed by the horrific scene she'd walked into earlier that day. Suspiciously serene, in fact. She didn't say anything, just waited for them to ask their questions. Claire leaned back, content to let Bud take the lead.

"Thank you for waiting so long, Mrs. Sherman. My name is Bud Davis. This is my partner, Claire Morgan. We're both homicide detectives at the Canton County Sheriff's Office."

"How do you do?" she replied. A very polite woman, it seemed. As the truck became warmer, Barbara took a moment to shed her puffy black insulated jacket. She had on a Christmas elf's costume underneath: red corduroy jumper shorts with a red-and-white-striped, long-sleeved T-shirt, knee-high candy-cane-striped socks, and red ankle boots. This night was so way weird that Claire was getting a little overwhelmed by the sheer absurdity that kept slapping her in the face.

"I'm sorry it took us this long to get done inside the house, ma'am. Officer Corrigan told us that you discovered the body; is that correct?"

"Yes, sir. I came out here a little early, you know, just to check and make sure everything was in good order before the tour started. But I'm not really in charge of the tour groups or anything. I just enjoy dressing up in these cute costumes and taking folks through these beautiful homes. This holiday house tour is sponsored by the Chamber of Commerce and the Lake of the Ozarks Garden Club. They did a great job this year, you know, despite today's terrible tragedy. They ordered all those poinsettias you saw inside the house. They got them from Mexico. Had them shipped up."

Now there you have some useless home tour trivia, Claire thought. Mexican flowers were the last thing on her crime-scene-things-to-know list.

Bud continued. "Were you alone when you found the victim?"

"Yes, but only for a few minutes before the folks began to arrive. A few of them were already standing around on the porch, waiting for somebody to unlock the door and take them through the house. So I hurried so I could check out the house first, like I always do. I was already in costume and expected to stay for the second go-around slated for this evening at eight. It was cancelled, of course. All the tours are by now, I suppose."

"Do any of the guides wear angel costumes?" Claire asked.

"No, that was last year. This year, we can either choose to be an elf like this outfit I'm wearing, or there are flannel nightgowns, and old fashioned caroler outfits reminiscent of Dickens's London."

"We think our victim might be one of your tour guides. They'll probably have her name and address somewhere, right? Did you happen to know her personally?"

"No, I'd never seen that poor little thing before."

"Okay," Bud said. "Tell us exactly what happened when you got here. Everything you can remember, no matter how small or seemingly insignificant."

"Well, I went ahead and did a walk-through before I took anybody inside the house. I don't know why, but I like to do that when I have time to. Maybe I had a premonition or something about today. I just felt like I should look around and make sure everything was okay. I have to light the display candles anyway. So I had the visitors come inside out of the cold and wait for me in the kitchen. We had provided hot cocoa and coffee and had some sugar cookies sitting out on the counter for refreshments. But then, when I walked into that library and saw that poor child, oh my goodness, my heart practically stopped. It was just horrible. I just froze in my tracks, because I couldn't even believe my eyes. Then I saw how her eyes were staring down at me, like she was really perched on top of that tree and looking right at me, and then I realized she was dead, really dead, and I'm afraid I pretty much just lost it. I ran out screaming, and that panicked everyone else, so they all ran out of the house, too. Some man in the group had the wherewithal to call 911." She stopped talking long enough to inhale a deep breath. Her voice was shaking. "I still have trouble believing this kind of thing could happen right here on our lake. Don't you?"

Both of them nodded, but they had been homicide detectives far too long to disbelieve anything they found at a crime scene. Murderers found victims everywhere, even at Lake of the Ozarks. "Did you touch anything when you were in the library? Did you go up on the balcony and touch the body?" Bud asked her.

"Oh heavens above, no. Why would I want to do that? I could barely even look at her up there, you know, all that blood soaking that white gown. Oh my word, I still cannot believe it. I've never seen a dead person like that. Somebody who has just been murdered. Except on TV shows."

"And you're sure you don't recognize the victim?"

"Well, no, but I didn't look at her all that long. I just saw the blood and those eyes. My thought was that she was a guide dressed up like a living angel. One of us. Most of the younger guides are about her age." She clasped her hands together tightly and kept shaking her head as if completely befuddled. "It looked like one of our costumes from last year, truth be told. They just used long white nightgowns."

Claire thought the poor woman might be suffering from shock. She didn't really act like it, though, which seemed odd. A Chatty Cathy type, but seemed to be telling the truth. Maybe. "Who could we contact that might be able to give us the victim's name and address? We will need to notify her next of kin as soon as we verify her identity."

"I have no idea, unless, of course, she was a guide, but I don't think she was. But if so, I guess you'll need to find out who hired her and question them. I'm not sure who's in charge of that kind of stuff this year. I've been leading tours for them going on ten years, but I certainly don't keep up with the ladies in charge of recruiting the guides. I just try to make sure everything in the house looks the way the garden club left it. You know, pulling out dead branches from the fresh arrangements and lighting the candles, things like that. "

"Did you see anybody, either inside or outside the house, when you arrived here today?"

"No, sir." Mrs. Sherman stared at Bud a moment. "I did happen to notice, however, that the patio door was unlocked. That observation was, of course, before I turned around and saw the dead girl up on the balcony."

Claire had already checked out the doors. She had found no footprints inside or outside the patio French door, so the killer must have come in a different way, or broken in and concealed himself in the house before the victim arrived. "And you're sure you didn't touch anything? Or see anybody loitering around?"

"Of course I'm sure. I know better than to do that, even as creeped out as I was. I watch *NCIS* every week. Well, at least I did until Ziva left the show. Didn't like it so much after that. She and Tony were so good together, don't you think? It's a damn shame that such a good actress had to leave. I heard she only left because she wanted to be with her boyfriend down in South America. Such a shame for Tony. He was never the same without her."

"Ain't that the truth? Ziva was badass, too. Man, could she take down guys, or what?" Bud happened to be a TV aficionado. In fact, he knew every single program and every single character on every single channel and who they were dating or cheating on. His recall was amazing. Claire only liked programs like *Supernatural* and *Arrow* because they were both pretty much about teams of badass fighters out for justice. Like she and Bud. Bad thing, though, probably, since she was a cop and those characters were pretty much vigilantes. The mention of the *NCIS* characters, however, seemed to warm up Mrs. Sherman toward Bud. They were smiling at each other now like they were good old TV friends. Bud did have a knack for connecting with people, and he was especially good with women. Any woman. Any age. Always had been. But alas, his amorous endeavors had dropped a couple of degrees since he'd hooked up with his beautiful and leggy model, Brianna.

While they smiled at each other, still in the throes of NCIS nostalgia, Claire assumed, she took over the interview. "Did you notice anything unusual outside the house when you drove up today? Anything out of the ordinary? A repairman, maybe? Somebody walking a dog? Shoveling snow? Tire tracks? Anything like that?"

"No, I'm afraid not. This entire property is surrounded by all those big trees. You know, it's so extremely isolated up here, even from the neighbors on the next property over. But I never would have expected that it would become a place where a young girl could be murdered. It's just so frightening to comprehend. But I guess you've seen a lot of horrible things in your line of work."

Now that was the understatement of the century, Claire thought. Oh yeah, she'd seen plenty of things every bit as horrible as that dead angel inside that house, even things that were a hundred times worse. Yep, she and Bud had pretty much looked the devil in the face, more often than not, and both on and off the job. "Okay. We understand that the singer Jonesy Jax owns this house. Can you tell us if that might be true or just a rumor?" *Please God, let it be some hellish rumor.*

Barbara Sherman nodded. "Yes, I've heard all about that. I believe he just bought this place recently. He's that famous heavy metal rocker, I guess you know of him. The nasty one with white hair, the one who looks so dirty and disheveled all the time."

Talk about hitting the nail on the head. "We just need for you to verify that he is the actual owner of this property."

"Well, I'm not able to verify it, per se. All I can tell you is that the Christmas tour contact, you know, the realtor, told me he owned this place. Mary Lynn McPhee is her name. She said she got permission directly from him to decorate this house, but he wanted to wait until the tours were over before he moved in. She said he was willing to wait until Christmas Eve. He didn't want his fame to overshadow the tour by being here on the property himself. That was rather kind of him, I suppose."

"Has he arrived here at the lake?" Claire asked with severe and unsettling dread.

Mrs. Sherman shrugged. "I don't know. Mary Lynn sounded as if he was still out in California when she talked to him. Or maybe, come to think of it, she said he was on a tour stop in Chicago. Yes, I believe that's what she said. That he had a big show up there, right before Christmas. I can't really remember where he was."

"Did she tell you anything else about him?"

"Well, she did say that he was extremely polite during their video conference. She said he was nothing like the despicable person he is on stage."

Well, that was a load of bull. Claire had been up close and way too personal with the lecher. Give him time and a bottle of whiskey and he'd be breaking his guitar over some lake-dweller's head before you could say "drunken jerk." "Did she say anything else about him?"

"Apparently, he visited here once before, for some reason or another. Or maybe he was born around here. I declare, I just can't recall details anymore. He did say he liked it out here in the sticks. I do remember Mary

Lynn saying that. Something about needing a quiet place to come to when he needed to get his head on straight."

And that would be all the time, Claire thought.

"He's the one who insisted they put up all these Christmas lights. He said he wanted both the exterior and the interior to be lit up so much that the astronauts could see it from orbit. Said it would be his Christmas present to them."

Yeah, that's the way certified morons thought about things, too. Just the idea of trying to deal with Jonesy Jax was beginning to ruin her fabulous, happiest-ever Christmas. "So, ma'am, do you happen to have a phone number for him?"

"Yes, she gave it to me since I was the guide for his house. But he's never answered when I've called. I tried again while I was waiting out here with the other officers."

"Okay. Give us his number and I'll keep trying to contact him," Bud said.

"I did find out that it's not his cell, but the phone number for his Malibu beach house."

"Bet the neighbors just love him living close by. Probably like holes in their heads," Claire said. "But I suppose it's close enough to L.A. that just about anything goes. Even crazy loons are loved and paid big bucks for their unlawful antics."

"Well, he is allowing us to use his house for our charity," Mrs. Sherman said with a bit of a huff. No doubt thinking: *How dare that damn detective show contempt for a man gracious enough to lend his house to our tour.* Apparently, it didn't matter how addled in the brain the guy was. Then again, Mrs. Sherman hadn't met the guy in person.

"Yes, ma'am. He's a prince, all right."

Mrs. Sherman gazed back at her, not sure if Claire was being snarky, or not. It was snark, all right. Up front and meant as disdain.

Bud looked at Claire's expression and decided it was time to take over. "After you called 911, did you or anyone else go back inside where the body was?"

"Oh my Lord, no. Once I saw that poor girl, I knew that she was dead. I wouldn't have gone back inside that room for any amount of money."

"Okay. Anything else you can tell us? Anybody make threats about this house or any other house on the tour? This year or in past years?"

"No, sir, we really hadn't even named the houses to be included in our tour until a couple of days before we started. Members of the garden club were the only ones allowed inside, and that was only for decorating purposes. They bought all the supplies and took care of everything. I just happened to be here today. I never could've imagined anything like this could ever happen. Not here. Not on our lovely little Christmas tour."

Claire listened politely. The woman was handling it better than most witnesses would after happening upon a brutal, bloody crime scene. Claire wondered why. Maybe they should look into this sweet little lady. "And Jonesy Jax was never here at this house? You're certain about that?"

"No. At least, I don't think so. She said he gave his permission and then left the room before they finished their video conference. His agent inked the contract and took care of all that."

"Did he charge you for using the house?"

"Oh, no. The contract was mainly about his privacy; we were to make sure his groupies and fans weren't allowed inside. He didn't want anybody to know he was settling here in Missouri, or that he had bought this house."

"And his agent's name?"

"Candi Kisses."

"Nuh-uh," said Bud. "No way."

"I know. I admit I rolled my eyes to high heaven when I heard that. He said she made it up so she would be remembered."

Remembered as an imbecile, Claire thought.

"Maybe he was just messin' with you," Bud suggested. "You know, everybody knows he likes to joke around."

"Mary Lynn said Ms. Kisses was right there sitting beside him at the table and was introduced as Candi Kisses. Nobody seemed to think it was unusual."

Claire felt like she was going to gag. This case was going to turn into a nightmare of enormous proportions. She just knew it in her gut. This murder was a harbinger of bad things now galloping down the road to run her over, and she was pretty damn sure she would soon get flattened like Wile E. Coyote. Most movie types she'd met had the IQ and personal habits of alley cats, save for a few nice guys, and most of their temperaments were not conducive to normal human interactions. Arrogance was a necessary state of being famous in Tinsel Town, she'd found. Well, maybe not all actors were monsters, but, say, 99.9 percent were. Jonesy Jax would be the president of the Actor-Singer Cray-Cray Club.

Claire leaned forward. "Okay, thank you very much, Mrs. Sherman. I guess that's all the questions we have for you right now."

"Would it be all right if we called you again, if we have more questions?" Bud asked.

"Of course. I'll be glad to help you in any way that I can."

"Would you mind to write Jax's Malibu number on the back of my card?"

"All right, of course. But I really need to be getting home now. My husband will worry about me. I usually get home before he does. I took an anxiety pill while I was sitting out here a while ago, and I think I need to lie down and rest. All of this has really been quite upsetting."

It didn't seem to have gotten to her all that much, not under Claire's observation. "Of course, ma'am. Again, thank you for waiting out here so long, Mrs. Sherman."

Claire took the card after Mrs. Sherman scribbled the number on it, and Bud walked around the car and opened the door for the woman, because he really was as polite as hell where ladies were concerned. Mrs. Sherman hurried across the snowy drive to her late-model gray Mercedes and took off down the road. Everybody else had already gone. Bud and Claire stood in front of the truck for a moment, looking up at the sparkling lights. Maybe the astronauts really could see it. Maybe they were enjoying it more than she was. But that wouldn't take much.

The air was really frigid now. Claire hoped Black had all the fireplaces in the penthouse built up high and blazing like crazy. Or, better yet, maybe he'd be ready to warm her up in the special way only he could. That sounded even better to her. Or both him and the fire, maybe.

Bud blew his breath into his palms. Yes, he was getting his warm clothes before Christmas. "Okay, we'll have to get a bead on Jax's location first thing in the morning. Maybe he'll know who this kid is. Otherwise, we've got exactly nothing."

"That's for damn sure."

"Let's take another quick look around inside for ourselves," Claire said, "just in case Corrigan and his jerk partner missed something. I want to see the master bedroom where she might've been staying."

So that's what they did for the next hour, but with no luck whatsoever. The interior of the house was beautiful, fully decorated by some Beverly Hills whiz kid, all right. At least that's what the card on the kitchen island read. But the place was definitely brand new, all the wood ceilings giving off that rustic, raw wood and varnish smell. At the end of the search, Claire was pretty sure that the drunken rock star had never stepped foot inside that house, and maybe never would. Hell, he had probably bought the place while in a particularly mind-blowing pipe dream.

If he had been inside, he hadn't brought along any clothes or shoes or coats. No nothing, in fact. No food in the fridge, no supplies in the kitchen cabinets. It was pristine, like a model house in a new subdivision, but one built on a budget fifty times bigger. Top of the line in every way. She wondered if Jonesy Jax really would show up. He probably just bought houses here and there for the hell of it. Of course, Black had a habit of doing that, too, but at least he spent time in them once in a while and considered them investments.

The only room in the house that looked lived in was the master bedroom. It had a suitcase in the closet with a minimal amount of clothes on the hangers, but they were clothes that would fit their victim. She had been staying there, but it didn't look like she'd been there long, like the officers had said. Nothing much to see inside that bedroom except for a few bathroom toiletries and dirty clothes strewn about. It was strange, and hard to figure exactly what she was doing there. Maybe she had been a squatter or a druggie who had broken in and made herself at home. But how would she have even found the place, way out here in the sticks? Someone who'd been on the tour, maybe?

Claire sighed, feeling weary all of a sudden. "Okay, let's just go home, get some sleep, and start again in the morning."

"You got that right, partner. Music to my ears." Bud smiled mischievously in a way she knew very well, and she braced herself for whatever was incoming. "I need to read that article about Black and admire you in that bikini before I go to bed. I just can't get enough of you famous celebrities. Know what they're calling you two on TMZ? Blair. Get it? Black and Claire combined. Only the biggest celebrity couples get a tag name like that. You've made it to the top, darlin'."

"Shut up, Bud. I mean it. Enough, already. That's just stupid. Blair. How stupid. Are they really calling us that?"

"Yep." Bud laughed at her and headed around to the driver's side of his truck. Claire smiled a little, too, and pulled open her door. She had missed the heck out of being around Bud. On the other hand, she was eager to get back home, because she missed Black and Rico and all their ridiculously overdone excitement about Christmas. She wasn't used to being away from them for so long, not anymore. Her work hours had become irregular again fast, and the crime scene had taken longer than she'd figured. It was a school night for Rico. Unfortunately, they'd probably have to wait on decorating the tree until tomorrow. Probably a good thing, because after seeing that young girl's body, lit up and perched at the top of that tree, Christmas tree decorating had lost its appeal. Imagine that.

Play Time

For the next few months, Junior and Lucky were extra careful about not being seen together. They met up a lot in secret, however, always in small, out-of-the-way restaurants and malls, usually down in Oceanside or out in Santa Clarita. Sometimes they hooked up in luxury hotels in downtown L.A., usually reserving a large suite under an assumed name, playing video games all night and ordering pizza and beer and women and anything else they wanted. Lucky was turning out to be a great guy, a really good friend, even if he had screwed Junior's mother in Junior's house. That fact was sickening to think about, and sometimes Junior did dwell on it. But he decided to let it be.

Truthfully, however, Junior liked Lucky even more than he wanted to admit. They thought alike. They both had dark, creepy thoughts that they wanted to pursue for real. They had killed together for the first time, had done it well and gotten away with it. As time went on, they craved doing it again. They wanted that lovely adrenaline rush and final burst of pure ecstasy when their target finally bit it. Both of them were interested in having beautiful women around, too, but neither had a real girlfriend. Girls liked to talk too much. Girls loved to gossip with other girls and share all their secrets, and that could be a dangerous proposition so soon after their first kill. Not a good idea. Girls got jealous and caused trouble and made scenes. Girls listened to them when they got drunk, and they might slip and mention the murder. Besides, there were prostitutes galore in L.A., good-looking ones for when they wanted sex, call girls, and they liked to use them together. It was all great fun and they were so happy to be alive and such good friends.

After his mom had been rotting in her grave for six months, they started hanging out in public together. They'd already graduated from high school and didn't have to go to class anymore or worry about graduation. At first they went out to trendy clubs together, a one-toe-in-the-water kind of thing, after all his mother's phony, slutty friends had stopped checking on Junior and bringing all those disgusting casseroles made by their cooks and left by their butlers outside his front door. They finally lost interest and returned to their shallow, self-involved lives and forgot all about poor young Junior who no longer had his plastic-coated mom around. He had told everyone he was thinking about going to St. Andrew's College in Edinburgh because that's where Prince William had gone. They all believed that ridiculous lie, too. They believed all his lies. He had turned out to be an exceptional liar, and that was a good thing. But he'd always been, really. He was getting even better at it as time went by.

The more he hung around with Lucky, the better he liked him. He especially loved the fact that Lucky liked to play board games. The basement game room was a veritable arcade, with just about every video game and board game and pinball machine known to man. They spent hours down there together, trying their level best to beat each other at everything. They found out that they were both highly competitive in their own ways and neither took prisoners because winning was the most important thing. Both of them loved to best the other more than anything else in the world, and neither of them lost graciously. In fact, they often came to physical blows over close scores and accused each other of cheating, but that usually happened when they were halfway drunk. Especially Lucky, and he got drunk a lot. That's when they pretty much attacked each other and wrestled on the floor, scratching and punching and ending up all bruised up with black eyes and bloody noses. But they didn't care. They always got up and shook hands afterward, and then had a beer as their red fits of anger dwindled and their hazes of rage slowly faded away.

Junior was finding out that Lucky was a lot smarter than he had first thought. Not brilliant like Junior, of course—nobody could be as smart as he was. But Lucky had proven to be very bright and often came up with great ideas. Even though Lucky had concentrated on sports in school, he knew lots of other interesting things about different subjects and areas, but that only meant that they could teach each other new stuff. They just clicked. They snapped into place like Lego blocks, as if they should have been born twins. It was so great to have another guy that Junior could trust. Somebody like a real brother, like family. Somebody who truly liked him and treated him with respect. This was the best time in Junior's life, bar none.

Another thing they found out they shared was an intense love of horror movies. There was a home movie theater in Junior's basement, and they'd relax in two big, leather recliners, eating cheeseburgers and fries from In-N-Out Burger and drinking beer all night long while they watched one film after another. They liked to watch flicks with lots of blood and gore and strangling and maiming and butchering, and then they'd discuss how they could have committed the murders better and without getting caught. They loved the cruelty and the mind games and the screaming of victims, and the more they saw, the better they liked it. It was exciting and horrible and mind-blowing. Soon those kinds of films became their obsession. That dark basement room filled with endless depictions of murder and death and destruction was what they lived for.

Chapter 7

Nicholas Black sat in a comfortable maroon leather wing chair in front of the living room fireplace. He was waiting for Claire to get home from work, staring into the fire, his feet propped on a round hassock. Rico was sitting on the couch, his fingers working fast and furiously on the keys of his iPhone. He was playing a new Star Wars video game that Black had downloaded for him a couple of weeks ago. All sorts of ringing and exploding sounds were disrupting the quiet room. Black grinned at the expressions flitting across Rico's face as he concentrated on the keys. He loved Star Wars more than just about anything. The penthouse no longer lay silent when Claire was gone, that was for damn sure. Since Rico had come to live with them, the ten-year-old boy had always been on the move, running from room to room and laughing and talking with nonstop excitement. Tonight was no different. They had already put up a small Christmas tree in the boy's bedroom, but Rico had wanted to wait for Claire to come home before they decorated it. Now, however, Rico was waiting for Claire's good friend, Harve Lester, to come pick him up so he could help decorate Harve's tree and spend the night at his house. Black looked forward to some private downtime with Claire, and that meant the kind they enjoyed the most.

But now she was late coming home, and Black and Rico were both becoming impatient. Being late was always okay with him until it became *too* late, and then he started getting worried. God knew he had reason to be. She had been late in the past for some very dangerous, life-threatening reasons. He shot back his sleeve and looked at his watch. Going on three hours late now, but he couldn't say he didn't expect that to happen now and then. Homicide detectives worked crazy hours, and she and Bud had just caught a murder that they had to investigate. He understood that and tried to be reasonable. Sometimes it wasn't so easy. Like right now.

For a long time, he and Claire had worked around her crazy detective schedule. That's when he had really been concerned about her safety. She had this bizarre tendency to get caught up with serial killers, one right after another. It was uncanny, actually. Hopefully, this time, the murder would be an easy one to solve, with enough proof at the scene to make an immediate arrest. But he wasn't counting on that. Few of her murder cases had ever been simple, but she always somehow managed to solve them. She was damn good detective. But these late hours were one reason she had agreed to open her private investigation firm. Nothing had ever made him happier than that decision.

At the moment, however, there was a holiday lull in her active PI cases, and her partner, Will Novak, was off somewhere in Central America. Claire had jumped at the chance to return to the sheriff's department and partner up with Bud again. Black was fine with that, because it made her happy. Still, he had not missed these long nights of sitting and waiting for her, most of the time without a clue to where she was or what she was doing or what kind of danger she was facing. He'd done that too often since he'd met her. "Hey, Nick, I'm stuck on this level," Rico said, getting up and coming over to his chair. "Will you help me? You're good at these games, aren't you?"

"Yes, I am. Come on, we'll do it together."

Rico climbed up onto Black's lap. It felt good to have a little kid sitting on his lap. He'd always wanted a son, and Rico was just the best little kid in the world. Black already considered him a son. Black smiled at how excited Rico was as he explained the game and what he was having trouble with. This kid was something else.

"Okay, look, take the catapult back and aim higher and it will drop down and topple the enemy's fort. See, let me show you."

Black demonstrated and managed a bull's-eye, and Rico laughed when the entire structure crumbled into the moat. "Cool, that's so cool. Awesome, Nick. Okay, let me try, let me do it."

Black handed the phone over, and Rico frowned in concentration as he continued to play. Rico was a whiz at anything computer related, learned quickly, and loved his electronics more than anything else he had. Black smiled at his enthusiasm, so happy to have the boy living with them. Now if Claire would just get home so he wouldn't have to worry about her.

Other than Claire's late arrival and the blasted media hounds down in the lobby, he was more content than he'd been in years. Everything had been going so well. Now that they were married, he and Claire were in a really good place. A fantastic place. Rico had a lot to do with that, too. All three of them were doing fine after barely surviving some dicey situations the summer before. But who was he kidding? They'd survived because of Claire. Her courage and determination had saved his life and Rico's, but Rico had been a little hero, too. Now life was finally getting halfway back to normal. They were home at the lake. He was seeing patients, and not just at Cedar Bend Lodge but at his private clinics in other cities, too. He would have to start traveling again soon, maybe even a trip to New York later this week. Right now, though, he was simply glad to be home at the lake where it was nice and quiet. Most of all, he was happy that Claire was his wife and Rico was still living with them. Black was pretty much glad about everything he could think of—except for those damn tabloids. His jaw hardened again when he thought about Claire's picture in that bikini. He'd been angry about it all day long, couldn't seem to shake off his resentment. Now he wished he hadn't ever bought that thing for her.

"Hey, I know I'm really late. Sorry."

Black turned around at the sound of Claire's voice. Immediately relieved, he got that little thrill that shot through him each time he saw her come home from work safe and sound. He got it every time he saw her, period. Rico jumped up and ran to her, and she leaned down and gave him a big hug, then bent down and listened to the boy's excited chatter about the computer game.

"Harve's gonna be here any minute to pick me up," Rico was telling her. "I'm going to help him with his Christmas tree."

"Hey, tonight's a school night."

"That's okay. I've done my homework and Harve says he'll take me to school. Nick said I could go."

As if scripted, Black's phone vibrated and a text from Harve popped up. "He's downstairs waiting with Isaac by the elevator. I've got your backpack ready to go. Don't forget to brush your teeth."

"Okay, then I'll see you tomorrow after school," Rico said, rushing to give Black a hug and then grabbing his backpack before returning to give Claire a quick kiss. "I gotta go. Harve'll be waiting for me. We're gonna make s'mores and cocoa."

Then he was gone in a flash, a clatter of running footsteps receding down the hall, leaving Claire and Black looking after him. Claire turned and smiled at Black as she slipped out of her parka and pulled off her gloves. She crossed the room to him, her face flushed from the cold, cheeks pink and glowing. God, he was glad they were finally married. All she had to do was show up and he wanted her. It had always been that way. He watched her shrug out of her shoulder holster and put it down on the coffee table. "Good God, is there anything on earth sexier than a woman wearing a shoulder holster?"

"You are, according to *People* magazine."

"Don't get me started. I'm still pissed off."

"That is putting it mildly. But that's okay with me. Just so long as you remain calm around me and Rico." She glanced around. "It's too quiet already. That kid. How'd we ever get along without him? And where's that best and biggest tree ever that you've been bragging about?"

"When you didn't show up for dinner, Rico decided he wanted to go over to Harve's house and help him put up his tree. So I said he could, and that we'd wait and do ours tomorrow night."

Claire sat down and started unlacing her snow boots. "Black, it's a school night. He needs to get to bed early."

"Harve knows that. Besides, Rico can miss a day of school now and then. His IQ is through the roof. I tested him the other day."

"You don't have to tell me that. On the other hand, he still needs to learn the basics, you know, like multiplication tables and state capitals and verb tenses."

"He probably already knows them. Besides, I got him a new Apple Watch so he can look all that up whenever he needs to. You know how interested he is in just about everything. That will be a good incentive to satisfy his curiosity."

Claire sat down on the arm of the couch just across from him. "Yeah? Know what, Black? I think we need to talk about how much you spoil that boy. You are now edging up to win the most super indulgent parent who ever lived award."

Black only smiled. "I'm not spoiling him, I'm rewarding him. He saved our lives in Sicily, if you recall. He's a good little kid, despite all the bad things he's been through."

Claire looked unconvinced, but Black's gratitude for what Rico had done was endless. Rico had helped Claire get Black out of a very dire situation with some equally dire bad guys. They both owed the kid for that little miracle of youthful ingenuity. Still, he was only ten years old, turning eleven in another month or so. He needed structure in his life, and he was getting it. Claire didn't need to worry about that.

"All true," Claire was saying, "but he's still stealing things around the resort. That's got to stop."

"He had to steal to survive when he was on that island. You know that. He stole stuff that saved our necks, if you'll recall."

"I am as grateful as you are, Black, and I love him as much as you do, but he has to learn right and wrong, and that he's got to follow the rules just like everybody else. Or we're gonna end up with a little juvenile delinquent on our hands."

"No, we won't. He knows right from wrong as well as you and I do."

Black watched her roll her neck around and stretch her shoulders, and then he stood up and walked over to the couch. He sat down beside her and pulled her off the arm of the chair down onto his lap. He put his arms around her waist and laid his head against her breast. He could hear her heart beating, and it began to speed up. He smiled, liking that. She slid her arms around his neck, snuggled closer, and laid her cheek against the top of his head. That's all it took. He wanted to kiss her, just like he always did. He closed his eyes as she tangled her fingers in his hair. It felt so comfortable, the two of them together, married, happy, felt so damn right, felt perfect. He sighed, glad she was finally back home. But Rico's stealing had become a bone of contention between them. He didn't think it mattered since he owned everything that Rico had taken from the hotel. Claire felt differently, and as a law enforcement officer it bugged her big time. "You know, Claire, it doesn't matter what Rico takes, anyway. I told the resort shops and restaurants to let him have what he wants and charge it to me. So he's not really stealing. Technically."

Claire leaned back and stared down into his face. "Black! What the devil are you thinking? He cannot be allowed to just take things off store shelves without paying for them. Not here, or anywhere else. That is a bad habit, and a dangerous one, and you have to know it."

"It never amounts to much, just a few cans of soda and some candy, usually, for himself and the other kids. He's not robbing cash registers."

"What other kids?"

"Kids whose families are staying here. He's mentioned somebody named Ollie, who's on vacation here, and there's a Jonathan, and there's a Katie, I think. I always confront him when I get the bills and tell him it's wrong and that I'm taking the cost out of his allowance."

"Why does that sound ineffective to me? Besides, I think a hundred dollars a month for a ten-year-old's allowance is going a little overboard. Surely you see my point?"

Black only smiled. "Most of it goes into his savings account. And I told you. We owe that kid. I am grateful, and I always show my gratitude in a big way." He picked up her hand and pressed the back of it to his mouth.

Her skin smelled good. Irish Spring soap. He turned it over and caressed her palm with his lips because he knew it turned her on. Then he sat up and pulled her around to straddle his lap. He slid his hand up under her sweatshirt. "My God, you feel good. I'm suddenly very pleased that we're home alone tonight. Let me take off that shirt and see what happens."

"I know what's gonna happen, and so do you. But I'm in, one hundred percent. Trust me. You need to warm me up, anyway. It's cold outside."

Claire moaned softly as he pulled the sweatshirt over her head. "Now this is something I have sincerely missed, Claire. I'm not used to having a kid in the house twenty-four seven. It's cramping my style."

"Well, I haven't noticed much of that. Think back. Last night. Long, hot, sexy, soapy shower together. Or did I dream that?"

"Nope. That was as real as it gets. I think we need a reenactment. Right now would be good."

"Wow, you have calmed down considerably since your ridiculous tirade this morning." Claire laughed softly as she said it, her lips moving across his cheek until she found his mouth. "I think you've got a dandy idea going on here, though. So feel free, sweetie pie. Have at it. I am yours for the taking."

"Then hold on tight, because I have missed the hell out of you today." Having at it was what Black had in mind since she left the breakfast table that morning. It had been a long day of wanting her. He turned and lay down on his back and pulled her on top of him. Then he began to kiss her, both hands tangled in her hair, slowly and thoroughly at first, but that never lasted long. She responded in kind, and their lovemaking shot into double time pretty damn quick.

Black sat up and pulled off his own shirt, and then his mouth found hers again. That was pretty much all he thought about for the next ten minutes, except for some heavy breathing and pleasurable moans. It was always like this, always so damn good, and it had only gotten better since they'd been married. She was responding, her palms sliding up his bare back. Yeah, things were good, all right. At least, they were until Claire's cell phone vibrated inside her jeans pocket. "Gotta take this, Black," she muttered hoarsely, sitting up astride him.

"Hell no, you don't. Call them back, for God's sake." Black pulled her down against his chest again, not prepared to stop anytime soon.

Claire let him do that, but then braced her elbows on his chest as she pulled out the phone. She frowned as she read the screen. "It's the front desk. It might be about Rico. I better answer."

"The desk usually calls me when it's about Rico." But Black let go of her and watched her sit up and answer the phone. He worried about Rico as much as Claire did, but not so much when he was staying with Harve. Claire listened for a moment, and then she said, "No, wait, wait a second, don't send him up here. I'll come down." After that, Claire sat up in a hurry and started pulling on her clothes.

Black sighed. "What? Can't it wait?"

"No, unfortunately. She says there's an FBI agent down in the lobby insisting that he talk to me tonight. Said it concerns an extremely urgent matter."

"And that would be your murder case, I take it?"

"Yep, afraid so." Claire stood up, hastily pulled on her snow boots, and started lacing them up.

Black watched, not happy about the interruption. "I'd almost forgotten the joys of your being a law enforcement officer. At everyone's beck and call."

"We can make love any old time, all night long if you want. Suits me fine. But if there's a federal officer downstairs demanding to see me, something important is going on. And it probably does concern this homicide. On which, by the way, we have exactly zip."

"You haven't told me about your case. So why don't I tag along and see what's so important? Maybe I can help."

"Okay with me. He might object, though. You know how uppity FBI agents can get."

Black got dressed quickly. He was a forensic psychiatrist; he was always interested in her cases, and Claire had solved some doozies. Mainly, he liked to help so she wouldn't get shot or beaten up again.

Minutes later, they were inside the private elevator and on their way down to the lobby. Two Cedars restaurant was still open, and so was the adjoining bar. Both places were fairly crowded. Probably late Christmas office parties. They had a ton of bookings this year. The bar looked jam packed. All the hotel boutiques were still open, too, and would be until midnight. Black was pleased with Cedar Bend's bottom line. It had become the place to go at the lake and was always busy and buzzing with excitement. Better yet, he didn't see any paparazzi or reporters anywhere. Either they'd given up for the night or something notable was going on somewhere else.

"That must be him," Claire was saying, looking toward the main fireplace. "See that guy sitting in the rocking chair? He's the only man I see who's not with a group."

Black found the guy she was talking about and watched him for a moment. There were leather couches and chairs all around the raised hearth, the fire built up high, logs blazing and snapping. People sat everywhere, conversing or enjoying cocktails and the warmth of the fire. The FBI agent sat off by himself, so Black and Claire walked over to him together. When he saw them approaching, he stood up. His eyes riveted solely on Claire, really scorching her with the kind of masculine stare that Black understood all too well. He didn't like it. He didn't like him.

When they reached the guy, he said, "You're Claire Morgan; is that correct?"

"Actually, she's Claire Morgan Black now," Black told him. Nope, he did not like this guy at all.

Claire jerked a surprised look at him, and the Fed swiveled his attention to Black. He hadn't seemed to notice Black before that. They stared into each other's eyes for a second or two, and then the agent's mouth curved into a slow grin. Smug as hell and openly showing it. "I take it you must be her possessive husband." He had uttered it with a benign smile but it was meant as an insult. Black saw that; he wasn't obtuse. He took it for what it was.

"I'm Nicholas Black. Who are you?"

"Well, with all due respect, Dr. Black, this is a private law enforcement matter that I need to discuss with your wife. You know, with Mrs. Claire Morgan Black."

There was a barb in that, too, a direct challenge, and Black received it loud and clear. This guy was taunting him, no doubt about it. What's more, he wanted Black to know it and react negatively. Black wasn't one to be baited, but he did appreciate the heads up. No way in hell did he want this guy around Claire. Something was very off here, and Black wanted to know what it was. No legitimate FBI officer would behave in such a disrespectful way. But he'd go along with whatever game this jerk wanted to play, at least until he found out what his game was.

The agent kept up the smiling at him. They were about the same height. Eye level, which was a little unusual; at six feet four inches, Black rarely met anybody as tall as he was. "No offense meant, Dr. Black, but this is an official FBI matter. It's confidential, you understand. I'm afraid you'll have to go."

"No offense taken," Black answered calmly, but that was a damn lie. All of them knew the agent was needling him. Claire's eyes had narrowed. She was searching the agent's face for his motivation, too. "No problem," Black said with a smile. "I'll just wait for you over at the bar, sweetheart."

Black walked away, but he'd be damned if he'd go upstairs and leave Claire down here alone with that guy. He was going to watch their little private meeting and see what the hell this guy was up to.

Chapter 8

Claire watched Black walk off, all smiley and easygoing, but he didn't fool her, not for one single second. She knew him better than that. His jaw was flexing under his tanned cheek. He had suddenly become all loose and relaxed and calm. He was ticked off big time, all right, and for good reason. Just like the man standing beside her had intended him to be. She didn't like that much, either. So she turned her full attention back to the so-called FBI agent, searched his face, and wondered why he was intentionally provoking her husband. It took her about five seconds to size him up.

In the looks department, he was smokin' hot as hell. Not as handsome as Black, of course, because he was hard to beat, with that jet-black hair and those sky-blue eyes and sexy dimples, not to mention all those hard muscles. Just ask *People* magazine. But there was something behind this Federal agent's good looks that was vaguely disconcerting. He looked somewhat familiar to her. She felt some kind of vibe start quivering, but she couldn't quite identify what it meant. He just stood there, tall and imposing, smiling down at her, as if they had some kind of significant secret crackling back and forth between them.

Claire decided that she didn't like him. Snap judgment? Oh yeah, but usually she was right on with that sort of thing. "You got a name, agent, or is that confidential, too?"

Their eyes met and clicked together like a stiff hinge on a new gate. That was the moment that Claire realized what was so sexy about this guy: It was definitely his eyes. He had the most intense eyes that she had ever gazed into. They were sort of green but maybe more hazel, because there were lots of brown flecks inside the irises. He apparently liked to pretend they were twin laser beams, destined to hold one's audience enthralled, immobile, and unable to speak for lack of breath. What was more, he had them focused on her now, and they seemed to crawl all over her face as he leaned his body in closer to her. He was trying to control her stare so that she couldn't look away, she realized. So she looked away.

When she returned her attention to him, he still had that unnerving intensity in his gaze. He was staring at her like she was the only thing on earth that he was interested in, like she was a big slice of Pizza Hut Deep Dish Super Supreme and he was a hungry critter. No, actually, the look was more like they were the only survivors on a deserted island and he wanted to jump her bones and then do it again. It felt as if her attention had been expertly lassoed and he was slowly hauling her into his personal space so he could grab on to her. What the hell was with this guy and those hypnotic eyes? Claire broke eye contact again, glad she could. She almost felt compelled to look back at him, like all those women glammed in teenage vampire movies. Well, glammed wasn't exactly her thing. It just wasn't gonna happen. This guy was big trouble, and he reveled in it, but she was about to stick a pin in his self-absorbed, self-satisfied bubble.

"Okay, that hole you're staring through me? I think it's deep enough now. Didn't work. Not charmed. Not intrigued. Not anything. So you can put away your eyes and that intense yearning look you've got going on. I'm married to that guy over there at the bar. You know, the one you just insulted, so if this is a clumsy come-on or an attempt at flirtation, you are wasting your time and mine. His, too, I might add. You're lucky he didn't knock you flat on your back. He's totally capable of it; don't think his sophistication is all he's got going on. Okay? Get it? So turn off your eyes and give them a rest for the next gal. Who are you and what the hell do you want? We were busy when the desk called."

The lasers continued to burn. Good grief, what was with this guy?

"You're very direct, Detective. Very beautiful, too. Especially now that you're angry. I bet your husband over there riles you up just so you'll get that kind of fire going on."

Was this guy serious? One thing was for sure: he was no special agent of anything. Huh uh and no way. So why was he masquerading as one? She heaved one gigantic sigh. "That all sounded incredibly stupid and adolescent, but you must know that. So here's hoping you are as direct as I am, because you interrupted us while we were in the middle of something important. Therefore, you and I are going to make this conversation short, starting the countdown right now. Do you plan on introducing yourself, or are you always this rude and keep people guessing your identity?"

Claire was extremely put off by everything this guy had said and done so far, and she hadn't even gotten his name yet. A new record for her instant I-hate-you meter.

"Oh, so sorry, looks like I might've offended you. Didn't know you were so thin skinned, Claire. I'm Special Agent Oliver Wood, out of our Kansas City office."

"You got a badge to prove that? I thought you guys wore suits and dark glasses and were halfway professional." Claire moved her gaze down to his black V-neck sweater and faded jeans. He also had a scruffy goatee that hugged his jaw line, and a mustache, both cropped close to his face. It was auburn like his gelled-up hair. Hair that was short, but way too long for any clean-cut, well-trained Fed. Shoulda shaved if he wanted to fool her.

"I'm off duty. Even Federal agents get to dress casually on their off hours. So do you, by the looks of that old sweatshirt, which is on backwards, by the way. Guess I did interrupt something important."

Aware that that could very well be true, Claire glanced down at her shirt but found it looked fine. He'd been mocking her, and she'd fallen for it, which was doubly irritating. Then he smiled when she frowned at him. Maybe she should report him to the President. "Why are you here? And you can show me that badge anytime now, because I don't think you're an FBI agent, or any other kind of law enforcement officer. I think you're a phony, and not a very good one."

Oliver Wood didn't answer her questions. He just picked up his coat, reached into its inside pocket, and pulled out a badge folder. He flipped it open and held it up in front of her eyes, dangling it there like a real jerk. Nope, she and this Wood guy were not gonna hit it off. Ever. She glanced over at the bar and found Black sitting on a barstool with a short glass in his hand, leaning his back against the bar and watching their little tête-à-tête. His expression did not bode well for her guest. Probably a good thing if she and Laser Eyes ended up coming to blows. Black could step right in and help her beat the guy to a bloody pulp. He could hold him down while she pummeled his smug yet unusually handsome face. It sounded lovely to her, even on such short acquaintance.

"Okay, now that you've got all your smartass crap out of the way," she said to him, "maybe we can actually have a professional conversation." She looked at his badge again. "That badge isn't fake, is it? It doesn't look all that legit to me. You know, the misspelled words."

Slow smile, and then, "No, ma'am. It's real, official and everything. I promise."

Claire considered walking away from the guy. She took the badge and examined it closely. It looked like the real thing, but he certainly didn't. Maybe he stole it from a real agent. Yeah, that was probably it. "So tell me, Special Agent Wood, what exactly do you want? Also, you might want to add why you intentionally antagonized my husband a minute ago. That something they teach you at Quantico nowadays? Annoy the hell out of people that you request a meeting with?"

Deep inside all that brown-green intensity, she saw those incredibly expressive eyes react to her words, very briefly, and then all reaction disappeared. Instead, he showed her some impressively white teeth. "I have offended you, Claire. Is that what's got you all hot and bothered? That is what's happening here, right? I've hurt your feelings?"

"You couldn't touch my feelings with a ten-foot pole. Quit staring at me like that. You are really coming off creepy now. Like some kind of pervert."

After that, Wood presented her with what looked like a normal grin, which made him look even better. "I'm not supposed to look at you while we talk? That's what you want me to do? Where would you like for me to look? Over there at your doting husband?"

This guy was really getting on Claire's nerves. She took a few more seconds to search his face, now rather intrigued as to his motive, if nothing else. He was jabbing her now, and that, of course, was unprofessional. She wasn't handling him all that well, either. Never had been a woman who responded favorably to obnoxious men and chauvinistic banter, and that's what she thought he was all about. Maybe he didn't like women police officers. Maybe he thought she should go barefoot and pregnant, and all that sexist crap. Her aversion shot up into the stratosphere. She wanted very much to tell him where he could put his badge, and in some colorful, less-than-complimentary four-letter words. He was goading her on purpose, and it wasn't the least bit professional to let him get to her that way, so she went completely calm.

When she said nothing, he smiled some more. Tacky. He was just damn tacky. "It's just that I feel like I know you pretty well already," he told her then, smiling down into her eyes. "I read the *National Enquirer* faithfully, you see. The latest edition kept me enthralled on my flight down here."

Claire smiled back. "So you admit freely to being intellectually stunted. I can see that in you."

Her retort made him laugh. Maybe he was just stupid. Or socially awkward. She had a good friend named Laurie Dale, who happened to be an FBI special agent. A woman who'd saved Claire's life once upon a snowy night not so long ago. Laurie was serious-minded and well-trained and not a jerk with glowing eyes and clumsy put-downs. This guy must have got his training at a comedy club. Her suspicious meter just would not stop dinging.

"You're not very professional, are you, Wood? Maybe I need to reexamine that badge. See if it's as phony as the rest of you."

More staring, more trying to mesmerize her. Fat chance. He handed his badge over again. "You're everything that I heard you were, Mrs. Claire Morgan Black."

God, he just would not stop. So Oliver Wood was a gargantuan smartass. She usually liked that in a person—if she liked that person even a little bit, but that didn't apply here.

"I think I would rather speak to your partner, or better yet, your SAC in Kansas City. You grate on my nerves, to be perfectly honest, and vice versa, it appears. And gee, we've only been talking for what? Two minutes. Maybe three. So where's your partner? Don't you Feds always travel around on tandem bikes?"

"She's interviewing your partner as we speak. Bud Davis, right? Hope their collaboration is going better than ours. Shall we start over? Pretend we want to cooperate with each other?"

"By all means. So, what the hell do you want? Tell me quick. Like I said, I'm busy."

"I can imagine." Wood glanced at Black with a highly suggestive smirk on his face, just so she'd know exactly what kind of scene he was imagining. He was right on target, but he'd never know that. She didn't bite this time, just put some freeze in her eyes and laid it on him. He examined her face in detail. "I'm here to discuss the homicide you picked up today. The young woman who was murdered at the holiday tour house. That is your case, is it not?"

"That's right, it is. We haven't been able to identify her."

"I know."

"How do you know, pray tell?"

"Because you haven't had time to find out."

"We're not amateurs, Wood. We've done murder investigations for a long time, and with good results."

"Oh, I know all about that. You have quite a reputation for solving difficult cases…and for other things."

He wanted her to ask what other things, so she didn't. "I suspect you do some other things yourself. Badly."

He laughed out loud, but it was slow and enigmatic and magnetic as his hazel eyes continued to try to subjugate her gaze. Again she felt as if she couldn't look away from him. "Detective Morgan Black, we happen to know your victim's identity. Her name is Heather Cantrell. She managed to slip away from us, and we've been looking for her for the last six months."

"Didn't solve her case in under two minutes, huh? Maybe she ducked out on you while you were busy being rude to somebody. Bud and I can give you some pointers in protecting witnesses, if you like. No problem, really. Don't be shy, just ask us."

Wood didn't bite, just let his eyes skewer her some more. But then, finally, he was ready to stop with his cute games and get down to business. "The victim was a Federal witness that was slated to testify against an important member of the New York mob. She's been in witness protection for over a year, but she got away from us. I'm here to advise you of that, and to let you know that we will need to review your file and take a look at the body. I'd like to do that right now, if you don't mind."

"Like hell, Wood. You're going to have to go through official channels for any kind of collaboration between us, especially getting access to my murder file. You should know that without me having to tell you."

"Not the way it works, not this time."

Claire could not believe this guy. Talk about cool self-confidence. And then there was that sex appeal, just oozing out of his every pore while he intentionally tried to make her angry. His eyes were disconcerting to her, even with Black sitting right there in the lobby, watching their every move. Good thing Wood was such a loser or she might just swoon away like Scarlett O'Hara with that frail and puny Ashley guy. As if.

Unsurprisingly, Claire was nowhere close to buying what he was selling. "Don't kid yourself into thinking I'm naïve or inexperienced, especially when spotting phonies. I don't trust you, and I go by my first impressions. So what's your real game here, Wood? Why does the FBI want in on my homicide case? Seems perverse to me. Then again, everything you've said seems perverse to me."

More staring. But he was going for earnest now. Switched straight over into truth-and-sincerity laser mode. Dim the lights, charm the target. He was maybe even faintly puzzled by her scorn, poor guy. She resisted the urge to put one hell of a punch into his stomach.

That overwhelming desire was saved by her good sense and Wood's cell phone. The ring tone was the old fashioned kind, like those old ancient rotary phones. Loud. Annoying. He pulled it out of his pocket, glanced at the caller's name, and said, "Please excuse me. I have to take this."

Glancing over at Black, she rolled her eyes and made a face that could not leave her disgust for this guy unknown. He smiled and took a swig of his drink. Waiting, but not exactly patient.

Chief Crazy Eyes was soon back. "Now, where were we?"

"Pretty much nowhere."

Then his eyes left her and moved around the lobby. His perusal stopped near the front doors, and his whole persona changed in a nanosecond. He looked shocked, and then he tried to hide it. Claire turned quickly and looked where he'd been staring. Two guys had just entered the lobby. One was coming in the door, rolling a black suitcase behind him, and the other man was heading for the check-in counter. It didn't look like they were together. Maybe, though. The guy with the luggage was shorter and dressed in a red and black running suit and a Toronto Blue Jays baseball cap. The other guy was dressed in jeans and a St. Louis Cardinals T-shirt, tall and blond and cute.

Wood turned to Claire in a hurry. "I'm sorry, but I've got to go. I'll contact you again soon and we'll go over the file."

Surprised, Claire stared at him. He had dropped his attitude and was now in a big hurry. Why would that be?

"Aw, shoot. We were having so much fun. Before you go, know that there's no way in hell you're getting your hands on my file unless you go through my sheriff. Our jurisdiction, our case. You got that, Wood? Don't even try it without official documentation."

He gave her a quick yet arrogant smile. "I'll contact you again, and maybe we can both be more professional next time." He was waxing serious now, but his sober expression was telling her that either he was a super serious guy behind those weapon eyes and that smartass talk, or he was a damn good actor. She watched him walk swiftly across the lobby, avoiding the two men that he'd seemed so interested in. He was talking on his phone again as he pushed out through Black's bejeweled front doors and into a dark and snowy night. Good riddance. Maybe Bud was sparring verbally with Wood's partner and she had sent Wood an SOS. If so, Claire's money was on Bud any day of the week—unless his partner was a tall, willowy blonde with a Scandinavian accent. If that was the case, Bud was a goner from minute one. He had a type.

Black joined her about five seconds later. They turned and walked together toward the elevator. "Well?" he said. "Who is that guy, really?"

"Well, I think I just met next year's Sexiest Man Alive. At least in his own mind. Unfortunately, he's also the Most Obnoxious Man Alive."

"He can have the title right now. I sure as hell don't want it. Why was he trying to offend me?"

Entering the elevator, Claire waited for the door to slide closed behind them. She looked up at him. "Why did you let him get to you? He's an idiot."

"Because he interrupted something very special that I'd been looking forward to all day."

Claire laughed. "But that's still on the agenda, right? You haven't lost your urge?"

"Damn straight. I haven't lost the urge since I first laid eyes on you the day we met. Oh, and by the way, I snapped a picture of your friend down there. Thought you might want to check him out on a facial recognition database. If he's an FBI agent, I'll eat my hat."

"You are just so accommodating and brilliant, now aren't you?"

"You haven't seen accommodating yet. But you will, as soon as we get in bed."

"Sounds good to me."

Once they hit the penthouse, they headed for their bedroom and let Black's accommodations begin, all of which were quite entertaining and long lasting. It was definitely the fun kind of accommodation. The kind Claire liked the most.

Play Time

One night after Lucky had moved all his meager possessions out of the YMCA and into his own room in Junior's plush Beverly Hills estate, they sat downstairs in the game room. For the first time, Junior was playing his dad's music for Lucky. Lucky kept nodding his head and smiling, thinking his dad's hard rock sound was as cool as hell. Secretly, Junior did, too, and he loved it when his BFF said that Junior looked a little bit like his dad. Still, he outright hated his father for leaving him alone with his monster mother all those years ago, so he always insisted to Lucky that his dad was just a drunken jerk.

After they got tired of listening to music, they decided to play a game called Detection, and this time, they made bets and played for money. Junior had told his attorneys that he'd hired Lucky as his personal assistant and security guard, and he instructed them to pay Lucky a huge salary every month so his best friend wouldn't have to work or resent having to ask Junior for spending money. Sometimes Lucky acted mad about being so broke, and Junior wanted to make things easier for him.

Detection had become one of their favorite pastimes because it dealt with murder. Whoever guessed the right killer and the right weapon and the right room where the murder had been committed won a thousand dollars for each right answer. They were really going through his inheritance at a rapid rate, enjoying month-long spending sprees where they bought themselves expensive clothes and luxury cars and lengthy trips to Europe and Japan for wild, exciting adventures. But the money was endless and just kept building back up, thanks in part to interest but mostly to Junior's dad's world tours, which kept on filling up Junior's coffers. They had worlds of fun and remained exhilarated most of the time.

After a while, though, all the hedonistic fun and excitement started to wear thin, especially for Junior, because he'd had pretty much everything he'd ever wanted his entire life, especially when he was little and his mother liked to show him off and brag about his father's fame. Tonight, they were both in terribly foul moods, pretty damn sick of hanging out exclusively with each other, and of just about everything else in their lives.

So they sniped at each other, and drank too much beer and whiskey and threw dice, and argued about silly stuff. Lucky was winning most of the time, and Junior really hated that. It annoyed the absolute hell out of him. He was smarter and nicer and more grounded, yet Lucky won everything. He stared at the poster he'd tacked up on the opposite wall. It depicted the cruelties performed in his favorite torture porn movie. He smiled to himself and felt a little shiver wriggle its way up his spine. That movie was so scary and gruesome that it had turned him on and grossed him out at the same time. But now, sitting there, gazing at that poster, he began to get the most intriguing idea. Junior and Lucky had watched the movie together, over and over, and then they put on the second one, and then the third. They loved everything about those movies, especially the utter inhumanity. They reveled in each act of torture and each drop of blood. The films were morbidly fascinating.

Recently, Junior had been spending a lot of time reflecting on the way the two of them had banded together to commit murder. They had worked together so well, and so unexpectedly, and they had been a team when they held his mother under the water. It had been deliciously easy, really, downright comfortable, with both of them pitching in and acting toward one goal. More important, they had gotten away with it, and as slick as warm gut, too. He liked the feeling. Such power. Strength. Omnipotence. He loved it even more every single time he relived it, and he was beginning to think about it nearly all the time. Most often, though, it was when he was in bed at night, all alone with his dark needs and thoughts and desires.

"Know what, Lucky?"

Lucky glanced up from his cards and took a quick swig of beer. He was scowling. He was in a mean mood. "What?"

"I want to kill somebody."

"Well, you better not mess with me. I'm not in the mood, and I've got a big bowie knife on my belt. I'll carve you up good."

"Not you, you idiot." Junior had to laugh at the idea. "Don't be so stupid. You're my bro. I'd never hurt you."

"Who then? Those moron lawyers of yours?"

"Can't kill them. I need them. They make sure I get my money. All I have to do is snap my fingers." Junior picked up the dice and tossed them onto the board. "Besides them, I don't care who dies. That's not the point. The point is we are getting bored messing with each other, you know, arguing and getting on each other's nerves, because killing Mom was the biggest high we've ever had and nothing else equates with that day. Go ahead, Lucky, tell me I'm wrong."

A familiar expression slowly overtook Lucky's face. He looked pleased. "You're not wrong there. Nothing else gives us that kind of thrill, does it now? But we can't just go around killing people for sport, now can we?"

Junior raised a brow. "Why ever not?"

"Because we'll get caught if we make a mistake, that's why ever not. And then we'll end up on death row."

"Not if we play it smart and do it right. You know, plan it out down to the very last detail. Make sure there's no way we can get caught. We are both smarter than anybody else. We can take our time, figure out the perfect crimes, and commit them."

"Still might get caught. You know it, too. We watch *CSI* and all those kinds of shows. We know all about DNA and that kind of stuff."

"That's exactly my point. We know what *not* to do. And we can find out more. We can study up before we do the first one. We can take classes, or hell, we can sign up for the police academy or the FBI. That would be the smartest thing to do: live two lives. Work inside the system against the system. Exemplary and evil. The two Es."

"All that's true, I guess." Lucky shrugged it off and shook his head. "Whatever. If you want me to kill somebody, just say the word. I'm game. I do like the idea of training ourselves in law enforcement so we can fool everyone."

Junior was pleased, but sometimes Junior felt as if he liked Lucky a lot more than Lucky liked him. Lucky still kept some other friends down in south L.A., maybe even had a girlfriend down there. Junior suspected he did. He went off sometimes and hung around with them and left Junior to his own devices. At times, Junior liked that—he needed some time alone—but sometimes he felt lonely and resentful. Junior didn't have anybody to be with but Lucky. He had pretty much cut off every other person he knew. Occasionally, he went to chess and math tournaments but he didn't let anybody get too close to him. Didn't say much to anybody, and certainly didn't say much about his past and what he was doing at present. Sometimes he worried that Lucky might get drunk and his tongue might get loose and blab their secret to his other friends. It really upset Junior to think that way.

"This game's stupid, and no fun," Junior growled suddenly, pushing the Detection board away and knocking over the tokens. "I don't like any of these games anymore. They're too simple for people like us. We need a game that'll make us think."

Lucky leaned back, drained his bottle, and stared at him. Then he belched and didn't cover his mouth. "Okay, let's play a video game. Which one would you like?"

Junior smiled. "None of them. We've played them all a million times. There's no challenge anymore. I've been thinking: I want us to make up our own game. A killing game. We can call it 'Live or Die.'"

"Live or Die?" Lucky stared at him, but Junior saw a little glimmer show up in his eyes. Lucky had these real expressive eyes that Junior could read pretty well. Lucky was interested, all right. He liked the sound of Junior's idea. Junior grinned, inordinately pleased.

"What kind of killing game?" Lucky asked. "Some torture porn thing, I bet, since those are your favorite movies. If so, count me in."

"Well, yeah, sometimes we could do that, I guess. But those kinds of murders are really complicated and require intricate lairs that would be really hard to set up. And they create lots of unwelcome attention in the press. We need to do our own version of those movies. You know, just like the evil one always says, 'Play time. Murder time. Who's game?' Remember that? We need a catchphrase like that. Something we always say to the victim right before we kill them. You know. 'Live or die?' Get it?"

"Yeah, that's so freakin' cool, Junior." Lucky thought a moment. "Or how about sayin' 'Game on' when we've got them captured and under our control?"

"Maybe. But I was thinking about something a little more, well, you know, terrifying. We need to say something that will scare the hell out of our victim right before we kill them."

"How about something like this: 'You, my friend, are gonna be dead in exactly one minute,' and then we start a stopwatch!" He laughed, and then he said, "You know, so they have to watch the last seconds of their lives tick down to zero." Lucky's eyes were shining with humor. Junior loved it when Lucky was this happy. "That ought to make them wet their pants. We could even use one of those timers with a bell that dings so they could hear their own personal death knell."

"Now you are definitely getting the picture, Lucky, my man."

Junior glanced down at the Detection board. He picked up the little metal game piece between his thumb and forefinger. "Know what, Luck? We could use the Detection format as the basis of our own game. Maybe we could use the same game board, and designate these little game tokens to pick our murder weapon, but get this: we'll use the real things instead. Let's see, that would give us lots of stuff to kill our victims with. We could always add more weapons later if we get tired of using the same ones over and over."

"Over and over? God, how many people do you want to kill?"

"As many as we can. I've decided I like to kill people."

Lucky threw back his head and laughed. "You are something else, Junior. I thought I had a warped mind, but you, hell, you just take the cake. You are a true-blue born killer, bloodthirsty as hell. I knew I liked you better than anyone else for a reason."

Junior was extremely pleased by Lucky's compliment, but he tried not to show how much it meant to him. "So, looks like we got ourselves this candlestick, and there's a tire iron, and a sword and a rope garrote. See where I'm going with this? The Detection weapons will give us variety so we don't get bored. Shooting somebody's pretty damn quick and easy. The fun doesn't last long enough."

"Awesome, man. That gives us lots of bloody options. But how do we choose? Whatever catches our fancy in the moment?"

The two young men looked at each other, and it was clear that both of them were getting really excited. *Now, this is going to be fun*, Junior thought. All they had to do was figure out the details and pick out some victims. He couldn't wait to get started.

Chapter 9

The next morning, around eight-thirty, Claire and Black sat across from each other in the breakfast nook. As usual, Black was dressed immaculately, in a navy suit and red tie and the usual crisp white shirt with his triple monogram on the cuff. He looked good, too, in a sexy, rich, corporate sort of way. Claire still liked him better in his T-shirts and jeans. She, on the other hand, still had on her flannel pajamas and matching robe, and hadn't bothered to comb her bed hair. She wasn't a morning person like he was: never had been, never would be. Yes, that was one more glaring difference between their personalities that didn't matter in the least. She was only up with him because she woke at the crack of dawn worrying about the Heather Cantrell case and the total lack of concrete evidence to point Claire in any pertinent direction. That is, if the unsavory Fed from the night before had even given her the girl's real name.

Black had ordered up bacon and eggs and biscuits from the restaurant, along with a selection of flaky pastries, and Claire poured two glasses of orange juice and made them both a cup of coffee. Black always chose the kind of brew that resembled black and completely undrinkable mud, no doubt because he grew to manhood in New Orleans, where chicory was the name of the game, as unpalatable as it was. Claire had a tendency to go for normal stuff, certainly no lattes, cappuccinos, or diet this-or-that, and definitely no non-fat anything. She drank coffee for the caffeine, for the pep to get going in the morning. Hell, if she wanted to lose weight, she'd add another couple of miles to her daily run. But she never cared about that. Black liked her the way she was, and ditto for her opinion of him.

Glancing at Black, she unfolded her napkin and grabbed the biggest jelly donut from under the silver dome. "I'm still trying to figure out what that guy was trying to prove last night," she told him, taking a sip of the fresh-squeezed orange juice. It tasted good, icy cold and sweet.

"Got me," Black answered. "What we probably should do is check out his credentials, because I don't think he's FBI or anything close to it. I think he's probably some crackpot reporter who wanted to get close to you for a story."

Claire contemplated him. "Or to you. I think he was after you the whole time. He was definitely baiting you, trying to make you angry. If he could get you to take a swing at him, they could sell one bombshell photo to the tabloids."

"He didn't take his eyes off you the whole time. And I had to sit there and watch it. It was not something I enjoyed."

"Well, after you didn't bite on his jabs, I think he tried to intimidate me. Nothing he said made much sense. It was like he was just playing around with me. Saying whatever came into his head. It was strange, and I was glad when he took off, believe me. I texted Laurie Dale last night and asked her to run a check through the Bureau databases and see if he's a real agent. She's calling me back today."

"Are she and Scott up at the farm?"

"No, they're still down in Springfield. She's working some important case down there."

"Maybe it's related to yours."

"Maybe. I didn't ask her. I'm anxious for her to call me back. That guy was downright irritating."

"So, tell me about your case. See if we can find any connection to the guy last night. We didn't get to talk much after we went to bed."

"Yeah, no joke. Your mouth was way too busy to say much."

"Talking in bed is highly overrated. I can think of better things to do with you than have a damn chat." His dimples showed up and wowed her, as usual. "And I wasn't in that big of a hurry, if you'll recall."

Claire remembered, all right. She smiled her gratitude for all those lovely pleasures. He smiled back, promising more. Okay by her. "Trust me, I'm not complaining. But to answer your question, that jerk—and for the record, I don't think there's a chance in hell that he's legit, either—told me our victim was in the Bureau's witness protection program. He said she disappeared, and that she ended up at the lake, dead at the top of that Christmas tree."

Black placed his cup down on the saucer and gave her his full concentration. "That changes things. What else did Wood say last night? When he wasn't undressing you with his eyes."

"I thought once we got hitched you'd stop with that jealousy thing."

"That's true, but that guy was about as blatant as he could get, and I just had to just sit there and watch it go down."

"You didn't have to watch."

"I'm pretty sure I did."

Claire laughed at his expression. "Well, after he was done provoking me, he informed me that he wanted to go over my case file and take a look at the body. Just like that. Pretty much a 'hand it over, lady, and don't ask too many questions.' As if that's ever gonna happen."

"No FBI agent would want to step on your toes like that, not blatantly, in any case. They try to be diplomatic when they take over for the locals."

"*Au contraire.* They do step on local toes. Lots of them have, in fact. My toes have been black and blue from said encroachment. My question is this: if he's not FBI, what's he trying to do, and, more importantly, why the hell does he want to see that girl's dead body?"

"You asked him that, I presume."

"He wouldn't say. Or couldn't. Probably didn't have a good reason. Or, no, make that he didn't have a *legal* reason. I have a feeling he thinks I'm a small-town pushover that he could dictate to. You know, wave his hand and it shall be done."

"Then he doesn't know you very well."

"Thank God. He knew about those pictures in the *National Enquirer* and enjoyed rubbing my nose in them."

Black put down his coffee cup. "What did I tell you? Every man in the country is going to buy that damn tabloid."

"Give it a break, Black. Forget those stupid pictures. Wood got a mysterious phone call, after which he looked worried, and hightailed it out of there like nobody's business. Or, he might've seen somebody that he didn't want to run into. I watched him get all antsy when a couple of guys showed up down in the lobby. I don't think they were together, maybe just walked through the door at the same time. He couldn't seem to take his eyes off them while he was on the phone. And then he took off in a hurry and made a point to avoid them on his way out."

"Who were they? Did you know them?"

"Never seen either of them before, but I need to get their pictures off your security cameras ASAP. If they're staying here at the hotel, I want to have a word with them. Today. And text me that photo you took of Oliver Wood. I intend to ask around about him, too."

"I already called the security office. They're going through last night's lobby tapes, and they'll call if they find out anything. Shouldn't take them long to find what we're looking for. I told them it was urgent and to get right on it." Black eyed her for a moment. "I'm surprised he could tear himself away from you long enough to notice anybody else."

Claire shook her head. "I cannot believe you're actually jealous of that creep. Give me some credit, why don't you?"

"I'm not jealous. But I don't like him coming on to you the way he did. Especially since he did it on purpose. Why he did it is a much more interesting question."

"Know what I think, Black? I think that guy wasn't flirting with me as much as he was pulling your chain. Looked to me like he was trying to get you all hot under the collar so you'd get angry. Like I said, he was goading you to knock his block off and cause a scene. They'd pay big bucks for a picture of Nicholas Black losing his temper, since you never do. I hate paparazzi." She frowned as a thought occurred to her. "Do you know him from somewhere? Did he look familiar to you at all?"

"I've never seen the guy before. But don't kid yourself. He might've been trying to make me angry, but he was definitely interested in you. You were the target, not me. That was easy to see. I didn't like it then, and I don't like it now. I don't care what his motives were."

"Well, me either."

"Tell me again everything he said to you."

Claire repeated their conversation in as much detail as she could recall.

"That's not much, all right. I can see reading the file, but why would he want to see the body, except to get an official ID?"

"He's so weird, it could be anything." Claire sighed heavily and took another bite of her donut. Did she ever love jelly donuts. She finished it off in a hurry. "I need to call Bud and find out if Wood's partner visited him last night like he said. Or maybe I'll just wait until Bud shows up. Should be here soon." She pushed her plate away, suddenly feeling sick to her stomach. A vision of half of that teenage girl's head lying on the floor made it worse. She swallowed hard and took a drink of juice. "Oh, yeah, and the worst part of the whole thing, Black? Guess who owns the house where we found the victim?"

"Who?"

"Well, let me give you a little hint. This idiot's the biggest loser in the universe. Ready to be sick? It's no other than Mr. Jonesy Jax. You've heard of him, right? He's the heavy metal rocker with all that long, bleached-out white hair that he wears in braids. He only wears black clothes on stage." A mental image of the white-robed angel splattered with blood made Claire's stomach pitch some more. "And he's a real-life moron, if you don't know him. Unfortunately, nobody seems to have a clue where he is or how we can get in touch with him. So, as of now, we have a deceased young girl with a name we don't know is legit, found dead and posed atop a freakin' Christmas tree. Happy Holidays, everybody."

Black had forked up a bite of scrambled eggs but stopped his hand before it reached his mouth. He stared across the table at her. "Jonesy Jax owns the house where the body was found? Well, this is your lucky day, sweetheart. I know exactly where Jonesy is."

That pronouncement shocked Claire into momentary silence. "Really? Where is he?"

"Directly underneath us, in the honeymoon suite. Got here under strict confidentiality and checked in under an assumed name."

"What? Why didn't I know about this? Why didn't you tell me?"

Black lifted a shoulder in a careless shrug. "I didn't see any reason why you'd be interested. You're pretty upfront with your disdain for rock stars and their music."

"When did he get here?"

"Almost a week ago. He told me he bought a house overlooking the lake out on some cliff, but I didn't put it together with your case until now. He said the house wasn't ready for him to move in, so he was checking in here. He wanted to avoid the paparazzi as much as he could, so I flew him and his friend in on my Gulfstream around midnight a week ago Sunday."

Claire scoffed. "And how'd that work out for him? The media's already here, down in the lobby every single day. Guess he's ringing up a lot of room service."

"I suspect he is. But those jackals down there are here for us, not him. They have no idea he's here, or those vultures would double in number overnight. I hope they don't find out. Nobody knows except for me and a few of the maids. I told them not to breathe a word to anybody about his presence and gave them a big Christmas bonus to keep it to themselves. I figured they deserved it. He's a slob, but he wants privacy. As you know, that's the main reason my celebrity patients come out here instead of my clinics in L.A. and New York. Anonymity. That's what they all want. That, and the top-notch security that I can provide. He preferred to stay in the hotel this time, but last time he was here, he holed up down in the bungalows with the other celebs."

"Why was he here the other time?"

"You know I can't divulge that. Not even to you. And I love you."

"Doesn't matter. I can guess. Alcohol, drugs, sex, probably sex addiction is the big one. Throw in depravity and misogyny, for good measure."

"I seem to be getting the impression that you don't care for the guy."

"You're just brilliant. I always have said so."

"You're being a tad hard on Jonesy, don't you think? I've spent time with him, and he's not the man he portrays himself to be up on stage in front of thousands of maniacal fans." Black drank more coffee and made no further comment.

"I cannot believe that you're taking up for that sleazebag, or that you ever hung around with him for even one minute. Oh, and by the way, I've spent time with him, too. I had to get up close and personal at a traffic stop, and he was about as despicable as any man could be. I tagged him as a sicko pervert from minute one. Please tell me that you don't socialize with him."

"Then you met him a long time ago. Actually, I've been helping him get his act together. After about a year of treatment, he got his life back under control. And, yes, I have seen him socially, on occasion. Before I met you. Mainly when I was working in Los Angeles. I've gone to his concerts when he sent me tickets; he asked me to come watch his show as a favor to him. He felt more secure getting through it when he was sober if he knew I was in the audience for moral support."

Claire shook her head. "So tell me, Black: you catch any of those pills that he threw out to the underage kids in the crowd?"

"Those pills were just candy. That incident happened before I treated him."

Claire was absolutely incredulous that Black was fond of Jonesy Jax. The two of them were diametrically opposed in every single way that she could think of. "You hang out at any of those wild parties he gives? You know, the ones with naked women jumping out of cakes and strippers on his roof?"

"Of course not. He's a patient. I don't party with patients. Our friendship was business-related, and never about doing drugs or being with women, which you should already know. I'm more fastidious than that, even when I was single. Jonesy and I played tennis occasionally, when I happened to be out on the West Coast. I've treated him in my Beverly Hills clinic a time or two, when he fell off the wagon and binged on drugs or alcohol. But it's not always about his problems. Sometimes he wants me to help the people he cares about. Some of his friends have addictions, too."

"Wow, as if that's a news flash." Claire still couldn't believe Black and Jonesy were friends. Black was painting her a picture of a real, live, functioning human being. No way was Jonesy anywhere close to that. "So you are telling me that Jonesy Jax plays tennis? Sorry, but I find that really hard to believe. You mean he can actually track the ball when he's usually spiked up on coke?"

"He's sober now. At least, he is until around noon. After that, all bets are off. Still, he's no longer out of control. He can stop boozing when he wants, and he doesn't do the drugs much anymore."

Claire didn't really give a rip about Jonesy Jax's problems, but she did want to interview him and see what he could tell her about their victim. "So how about coming downstairs with me and paying him a little visit? Waking him up before noon appeals to me. He needs to be at least halfway sober when I talk to him."

"Sure, right after I finish breakfast. You should eat more than that donut, you know. You haven't had much of an appetite lately. Do you feel all right?"

"I feel fine. Not so fine about this case, though. First off, some creepy Lothario type full of sexual innuendoes shows up out of the blue, one that I swear can look straight into my brain. One who might not even be a real FBI agent. Now I find out the murder scene is in the home of a drunken reprobate and skuzzy hard rocker. And it's only day two of the investigation. Just what I wanted for Christmas. Hell on earth. Forget the peace thing."

Black only smiled. "Again, Claire, I think you're being a little hard on Jonesy. As for Christmas, this is going to be the best Christmas we've ever had. Our first Christmas with a signed marriage certificate framed and hanging on the wall. That's enough to celebrate right there, since I never thought it had a chance in hell of happening. And then there is little Rico, and he's enjoying the hell out of the holidays. You'll see. I intend to make everything absolutely perfect for both of you."

Claire relaxed. "Well, of course, you will. It's in your nature."

Black looked as pleased as punch. She had no doubt that he would definitely try to make it perfect. He wouldn't stop until everything was exactly so. But she liked that about him. She liked a lot of stuff about him. Nearly everything, actually. When he walked down the hall to his office to review his daily agenda with his assistant, Claire took a quick shower, and then dressed in an old black departmental T-shirt, faded jeans, and leather snow boots, then looped her badge around her neck and holstered her Glock 19 under a nice, warm, fleece-lined gray hoodie. Okay, she was ready to face the nitwit downstairs who was probably sleeping off one gargantuan hangover. She phoned Bud and told him what she knew about Oliver Wood and Jonesy Jax. He said nobody had come to see him last night, but he had been called in this morning to testify in court, which could last all day, depending on the docket. So Claire decided to go ahead and interview Jax on her own. Well, maybe Black could tag along and keep him from molesting her. Bud said he'd call as soon as he finished testifying.

She took a deep breath and went in search of Black. Claire found him in his office, watching the videotapes from the lobby.

When he saw her, he said, "Come over here, Claire. I just got this tape from security."

When she joined him behind his desk, he started the security tape, and they watched silently as people came in and out of the lobby. "Do any of the security people know those two guys?"

"A couple guys said they'd seen them around and thought they were guests here. More importantly, they recognized Oliver Wood, too."

Claire perked up. "No joke? He's staying here?"

"No, but they say they've seen him around the resort. And what troubles me is that a few of them have noticed Wood on the shop concourse talking with Rico."

"Oh my God. You think he's after Rico?"

"They said it all looked innocent and casual. Usually Rico and Wood happened to play video games next to each other in the computer room. Nothing appeared out of line or looked inappropriate or they would've intervened. I'll ask Rico about him when he gets home today."

"Well, I think it's highly inappropriate. What the hell is an older guy like Wood doing down there with all those kids? Especially if he's not a guest?"

"Lots of grown men play video games down there, but I told the security guards to call me if they spot him again. I think this gives credence to our theory that Wood might be a photographer or a reporter, trying to get close to one of us for a story."

"I don't like it, Black. Maybe you ought to tell your guards to escort him off the property if they see him again."

"I already have, but not until after I talk to him myself."

Claire searched his face. "You're more worried why he's hanging around here than you're letting on."

"No, I'm just cautious where Rico is concerned. There's going to be a bodyguard on him all the time, and I've instructed all the staff to keep a closer eye on him from now on. I'm to be called if Oliver Wood shows up anywhere at the hotel. I think that's enough to keep Rico safe."

Claire did feel better with the new precautions, but she didn't trust Oliver Wood, not even a little bit. Who the hell was he, anyway? " I hope you're right. Are you ready to go downstairs and face your repulsive, hard-rock, lowlife, bottom-feeder buddy with me?"

"That's one way to put it."

"That's exactly the way to put it. If you can get loose now, let's go ahead and talk to him. Bud's in court. But I predict it will only take three, maybe four seconds for him to do something stupid and insulting. Want to lay a bet?"

"Snap judgments are not good things."

"Nothing snap about it. He came on to me when I was an L.A. police officer. Maybe it's just a quirk, but that annoys me."

"Well, I don't like it, either. What did he do?"

Claire told him in brief but belligerent fashion. Black listened and said, "He better not do it again, or he'll regret it."

"My hero. So, c'mon, Black, let's get this over with."

"Promise me you'll give him a fair chance."

"Why would I ever make a promise like that?"

Black shook his head and stood up. Claire laughed at his worried expression. She had been joking, but the truth was, if she ever got a legitimate chance to knock some sense into Jonesy Jax's addled head, she would be more than pleased to do it.

Chapter 10

A few minutes later, Claire and Black stood in front of the elevator, ready to roll. "We probably ought to call his suite first," Black told her, pressing the button. "It might freak him out if we just show up out of the blue with a badge and start questioning him about a murder."

"No way. I don't want him to have time to make up some story or call in his lawyers. He's probably got a whole team of them at his beck and call. He certainly had enough of them when I arrested him in Los Angeles."

"Are you telling me that you're planning to arrest him when we get down there?"

"No. I can't prove anything yet. But he's up pretty high on my suspect list, unless he's got a rock-solid alibi. You treated him. You think he's capable of murder?"

"I think anybody's capable of murder under the right circumstances. In his case? Maybe, if he was high on drugs at the time. But he's pretty much off the hard stuff now. He's not an evil person, if that's what you're thinking. Let me warn you: no telling what we'll find going on inside his suite. He's been known to do some rather strange and unpleasant things."

"I've seen lots of strange and unpleasant things in my lifetime. Let's go."

When they stepped off the elevator on the floor below, a couple of Black's burly security men were standing around—no doubt on double duty guarding Jonesy Jax from his druggie fans—looking sharp in their Cedar Bend black and tan uniforms. Down at the east end of the hall, in front of the double doors leading into the opposite suite, a couple of guys carrying shopping bags were entering their room. On the west end of the hall, a big black guy stood guard in front of Jonesy's suite. This had to be Jonesy Jax's own man. He looked like he pumped iron and ran twenty miles a day and fought grizzly bears on the weekends. He knew Black, too. But who didn't? Her guy was famous.

Black was just so polite—most of the time. He started with the introductions. "Claire, this is Benjamin Hargate. He's been Jonesy's personal bodyguard for as long as I can remember."

"How do you do, Mrs. Black," Hargate said to her. Also polite, no doubt unless they tried to break down the door or touch his unsavory rock star. He was acting like a regular human being, even after being in close association with Jonesy Jax for so long. Good sign, that. Maybe a miracle, in fact.

"How you been, Dr. Black? Congrats on your marriage."

Black said, "I'm good, Ben. Thank you. How are you?"

The guard nodded, then turned and tapped on the door with one large knuckle that appeared to have been broken on somebody's nose several times over. They waited. He tapped some more. Finally, about ten minutes later, it seemed, the door swung inward and revealed a young woman standing before them in a slinky black lace teddy, a garter belt, and black fishnet stockings. Hooker high heels, of course, just to lounge around the suite, because it all looked so comfortable. Luckily, she also had on a short black silk robe, which was unbelted and hanging open, for easy access, no doubt.

"Good morning, Ms. Kisses," Black said, still being mannerly, not laughing at the woman's ridiculous made-up name. Probably a former, if not current, porn star. "We need to speak with Jonesy. It's important that we see him. Is he up yet?"

"Well, no." The woman was clearly of a sarcastic bent, and gave them a short but effective guffaw at Black's bizarre notion. "It's just ten. Get real, dude."

"Are you Candi Kisses, ma'am?" Claire asked, but it didn't exactly roll off her tongue with ease. In fact, she almost choked on the sheer absurdity of having to say it out loud. It was just such a moronic thing to have to say that Claire couldn't quite get a handle on it. She grimaced instead and let that be enough.

"Of course I am."

Of course you are, and you're an imbecile as well, Claire thought. *Another Hollywood nutzoid working for a lunatic.*

"Who the hell are you?" Candi looked at Black. "I can't believe yous just showed up here at Jonesy's door without calling me for permission first. That is just so crazy rude. Yous can't do that."

Claire could only stare at her. Okay, she was a nutzoid from Brooklyn. It was plain to see that this kid was as clueless as a blind poodle on a computer keyboard—maybe even more so. Even Jules Verne could chase a ball and bring it back. This gal would need instructions. Black was saying nothing. It was Claire's game and she had to play it, even with a saucy little twit with an idiotic name. She inhaled a deep breath and dealt with the girl, kid gloves still folded in her act-nice drawer. "Well, yes, we can most certainly do that, Candi Kisses. See this guy standing here beside me? He owns this hotel and everything in it, including your suite. And I am a Canton County Sheriff's homicide detective, with a badge hanging right here around my neck and a big old Glock under my arm and the power to throw you in jail lickety-split for noncompliance. That a good enough invitation for you, Candi Kisses?"

Jonesy's girlfriend blew out a breath that was soaked with rum and a strong odor of nicotine. Unpleasant up close ? Oh, yes, very. "Well, I guess I can't stop yous from coming in here then, if he owns the hotel, but we are pretty busy. Why don't you just come back later, after you're invited?"

It was difficult, but Claire ignored most of that annoying prattle. "Busy doing what, Candi Kisses?"

Black glanced down at her, disapproving of her mocking tone. Imagine that.

"Busy minding my own business. How about you do the same, lady?"

So it wasn't an act: This girl really was incredibly ignorant. Twenty-ish, and brain already fried to a crisp, like a cracked egg in grease. Like the employer, the employee goes. Or whatever function the nearly naked girl was slated to serve for Jonesy Jax. "Do you really want to see the inside of a jail cell, ma'am? That won't be a problem, believe me. Don't know if the orange jumpsuit will flatter your pink hair, though."

"Ha. Aren't you hilarious."

A great and steadily building wave of loathing was rising up inside Claire's chest, like a tsunami wave of destruction, and after only one and a half minutes. That was a new record for Claire. Usually it took two minutes for annoying X-rated womenfolk to enrage her. Black was watching her warily, as if she were going to do something rash to the silly little bubble brain, like bust her in the nose with a fist. It was a nice fantasy, but she would waste too much time mopping up the blood, and it would be hard for Candi to answer questions with cotton stuffed up both nostrils. Otherwise, it was a grand idea.

"We're here to see Jonesy Jax. Not you. So go get him, ma'am." Claire held up her badge right in front of Candi's eyes. "Now."

The woman invited her to participate in a flat-eyed stare-off for approximately five seconds, and then she flounced off in her skimpy attire. Claire and Black stepped inside and closed the door behind them. Ms. Sexpot stripped off her robe as she crossed the room and glanced back over a naked shoulder to see if Black was watching her smut show. Flirting at its most pathetic.

"Bet that sexy stunt got you goin', huh, Black?"

"I'm more concerned with the murderous look on your face."

"I don't care for Candi."

"No kidding."

"But, no worries: I'm not going to shoot her. Pistol-whipping might be in the cards, if she takes off anything else to entice you."

Black just shook his head.

"Okay, I was told last night that Miss Candyland is his booking agent. Surely that cannot be true: she's not old enough to drive yet."

"Afraid so. If I recall, Jonesy usually makes his current lover double in that regard so she can travel with him."

"This case just keeps getting sleazier."

"It can get a lot worse than this. Let's just hope it doesn't."

Claire glanced around the giant living room. It was as beautiful as the rest of Cedar Bend Lodge, of course. A bit more enthusiastically decorated, to wow a bride and groom, she assumed. It was rustic in a high-end, expensive-decorator kind of way. Big sliding doors opened onto a long balcony overlooking the frozen lake. The porch was covered with snow drifts that slanted up one wall. Frost had configured icy snowflakes on the plate glass. Everything in sight was frozen and dead and waiting for the spring thaw. The gas fire logs were dancing and burning hot in their artificial way, but the room was quite dim because of the never-ending dark clouds pressing down over the water.

At the moment, however, Black's major luxury suite was a total disaster area. There were discarded clothes flung everywhere, lots of black and red teddies lying about, and other unmentionable things that Claire wished she hadn't noticed. Empty rum and whiskey and beer bottles littered the giant white coffee table, and ashtrays overflowed despite the fact that Cedar Bend was smoke-free. Guess rock stars got to do anything they wanted. The acrid stench of cigarettes hung in a dark cloud near the ceiling. Yuck and more extreme yuck.

"Better put up some more no-smoking signs, Black, before these people choke to death."

Black didn't look pleased at the state of Jonesy's housekeeping, either. He had always been the super orderly type: his extensive military training, no doubt. "He keeps sober better if he gets to smoke. We found that out in therapy. I can let things slide now and then if it's good for my patient's mental health issues."

"This is all so utterly distasteful that I think I'm gonna break out in hives, especially the fact that he's got an underage nympho staying in here with him."

"She's not underage. I asked to see her driver's license when they checked in, just to make sure."

"Very astute of you, dear. How old is she?"

"Eighteen."

"Trusting that it's not a fake ID, huh?"

"Can't guarantee that. I hope it's not."

It took Jax some time to show up. After fifteen minutes, Black sat down beside the fire and Claire chose an easy chair near the balcony doors, where the cigarette smoke wasn't so thick that it gagged her, and waited silently—if not happily—for the next fifteen minutes. Not the most patient detective in the world, Claire got up and opened the sliders to clear some of the acrid smoke out of the place. The cold, fresh air felt good and smelled clean and the snow was coming down again in light and fluffy flakes. Lake of the Ozarks was absolutely beautiful in the winter, especially when it snowed this much. She enjoyed the view for a while.

"Shut those goddamn doors," came a low and hoarse voice from somewhere behind her.

Claire turned around and found Jonesy Jax standing there in the flesh—literally. He had on a pair of tight black Jockey briefs and nothing else. It was not a sight anyone wanted to see this early in the morning. Or ever.

Black took offense to his guest's language and attire, or lack thereof. "That's my wife you're talking to, Jonesy. And put a robe on, for God's sake."

Jonesy jerked his head around to Black, apparently unaware of his presence. "Wife? You get married, Nick? When?"

Nope, Claire's hatred had not dried up. Both he and Candi just made it so damn easy to despise them. Who could blame Claire? Who in their right mind wouldn't hate them?

"Claire and I got married last summer. I'm surprised you didn't see it in the tabloids. Everybody else on earth did."

"I quit reading those stupid things. Got tired of all those lies they told about me and my ladies."

Ladies? Yeah, right, Claire thought. She'd met him for the second time half a minute ago and now would believe anything horrible that anybody said about him. He looked older now, quite haggard in the face, his skin tinged a little gray. Her take? He had better see a cardiologist, and quick. He still had his long hair woven into those ugly bleached white and braided pigtails. He had tattoos all over his body, and that meant everywhere she could see skin. The ink alone must have cost him a fortune.

Jonesy looked back at her, as if sizing her up as a wife suitable for his friend and paid shrink. Then he suddenly yelled out at the top of his lungs: "Bring me a robe, Candi, damn it!" Claire jumped slightly but was chagrined about it. Then the fabled rock star looked back at Black. "Sorry, man. I just woke up. Still a little wasted, I guess. You know how it is."

"Actually, I don't." That was Black, the disapproving head doctor dripping recriminations.

Claire walked over and stood a few feet from Jonesy, but not too close for fear of catching something nasty. She didn't shut the sliding glass doors, either. She wouldn't close them now if he said "please" and paid her ten thousand dollars to slide them together just one inch. Candi appeared swiftly and held out one of Cedar Bend's white monogrammed terrycloth robes to Jonesy. He poked his arms through the sleeves and belted it, all the while staring at Claire.

"Well, you got yourself a looker there, Nick, I'll give you that. Maybe I can put her in my next video. But she'll have to dress sexier than those jeans. Can she dance?"

Her deep dislike plummeted to sheer abhorrence. Claire stared at him in a way that even a plastic mannequin could understand. Black said nothing, used to that look. This was her show. He knew that, and he also knew she could handle it without bloodshed. "How I dress is not pertinent to my investigation, sir." That last polite reference to him galled her, but hey, she could be professional. Even when it was uncalled for.

"Investigation? What's that supposed to mean?" Jonesy stated with a furrowed brow and a confused expression.

"What that is supposed to mean, Mr. Jax, is that a woman was murdered there yesterday, inside your new residence. So tell me, where were you yesterday?"

Jonesy's bloodshot eyes widened. They were swollen, with whites the color of tomato sauce. Jeez, the rock star was all discombobulated. "What do you mean?"

Crap, she needed a kindergarten teacher to translate for her. Claire lifted her badge and showed it to him. "Maybe you should splash some cold water on your face and get yourself a couple of pots of coffee. Maybe even brush your teeth. Make yourself presentable for this official police interview. Then you might be able to answer my questions."

Black slanted her one of his warning looks, recognizing the signs of her annoyance, but he elected to stay out of their conversation.

On the other hand, Jonesy didn't seem to care for her. "Yeah, and maybe I ought to call my lawyer, too. I don't like fuckin' cops."

At that, Black rose up to his full six-feet-four-inch height. He looked deceptively calm, but deadly. Funny thing, he had always hated it when people called her a fuckin' cop. It simply irked the hell out of him. Sometimes it even shook him out of his psychiatric serenity and into protective husband mode. Like now. "Watch what you say to my wife, Jonesy. You do whatever you want. Go ahead. Call a lawyer. Be stupid some more. My wife is a police officer and a good one. She's not going to put up with your crap, and neither am I. You insult her like that again, and you're gonna end up on your back on the floor."

Claire beamed at her dear husband. Good job, Black. Threats of physical violence and everything. How sweet. She was gonna keep him. Usually he was just an observer, tagging along to keep her calm. Maybe he didn't like Jonesy Jax as much as he had professed.

Jonesy appeared as if he didn't want Black to knock him down and disfigure his face, but didn't care to admit as much. "Okay, Nick, just cool it for a minute. I'm just not awake yet. Still a little high. Don't even remember last night, or what I took. Gimme a break."

Claire reentered the friendly conversation. "Well, you better get awake, because right now you are wasting my time. Also, it's not exactly brilliant to openly discuss your drug habits with a cop present."

She and Jonesy had one heck of a mutual hatred, and they stared at each other in a death duel for about twenty seconds. She knew this was going to happen. She remembered what he did when she'd stopped his limousine. After a few seconds, however, Jonesy turned around and headed back into one of the bedrooms. A moment later, Candi Kisses slunk out, still in her come-hither underwear but sans robe. "He says he's gonna take a shower and brush his teeth and put some clothes on, and take a bunch of Excedrins and a belt of whiskey and then he'll be back."

That was putting a load of specifics on things. But Claire approved. "Maybe you should do that, too, Candi Kisses. Especially the clothes part. It's snowing outside. You know, twenty degrees, or under. You'll catch cold, if you're not careful. But that's strictly up to you."

Candi shrugged, ran over to the balcony doors, and slid the door closed. "Well, this is all just too fuckin' boring. I'm gonna go back to bed."

"Thanks for sharing," Claire told her. She turned to face Black. "I cannot believe you ever spent time in the same room with these people," Claire muttered softly after the girl had sashayed out of the room. "Makes me worry about your, you know, good judgment and healthy habits."

"I've had to deal with a lot worse than Jonesy Jax."

"Poor you."

Black only shrugged. Claire sat down beside him and waited. They watched the snow float down for at least thirty more minutes before the rock star finally strolled back into the room. This time, he had clearer eyes, but the famous swagger was alive and well. Good thing was, he had some sweats on: all black, his name and picture emblazoned on the front and the back.

Claire wondered if Jonesy had taken a hit of cocaine to help pull himself together so fast. He walked straight over to her and extended his hand. "I'm sorry, Mrs. Black. I was an asshole earlier. I hope you will overlook it. I didn't mean to offend you. Or you, Nick. I wouldn't ever want to do that."

Loathe to touch him, to actually have her flesh press up against his flesh without a protective covering, Claire hesitated, but then she extended her hand in an act of distasteful reconciliation. They shook, and then he smiled. He was not bad looking, not once she saw him close-up and not almost nude. Then he walked over to Black.

"I'm sorry I spoke to your wife in that disrespectful manner. I was wrong. I shouldn't have done it."

Black readily agreed. "She's a police officer, Jonesy. Better remember that. She can lock you up."

And throw away the key, Claire finished for him, pleasantly jacked up by such a lovely fantasy.

"Sit down, please. Would you like some coffee, Detective? I've ordered a couple of pots to be brought up. Got some cheese Danish coming, too, and blueberry muffins. The works."

Claire shook her head. "No, thank you, we had breakfast earlier."

Jonesy was staring at her. "Hey, you look kinda familiar. We met before?"

"I think I might've arrested you in Los Angeles once, for numerous counts of misdemeanors and felonies."

Jonesy laughed, thinking Claire a real jokester. Then he got serious. "Okay, I guess I'm ready. Now what's this you're telling me about my new house? Do you mean the one I just bought out on the lake, that one up high on that cliff?"

Claire wondered how many houses he had bought in the vicinity. "Yes. The one you approved to be featured on the Christmas at the Lake tour. You did know that it was being used in that regard, did you not?"

"Sure, I knew about that. No big deal. I wasn't ready to move in, anyway. I've been waiting for my daughter to show up. I sent her the key, and she's supposed to call me as soon as she got out here. That's why I bought the place, so she'd have a house in a safe area where she can live when I'm out on the road. Life on tour is no place for a girl as young as her."

Claire stared at him. Hypocrite, anyone? What the hell was Candi of the Kisses if not an exploited young girl? Then, all of a sudden, in a flash of intuition she did not wish to examine, Claire sucked in her breath. A very awful thought had blazed its way across her conscious mind. Her belly gave a little quiver of sick. She turned to Black and knew instantly that he'd already come to the same unwanted conclusion. Oh God, this interview was not going to turn out well. She knew it. She felt it. She heaved in a deep, bracing breath. "I didn't know you had a daughter, Mr. Jax."

"Call me freakin' Jonesy, okay? Everybody else does. Hey, I was rude this morning. I know it. I wasn't sober yet. But I'm not the man in the tabloids anymore. They exaggerate everything about me. I'm okay now. Nick'll tell you that."

Claire knew all about the media, that was for damn sure. She waited a few seconds and then asked the question that she had to ask but didn't want to. "Can you tell me where your daughter is right now? Is she here? In your suite, maybe?" Claire realized how hopeful her voice sounded. She stood there and waited for the boom to drop, because she had a feeling it was coming down hard on top of them.

Jonesy actually smiled. He looked totally different with that smile. It was real, too, not the maniacal one he manufactured to wow his crazed groupies. "Not yet. She was supposed to get out to the house yesterday but didn't show. Guess bad weather must've messed up her flight."

"Have you tried to contact her today?"

"Yeah, sure. So did Candi. But she's not picking up. She does that to me sometimes. You know, just wants to do her own thing." He shrugged. "Don't want Daddy checking up on her, and all that. So I give her space. She's a good girl."

"So she's an adult?"

"Yeah. Almost nineteen. Will be in January. On the fifth."

"You never told me you had a daughter," Black said, looking very sober now.

"I didn't know it myself until about a year ago. I've kept it quiet, didn't want her in the spotlight or her pictures to get out in the tabloids. She's kinda quiet and shy. I didn't want the paps to chase her around like they do me."

"Why didn't you know about her?" Claire perked up at that. Maybe the bludgeoned girl was not his child. Maybe she was a random victim, chosen by the killer and brought into his house because of its isolation. Maybe his kid was snowbound in some dink airport somewhere. God, she didn't like Jonesy Jax one bit, but she wouldn't wish this kind of terrible grief on anyone. But maybe she was wrong. She hoped she was.

"Her mother was a girl I dated for a while. She got pregnant and didn't tell me. She didn't like my lifestyle, so she took off. Can't say I blame her. That's how I didn't know anything about it. She just showed up after her mother died. Said her name was Heather Cantrell, and she had a birth certificate with her that named me as the father. Of course, that happens all the time, so I took a paternity test and it turned out positive." He smiled at them, eyes filled with happiness. "Once I got over the shock of having a teenaged kid, it seemed like a fuckin' miracle. A fuckin' Christmas miracle. I've already given her my legal name. Now she's Heather Jax and just the greatest kid to have around. You'll see that when you meet her."

"I see," Claire said, and she did. Heather Cantrell was the name given to her by Oliver Wood.

She sat on the chair across from him and looked down at her lap for a moment because she knew, she knew in her gut that the dead girl in that house had to be Heather Jax. Now she was going to have to tell him that his daughter was gone again, for good this time, and in a terrible, horrible, inhumane, murderous way. But she had to be sure first. Black was watching her now, his eyes telling her loud and clear: *want me to tell him for you?*"

She did indeed, of course she did. She would've loved to pass that awful task onto Black's shoulders, but she couldn't and wouldn't. It was her job and her place to break the news. But she had to know for sure. "Do you happen to know anything about a tattoo of a grim reaper holding a scythe?"

Grinning, he pulled back his sleeve and showed her his forearm. "This what you're talking about? It's the logo of my band. Got it on the front of all my albums. Heather got one, too, once we got together."

"Would you happen to have a photograph of your daughter, Mr. Jax? A recent one, preferably."

Jonesy jerked up his head and held her steady gaze, not as dimwitted as she'd always figured. The calm look in his eyes slowly turned to panic as his mind fumbled to put together her words and what they meant. He was breathless with dread when he spoke again. "Why? Why do you want to see a picture of her?"

"Please, sir, just allow me see a photo, if you've got one here at the hotel."

Jonesy jumped up and grabbed a small framed picture that was propped up on the mantel. He hurried over to her. The photograph depicted Jonesy Jax and a pretty young girl. She had a tight grip on his arm and was leaning into him. He had his arm around her. Both had on bathing suits and L.A. Dodgers baseball caps, and they were standing out on some deserted beach somewhere. They had big, happy smiles plastered across their faces. Crap and damn it to hell. The kid in the picture was her victim, all right. There was absolutely no doubt in Claire's mind. She wished she had thought to Google Jonesy's family before coming downstairs to do the interview. It just hadn't occurred to her that Jonesy could have a grown daughter living here at the lake. She held the photo in her hands and kept staring down at it. She was trying to come up with the right words. Words that wouldn't devastate him. There weren't any.

"Oh my God, my God, don't, don't, please, don't." Jonesy jumped up and then squatted down in front of her. "I can tell by the look on your face. She's the dead woman you found in my house, isn't she? Oh no! Oh God, fuckin' no. Tell me, tell me, it's Heather, isn't it? She's dead, isn't she?"

Claire met his eyes. They looked wild with grief, and his expression was so stricken, his face so white with dread. There was absolute horror inside those eyes. She could barely force herself to maintain eye contact. "I'm so very sorry, Mr. Jax. I had no idea who she was when I came here, or I would have handled this interview much differently. I promise you that."

Jonesy Jax stared disbelievingly at her. He was too devastated to speak. It was obvious to all three of them. Then, suddenly, he lost it completely, just freaked out, and laid his head in Claire's lap and grabbed her legs and started in with the most heartrending low keening cries. Then he let her go, and slid down all the way onto the floor and curled up in a fetal position, his head buried in his palms. Utterly distraught. Groaning and moaning, prostrate with grief. Claire leaned forward and placed a comforting hand on his back. She felt sick to her stomach again. "I'm so sorry that I had to bring you this terrible news. I am so sorry for your loss, Mr. Jax."

Claire looked to Black for help. He came quickly, thank God. He knelt on one knee beside the weeping man. "Come on, Jonesy, let me help you up. You've had a terrible shock. It's going to take some time to pull it together, I know. I'll be here for you. I'll stay right here and try to help you deal with this. Let's go back to the bedroom where we can talk privately. Do you think you can stand up? I can give you a sedative that will help you calm down, if you want." Then Black turned to Claire. "Are you okay?"

She nodded, but she knew exactly why Black was asking her that. He knew this show of grief would make her relive the moment of her son's death. Her precious little baby boy named Zachary. He was right; she was reliving it. She was fighting down her own demons that clamored inside her head, just like Jonesy Jax's. She knew exactly how the rock star felt right now, down there on the floor at her feet. The horrible realization that his child was gone from him forever, that he'd never see her alive again, never talk to her, hug her or kiss her, not ever again. Claire had balled up like that one night on a busy ER floor when her toddler had been killed. She had wept inconsolably, too. She still wept like that sometimes, when she was alone and reliving that nightmare. Claire stiffened her jaw and tried to force out the image of her baby, shove him back behind the shadowy blackout curtains of her mind.

Jonesy was still sobbing when Black helped him up. He grabbed hold of Black's lapels and buried his face in his chest and wept harder. Black kept patting his back and telling him softly that he needed to lie down, and finally got him headed back toward the bedrooms. The rock star was about as distraught as anyone Claire had ever seen. It was going to take him a long time to accept that his child was gone—if he ever did—and he would never, ever get over it. All Claire could see right now was Zachary's little face peeking out from between those heavy black curtains inside her mind, his big, innocent blue eyes laughing, his blond hair curling down over his ears. He was so very real at these moments, and she could hear his chortling little laugh as he ran to her so fast on his chubby little legs. Suddenly, she knew she had to get out of that room and away from Jonesy's loud wailing.

Shaken and trying to pull it together, she headed for the door and slipped out into the corridor. She stood with her back against the wall for a few moments, chest heaving. Jonesy's bodyguard looked curiously at her when she bent over and sucked in a lungful of air. Okay, she had to stop this. It had been years since her baby had died. She had to shake off this panic attack, or whatever it was. She hadn't broken down in a long time, but this one was bad. What she needed to do was call Bud and find out when they could get back to work. She and Bud would have to come back to this suite and interview Jonesy Jax and tell him all the cruel particulars of his daughter's violent death. The idea absolutely made her ill.

Play Time

The more Junior and Lucky discussed their killing game, the more enthusiastic they became. They discussed it endlessly, and planned it out in specific details. Sometimes they didn't agree and debated the rules. That's what they were doing at the moment, sitting at the game table, drinking beer, and figuring out the best way to commit their second murder together.

"I still say we ought to just pick out whatever Detection weapon we like best. I like knives and ropes and running people down with cars. Yeah, those're my favorites. Clean and easy, and the car's always a quick getaway," Lucky was telling Junior.

"Huh uh, choosing the murder weapon yourself won't be any challenge. C'mon, Lucky, what's the fun in that? We need to draw the murder weapon out of a little pouch and let it be a big surprise. That'll make it super exciting. And a hell of a lot more difficult. Like, what if we got something that we don't know how to use? Like a chainsaw, maybe. Then we'd be new at killing with it, and it would make murdering the victim a whole lot harder. It would make us better at it if we had to learn to do it in different ways."

Lucky stared at him. "So you're sayin' that we go with whatever weapon we draw, whether it's a good option under the circumstances or not." He considered it briefly. "Well, you know, I think you might be right. That'll surely keep us on our toes and make us use our heads. Stands to reason we'll plan it better if we hold our feet to the fire like that."

"Now you're talking. A gun's always gonna be easier than killing somebody with a rope. Especially when we get those silencers we ordered. Okay, so we're both good with the how and the why of the weapons, right? So how do we choose the victims?" Junior smiled, getting really excited. "Maybe we could just drive around and point out somebody walking down the street. You know, real random like. That would make it really hard for the cops to connect us to the murder."

"Or it could be someone we just want to see dead. No reason necessary. Maybe we see 'em and just don't like 'em."

Junior found that amusing. "You mean, pick out somebody that rubs us the wrong way. Like that cashier at Staples who gave us shit the other night. Remember her? What a bitch. She kept looking at us like we were dirtbags or something."

Lucky jumped up and strode across the room. He sorted through the games on the shelves for a moment and then pulled out a box and brought it back to the table. "Or, my friend, we could use this. I used to play this all the time when I was in grade school. We could use its game board to choose what kind of victim. And that way, everything we do decide on is totally random. Cops would go crazy trying to trace victims back to us, or to each other. Maybe we could even leave them some stinkin' clues. That'd drive them nuts. And they're gonna need them if nothing we do connects in any way. Hell, this's gonna be fun."

"Well, now that is just brilliant, I've got to say."

Lucky grinned, pleased by Junior's rare compliment, no doubt. Junior watched him set up the board between them. "First off, you gotta choose your path in life. Remember how this game's played? You figure out how you want to start off in your adult years, okay? What you want to do for a living, where you want to work, all that kind of crap. See here? It says: Career or College or Travel." He glanced up. "So what's your choice?"

"College, I guess, since neither of us plan on attending. Besides, those college kids look down their noses at anybody who doesn't have a degree. It irks me, since I'm smarter than all of them put together. College chicks don't even look at guys like us unless we throw around our money."

"Okay. Done. We'll choose a college kid to kill. Hey, maybe we can make it a competition of sorts. You against me."

"As in, we both choose a victim and see who can perform the best murder without getting caught? That what you're talking about?"

Junior was getting pumped now. "OMG, this is just gonna be so freakin' cool, dude. But there's gotta be a time limit. So how long do we have to get it done?"

"Well, let's say we just spin the wheel or throw the dice to get that stuff. Whatever number comes up, that's how many days we've got to murder our victim and get away scot free."

"Great idea!" Lucky said. "Just pick some poor guy and whack him good. Awesome, man!"

"Maybe." Junior contemplated Lucky. "Or, it might make the game more difficult if we just decide on the type of person we want and look for somebody who meets that description. Maybe we should pick a picture out of some magazine or newspaper or find somebody interesting on TV. Choosing a type out of a magazine would probably be better. My mom's still getting a ton of subscriptions."

"Where are they? Let's look through them."

"Over there, on the end table."

Lucky gathered them up, brought them back, and spread them out on the table. "Okay, watch and learn, buddy boy." He picked up a magazine with a slick photo cover. It was a woman's magazine called *Cosmopolitan,* which had been Junior's mom's favorite reading material. Lucky shut his eyes, opened the magazine to a page near the middle, and then stabbed his finger down on the page without looking.

Eager to see what kind of person would be the first to die by their hands, they both leaned in close. "There you go. Victim number one, right here on the page in front of us."

Junior could not hide his excitement. "What we've got here is a young girl with lots of long red hair and one very short skirt. Yum yum. Is she hot, or what? Maybe we ought to have some fun with our victim before we put her down."

They both nodded, liking the sound of that. Especially Junior. He wasn't as good with women as Lucky was. Lucky always bragged about having sex with at least a hundred women. He probably had, too. Women took one look at him and dropped to his feet. They liked his eyes and his self-confidence. All he had to do was stare at them for a while and they melted. Junior had never seen anything quite like it. "Sounds like a plan, Lucky, my man."

"Sounds like a lot of fun, too."

"Maybe we should do this first one together, hone our skills a bit, you know, before we start competing for cash. Have a trial run, just to get the hang of things. Might take two of us at first to take somebody down and make sure they don't get away and call the cops."

"So now we've got to go find us a girl with red hair and a short skirt. One of those stuck-up college coeds would be perfect. Then we kill her off with a candlestick, right? Spin and see how long we've got to get it done."

They spun the game wheel and both boys watched it slow down and finally stop on the number three.

"Awesome. Three days to get it planned and carried out." Lucky raised shining eyes to Junior. He looked...well, he looked really turned on.

Junior's heart was racing. "Then let's do this thing. The UCLA campus is a perfect hunting ground and just full of girls in short skirts. Good-lookin' ones, too. I want to get a pretty one. The one in the picture is hot."

"Three days to find a woman we like the looks of and is similar to this picture." Lucky ripped the page out of *Cosmopolitan.*

"No problem there. You see redheads everywhere nowadays. It's the new fad. Too many blondes, so they go red to get noticed."

"Okay, cool, but after this initial kill, we go into competition to see who gets the cleanest murder the fastest. Hey, maybe we should come up with a specific dollar amount for the prize. How about a hundred thousand dollars? Or a new Porsche? My dad's on tour again. He's making tons of dough that'll trickle down into my bank account."

"You got it, bro. I would just love me a Porsche. A shiny black one. But now let's go find us a pretty little redheaded gal." He laughed. "Just like Charlie Brown's girlfriend. But first, let's pick up a pepperoni pizza. I'm hungry."

Satisfied and excited, they headed up the steps and made a beeline for the garage. Game on. Oh yeah. Game is on, all right. Time to rack up some serious bloodletting fun.

Chapter 11

Bud didn't arrive at Cedar Bend Lodge until just after one o'clock. That was a good thing. It gave Claire plenty of time to grab hold of some shaky emotions. She didn't understand why she had spiraled so quickly about Zachary—it was rare now to hit her so hard and so brutally. But she would be all right. What she needed was to get back to work. Work was always a panacea for dark days. Black was gone, already down at the exclusive bungalows seeing his patients. By the time Bud finally showed up in his truck, Claire was already downstairs in the back corridor, watching for him. Unfortunately, the paparazzi had caught wind of the private elevator. Fortunately for Claire, Black had ordered barriers set up to bracket the back drive and manned them with security guards. That helped them some, but not enough, as they soon found out.

The photographers had their tripod cameras set up just outside the ballroom doors, every one zeroed in on Claire's private entrance, ready with their big-zoom, we-got-you-sucker lenses. Snow muffled the sounds of the day and made everything quiet, so Claire could hear the snapping and clicking of shutters as she walked down the sidewalk. Averting her face to ruin their shots, she kept her hood pulled up, head down, and wore a pair of big, round black sunglasses so they wouldn't have squat to sell to the tabloids. Even those despicable rags didn't buy bad shots. They paid the big bucks for juicy ones that sold copies and ruined lives. Nobody followed them around the hotel to the exit drive, though, probably because Bud had slapped his flasher on top.

"So, you're sayin' the victim turned out to be Jonesy Jax's daughter? You got a positive ID on that yet, Claire? That is going to cause all hell to break loose around here. You know that, don't you?"

"Jonesy showed me a recent picture of Heather Jax. He adopted her and she took his name. Used to be Heather Cantrell, her mom's maiden name. I could readily identify her off that photo. It's her, all right. And that's not all: He's got the same tattoo that she has, and it's his business logo." Claire turned in the seat and started outlining everything else she had on the case so far, but Bud interrupted her almost at once.

"You got to meet him this morning? Did he remember you arrestin' him that time?"

"I don't think so, and I don't give a rip. He started out as his usual nasty self, but after he got his head on straight and realized his daughter had been killed, I felt sorry for him. He took it very hard. He was still getting to know her, but he loved her. I have no doubt about that."

"And you're absolutely certain she's his kid and our victim?"

"He did a paternity test. It came back positive. The picture he showed me this morning was recent, and it was a spot-on resemblance, Bud. It's either Heather Jax, or she's got a very unlucky doppelgänger here at the lake. It was a bad scene when I told him. Count yourself lucky you weren't there. Black was, thank goodness. He's good at times like that. Jax grabbed him and wept on his chest like a baby. Black says he's still distraught. He finally had to sedate him."

"Sounds like a bad scene."

"Yeah, to say the least. Unfortunately, you and I have to interview him again. Worse than that? He's got to do the official ID at the morgue. To tell you the truth, Bud, I'm not sure he can handle it. That's how hard he's taking this. Black says he'll pull it together eventually, but I'm not so sure. I guess we've gotta wait and see."

"Everything about this case sucks. It's ruining the hell out of my Christmas fun."

"Yeah, me too. It's obvious that Jonesy loved her. But her showing up out of nowhere and claiming to be his daughter, and then getting killed by some maniac in Jonesy's own house, something about all that doesn't add up. There's more to it, I'm telling you."

Bud slowed down, stopped at the big rock entrance sign that led into Cedar Bend Lodge, then hit his blinker. "Yeah, I think so, too. Lots of things going down around here all of a sudden. Guess you brought some bad luck back to the lake with you."

Claire winced at that remark, but it was true. "Yeah, I usually do."

Bud darted a quick and regretful look at her. "Hey, wait, Claire. I'm sorry. I didn't mean that the way it came out. Really. This case has nothing to do with you bein' back here. It's just been pretty quiet since you left the department and got married, that's all I meant."

Claire wished that were true, but bad things did seem to follow her around. As if some black macabre shadow stalked her day and night, hanging back out of sight but always there to lunge at her when she least expected it. Sometimes she wondered if her friends thought that, too. Even Black hadn't escaped her curse; he had lived a fairly charmed life until they hooked up. Truth was, he'd started worrying about her since the day they'd met and hadn't stopped. They'd faced off with death way too many times, both of them. Black was the sunny spot in her life, he and her friends at the lake. And Rico, too, of course. That kid. Talk about brightening up their lives.

"Hey, Bud, you sure you didn't hear from the FBI last night? Was your phone off or anything? Could you have missed a call?"

"Nope, my phone's never off. Last night Shag and I hung out at my place and watched Superman mess it up with Batman. We're pissed how they went up against each other. It wasn't Superman's fault aliens came to Earth and made him take them out in the middle of the city. But I was asleep in bed by midnight, phone beside me. No FBI contact."

"I just can't figure why that guy came to see me. He stood there and lied to me. Flipped open his badge folder and demanded to see our murder file. He was a strange man, Bud. Told me our victim was in witness protection, and he knew her name. Insisted that I show him the file and wanted to view the body. Worst thing? He was probably the biggest jerk I've ever met. He really got under Black's skin, and nobody but nobody gets under Black's skin."

"Mr. Unflappable got riled up? I would've liked to have seen that."

"Black's been edgy the last few days, anyway. You know why, so let's not mention it aloud ever again."

"I'd be mad, too, if I were him, married to you when those pictures came out. Luckily, I can just laugh at you both."

"Yeah, I noticed."

"Just kidding." Bud maneuvered around a car that had stopped in their lane. "No way is that guy gonna horn in on this case. Even if he's legit. You didn't tell him anything pertinent, did you?"

"No, I didn't trust him or his motives. The badge looked real—the rest of him didn't. I've got Laurie Dale looking into him. I can pretty much guarantee that this guy isn't on the up and up. He told me his partner was interviewing you while he was with me. He just made that up. Why, is the question. He knew I could find out the truth when I talked to you."

"What do you think he was after?"

"That's a good question. Black rode down to the lobby with me, you know, to fight off the media if they started hounding me." She glanced over at him. "You should've seen it, Bud. That creep tried every trick in the book to make Black mad, you know, just little jabs about me and those pictures in Hawaii. No FBI agent would behave that unprofessionally. If he was impersonating one, why blow it like that? That's just stupid."

"And Black really didn't deck the guy?"

"He wanted to, but you know him. He prefers to sit back and analyze what the guy was really up to. But he didn't like it much. He was grinding his teeth at one point."

Bud laughed. "He's lucky Black's got self-control."

"Black did snap a picture of him, though, and sent it to my phone." Claire pulled it up and showed him when he stopped at the next traffic light. "Ever seen him before?"

He shook his head. "Nope. Not that I recall."

"I'm sending it through face recognition today. He told me his name was Oliver Wood, and he spent the conversation picking at Black and me. It was crazy. Then, after a little while, he took off in a hurry. I mean, he practically ran in the other direction. I think he saw somebody he didn't want to run into, somebody who's registered at Cedar Bend. If we can find out who that is, we need to talk to them and see what the connection is. Some of our security guards have seen him around, but nobody noticed anything suspicious."

"So Laurie's here at the lake?"

"She and Scott are coming up for Black's Christmas party. You're coming, too, right?"

"For sure. I just hope Brianna gets here in time."

"Me too." Claire stared at the back of a Ford Fusion, which was driving way too slowly in front of them. "Tell you one thing I dread: attending this autopsy."

"Buck's probably finished by now."

"I can't stop thinking about that Oliver Wood guy. He's got these really unusual eyes, Bud. I mean, super intense. Sort of like he could look at me and pull out my innermost secrets. It was unnerving."

"Doubt we can find anybody with laser eyes outside of Marvel comic books. But people are gonna remember that about him. He sure as hell made an impression on you. Nobody's ever looked down into my soul, thank God. Except maybe Charlie, when he goes into one of his rages."

Claire had to laugh. "Yes, sir, the sheriff can jerk your soul right out of your body, all right. How's he feeling, by the way?"

"Everybody's afraid to call and ask. You know how he is when he's confined to bed and has to miss work."

"Well, I'm not calling him."

"Me, either."

The medical examiner's parking lot was deserted, packed down with dirty ice and piles of snow, but the plows had scraped a wide path right up to the front door. Snow banks rose to the top of Bud's tire wells as they drove in. The air was bitter but the temperature hadn't made it down past zero yet. The sun had come out but wasn't having much luck with the warming thing. They were definitely going to have a white Christmas, which pleased Claire. For one thing, Rico had never seen snow until coming to the lake. Born in California, his family had eventually moved to a sun-drenched Sicilian island, and neither locale was exactly known for frigid weather. He'd already built half a dozen snowmen over at Harve's house. Just thinking about Rico made Claire smile.

The front sidewalk had been cleared, so they climbed out and carefully made their way to the front door. The ice had been salted but was still slippery. When they walked inside, they were met by the distinctive odor of death, chemicals, and floral-scented room fresheners, which weren't working. Claire hated morgues. Hated attending autopsies most of all. That was one thing she definitely did not miss about working homicides. Watching Buckeye insert the sharp tip of his scalpel into muscle tissue and carve a giant Y-cut was not a whole lotta fun, huh uh. She hoped he was done with the body and had the victim covered with a sheet.

The morgue was silent, unusually quiet as they walked down the deserted hall toward Buckeye's office.

"Hey, guys." Shaggy looked up from his microscope as they entered his office. He leaned way back in his swivel chair and presented them with a huge grin. Never, ever in a bad mood was Shaggy. Well, maybe once in a blue moon, but no more than that. He wore jeans, snow boots, a black tropical shirt with palm trees and suns, with a black hoodie. The jeans and hoodie were unusual—maybe he was finally giving in to the Missouri wind chill factor.

"Did we miss the autopsy?" Claire asked, hope in her voice. "Please, please say yes."

"You're in luck. Buckeye was in a hurry to get it done. He wants that trip down to the Caribbean in the worst way."

"Did you find anything we can use?"

"No fingerprints or DNA on the body or the trophy. But we did find something that wasn't supposed to be there." They waited silently while Shaggy lengthened the suspense. Whatever it was, Claire did not think it was going to be appetizing. "Guess what was in her stomach?"

A few things ran through Claire's mind, all of which turned her stomach. "Oh God, I don't know. What?"

"Please don't let it be a roach or something. Or even worse, some kind of hairy spider." Bud was creeped out by insects, especially eight-legged ones. In fact, he verged precipitously close to arachnophobia. He'd doubled his fear a few years back on a particularly gruesome murder cases that dealt with lots of creepy crawlies. Claire felt a swath of goosebumps race up her arms just thinking about that one. That's when she'd gotten into the habit of shaking out her shoes and garments before putting on her clothes.

"No bugs. Better'n that. Or worse, depending on how you wanna look at it. Wanna see it?"

"That's why we're here, Shag."

Shaggy picked up a clear plastic baggie off the desk. He held it up. "Know what this is?"

They crowded in behind him. Claire bent down and looked closely. "What? That looks nasty."

"It's the victim's stomach contents."

Both of them stepped back, grossed out. Pathology humor was just sick.

"Shit, Shaggy, put that green stuff down," Bud told him. Bud was a big, strong guy, but someone's stomach contents in a baggie got to him. Made him gag, even. Claire, too, but not as bad.

"So, what's it got in it?" Claire asked him, but she didn't want to look at it any longer, either. She felt like hacking.

"Well, this stuff in this little baggie you see here, my friends? It's gonna tell us where she ate her last meal."

Okay. That did sound like a clue that could be helpful. "Where? And hey, don't you have a jar or something to put that in? That baggie is just disgusting."

"I just got finished with it. It'll go in a jar in a minute."

"Well, where'd she eat?" Bud asked.

"Bud, you remember that game store we went to last year? She ate right there at their snack bar. Bet on it. They're the only ones in town who have pineapple and papaya pizza on lemon crust. I know, because that's my favorite, and it's the only place I can get it. And that is precisely what is in this little baggie I hold in my hand. And some peanuts and traces of beer, too."

"Well, ugh. That sounds almost as bad as it looks." Bud looked away.

"What game store?" Claire asked.

"It's called Games Galore. Over in Osage Beach. But that's not all I found. There's something else that's really bad. Even I thought it was sickening."

"Oh, please," Claire said. "Just tell us already, Shaggy. Enough with this drama."

"Okay, but you sure are pissy today." He picked up a different bag. This one held some sort of little round silver disk. "Know what this is?"

Bud took the bag from him and examined it. "Looks like a dog tag to me. Where'd you get it?"

"Inside her stomach, with that liquid pineapple pizza."

"Oh God, Shaggy, just stop, or I really might throw up." Claire shook her head. Her stomach was reacting more than usual to all the yucky talk, and she was sure as hell not in the mood for discussing Shaggy's gross specimens. God, it had been one terrible day, ever since she first opened her eyes and rolled out of Black's arms. Now she wished she hadn't gotten up at all. Being in bed with Black sounded pretty good at the moment, with her eyes shut to everything happening outside their bedroom. "Just tell us where you really found it and quit jerking us around."

"I'm not jerking you around."

"Shaggy. I am not in the mood for games. Not today."

He laughed some more. "You just made a pun and didn't even know it."

"Tell us."

"Okay, okay. Apparently, the perp made this really deep slit through her abdomen right around here." Shag pointed to a spot on his own torso. "Then he sort of whittled a deep hole down through her tissue and muscle. It's hard to see. We almost missed it at the scene. I think he must've pushed that little disk down inside her stomach with his forefinger or his knife or some kind of long object."

"Oh my God." Bud sounded revolted.

Claire stared at Shaggy. Everything about this case so far was gross. Whoever did this was so warped in the head it scared her.

"I think she might've still been alive when he did it. But maybe not." Shaggy looked serious now. "Maybe he did this right after he hit her with the trophy and she wasn't gone yet. No prints left on anything. He wiped everything clean and wore gloves, I'd say. Nothing on the evidence found in the room, either. But wanna hear the clincher? Ready?"

They looked sourly at him.

"Okay, this little disk? It is a dog tag. See the little hole? And it's engraved with a special message."

Claire grabbed the bag out of his hand and turned it over. And there it was, as plain as day. She read it out loud. "It says, 'Love, Dad.'"

"Love, Dad? What the hell?" Bud said.

Claire blew out air, very glad now that she'd only had that one donut for breakfast. "Jonesy Jax is her dad. So apparently he's involved somehow, or the killer wants us to believe he is. Maybe the killer knows him or hates him or wants to get even about something."

"Or Jonesy might have done it," Bud countered.

"I can't believe that. I was there this morning. I saw the shock on his face when I told him his daughter was dead."

All three of them stood there a moment, silent and staring at the silver dog tag.

"Well, this means something significant. It's another clue he left for us," Bud said. "He's playing games, all right. Maybe we can figure out where it was engraved, get a lead on the killer that way."

Claire shook her head. "You can buy dog tags anywhere in town. You realize how many people have jewelry engraved every single day? It's not exactly uncommon, nor is the message. We've got to figure out what the killer is trying to tell us here. It's got to refer to Jonesy Jax. Unless Heather has a stepdad somewhere, maybe a guy who was around when she was growing up, her mother's husband or boyfriend, maybe. Before she found out Jax was her real father. Maybe he didn't like her reconciling with Jonesy."

Bud shrugged. "Could be a jealousy thing, I guess. If she took Jonesy's name already."

"She did." Claire turned to Shaggy. "Is Buck still back there?"

"Yeah."

They left Shaggy with his grotesque specimens and found Buckeye right next door, standing at a stainless steel autopsy table. Their victim was laid out on her back, her head on a molded plastic block. She was completely nude, and Buck was examining the sutures of the Y cut. Buck sewed up corpses with the precise stitches of a Calvin Klein seamstress. A regular Betsy Ross, he was—but only on cold, dead flesh.

He glanced up from his work. "Hey, Claire, come over here. I want you to see this wound. Did Shaggy tell you about the dog tag?"

"Yes, and it's pretty damn gruesome, I've got to admit."

"Cruel, is what it is. Sorry I went ahead with the cut, but I'm out of here after we get all the reports done—if our flight doesn't get snowed in."

Bud was staring down at the body. "I wasn't expecting this one to get this kinky. I thought it was gonna be a run-of-the-mill murder by a blunt instrument. Theatrical, true, but this sounds to me like we've got us a real nutcase. One who likes to play games.

"Let me show you where he forced that thing all the way down into her stomach."

Bud and Claire stood silently, grimacing in tandem as Buck pointed a gloved finger at a small, round cavity in the girl's upper abdomen. Looked like something a drill would make, and what an awful thought that was. He pulled the edges open with his fingers. Such a gaping hole in her stomach was not a sight they'd easily forget, no matter how hard they tried. Claire's gaze didn't linger long on that ugly wound. She got the idea. If the girl was alive when he jammed that dog tag through her body, it must have been excruciating. She got a clear visual of the act, and then shoved it out of her mind. But why would anyone do something that unnecessary? It had to be a daddy thing, but it didn't make a lot of sense. She'd hoped Shaggy was wrong, that the girl had been bludgeoned first and died instantly, but she was pretty sure it hadn't happened that way. If Shaggy was right, this young woman had suffered—the killer had made sure she had.

Instead, Claire studied the dead woman's face. She was definitely the young girl in Jonesy's photograph, there was no doubt in her mind. But they didn't have to tell Jonesy about the dog tag. No way would Claire do that to him. Heather Jax looked halfway peaceful now, since Buckeye had closed the eyelids of that empty, staring gaze. She had barely been old enough to vote, and she'd died for a killer's warped pleasure. Life was not fair. Life was a crapshoot, and always had been. Or just plain crap, in this instance.

Her baby's life had been short, too. Zachie never made it to preschool, never swung a bat, never drove a car. He had only lived to celebrate two birthdays. Claire turned away from the table, shoved down hard on rising emotions. *Don't think about it*, she told herself. *Don't picture him in your mind.* But she did. Standing up in his crib and sucking on his pacifier and pulling his red wagon around the house. *Don't remember him hugging you so tightly around the neck.* Oh, God help her, she had to get a grip. She was working a murder. She tried to remember the coping mechanisms that Black had taught her. Most of the time they worked okay, but not today. She forced herself to listen to what Bud was saying.

"Find anything else that'll help us?"

Buckeye said, "She's got that reaper tattoo, but I found another one that's a bit unusual. Maybe you could get an ID off it."

"I know what the reaper stands for," Claire told them. "Jonesy's got one, too. It's his band's logo."

"I think I remember that now, come to think of it," Bud said.

"Well, I found another one." Buckeye lifted the girl's right hand. He pulled apart the thumb and forefinger and revealed the web of skin. A tattoo was etched there. Two tiny letters: JJ. Meaning Jonesy Jax, no doubt. It was an interesting place to have them inked. Nobody would see it unless she spread her fingers apart.

"A tribute to her dad?" Bud said. "Before he owned up to it?"

Claire pulled over Buckeye's magnifying glass and examined the tat closely. "Got to be. Maybe she did it when she found out he was her real father but before she decided to contact him. Maybe she didn't want some possessive or jealous stepfather to see it. Or boyfriend."

Buckeye stretched tired muscles and snapped off his gloves. "I'm ready to get out of here. This was a bad one."

Claire could relate. A nice warm beach a thousand miles away from this morgue and its foul odors sounded damn good to her. "Maybe you could catch a late flight, Buck. Charlie would okay that, I bet."

"He's way too ill right now to care about my time off, one way or another. First time I remember him getting down with the flu this bad. I hope to heck we can get out of here, though. I've had enough of this snow and ice to last me a lifetime." He shook his head. "So she really was that rock star's kid? And he's now gonna live here, on our lake, and make trouble for everybody? You met him?"

"Unfortunately, yes. I even got the dubious pleasure of meeting his girlfriend—a sassy little vixen by the name of Candi Kisses." The two men laughed together. Claire frowned. "I guess we shouldn't make fun of him. He was planning his first Christmas with his newfound daughter out in that mansion in Cliff Point, but this murder ended that storybook happily-ever-after. I'm telling you, he loved this girl, I don't care how long he knew her. He pretty much fell apart right in front of us."

Buck clicked off the bright light over the table. "We can have the autopsy reports on your desk by late this afternoon."

"Okay, good luck getting down to the islands."

Buckeye nodded and turned to wash his hands. Bud and Claire walked out of that cold and dreary place, glad they could get away from that mutilated body and breathe in some cold, fresh air. Morgues—and everything about them—sucked.

Play Time

The first redheaded girl in a short skirt that Junior and Lucky found as they cruised up and down the dark roads in and around the UCLA campus turned out to be a young prostitute plying her trades right outside the south campus gate. She didn't appear to be a coed, not unless she was moonlighting for tuition, which could have very well been the case. It had happened before. The important thing was that she was pretty good-looking, a hooker on the prowl who met their designated description. She wore black fishnets, firetruck-red six-inch heels, and a short white skirt that showed off some shapely legs. Her top was low enough to reveal two other impressive attributes that they both deemed highly important. As they drove slowly past her in Junior's red Mercedes, she smiled and waved at them by lifting the hem of her skirt—which pretty much did the trick. Yes, they liked that about her.

"What'd you think, Junior?"

"I think she just looks good enough to eat. She's a little-bitty thing, too, so she shouldn't cause us much trouble if she starts fighting. She'll probably be too scared, though."

"Okay, she fits the criteria, so let's do her. We can get us a college kid next time if she's not enrolled. This is only a trial run, anyway. Who knows, maybe she goes to classes in the daytime."

Junior drove the length of the block and turned the car around in a private driveway. Then he came back and stopped right in front of the willing young woman. She looked older than they'd first thought. Still in her twenties, or most likely thirties. Like a graduate student, maybe. Junior hoped she was in college. He wanted to keep to their plans and make their board choices sacrosanct. He was anal that way. But whatever, she did meet most of their standards. So Lucky slid down his passenger window and called to her. Junior decided that she was really good-looking under all the makeup she was wearing. More important, it would be easy to crack her skull with the heavy silver candlestick they'd chosen as a weapon, the one his mom always used in the middle of the table at Christmas dinner. They needed to get her inside the car and back home quickly and efficiently, before anybody saw them talking to her, much less saw her getting into the car. He decided that they needed to buy an old car in which to pick up their victims, one that wouldn't be so easy to identify.

"Hey, handsome," she said to Lucky, leaning down close so he could look down her blouse. Junior could smell her perfume all the way over on the driver's side. She smelled damn good. Nice and sweet. He thought he recognized the scent as Juicy Couture, because his mom used to wear that sometimes. Now the little redhead was smiling across the seat at him. "Oh wow, this is my lucky day. Two hot guys in a hot car."

"You do two at a time?" Junior asked.

"I do two and three and sometimes four, baby. But it'll cost you double for the both of you. Triple if you want a threesome."

"Yeah? How much?"

"A hundred bucks each for an hour, higher if you want some kink thrown into the mix."

"Seems a tad pricey to me. Think you're worth that much?"

She only laughed and shook those long russet-red curls. That's when Junior thought she might have on a wig. Her hair just looked too perfect. "I'm worth a lot more than that. I hone my talents. You'll see."

Lucky was still looking down her gaping blouse. "I think you're exactly what we've been looking for, baby."

"Yeah, me too," agreed Junior. "Climb in. We want to go somewhere nice and private. Campus cops patrol around here."

The redhead climbed into the back seat, raring to go, it seemed. Probably envisioning lots of dollar signs. Junior glanced at Lucky and smiled, and then he took off. He made sure he did not exceed the speed limit. It was late now, well after midnight. He took as many side streets as he could while Lucky flirted with the girl. He glanced back at her. "You okay with going to my house? Nobody's home this weekend but us. We'll have it all to ourselves."

"How far is it?"

"Beverly Hills."

"Really? You live there?"

"Yeah. I got lots of money."

She looked skeptical, as if she didn't believe him. "So tell me what you've got in mind. There are some things I won't do. No exceptions."

"Don't worry. We aren't weirdos. We like to play strip poker with girls like you, you know, the pretty ones." Lucky rested his arm on the seat and looked back at her. "You up for some fun and games first?"

"Sure, I like to play games." She giggled a little. She might even be in her mid-thirties, Junior thought. But she was still really cute. They had lucked out this first time around.

"What's your name?" Lucky asked her.

"Rosie."

"That your real name?"

"You don't get to know my real name."

"That's okay. You don't get to know ours, either. You work the streets every night around campus?"

"Unless I've got a final or something the next morning."

Junior and Lucky looked at each other again. So she was a college student after all. After that, Junior picked up speed, getting eager. He hit an on-ramp and headed for home. When they entered the quiet streets of his exclusive neighborhood, Rosie appeared impressed. "You guys must be as rich as Mark Wahlberg, living in houses like these."

"Yeah, we pretty much are. Maybe you'll get a big tip if you do things our way."

"No problem. I can stay as long as you want. But it'll cost you. I'm short on tuition."

"No problem," said Junior. "We're both loaded."

By the time they got Rosie the Hooker down into the game room, Junior was beside himself and antsy with anticipation. They had planned it all out in specific detail while they'd driven around eating pepperoni pizza. They had made up some game cards to play, cards that listed which piece of clothing the player who drew it had to take off. Once he'd seen how enticing her body was, he wanted the game to last longer before they revealed their true intent. But killing her was their objective, so that's what had to take priority over other prurient pleasures. They could find a call girl any day, but murder was the goal tonight—and that was pretty damn erotic. At least, it was to Junior.

The three of them sat down together at the round game table in the center of the basement. Rosie kept looking at Junior, even more than she looked at Lucky. That was unusual. Girls always looked at Lucky the most, and told him what pretty eyes he had and how handsome he was. She had great eyes, too, big and black and so heavily drenched with black eyeliner and black shadow and false eyelashes that it was hard to tell what they really looked like. Junior was pretty sure her hair wasn't naturally red. It really did look like a wig, now that he saw her close-up. At first, he found that disconcerting. If she wasn't a natural redhead, that would disqualify her from one of the major requirements they'd deemed necessary for their victim. Then again, he guessed it didn't really matter. She was gonna have red hair at the moment of death, and that was the important thing.

"What kind of poker do you guys play? Five card draw? Texas Hold'em?" she asked. "I like them all."

Lucky laughed. "We usually just skip the poker and get down to the stripping part."

"Sounds okay to me." She reached under the table and squeezed Junior's thigh, up high, where it counted. He was already incredibly turned on by the idea of murdering her in cold blood, and her familiarity and obvious come-on just made it that much more intense. He'd never picked up a hooker off the street before. Not like Lucky had. Lucky liked to boast about the hookers he'd had, and he bragged about never having to pay them a penny. Junior was pretty sure he was lying about his prowess, though.

Now Lucky was explaining the game to Rosie. "Okay, we're just gonna draw one of these cards right here, the black ones, and do what it says. Okay?"

"Sure. Sounds like fun. It's your money."

"All right then, you go first. You know, we're gentlemen. Ladies always go first."

"Oh, wow, I do like manners in my johns. Don't see all that many nice guys like you, not around campus. You sure you don't want to just get it on? The three of us? I don't think I'd have to pretend with you two."

"Aw, you're so sweet. But we can do that in a little while. I wanna play a game first." Junior spoke the last part in a creepy voice. Rosie gave him a startled look, but didn't seem to get the connection to the torture porn movies. Poor little thing, she had no idea what kind of horror was headed her way. But he couldn't let himself feel any empathy for her. She was a means to the end. Besides, the die was cast. She was in the lion's den with two very deadly and bloodthirsty big cats. That analogy made him smile.

"Okay, I'll draw first," she offered. "You boys got anything to drink?"

"How about a glass of champagne? We bought it to celebrate with you."

"Really? What are we celebrating?"

"Oh, just the first step in a big project of ours."

"I love champagne. I've only had it once, on New Year's Eve."

Junior went to the bar and poured them all champagne in his mom's best crystal flutes. Rosie held hers up, examined the etching, and exclaimed over all the bubbles. She was coming across as a very innocent girl. After she took a drink, she put her glass down and reached for the top card of the stack. She had long nails painted dark blue. Junior was going to have to watch those nails when he grabbed her, or she would most certainly use them like talons and gouge his face. Girls always went for a guy's eyes when he got too carried away.

"Why, look here, guys. This card says for me to take off my skirt." Rosie jumped right up, eager as hell, it seemed, unzipped her tiny white leather skirt, and let it drop down to the floor around her feet. All she had on underneath it was a black garter belt and the fishnets. She looked as sexy as hell standing there in front of them. She was as pretty as the high-price girls they called in from time to time.

"Nice," Lucky said. His tongue swiped over his lips. He found her desirable, too. "You look real good, Rosie."

Junior could tell that he meant it. She was fine, and she was sexy, and she was ready to roll. A captive audience, in fact. For a second, he thought about taking advantage of her chosen profession and having a bit of fun before they did her, but then he realized that that wasn't in the plan. They had to treat their new game in a businesslike manner if they wanted to succeed. This first selection was an important step. They had to do it well, do it together, and get away with it, without any hitches.

Junior elected to draw next. His card told him to remove his shoes. So he kicked off his black tasseled loafers.

Lucky's card said to take off his shirt. He pulled his T-shirt off over his head, and Rosie reached over and rubbed her palms on his bulging pecs, then trailed her fingers down over his six-pack and below. Now Junior thought what a pity it was that she had to die tonight. She really was a nice girl, and smelled so great and sure as hell was hot to trot. Then again, she was nothing but a cheap streetwalker, so far beneath them that what did it really matter?

They joked and flirted with each other, and drank their bubbly and played the game for a while until each person had drawn twice and removed two articles of clothing. Then the girl drew the card for which Junior and Lucky had been waiting on pins and needles. "You just won a special surprise," she read off the card. She looked at each of them in turn, smiling. "What's this one mean? Do I get a bonus?"

"It means this," Lucky said. "Watch closely now."

Junior felt his muscles draw up and get all tense, and he veritably held his breath. Lucky leaned down under the table and got a firm grip on the heavy candlestick. It weighed at least five pounds and was almost a foot tall. Pure sterling silver. A pair of them had cost his mom a bundle at Tiffany's. Junior sat tense and rigid as Lucky stood up and held it out for Rosie to see.

"Oh, that's so pretty. Is that my prize? Do I get to keep it?"

"Sure," Junior said. "It's all yours."

When Rosie glanced over at Junior, looking absolutely delighted, Lucky smiled, too. He was now standing right behind her. Then he said, "Die, bitch!" He swung the candlestick down hard and smashed it against the side of her head. Blood came flying out, spattering crimson droplets all over the table and game cards. Rosie fell forward onto the tabletop, then collapsed sideways off her chair and went down onto the rug. She was moaning a little, barely conscious, already close to dead. Lucky stood over her, still breathing hard, his nostrils flaring, his muscles flexed. Junior could see the blood spatter all over his chest. Then he looked at Junior and laughed. He took one hand and smeared the girl's blood around on his bare skin, as if he relished the feel of it. Junior backed away from the carnage and couldn't stop staring at the girl's busted skull. He could see some of her brain, for God's sake, and some sharp shards of her skull sticking out through her hair. It wasn't a wig, after all. She was a true redhead. He supposed that was a good thing.

"Your turn, Junior. Just like we agreed."

"She's already dead, I think."

"Don't care. You have to do it, too. We agreed. Don't be so squeamish."

So Junior stood up and took the bloody candlestick out of Lucky's hands. He hesitated a moment, and then he lifted it high over his head and brought it down on her like an axe splitting wood. After that, her head was nothing but a thatch of red hair and pulpy gore. The two boys stood side by side and stared down at Rosie's body, both a bit shocked by what they'd just done. On the bright side, they had chosen a victim, and now she was dead and nobody was any the wiser. All they had to do now was dispose of the body and they'd be home free.

"Good job, Lucky," he said, but his voice sounded shaky, and that embarrassed him.

Lucky gave a little butler's bow. "We are gods now. We decree life or death."

"I can't believe we really did this."

"Yeah, well, we did. Simple as pie. And you know what they say: the first time is always the hardest. Here's to many more games." They lifted their champagne flutes and clinked them together.

Feeling giddy, they started to laugh and staggered away from the dead body. Junior felt as if he'd released some kind of black-cloaked demon that had been lurking deep inside his soul since he'd been born. Lucky just looked pleased that they'd pulled it off. Fortunately, there were a lot more devils deep inside both boys, devils that would rise up and help them when they needed someone to die.

Junior became a bit more subdued after his initial elation faded. Actually, he felt a little nauseous when they wrapped her body up in a long plastic tablecloth they found in kitchen pantry. They shoved her into the trunk of the car and drove way up into the hills, ending up on Mulholland Drive.

There, in the darkness, with all the lights of the valley stretched out below them, they dragged her over to a steep incline thick with weeds and underbrush. Then Lucky put his boot on her back and shoved her off the cliff. They both watched the body roll and tumble down the deep ravine, wrapped up tightly in the tablecloth, the little candlestick token they'd taken out of their Detection game wiped clean of fingerprints and adhered with superglue inside her closed right fist. It was a little flourish they'd agreed upon, a tiny clue for the cops to fret over. But who were they kidding? Nobody would ever find Rosie's body. They had done their first victim, done her well and got away clean. Boy, did that ever feel good.

Chapter 12

Standing just outside the morgue's front door, Claire and Bud looked up at the heavy snow clouds that colored the sky dark enough to match their moods. Hell, the sun must've boarded a plane and zoomed off to the Bahamas like Buckeye wanted to do. Most lake residents would like to climb aboard with him. A brisk breeze flushed Claire's cheeks pink, and she gratefully breathed in a great big lungful. It felt bracing and very cold. It revved her up some, revived her after having to look at a corpse with a hole in its belly and think about the evil things that had been done to such an innocent human being. Hawaii had been wonderful, balmy and breezy and quiet, and every single day she and Black were there she had enjoyed its beauty and serenity. Still, she had missed the lake. Winter had always been fine by her, unless a blizzard raged off the plains and shut the lake down to a ghost town.

After a moment, they climbed back inside Bud's truck and sat silently for a moment while Bud fired the ignition and switched on the heater. Mentally, Claire was going over everything they knew and ticking off even more stuff they didn't. All she kept seeing in her mind's eye was that round puncture wound, a deep hole carved way down into Heather Jax's stomach. Then she visualized again how the killer must have stuffed that stupid dog tag down into her body. Such images were the stuff of nightmares.

"Well, okay, Bud, that distasteful visit took care of lunch for me. Definitely not hungry, not anymore. Maybe never again." She gazed at his profile. "I'm gonna call Harve and see if he can dig up some cases where the killers leave dog tags inside the victim's body. God, I hate even saying that out loud. It sounds so damn sick. What kind of person would do something like that, huh? And why, for God's sake? Give me a break already. I hate this case."

No doubt equally grossed out, Bud put the truck in gear. Claire pulled out her phone. Harve answered on the first ring. She quickly related their dilemma, and he told her he'd get right on it. He also assured her that he and Rico had a ball the night before decorating his tree, and that Rico had made it to school on time, even a few minutes early. Claire smiled and thanked him. He was so crazy about that boy. She clicked off as Bud waited for a snowplow to pass, then took a right and followed in its cleared wake.

"Maybe he'll come up with something. If it's out there, he can find it: no question about it. He always does. So what do you think, Bud? Is this case getting a little too bizarre, or what?"

"Definitely. A Christmas present from hell."

"One thing, though: Let's get hold of that dog tag and game token as soon as Shag's done with them. Maybe it'll turn out to be the clue we need. We can show them to people in jewelry stores, or even Walmart. Especially since we don't have anything else to go on. Nobody does something that horrific without good cause. I mean, this guy bored down through that girl's body, for God's sake. Who would even think of doing something like that?"

"Psychopaths. Nobody else that I can think of. Shag'll get done with the evidence later today, they said. I've been thinking about the game angle. The Detection piece was not there for nothin'. Games are a big deal right now, you know, popular culture, trivia and all that kind of stuff. They have tournaments everywhere, and all kinds of contests, and actually give out prizes and trophies for winning. In fact, there's a tournament going on right here at the lake. I saw it advertised the other day. It's being held at that specialty store in Osage Beach I was telling you about earlier, the one that sells nothin' but games. I've been there a couple of times with Shaggy. I'm telling you again: I know that trophy token came straight out of Detection. And it was meant as a clue for us. He is wanting us to play a game with him, so let's do it."

"Yes, he's challenging us, all right."

"Maybe he's obsessed with competition. Has certain games he likes to play and gets real seriously into them. Shaggy's that way about one called Cranium. We used to get together and play it all the time. He gets really wound up, you know, mad if he doesn't win. But he usually does win."

"Sounds like Shaggy. Okay, so how about we go over there and check out what's up at that tournament? Maybe we'll get lucky and find our killer sitting there holding a little trophy token in his hand." Claire felt her jaw grow hard. "I'm having a lot of trouble with it being inside her stomach. Why not just leave it in her hand or on the body? Bashing her head in wasn't good enough? He had to do that to her, too? Doesn't make a whole lot of sense to me. It's such a specific thing to do. That made it look personal. I've never heard of anything like that, have you, Bud?"

"No. Looks like a personal beef to me. Or maybe just a fetish he's got. He's nuts, Claire. No telling how his mind works. Still think it's a clue, and he's toying with us."

"Could be nothing but a thrill kill. Or some kind of perverted sexual thing. Or, more likely, some kind of witchcraft or devil worship. But they usually just cut out the heart or whatever organ they're into. They don't bore holes down into the body."

"The game is the key, I feel it. Wait until you see those highly obsessed guys playing down at Games Galore. Man, they get eliminated early and you'd think they're headed home to kill themselves. It's way weird to watch."

"Doesn't say much for their real lives, does it now? Our friend Jonesy might know why the killer picked her out and left that thing inside her. Could be his kid was into something dirty, something he didn't know about—or maybe he did. Maybe he encouraged some kind of drug involvement and was part of it himself. He met her last year, so she's been hanging around him for a while. And being around Jonesy Jax is scary. He could have corrupted her with sex and drugs, or both, although I'm tellin' you that he seemed genuine when he said he wanted to keep her safe and off his road tours."

"Safe to Jonesy probably isn't safe to everyone else. I assume he's got some big guard with him at all times, right?"

"Yeah, I met him this morning." Claire thought a moment. "Maybe Jonesy screwed somebody over, which I've heard he's done before, maybe a drug dealer or a dirty music producer or a vengeful female groupie. This could be revenge, the only way they could hit him back outside his fame and money, because this was so completely personal. There's no telling what he's done or said to people when he's high on cocaine or booze. He's a disgusting animal up on stage. That would tie in the 'Love, Dad' thing, maybe. Black says Jonesy's better now, has changed a lot, but that doesn't mean he's not crazy." Claire remembered how Jonesy fell on the floor and curled up. "I really can't stand that guy, but I did sorry for him. His grief was a terrible thing to watch. It really was. And it was real—I know it was."

Bud hung a right on Osage Beach Parkway North and headed for the game shop. "Fans of Jonesy Jax are super dark for the most part. Call themselves Jaxers. Could possibly be one of them, and he's got millions of 'em all over the world. I still can't see this as some random act by a stranger."

"Jaxers?"

"That's what people call them."

"The game theory seems more likely because of that token. It was left there for a reason, and the Detection game deals with murder. What if somebody simply decided they wanted to act out the game for real? That game's got certain places to choose for the murder scene, right? Maybe he played and then reenacted the murder in real life. Just to see if he could pull it off." She looked over at Bud. "I can't remember: does Detection have a lake house on the game board? Or a log cabin?"

"I remember it had businesses and shops and stuff like that as places for the crime scenes, so a library could've been one of them. A police station was definitely one. I do remember that, but I don't remember the others. Makes more sense than anything else we've considered, in a crazy, loony-bin, sadistic way."

"Yeah, well, that's what we've got here: a crazy, sadistic lunatic. Anything about puncturing the stomach in the instruction book? Is it a dark game like Dungeons and Dragons?"

"Nah, it's just a harmless family night kind of game. Clean fun, I guess, if murder can be described that way. Hadn't really thought about it being about homicides before, not our kinds of homicides. I played it with my parents when I was little, and I didn't come out warped."

"Well, it's still a little early to count on that."

Bud shot her a grin. "Shut up, Claire. You should talk."

Claire was glad they could still joke around. "Okay, I need to buy that game while we're in the store. Rico loves board games, and so does Black. Me? I can take them or leave them. Maybe there's something in the instructions that'll give us a good lead. Maybe we can figure out what he might do next. How long's it been since you played Detection?"

"A little while. I get enough murder and mayhem at work. Don't want to solve cases in my free time, too. Besides, I prefer to do other things with Bri when we're together."

"Yeah, I'm sure, but TMI." Claire smiled. The same applied to her and Black.

"This store we're going to?" Bud was telling her. "Let me warn you. This über-fanatical lady runs the place. She's pretty much an expert—aka know-it-all—on any game known to man. She hosts tournaments and stuff down there all the time. Today, I think they might be playin' chess. You know, she just lets anybody who comes in the store challenge anybody else who happens to be there. That makes it a sort of hit-or-miss tournament. Some of these guys are experts, believe it or not. The others just think they are. Sometimes the tournament's advertised, sometimes it's not. Shaggy says most of the time it's either Trivial Pursuit or Monopoly, you know, both of those are easier games to master. She might even be able to tell us if there's a Detection fan base around here and who might be crazy enough to kill somebody using it. Shag won a trivia extravaganza a few years back. Got a big trophy. Ask to see it next time you're over at his place. It'll make his day."

"That's because Shaggy knows everything remotely trivial," Claire said. It was the truth; Shaggy remembered everything. Just like her new PI partner, Will Novak. Novak had crazy-good recall and noticed everything around him, but that was a good trait to have in a partner. He had a lot of good traits. She wished he'd get back home, and they'd pick up an interesting case that did not include a morgue visit. But Black wished Will was here more: he was already tired of her demanding stint in homicide, temporary though it may be.

"I bought my mom Scattergories last Christmas. She really loves to play. Maybe we'll get lucky, Claire. Maybe we'll nab our killer at the tournament, and then I can go pick up Brianna in St. Louis tomorrow afternoon when her plane touches down."

"So she's making it back for Christmas after all. Well, good deal, Bud. I knew she'd find a way. She's so crazy about you. Don't worry about getting her here. Black can send his helicopter to pick her up at Lambert airport. We need to solve this thing before Christmas Eve, though I suspect Jonesy Jax is not going to get to host that Christmas rave after all."

"We need to go see him as soon as he's calm enough to talk to us."

"Let's check that out later this afternoon. Right now, let's go play some games."

It took about fifteen more minutes to reach Games Galore, mainly because the heavy Christmas traffic on the main thoroughfares made for slow going. The streets were clogged with vehicles, the falling snow not helping anything, but the snowplows were busy so traffic was moving, if only at a snail's pace. Despite the weather, the store's cleared parking spaces were full. So was the road out front, where a ton of parked cars lined both sides of the street. The name of the place was heralded above the front door in a flashing yellow neon sign.

The building looked to Claire like an old converted warehouse. Inside, it was one gigantic space with a few offices carved out in the back. There was a checkout register at the front that was manned by a girl who looked like a seventh grader. She had shiny silver braces on her teeth and wore her long brown hair in pigtails. Bud pulled open the door and stood back for Claire—down deep he was a true Georgia gentleman and always exhibited good manners. Women loved that about him. Claire loved that about him, although she was perfectly capable of opening any door she came across all by herself.

First thing that hit them were the delicious aromas emanating from the snack bar, the scents of hamburgers and pizza and popcorn and soft pretzels all blending together in a heavenly come-to-me. It made Claire hungry, until she remembered Shaggy's plastic baggie with all that green, liquefied pineapple papaya pizza inside. Nope, no snacks for Claire today. Big heaters hanging from the ceiling were straining to do their best. They gave off a low rumble reminiscent of distant thunder, but the interior was as warm as late August despite the cavernous space and high rafters. Rows of shelves radiated out toward the back, with every conceivable kind of game displayed from top to bottom. Rolling ladders were provided for items on the upper shelves, which had signs that advised one to help oneself, but if one fell, one paid for the medical treatment. Advance warning to bold rock-climber types. Claire pulled off her hat and gloves, unzipped her jacket, and welcomed the warm air on her face as the door closed slowly behind them with a soft and final pneumatic sigh.

Over to their right, the tournament was in full swing. A dozen card tables had been set up, all of which were manned by two people facing each other with a chess board and time clock between them. Folding chairs had been set up for spectators, and there were plenty of people watching, all enthralled with reverent silence. Looked to Claire as if she and Bud had definitely lucked out. It was indeed a shop full of aficionados who could answer any and all of their game-related questions, and perhaps even reveal to them the name of any raving, abdomen-puncturing maniacs moving about in their midst.

"Bud, you think that little dog tag could've been made here?"

"Who knows? We get a suspect in this place, then all we have to do is find a Detection game without that trophy in it."

"Yeah, right. I want to buy Detection and see how it's played. Why don't you come with me and brownnose that fanatical game lady? You have such a way with women."

"Hey, maybe we can get Shaggy to play with us down at the morgue. Stay in there awhile, where it's nice and warm."

Claire scoffed. "I'm not playing anything inside any morgue. My only desire when I'm in there is to get the hell out. Besides, what do you think Charlie would do if he heard about us goofing off in there?"

"Kill us? Ask questions later?"

"Yeah, pretty much."

They browsed around the aisles a while, and Claire marveled at what an incredibly large inventory the store held. Hundreds of games, and a big used game section, as well. Some of the boxed products on those shelves looked like antiques that had seen better days. Everything on the shelves and tables was stocked in precise alphabetical order, no exceptions. They located the D section easily enough and found both versions of Detection, old and new. Claire decided to buy one of each. Maybe she'd give them to Bud and Shaggy for Christmas after she had examined the boards and read the instruction booklet. Then they could play each other at the morgue to their hearts' content.

Lots of gamers appeared to be Christmas shopping. People moved about the rows and made the big space seem crowded. Claire held her games in one arm and followed Bud back to the office/return counter. A couple of old guys were standing there, two senior citizens, by the looks of it. Late sixties, maybe older. They were returning something they'd purchased that had a missing piece. They were not happy. In fact, their expressions indicated it was the true end of their world. She and Bud stood back and waited while the men enjoyed a spate of lengthy complaints. Claire wasn't waiting patiently for the elderly twosome's tirade to stop, but she didn't make a scene or threaten arrest.

Occasionally, at the front of the store, a spattering of applause would rise up to the rafters and be overcome by the loud heaters, she supposed when somebody got a checkmate, or a check, or something equally empowering. Claire had no idea what any of that meant, actually. She had never played chess well, or any other way, until Black had cajoled her into trying it once, because he was pretty good at it and wanted to show off. Or at least, he said he was pretty good. Claire's opinion? It was the most boring, tedious waste of one's time ever invented, but useful if one wished to fall asleep fast without sleeping pills. They'd sat across from each other for what seemed like six eternities, neither of them able to concentrate, because Black kept giving her these ultra-hot, sultry, I-am-so-gonna-jump-your-bones-after-I-beat-your-pants-off stares out of those crystal blue eyes of his while she contemplated how the hell the game was even played. His romantic moves worked better than his chess moves, as it turned out, and they happily ended up in bed sooner rather than later. Game on—and what a game it had been.

Everybody in Games Galore waxed as serious as sin. Observing and playing and no funny business, they'd damn you as an amateur if you even broke a smile. Claire and Bud didn't fit with the program, because nobody else in the building had seen that tiny little dog tag jammed down into a lovely young girl's body.

Finally, the two old guys finished with their damn petty haggling and complaining. The more outspoken of the duo took time to count every single penny of his return cash refund. Nobody's fool, that guy. Juno, the name of the lady game mistress, according to Bud, and hopefully their oracle of info, stood patiently waiting for the twin crotchety curmudgeons to take the hell off. She was an attractive lady, most likely in her fifties. Stocky, but in well-proportioned womanly curves. She was wearing a black T-shirt with a giant red chess piece on the front. It was a castle, if Claire remembered correctly. No doubt her salute to the tournament going on up front. Claire remembered seeing a sexy scene in an old movie where Faye Dunaway and Steve McQueen sat across from each other. The sexual tension absolutely dripped off them. It was pretty damn hot. Maybe Black had seen that one, too, and was reenacting it that night when they pretended to play chess on Kauai. Fine by her. Otherwise, that stupid game would've eventually forced Claire into sweet unconsciousness.

"Hello there, Ms. Juno. How you doin'?" Bud jumped headlong into the act of charming the curvaceous woman, no time a wastin'. His schmooze had sparked alive and was landing on her like a worker bee on a rosebud. He was amazing in that regard, his handsome face and honeyed words truly impressive, and it seemed to work on anyone with the XX chromosome: young, old, tall, short, whatever. Always had, always would—well, except maybe this time.

"Hello yourself," the lady said, her tone curt, her face stony and unfriendly. Probably still mad at the two old guys.

"Remember me?" Bud tried again, grin wide and affable. "I was in here last year at Christmastime. Bought a game for my mom. Scattergories. You recommended it."

"Yeah, to you and five hundred other people."

Yikes, Claire thought. Bud had better watch his step or he'd set off a land mine. The lady was not taking kindly to him.

"But you gave me a fifty-percent-off coupon. Surely you remember something that generous?"

That caused a tiny, baby little curve at one corner of Juno's heretofore stern mouth. Bud's legendary allure lived to see another day. Juno kept glancing over at Claire, or maybe it was the two games Claire was holding. Claire placed them on the counter, then held up her badge and got the ball rolling at a more suitable speed.

"Ma'am, I'm Detective Claire Morgan. This is Detective Bud Davis. We're from the Canton County Sheriff's Department."

"So I gathered. I can see your badges plain as day. I'm Juno Bradshaw. I own this store. What can I do for you?" Juno had long salt-and-pepper gray hair pulled back in a tight, fat bun at her nape. Not a strand had pulled loose. Looked concreted to her head with hairspray, in fact. She had the skin of a much younger woman, as if she'd learned about sunblock at the age of two or lived at the North Pole with Santa. Nice teeth. Nice smile. Nice manners, now that she was over her miff. Claire wondered if the Roman goddess of games had been called Juno. She stood back and let Bud do his investigatory magic. This guy was gold. She leaned on the counter and watched in awe. Yes, she had missed Bud a lot. She read the back of the game box, pleased to let Bud handle things until he needed her to play tag team.

Chapter 13

After a few minutes spent shooting board-games-are-the-bomb bull, so to speak, Bud was still holding his own. Claire had seen him in action many times during their years working together. They had always been close friends. She knew he took his time sweet-talking his way to the heart of the issue. Finally, he was getting down to the shiny brass tacks.

"We're working a homicide, Ms. Juno. We think it might be related to a certain game that you sell here."

"Indeed?" Ms. Juno perked up big time and appeared mightily intrigued by such a delicious idea. "Detection, I take it, considering your purchases?"

"That's right," Claire told her.

"Well, that's certainly apropos for a police investigation now, wouldn't you say?" Juno smiled for the first time. They both smiled back, the ingratiating detectives. "That is one of our bestselling games during the holidays, even after so many years on the market. Especially with the locals around here. I'm holding a Detection contest next week, as a matter of fact. You two will have to sign up before you leave. You'll need to get two more players in order to reserve a table."

"Could you give us a list of the people who've bought that game from you in the last six months?"

"I'm sorry, but I don't have that information readily available. I'd have to go through all my receipts by hand and write down the names. Sometimes I don't even get their names, not unless it's a credit or debit card purchase. I don't believe in computers, you see, not with all that hacking that's going on nowadays with that Internet nonsense."

"You don't use a computer program for the store? Seriously?" Bud looked genuinely stunned.

"No. Never did like those computers. Not even the little ones you hold on your lap. Old school, that's me. As you can plainly see."

Juno looked from one of them to the other, daring them to chastise her for being computer illiterate. Bud lapsed seamlessly back into charm city. "I don't like them, either, Ms. Juno. Too newfangled a gadget for me."

"Are you mocking me, young man? Because that's exactly what that sounded like."

Claire stifled her urge to laugh. Bud had met his match this time. Ms. Juno knew the ins and outs of snark. Time to jump into the fray. "No, he isn't, ma'am, he's much too polite. But I can tell you that this is a serious matter that we're talking about here. A young woman, who had every right to live her life to a ripe old age, is now lying dead in our morgue. We think the murderer is somehow connected to the game of Detection. We need to know what individuals bought those games from you, especially recently, or if a customer behaved in a suspicious manner while inside your store. A list of the participants in the upcoming Detection tournament would also be helpful."

Juno was clearly not appreciative of Claire's no-nonsense approach to law enforcement. Juno preferred Bud's kid gloves. Then again, most people they met up with did, too, but time was a wastin', and Juno needed to give her cranky attitude a rest. Claire frowned at her, and some of the anger flashing inside the woman's eyes died abruptly. Then, presto! she became as sweet as a pack of Valentine candy hearts. It was certainly an abrupt change of heart. Claire's frown had never held that high a level of threat before, but if it got them the information they wanted, so be it.

"Sure thing, I'd be more than happy to spend hours and hours just sitting by myself and looking through my invoices. No problem, Detectives. Not much around here for me to do except wait on my customers, stock inventory, see to the snack bar, call in orders to my suppliers, and oh, yeah, oversee the big important tournament I've got going on right now. Doing your research for you will give me something fun to do to take up all the hours of free time I don't have on my hands."

Whoa, and fifty times whoa. Sarcasm 101. Or maybe even the super advanced class of snotty and snide. Claire could learn from her, yessirreedefinitely. And to think Claire thought herself adept at applying the necessary put-downs when called upon.

"Ms. Juno, thank you so much for going the extra mile to help us out. We appreciate it, we truly do," Bud sucked up, and then gave her one heck of a blinding thousand-watt high beam smile. Love, incoming and super-charged. Claire was pretty rusty in that charm thing. Never had an ounce of it since birth, in fact. That was one more good reason for going into private work and partnering with Will Novak. He wasn't the least bit charming, either, and didn't give a rip who knew it. However, now, as a detective back at the sheriff's department with an official badge dangling around her neck, Claire had better buff up her 'yes sirs' and 'yes ma'ams.' If not, Charlie and Bud would axe her and find somebody else to fill in for future temporary assistance in homicide cases. Now that Claire was on board, with a brutal murder to solve, she wanted to find this sicko killer about as much as she'd ever wanted anything.

Bud and Ms. Juno continued to chat about some mutual knowledge regarding the ins and outs of Trivial Pursuit Genus as compared to the Anniversary Edition or the 80s Edition. Claire wandered away from their boring discourse and paused in front of a large cork bulletin board at one side of the counter. Lots of snapshots and pictures were tacked up there, most of which looked like shoppers holding up purchases. One section heralded winners of various tournaments, lots of them, in fact—from tiny tykes competing against each other in Candyland to grandpas playing hot games of checkers. Some of them held up little trophies: none that looked like the murder weapon, unfortunately. All were held high, with pride and wide grins, while they hugged or shook hands with an even happier-looking Juno Bradshaw. In fact, Claire espied several photos of people she knew personally, including a photo of Shaggy holding the winning trophy that Bud had mentioned. Another picture had one of the secretaries at the sheriff's office standing proudly with her husband and little preschool daughter holding a trophy for Chutes and Ladders.

Claire just couldn't see the appeal. She'd never had time to play games. Maybe she'd get the fever after she played Detection. Maybe it would change her life for the better. Maybe she'd win a tiny little trophy to tuck in among all Black's big, prestigious awards he displayed in his office. Maybe it would make her as happy as a singing Disney forest creature every minute of every day, bouncing off the walls from the sheer joy of it all. Nah, she was already pretty damn happy at the moment. Didn't need games to ring her bell. The lives she and Black were living couldn't get much more lit without throwing a breaker. They were as happy as the proverbial larks. Things had been so good that Claire was getting nervous, afraid something dark and wicked was this way a-coming. Yup, because that's what usually happened when she deigned to soar like an eagle with a fat trout in its talons. She thrust the bad vibes out of her head. *Don't chase trouble. Things are as good as good can get.* Except for that poor little angel with a big, round hole in her belly, lying on that steel slab in Buckeye's morgue.

Then, miracle of miracles, her intense scrutiny of the photographs paid off as it landed on one that looked suspiciously like the alleged Special Agent Oliver Wood—obnoxious jerk. Yes, it was definitely the guy who had hightailed it out of the Cedar Bend lobby after spending fifteen minutes irritating the hell out of her and Black. She tugged the picture loose from the staple holding it in place and stared intently at the guy's image. It was him, all right. Nobody could fake the intensity of those crazy eyes. Even now, they seemed to be trying to suck the camera into his head. Maybe he was an alien. It seemed more and more possible. He was standing in front of the shelves right behind Claire, the ones that had about fifty silver cups and trophies and blue ribbons displayed on them. So he happened to be a game player, huh? What a huge coincidence. Maybe one of his favorite games included extra points for bludgeoning angels to death and nailing them to bannisters. The Dead Angel Game, first edition, all rights reserved. Maybe Wood was the culprit who poked that token down through her flesh with those long, lean, strong fingers of his.

Claire took the photo back to the counter. Now Bud and Juno were discussing TV shows; the positives and negatives of comparing *Arrow* to the *Flash*. Juno preferred *Arrow*, of course, because Green Arrow was so handsome and that little Felicity that he loved so much was absolutely adorable. Bud went for the Flash because he ran as fast as lightning struck, whatever the heck that meant. Bud was in dire need of Brianna to get back soon, before he became a full-fledged nerd, a king couch potato.

"Excuse me, Ms. Bradshaw, sorry to interrupt. Could you please tell me the name of the man in this photo?"

Bud leaned close to look at it. Juno gazed at Claire, resenting the interruption of their television review. She took the picture. She studied it half a moment and met Claire's gaze again. "I don't believe I know that fella."

"You're in the picture with him, Ms. Bradshaw."

"Yes, I see that, but I'm in most of those pictures over there. Doesn't mean I know him personally or remember anything about him."

"It's dated one week ago. Want to look at it again and tell me the truth this time?"

Juno's regard registered as intense hatred, despite Claire's purchase of the two games that had totaled $47.50, plus tax. "All right. If you must know, I don't know him well. All he told me was that he's on vacation here at the lake. Been here awhile, he said. Didn't say for how long, but he's come back in to watch the tournaments now and again. I took that picture because I thought his eyes were so beautiful."

"Did he buy anything when he was here? A Detection game, maybe?"

"Not that I recall. No, I'd remember that. He didn't buy anything. He asked me if I'd seen two guys in here. He showed me their pictures."

Claire and Bud both stood up straighter. Interesting? You bet your life.

"Who were the other two guys?" Bud sounded eager.

"He didn't say."

Claire took over, rather excited herself. "Did you know them?"

"No, but they did look familiar."

"Have you seen them here today?" Bud asked, glancing toward the front of the store.

"I haven't noticed them. Been busy back here. You know, running the store and yakking with you two."

"Does he come in alone?"

"Yes, I believe so. He seems like a nice young man, but I don't know him from Adam. Not really."

"He hasn't told you his name, you're sure?" Claire prompted her because she was pretty sure Ms. Juno was a great big liar—or a dodge-the-question expert, at the very least.

Hesitation, big time, and a look that said: *Huh uh, no way, I don't want to tell you crap, lady cop.* Then she took a deep breath. "Oh, all right, his name is Oliver. Or that's what he said it was. Never told me his last name. But I don't think he's done a single thing wrong. He's very polite and well mannered. And he knows his games, inside and out."

Oh yeah, and that's the most important thing, Claire thought. She nodded. "We just want to talk to him, that's all. We're not here to run him in or get in his face." That was a lie—two lies in fact, but oh well. "Did he mention what he did for a living?"

"No, but he's quite intelligent. I could tell that, just by speaking with him. Good memory, and that sort of thing I take note of. A keen intellect is always impressive."

"What else do you remember about him?"

"Nothing, really. Last time I saw him, he asked me when the next tournament was, and he wanted a list of the upcoming ones."

Claire glanced at Bud. They both knew. They weren't morons—at least, most of the time they weren't. They were definitely on to something here. "What time did today's tournament start?"

"About an hour ago. It'll last all day and into the evening with this many players showing up. Even on a bad snow day like today. It's quite wonderful, really. I suppose people who want to get out of the house have little else to do."

"What did those other two guys look like?" Claire asked.

"I don't remember. One wore glasses, I think, black ones, maybe. They were pretty young. Well-dressed. They both had on baseball caps. I do remember that, for some reason."

"What team?" Bud asked.

"Don't recall that much. Might've been the St. Louis Cardinals. That's what I see the most in here. Some Kansas City Royals, too."

Claire was pretty sure their Bradshaw well had gone dry. "Okay, thank you so much, Ms. Bradshaw. You've been very helpful. May I keep this photo, please?"

"If you'll bring it back after you're done with it, you may."

"No problem. You'll get it back as soon as we make a copy of it. I'll bring it back in myself. Thank you again, ma'am." Then they turned and headed hastily for the front of the store. "What'd you think, Bud?"

"I think we ought to sit down and watch some chess for a while. Maybe we'll get lucky."

"You're a mind reader, you."

So that's what they did. Some little Cub Scout troop was selling candy bars and homemade lemonade over in the front corner, so Bud bought them lunch. Neither wanted to visit the snack bar, not with a clear-cut vision of pineapple papaya pizza reduced to glutinous green goo dancing in their heads. They perched on a couple of uncomfortable folding chairs in a spot where they could observe the entire audience, which was sitting around silently, watching the chess players sit motionlessly and stare at their boards. Yes, it was a lively, kickass spectacle. Claire kept scanning the tables and all the people standing around them, but didn't see her prey. Hell, she could probably pick him out from the white glow scorching out of his eyes.

Several hours passed, with several more winners who were delighted to have advanced into the semifinals. Everybody who won acted as if they had received the Pulitzer Prize for Literature or an all-expenses paid trip to Hong Kong. To each his own, but come on—they were playing a game, for Pete's sake. While Bud texted Brianna, to keep up with her travel itinerary and post sweet nothings, no doubt, Claire kept her own eagle-eyed gaze out for Crazy Eyes—without a lot of luck. Then, all of a sudden, the clouds parted, like a real-life miracle, and she saw him. He was sitting by himself in the back row on the other side of the competitor tables. Either she had missed him somehow, or he had just turned up.

"Hang it up, Bud, there he is. Let's go get him."

Claire maneuvered around the opposite edge of the crowd toward Oliver Wood, with Bud right behind her. She kept her hand inside her jacket near her Glock. The pseudo FBI agent was watching the game tables intently and didn't see them coming; those eyes must have been turned down to low beam. By the time they reached his chair and plopped down on either side of him, it was too late for him to flee like the felon he probably was.

"Hello there, Special Agent Wood," Claire greeted him. "Oh, but wait, that's right. I forgot. You're not a special agent. You were just feeding me lies. So tell me, who the hell are you, really?"

The so-called Oliver Wood stared at her, attempting his eye trick. He didn't seem surprised to see her. Didn't seem upset about it, either. Claire stared back, not mesmerized this time. Finally, he said, "I'm Oliver Wood. And I do work for the FBI."

Bud laughed. "Lying only goes so far, Wood. We know the truth. Quit playin' us."

"Apparently, you don't know the truth."

"Maybe you should come down to the office so we can have a long and drawn out and extremely tough interrogation. We'll give you a cup of coffee to keep you awake, and a donut, too, if you're good."

Still calm, Wood smiled at Claire. "Are you here to arrest me for something?"

"I didn't say that, now did I?"

"Because you can't. I haven't done anything wrong."

"Except for that little thing about impersonating a Federal agent."

"You've got everything wrong. I can explain."

"Be my guest."

During their less-than-friendly exchange, Wood kept glancing at the game tables. Claire followed his interest and found he was looking at one of the players, a guy who saw her watching and quickly looked back down at the chess board. He was fairly young, had on black-rimmed glasses, and had already made it into the semifinal rounds and was awaiting a new opponent. "That guy in the glasses a friend of yours, Mr. Wood?"

"Who?"

"The guy you were surveilling."

"Look, I don't know what your problem with me is. But if you want to take me downtown and question me, I've got no problem with that. I've got nothing to hide."

"Good, because that's gonna happen right now."

"Fine by me."

"Get up," Claire told him, tired of his cavalier airs. She stood up. This guy.
"Let's go," Bud said.

The three of them got up and walked along the perimeter of the player tables. The guy in the glasses was speaking into his cell phone now, not looking at them, as if he bore no interest whatsoever in what they were doing. Wood didn't look at him, either. Had their silent communication been Claire's imagination? She thought not.

Outside, they walked straight into a large crowd of loitering paparazzi. They started yelling her name and snapping pictures and asking her to stop and give them a good money shot.

"Damn it," she gritted through clenched teeth. She kept a tight grip on Wood's upper arm. "Just push on through them, Bud. How the hell did they find out I was here?"

"Told you that picture of you in that bikini was hot," Oliver Wood said softly to her. He was grinning, still not exactly terrified to be taken down to the sheriff's office.

Claire and Bud got on either side of him and held him tightly between them. They pushed their way through the cameras, heading at a fast walk across the street to Bud's truck. They were moving pretty good, but some of the media types were hot on their heels and trying to block their path. Halfway across the ice-slick road, a car came barreling down the street right at them, motor gunning. Claire whirled around and saw a brief flash of black metal before Oliver Wood grabbed her and shoved her hard out of the way. They fell together against the front fender of a parked car, Oliver on top of her, knocking the breath out of her.

Bud wasn't so lucky. The car swerved toward him, knocked him up in the air, and then down over the top and off the back of the speeding vehicle. He landed upside-down in a deep snowdrift pushed up under a lamppost.

Pulling her weapon, Claire tried to jump up and fire after the speeding car, but she'd landed so hard on her hip that her knees went out from under her when she tried to stand up. She'd slammed the side of her head, too, and could feel warm blood running down into her ear. Her head started pounding, but she was more worried about Bud. He wasn't moving, and Oliver Wood was already up off the ground and bending over Bud. "Call 911," he yelled at her. "I think his leg's broken."

Claire groaned, the pain in her head throbbing like hell, but she got her phone out of her pocket. She called 911 and asked for an ambulance. Then she struggled up onto her feet and braced her palms on the hood of the parked car. It felt as if her hip had been knocked out of socket, but it wasn't, or she wouldn't be standing at all. Photographers were all around her now, and Bud, too, snapping pictures as fast as they could. Nobody offered to help them, just took advantage of the accident, the jerks. When she looked back at Bud, he was moving a little and groaning. The car that had tried to kill them was long gone. So was Oliver Wood.

Play Time

Nobody found poor little Rosie the Hooker's body for a long time. Almost three months passed before a hiker discovered her bones and various tufts of russet-red hair that had not been dragged away by wild animals. But that was okay. The news of the murder hit all the Los Angeles newspapers, and Junior and Lucky bought up all the editions and pored over the articles and photos. Turned out Rosie was a runaway from Ada, Oklahoma. Her real name was Mary Sue Johnston. She was twenty-nine, a wannabe actress, and a UCLA film student. The newspapers said her life's ambition was to join the cast of *Grey's Anatomy*. The papers had printed her senior picture, in which she looked a lot younger and fresh-faced.

No clues found with the body, however, and no mention made of the candlestick token they'd left glued to her palm. Police were probably keeping that information secret in case a confession came in. Junior and Lucky hadn't made a single mistake, and that boded well for the next round of their lethal little game. They hadn't committed murder again, hadn't had the urge all that much. It had been a bloody affair, after all. Instead, they'd spent time in the basement, sitting at the table and remembering the shivery thrill of it all. They burned the bloodstained rug where Rosie had landed and mopped up all the spilled blood on the big white tiles with concentrated bleach water. Then they got serious about their game. For weeks, they sat and figured out the all the complicated rules of Live or Die, using elements from several other board games and eventually ironing out every detail that bothered them. They could not be careless or reckless. One thing for certain: In the future, they would kill their victims elsewhere so they wouldn't have to clean up such a big mess. That nasty task had not been pleasant, and the game room still smelled like blood. Cleaning up a murder scene sucked.

Months after Rosie had been located, Junior and Lucky huddled together one night at the game table. They were both ready—time to choose victim number two. Since they'd made the decision to kill again they'd been beside themselves with excitement. That was the best part about the act of murder, they had found: the intricate planning and burgeoning anticipation and nerves and fear, but, most of all, the ultimate high of taking a life. They talked a lot about watching a person die, watching a life end for good. How the light left their eyes. They liked that. The finality. The power they possessed. So they spread out the new game board they'd designed on the table and let the fun begin.

"Okay, first off: Career or College or Travel." Junior looked up at Lucky. Lucky's eyes absolutely shone with eagerness. He was really into the game now. "You know what, Lucky?"

"What?"

"I think we oughta make this one a contest. Show off our own personal skills and techniques. See who's better at the game of murder. See who can get the least blood spatter, stuff like that. We can make up a point system. That would be fun."

Lucky scoffed. "I'm better at killing, and I always will be. I killed lots of people before you even thought about it, if you'll recall? It's your turn."

"If this is a game, we need to treat it as a game. We'll choose our victims, and then we'll see who does the murder the fastest and the best, and maybe with the most imagination. Ten points for each of those, at least."

"You mean you really want to off two people at the same time?"

"Precisely."

"That'll just end up posing more chances for us to get caught. We don't need to go overboard and start pushing the envelope like this. No, you kill one. Then later, I'll kill one. Maybe later, as we improve with all this, we can go after two at a time. Don't get greedy, dude."

Junior was too jacked up on the idea to heed Lucky's fears. "Bullshit. Think about it: Maybe we could tag along with each other, but only to watch. Maybe one of us could film the other guy's murder. We'd be at the scene together, if that's what you really want to do. But the rule is that the guy with the camera can't help do the killing. That wouldn't be fair. No competition in that."

"We'll throw dice for who gets to go first."

"Awesome, man. Whatever."

"Man, do I love this game! My favorite thing ever. We are such badasses to do this and get away with it."

Junior grinned. He had always wanted to be called a badass. "Don't get so carried away. You've got to stop that or you're gonna make some careless mistake and get yourself caught."

It appeared Lucky didn't like Junior's criticism. He frowned and crossed his arms over his chest like he always did when he was ticked off. He had become so much more cautious than Junior. Who would have thought that? Lucky was the daredevil in the house. He was the one who took all the risks.

"Okay, c'mon, Lucky, let's just get this done. Forget the dice. I'll go first because this was my idea." He spun and smiled. "Okay, I'm gonna go with a professional person this time. Now for the weapon. Hand me the tokens."

Lucky picked up the small cloth pouch and handed it over. Junior pulled open the drawstring and reached inside. He pulled out a piece of coiled rope. "Ah, lookee here: I get to hang my first guy. I've been working on how to tie a hangman's noose. Pretty good at it now."

"Or you could use the rope as a garrote. That'd probably be less trouble for the kill. Hanging takes a lot of planning and finesse."

"Maybe if it's a big guy, I'll use it as a garrote. A girl or a little guy? I want to hang them high, watch their feet kick."

Lucky shook his head. "Why?"

"Because I'm not as strong as you are. I'll have trouble lifting somebody heavy. And you're not allowed to help, just watch. You've got to promise me."

"Okay. Unless you get yourself in a jam. Then all bets are off. But if you're going to do this alone, you need to hit the gym and get some strength in your arms. Some of these guys we pick out are bound to fight back. They'll be fighting for their lives, and they'll tear you up in about ten seconds."

"Shut up, Lucky. I can get the job done, so don't worry about me. Worry about yourself when you pick your own victim. Remember, sometimes you're too careless and reckless and don't plan things out. Just hand me the mags."

Junior decided to choose a college student like Rosie. He chose a magazine out of the latest stack: *Sports Illustrated*. The photo he chose at random was an advertisement depicting a heavyset plumber wearing a ball cap and holding a plunger as he fixed a toilet. The guy looked Hispanic, pretty sturdy and strong, and wore his cap backwards.

"He probably didn't go to college, Junior."

"Yeah, but he probably went to school to learn his trade, and there's nothing wrong with that."

"Piece of cake. He's not all that big. He's not gonna be a problem for you. Unless he's armed. We have to consider that, you know. Lots of people concealed carry now."

"Nah, I'm not worried. I'll just sneak up when he's least expecting it and knock him out. Or I'll get him while he's asleep. Then I can do whatever I want to him."

"My turn to pick my victim," said Lucky.

Lucky picked up a copy of *Fortune* magazine. He closed his eyes and stabbed his finger down on a page. It landed near a picture of a lawyer, a man sitting at the defense table in a courtroom. "Well, this ought to be fun. Lots of slick lawyers right here in L.A."

"Better watch it. An attorney might outthink you."

"Not if he's already unconscious. Let me pick a weapon."

Smiling at Junior, Lucky shook the bag and drew out the toy revolver. "Okay, good deal. I've got a gun I won in a poker game with the serial number already scraped off. And I've got a silencer I bought off a guy when we were down in Houston at that big gun show. Maybe I'll just shoot him with his own weapon, if he's carrying one. Make it look like suicide. That would be something new and different."

Junior leaned back and gazed at him. "Okay, then we're all set. Let's do this thing. Me first. I end the plumber."

"Game on," said Lucky.

"Game on," said Junior.

They both smiled.

Chapter 14

Nicholas Black was sitting in a business meeting, trying his best to shake off one extremely foul mood. He was still angry about the damn photographers camped outside his hotel. Most of them had reserved rooms under assumed names, an unwelcome outcome that he really couldn't prevent, so they were always hanging around, bothering his guests and the staff. He'd blocked off parts of the hotel grounds from their entry, including the bungalows on the point, out of security for his patients housed down there. He had hoped the ice, the plummeting temperatures, the heavy snow, and the holidays would wither up their obsession with Claire and him, and that they would eventually move on to other hapless celebrities victimized by the press. Neither Black and Claire nor Jonesy Jax intended to show themselves outside any more than absolutely necessary, hoping the vultures might lose interest in stalking their every move. Hell, didn't any of them have families or want to be at home for Christmas? Didn't they have lives outside of hounding people to death? He felt another swift onset of annoyance.

After Black had finished his therapy sessions that morning, he'd headed back to his office wing, where he'd been sitting in this endless conference ever since—a meeting that could only be described as long, tedious, and boring as hell. All the physicians in charge of his psychiatric clinics had come to the lake for their annual end-of-the-year patient progress reports. Most had brought their families along for a free vacation on the lake. One by one, they'd been filling him in on the mental stability of each patient under their care, including several well-known celebrities, and then had moved on to discuss the bottom line of financial operations.

Eight psychiatrists sat with him around the long, shiny conference room table, their leather briefcases full of reports and outlines and flow charts and patient follow-ups. He already knew the medical records of most of their patients, because he visited the clinics often and kept track of their progress with personal visits and/or conference calls. It appeared everything was going well, despite Black's four-month honeymoon. Everything appeared to be lucrative and well-run, with nothing for him to worry about. That's all Black really cared to hear. As far as he was concerned, a five-minute presentation was enough. He just wanted to get it done and get out of there. Right now, it was simply corporate minutiae that he could read over in his spare time. He hired the best people for every position he filled, people he could trust and who knew what they were doing, and success was what they gave him. Good news on every front.

Black glanced at the big clock on the far wall. Claire hadn't made it home for lunch today, but she rarely ever did when she worked homicide. She loved solving crimes and putting bad guys in jail, and her mood had ratcheted up enormously since she'd gone off with Bud that first day back on the job. As long as Claire was happy and safe, Black was fine with it. Soon he'd have to curtail the endless drone so he could pick up Rico at school. He could ask Harve to do it in a pinch, or if time was a problem. Then maybe they could have dinner together and finally put up their Christmas trees. Most likely, they'd have to wait for Claire to drag home before they hung the ornaments. Or, if he was really lucky, she might saunter back in early. Probably not now, though, not with a sticky murder case slapped down on her plate—especially one with Jonesy Jax involved.

His phone vibrated softly in his breast pocket, and he pulled it out in a hurry, hoping it was Claire telling him she was on her way home. It was Harve Lester. Black rose to his feet. Joshua Rhodes, the young physician in charge of his New York clinic, stopped his report in mid-sentence. "I'm sorry, Josh, but I've got to take this," he told him. "It shouldn't take but a few minutes."

The other physicians relaxed and murmured among themselves, as Black strode through the door that led into his private office, with its wall of windows overlooking the lake and the helipad out on the point. He punched on quickly. "Yeah, Harve? Everything okay?"

"No, it's not. You got your television on?"

Black frowned. "No, I've been in a meeting. What's going on? You okay? Is Rico okay?"

"We're both okay, but looks like Claire's having a pretty rough day. Turn your set on KY3 out of Springfield."

"Is she hurt?" Black asked quickly.

"I don't know yet. I think she's okay."

Alarmed, Black picked up the remote off his desk. A moment later, the news flashed on. Still holding the phone to his ear, he stared at the screen for a moment. Something was happening out in front of some kind of warehouse. There was an ambulance with its lights revolving, and cop cars parked everywhere. His heart stood still.

"Is Claire down there? What happened, damn it!"

"Keep watching. Sorry, Nick. You're not going to like seeing this. I didn't."

"Oh for God's sake, Harve, just tell me!"

About that time, the on-site video loop started over. And there were Claire and Bud walking out of the store, one on each side of the FBI agent who'd paid Claire a call down in the lobby. They were holding onto his arms and pushing their way through a throng of reporters. The paparazzi were following them and yelling questions, and Claire looked angry and was trying to hurry Oliver Wood across the street to Bud's truck. Then, while Black watched, a black Mustang came roaring out of nowhere right on top of them, speeding and swerving to hit them. After that, the camera started jerking around before righting itself again, and everything happened so quickly that Black couldn't really tell exactly what had gone down. His eyes had been focused on Claire until she'd disappeared off camera.

"Did the car hit her, Harve? Is she hurt?"

"I think she's gonna be all right. Hold on a second. They'll run a second camera angle next. I have a feeling she's gonna be sore, but not hurt too bad."

Then Black watched Claire on screen again, this time down on the ground in front of a parked car, trying to get up, unable to make it. It looked as if she was trying to get to Bud, who was lying on his back in the snow a good distance away. He wasn't moving. A couple of photographers had been mowed down, too. "Oh God, where'd they take her?"

"Canton County Medical Center, they said. They loaded them both in the same ambulance. That's gonna come on in a minute."

Black's phone buzzed again. This time it was Claire, thank God. His heart sped into overdrive. "She's on the other line, Harve. Thanks for letting me know."

Hastily, he clicked off and answered her call. "Claire! Are you all right? Where are you?"

"In our bedroom. Could you please come down here for a minute?"

"Are you hurt?"

"Yeah, kind of."

It took him about ten seconds to get to the penthouse wing. Claire was sitting on the edge of the bed, quite calm, totally unflustered. She smiled at him. She had a white gauze bandage wrapped around her forehead.

"Sorry I had to interrupt your meeting, Black, really, I am, but I need a good doctor who's not gonna talk to the press or take pictures of me all bummed up like this. So that would be you."

Black hurried over to the bed. "I saw you go down on television. What the hell happened?"

"Somebody tried to run us down with a car. Don't know who yet. But I'm sure as hell gonna find out."

"Where's Bud? Is he all right?"

"They admitted him into the hospital. I just came from there. His thigh bone is broken, a compound fracture of the right femur, but they've already set it. He's under sedation now, so I came on home for a while."

"No, you don't. You took a hard fall. How bad is that head wound?"

"Not so bad. Ten stitches in the ER. I banged my temple and ear against the front fender of a parked car, I guess. I'd probably be dead now if Oliver Wood hadn't pushed me out of the way. Bud wasn't so lucky."

"Yeah, let me see your hip. Looked to me like you landed pretty hard."

"It's a bit bruised up, but I'll live." Claire unzipped her jeans and pulled them down so he could look.

Black stared at the huge dark bruise that covered her entire hip and the side of her upper thigh. "Good God, Claire, that looks awful. Did they take x-rays?"

"Yes, of course. I didn't think it was really necessary, but they insisted. Nothing's broken or cracked or anything, just that big, bad bruise. It hurts like the devil when I walk or move much, I can guarantee you that."

"Why didn't you call me when it happened?"

Claire hitched a tiny shrug. "I was okay. No need to interrupt your work. And I didn't want another herd of press following you down to the hospital. I bet they've all already seen the news." She sighed heavily, and then she smiled up at him. "What I really need is a handful of some serious painkillers. That's where you come in, sweetie pie."

"Well, I'm going to examine you first. That fall you took was a hard one. Who took care of you in the ER?"

"Just the emergency room guy. I don't remember his name. He was good enough, I guess. And they gave me a very thorough examination, you can trust me on that." She stopped there and looked away from his searching eyes. He wondered if she was hiding something from him—and why. "I'm fine, Black, really. I was lucky as the devil. If you want to worry, worry on Bud's leg. They said he's going to be laid up for a while."

"You bet he is. Nothing else is wrong with him, I hope."

"No, just the leg. Some of the photographers said the car knocked Bud up into the air, and he came down hard, with his leg twisted up under him. They got that on film, too. I called his mother in Atlanta from the hospital, and she's on her way up here. Brianna's in the air. She's supposed to land tomorrow. You'll send your chopper to St. Louis to pick her up, won't you? I told Bud that you would."

Black couldn't believe Claire was worrying about that stuff. "Of course, I'll send the helicopter. I'm more concerned about you at the moment. You should stay in bed this afternoon. Now lie back and let me take a look at you."

"I don't think I'll be going anywhere for a couple of hours, at least. Not without some mighty potent magic pills filched out of your medical bag."

Black was not amused. "You could've been killed if you'd hit your head any harder. I thought we were done with trips to the emergency room. Guess I was wrong."

Claire gave him a look. "Like I said, Black, I'm fine. Just a little sore here and there, and suffering a giant headache from hell. We owe Wood a thank you for my ability to live and breathe. Too bad he disappeared right after he told me to call 911. Just melted away into the crowd of paparazzi and was gone."

"Forget him. Can you walk at all?"

"Of course. I got here, didn't I? I'm perfectly fine, Black, quit panicking and making a big deal out of this. I'm limping some and sore as heck. That's it."

"How did you get home?"

"I sneaked out of the rear entrance and called for an Uber. I made it upstairs without being seen, thank God. I guess the paparazzi are still down at the hospital, enjoying their feeding frenzy. There were tons of them at the ER entrance when I sneaked out."

"Tell me everything that happened, from the beginning."

"C'mon, Black. I just did."

"Tell me again, and don't leave anything out."

Claire spun the story, impatiently, as she was wont to do when annoyed. Black felt along her arms and legs, probing gently for breaks or sprains or residual pain. He removed the bandage from her head and examined the stitches. He could've done them better, but they would have to suffice. Then he applied a clean bandage, got her the painkillers she needed and a glass of water.

He sat down on the edge of the bed and stared at her. "Well, here we go again, Claire."

"Yeah, that guy tried to kill us, all right," she said, sighing heavily as she relaxed back against the pillows. "Or maybe he was just after one of us, and the other two were collateral damage. Personally, I think his target was Oliver Wood, not Bud and me. What do you think?"

"I think you were damn lucky to come out of this alive."

"Yeah, yeah, blah, blah, blah," she said, as cavalier as ever about her injuries. Then she smiled up at him, apparently trying to disarm him. That ruse usually worked. Not today.

Exasperated for about the millionth time since he'd first laid eyes on Claire Morgan, Black shook his head. He'd be glad when this damn day ended. Hell, it could not get any worse—he hoped. Claire groaned some when he helped her undress and slip into a nightgown, and then she lay back down and settled onto her uninjured side. He applied some salve on the bruise. "That should take away some of the soreness, but trust me, sweetheart, it's going to hurt like hell for a few days. You may not be able to walk tomorrow when the stiffness settles in. If that's the case, you are taking a sick day."

"We'll see about that."

Undoubtedly, Claire could be infuriating. Especially when it came to her work. She wasn't going to listen to him, no matter what he said, not when it came to a murder case. He knew that full well, so he changed the subject. "And you have no idea who was driving that car?"

"They got the car's description. The reporters around me said it was a late-model Mustang. I saw it was black, but it all happened so fast. I'm hoping they got a shot of the license plate. I called in a hit-and-run and officer-down from the scene, and they've got patrol officers down there interviewing the media. A BOLO's out all over the state now, but I hope they locate the car before it leaves the lake area."

"I saw it hit you. It happened quickly on camera, but it was a Mustang, all right. A sports coupe, I think. There are probably hundreds around here, and this guy's going to dump it or hide it, trust me." Black heaved a deep breath. "God, I hate it when you get hurt, Claire."

Claire took his hand and squeezed it. "I know you're worried, but it really is nothing this time. I lucked out. I should've been more aware, anyway. It's just that we were trying to get away from the cameras and take Wood down to the office for questioning." She sighed. "I guess we need to send some flowers to Bud. He's out for the count, I'm afraid. At least, for a couple of weeks. He's going to be so ticked off that somebody actually ran over him."

"A hell of a lot more than a couple of weeks. So tell me: Where does that leave you? You're not planning to work this murder alone, are you?"

"I don't know. Maybe. Probably. The sheriff's big-time shorthanded. That's why I'm out there, remember?"

"Well, you're in awfully good spirits after almost being killed by a hit-and-run driver, I'll give you that. Has your headache let up yet?"

"It's getting a little better."

"You need to stay in bed and try to relax that hip."

"Bud doesn't need to be by himself at the hospital. I've got to go down there in a little while and make sure he's okay."

"He's not alone. He's got the entire hospital staff to take care of him. He'll probably sleep through the night, anyway, if he's just out of surgery and sedated."

"That's what they told me, too. Look, I'm fine, Black, quit staring at me like I'm about to die or something."

"Hate to break this to you one more time, but you're not going anywhere today. Sorry, but those pills I gave you? They were rather strong sedatives."

Claire closed her eyes, the pills beginning to take effect. "I knew I couldn't trust you. You always take advantage now that we're married and I can't storm off."

"Why, oh why, Claire, do things like this keep happening to you?"

Claire's voice was already becoming slurred. "Maybe it's because we're chasing a real psycho who forced a dog tag down into that poor girl's stomach."

"What?"

"You heard me." She told him about the autopsy findings. Black just sat there beside her, listening in disbelief. He would have been incredulous by the killer's cruelty if he hadn't studied his share of sociopaths. Claire had met up with more than her share, too.

"It was probably him who hit you. Again, you were damn lucky you're not hurt worse than you are—or lying dead on the side of the road."

Claire opened her eyes. "Oh, Mr. Sunshine, please stop with the gloom and doom. I already feel bad enough."

"How about putting in an emergency call to Will Novak? He could be back in the States in a matter of hours. You need a helping hand on this case. We are talking about a crazed killer."

"I'm not going to bother Novak with this. He's unavailable, and for good reasons. You know what happened to Jenn in Mexico. He's helping her get through it."

"Then I'm going to put John Booker on this killer. Don't ask me not to. Let's see what he can find out. Maybe I could tag along with you until you get him."

Booker was Black's best friend and his go-to private investigator. He was a good one, too. Claire gazed up at him, her eyelids heavy now. "Great. I'm gonna need all the help I can get. You're too busy to take on anything else, though. Like I said, I don't think I was the target. Oliver Wood is in this thing up to his neck. I find him again, I get a lead on the killer. Mark my words."

"KY3 obtained a good shot of him slipping away from the scene."

"He did check on me and Bud first, though, before he disappeared. I'll give him that. He waited until he saw that I was conscious and trying to stand up."

"Sounds like you're making excuses for him."

"He saved my life. I owe him. You do, too."

"I do. But he's also your prime suspect, and his behavior in the lobby was unprofessional."

"Maybe. But I think he'll contact me again. He's still insisting that he's FBI."

"Laurie Dale told you that she couldn't find any record of him."

"I know, and I believe her."

Black didn't want to argue with her anymore. She was drifting off, and he wanted her to lie still and rest that hip. "All right, just stay off your feet and try to relax and get some sleep. We'll talk about this later. I'm going to put some ice packs on that bruise. Can you wiggle your toes on that leg?"

"Of course. You're getting all worked up for nothing."

"Okay, just do me a favor and stay in bed for a while. I'll be back soon, and we'll see if you can walk. You need anything else before I go?"

She smiled a little. "Are you pissed off? You look pissed off."

"No, I'm not pissed off. But you should have called me from the scene so I could've helped you, and you should've let the hospital admit you for observation."

"Why should I spend my hard-earned money on hospital bills when I've got my own personal doc waiting at home to lecture me on the hazards of my job?"

"Not funny."

"Thank you so much for being so sweet and taking such good care of me."

"I hoped to God this kind of thing would never happen again."

"Yeah, I know, but police work is dangerous."

"Thus, the joys of PI work."

"That's dangerous, too."

Black let that go, along with some of his frustration. "Well, excuse me, but I don't like seeing my wife run down by a speeding vehicle on my flat-screen television."

Claire didn't open her eyes, just murmured her answer: "Yep, that's always a bummer."

Black couldn't help but smile, but he didn't like anything about this. "He could've killed you."

"I've always been hard to kill. You know that. Maiming was a possibility."

"Don't particularly like the idea of you getting maimed, either."

Claire kept her eyes shut. "C'mon, Black, I'm trying to be stoic and brave with these awful wounds, but you keep hounding me. Take pity. Shut up, already."

"I'll tell you one thing: I'm going to make sure everybody in the country knows that the media almost got you killed. If they hadn't been chasing you across that street, none of this would've happened. You would've seen that car coming."

"Somebody must've alerted them that we were in that store. There were lots of customers in there. I guess somebody recognized me and tipped off the vultures."

"Okay, just rest now. I guess the silver lining is that you're home on time and well enough to eat dinner and decorate the Christmas tree tonight. I'll cancel my trip to New York tomorrow."

Claire opened her eyes. "Don't be silly. Rico will be disappointed. It's just a night or two, anyway."

"I don't like going off and leaving you injured and Bud in the hospital."

"I know. But it's okay to go, I promise."

Black's reluctance was not alleviated by her glib reassurances. He bent down, kissed her cheek, and left her lying there alone and drowsy while he walked back down the hall to rejoin his colleagues. Harve would pick up Rico, but school wouldn't be out for hours. Claire was resting, which he could barely believe she had agreed to do. Probably wouldn't have, if not for the sedatives. So that was one good thing—the only good thing at the moment, but he would take advantage of anything that actually went well today.

* * * *

By the time Rico got home that afternoon, Claire was awake, back on her feet, showered, and dressed in loose sweat pants and a soft red Cedar Bend sweatshirt. Black insisted on checking the head bandage again, so she humored him. The wound really wasn't half bad, not as her wounds usually went. She climbed back into bed to rest her hip so Black wouldn't get all bent out of shape. She was damn sore, but not enough to take her off the case. Claire had been thinking things through all afternoon and she didn't kid herself: Black was right. She could have easily been killed. Bud was nearly killed. Those realizations made her reconsider her evaluation of Oliver Wood. He was still a suspect for sure, but why had he endangered himself to save her? She had been taking him in for questioning; she might have locked him up for all he knew. Who was in that car? Whoever it was, she was convinced he wanted to kill Wood, not her and Bud. She'd go ten to one on that bet.

When Rico bounded into her bedroom around four-thirty that afternoon, keen to show her his latest drawing of a Star Wars battle droid, he skidded to a stop at the side of the bed and stared at the bandage on her head. His eyes got big and round and frightened. His voice came out in a scared whisper. "Did that woman on the island come back? Is she coming here to get me again?"

"No, no way, Rico. You know she's dead now. She's never coming back. Come here. Look, I'm just fine. See? All good. Just had an accident today. I almost got hit by a car when I was crossing the street." He still looked wary, so Claire changed the subject. "How was school today?"

"Okay, but how did that happen? You sure it wasn't that lady who liked to hurt me? You sure she really died and can't come back and get me again?"

Rico was reliving the nightmare in which they'd found him last summer. He had gotten so much better since he'd been with them, first in Hawaii and then here at the lake. Occasionally, though, he'd remember the cruel woman and her family who had held him captive. "Listen, Rico, you know good and well that she's dead. All of the people that hurt you are dead. I saw them die. They can't ever hurt you again. You are safe here at Cedar Bend with us. I promise you that. Okay?"

Huge dark eyes searched her face, sober and fearful. "But you got hurt today. Maybe they told somebody to come here and hurt you, and me and Nick, too. Maybe it was some of their men in that car. They'd do that to you, Claire, you know they would."

"No, it wasn't them, because they are dead, all of them are. This happened because I'm a cop, and I ran into some trouble with a bad guy. This kind of thing happens sometimes when you're a police officer. But I am right as rain now. I promise."

"I don't want you to die." Big, fat tears welled up in Rico's eyes, then oozed over and rolled down his cheeks. That was a rare thing for him, tears. Rico was very brave and resourceful, and about double his years in life-threatening experiences.

"I'm not gonna die, Rico. Do I look like I'm gonna die? Come here. Don't cry, please."

Rico got up on the bed and snuggled in along her good side. Claire held him tightly against her. "I'm fine," she whispered into his soft hair. "In fact, I'm feeling pretty great about now. Know why? Because we're gonna decorate all our trees tonight and make s'mores in the fireplace. We've just been waiting for you to get home so we can get started."

That cheered up Rico immensely and put his big smile back into place. "Can we have hot chocolate and marshmallows and maybe some cheeseburgers and French fries, too? From downstairs at the restaurant? They make them the best."

"Sure we can. We can order up anything you want. Just name it."

"Okay, let's go find Nick." He sat up, but then he started looking concerned again. "Does it hurt much where that car hit you?"

"It didn't hit me. I jumped out of the way and slammed my hip up against a parked car. I'm fine, I promise. Black's taking good care of me."

"I don't like it when you get hurt. You're the best mom in the world." Then he grinned, his face lit up with love. Claire smiled back; her heart was touched. She wasn't his mother. He'd seen his mother murdered right in front of his eyes, but he had survived that—and lots of other terrible things. He was just the best little guy in the world, as brave as anybody she'd ever met. A wonderful kid. No wonder Black doted on him. No wonder Claire loved him so much.

Their evening together turned out to be fun for all of them. They ate cheeseburgers and fries and German chocolate cake, and then they put on a Christmas CD and built up the fire until it snapped and crackled like crazy. After that, they decorated the absolutely huge pine tree that Black and Rico had cut down and dragged out of the woods behind her cabin on the cove. Black lifted up Rico and let him put the star on top. Claire sobered while she watched them, glad it wasn't an angel, because she couldn't get the image of Heather Jax up on that bannister out of her head. She tried to shake away the horror of the murder scene, because Rico was making their first Christmas together even more special.

It was almost as if they really were a little family. Almost as if Zachary had lived long enough to understand what Christmas was all about, had been allowed to grow up to the grand old age of ten, like Rico had. Thoughts of her little toddler always haunted her the most during the Christmas holidays, when she obsessed about all the things he'd missed out on in his short little life. But she couldn't think about that now. She was happy. She really was. She couldn't let herself dwell on death, not his or the one she was investigating, not right now, or her own homegrown, deep black depression would settle down over her spirit. So she pushed those dark thoughts away as she had learned to do. Not now. She just couldn't think about her baby right now.

Black glanced at her often and asked silent questions with that incredible intuition of his. She just smiled and gritted her teeth when she moved her hip the wrong way or sat down too long. She wasn't going to ruin their night and the memories they were making. Nope, she could suck it up for Rico and Black. But she was going to find Oliver Wood and make him tell her who had been driving that damn car, and why the driver wanted at least one of them dead.

Play Time

After their first stab at Live or Die went so swimmingly, Junior and Lucky both chomped at the bit to find another suitable victim. The chilling but thrilling demise of Rosie the Hooker was dying down some now, but their black souls begged for more spilled blood. The public outcry about the prostitute's brutal murder had waned considerably as the police floundered about with no leads, no witnesses, and one very cold case. The boys were just so damn good at their murderous game already.

Even so, they were way too smart not to be extremely careful the next time. They were damn tired of hanging around in Los Angeles anyway, bored with shopping on Rodeo Drive and clubbing at the popular celebrity clubs and drinking and smoking pot and sniffing coke. They craved a new and exciting kill in a new and exciting place. They wanted to go somewhere sunny and fun, with lots of tourists and lots of booze and pretty girls in tiny bikinis on warm tropical beaches. A place where nobody knew who they were or where they'd come from. More importantly, a place where nobody knew them well enough to identify them later.

Together, they decided Junior should get to kill his plumber as soon as they switched cities. They spent one evening on Google, searching ritzy beach resorts, avoiding the most famous and trendy ones, figuring there'd be lots of paparazzi hanging around looking for celebrities sunbathing in the nude and actors staggering drunk around their hotels with somebody else's wife. Those photographers also took random crowd shots, which could place them at the scene of the murder. They had to be unbelievably careful, especially if they chose to go to a foreign country. They'd have to use their heads and be even cleverer.

Still, they were both pretty damn savvy at this killing game they'd created. Junior was finding that Lucky was almost as intelligent as he was in many ways, that he also had the street smarts they needed for this kind of job. He wasn't any kind of dummy, that was for certain. He just hadn't cared about school enough to try to earn high grades. Lucky's favorite saying was, "It's better to be smart and lucky than just smart." Junior decided he was probably right about that.

Junior wasn't a lucky guy—never had been. He was talented, though, and brilliant. That meant a lot in life. But he did so love to kill people, loved the bright red color of their blood and the starburst designs flying blood made on hard surfaces. It actually turned him on physically. He was almost embarrassed to admit that. He should've been a police blood expert like Dexter Morgan on that TV show about murdering serial killers. He guessed they'd soon be serial killers, too. The idea appealed to him. It was exotic and intoxicating, so he was willing to let Lucky make a lot of the strategic decisions and calculations. His partner had a head for logistics in a way that Junior didn't. Just as long as Junior got to kill somebody, and watch them bleed out some, he was fine with whatever.

Junior now realized that he was afflicted with a malady called bloodlust, big time and over the top, too. He had become crazy about it, in fact, with an out-of-control need that needed to be fulfilled regularly. That's all there was to it. But that was okay; Lucky said he liked to be around crazy.

In the end, they chose Acapulco, a city way down on the southern Mexican coast. They liked the weather down there, and they liked the beaches and they liked the girls wearing almost nothing as they strode across the sand in front of them. The girls usually went for Lucky first, of course. He was super handsome and cool and buff from all that working out he did. More so than Junior, but that stood to reason. Junior always ended up with Lucky's leftovers, but those women were pretty damn hot, too. What the ladies liked the most about Junior was his endless stream of cash. He bought them expensive dinners and clothes and jewelry, and they tagged along after him two or three at a time, like little baby lambs. There were even two or three in bed, now that he'd slept with so many girls. Yes, sir, Junior and Lucky were living the good life.

After about a week of exploring the city and getting smashed and stoned every night with their small and loyal harem, they began their search for a suitably hefty plumber. There were lots of plumbers in the phone book, so they drove from one address to the next, finally settling on a man who looked about forty years old. He lived in an apartment over his small plumbing shop—alone, which was a good thing. They decided they should break in and surprise him in the middle of the night while he was sleeping. Then they would string him up and watch him choke to death on a hangman's noose. It had been a long time since their last kill, and they were antsy from sheer lack of good fun. Killing was their obsession now. It was an addiction that they loved more than all their other vices put together. It was simply sublime to exert power over life and death. Over another human being. Their choice whether he would live or die. They were like gods of the underworld, rising up to wreak havoc on the unsuspecting innocent. Beautiful and rich gods of death.

One night when they were following the plumber, he walked into a smoky saloon that the locals frequented and then came out three hours later, stinking drunk. Junior laughed out loud at his good fortune. Lucky scowled and said it wasn't a fair game, not unless his victim got to be drunk, too. Junior waxed magnanimous and told Lucky that okay, his next victim could be drunk, too. After all, fair was fair.

So they followed the stumbling, inebriated man home and watched him stagger around the side of his building to the alley alongside his shop and attempt to climb the steep steps that led up to his apartment. He fell twice along the way, he was so drunk. Then he went inside but left his door standing wide open. Man alive, Junior was getting off damn easy this time.

"You ready?" Junior said, glancing over at Lucky.

"This is not fair. You've got it easy tonight."

"Quit bellyaching. I already said your victim can be drunk, too. You're such a big crybaby sometimes."

Hell yes, Junior had gotten lucky. To be safe, they waited half an hour before they went in, wanting the plumber to be in a complete stupor. Or passed out—that would be even better. The light upstairs never went off, and the alley below remained shadowy and deserted. The plumber lived on a side street, with only a few businesses and no residences, so all remained calm and quiet. Nobody stirred. Just like the night before Christmas. They'd have to prevent the man from screaming, but they could do that with a rag stuffed into his mouth. After all, there were two of them. The last thing they wanted was to get thrown into some filthy, nasty Mexican prison for the rest of their lives. But the coast looked clear. They got out of the car they'd rented with fake driver's licenses, met at the front, and walked across the intersection and down through the alley. Pausing at the bottom of the steps, they listened for sounds of life above them. Nothing. They slowly inched up the steps together.

It turned out to be as easy as pie. The plumber had passed out all right, sprawled out on the floor right inside the front door. Triumphant, Junior and Lucky looked at each other. The time had come. All systems on go. Junior shut the door. They stood there a moment longer, listening to the plumber's low snores. Then Lucky walked through the small, messy apartment and found no one was there to get in their way. Wouldn't have mattered—they would've just killed him, too.

"Nobody home. Game on, my friend."

Waves of excitement shook through Junior. For a few seconds, he didn't move. This was his kill. His first solo flight. Finally, he was going to show Lucky just how badass he could be. Inhaling a bracing breath, he jerked off his backpack and pulled out the coil of heavy rope. He tested the tight knots of the noose, although he'd done it a dozen times prior.

The apartment had rafters, as if hell had provided for him. He tossed the end of the rope over the highest point, and then he set the noose around the unconscious man's neck. Then he hesitated. He actually had a fit of conscience. What had this man done to him and Lucky? Nothing. They didn't even know him, or anything about him. He swallowed down the hard lump at the back of his throat.

"Well, what? You losin' your nerve, Junior? I figured you would. Chicken, huh?"

Lucky made the sound of a chicken clucking.

That did it for Junior. He jerked the rope as hard as he could, but wasn't strong enough to get the guy all the way up into the air. Lucky grabbed on, too, and together they hoisted their victim up high. The plumber didn't even fight—he was just too drunk. They secured the rope around the bathroom door and knotted it tightly. Then the man just hung there, limp and loose-limbed, breath slowly cut off until his heart stopped. Junior watched for a moment, but found he didn't want to look at his murderous handiwork. The truth was he was having a twinge of guilt—he didn't take to coldblooded killing quite like Lucky did, not when it got right down to it. He had hated his mom, of course; she had deserved to die. And the hooker, that had just seemed like some kind of weird dream. But this man, he had just been minding his own business, living his life as best he could, fixing toilets and clogged sinks. He hadn't done anything to anybody.

Lucky outstretched his hand, and Junior took hold of it. They shook, right beside the plumber's swinging body. "So how do you feel, Junior? Feels damn good, don't it?"

"Oh, yeah, just like I thought I would. This is awesome." But that was a lie. As he followed Lucky down the steps and back to the car, he wondered if he might like it better next time. Maybe he only liked it when he got to see blood all over the place. Yeah, that must be the problem this time.

Chapter 15

By the time Black and Rico had finished packing for their quick jaunt to New York City, Claire was halfway regretting her decision to work homicide through the holidays. Yes, she wanted to go with them, but she'd made a commitment, and she was going to keep it. Charlie was already shorthanded at the station and now Bud was out, too. Besides, she was mad now. Whoever had run down Bud was going down, too. Count on it.

"Sure you won't change your mind?" Black said, pulling her close for a goodbye hug.

"No can do. Sorry, wish I could. You know why."

"And you feel all right? Still having pain?"

"Only when I move a certain way."

"Won't be as much fun without you bossing us around."

"True."

Black laughed and bent down to kiss her. Claire was all for meeting that sort of thing head on, and as often as possible. Black was one hell of a kisser. Nope, the marriage had not put out the fire crackling between them, not even a little bit. In fact, it had fanned the flames.

"Ew, gross! Stop, you guys are always getting so mushy."

That was Rico, making his disgusted face. He had his Star Wars backpack in one hand and his iPod and ear buds in the other. Claire and Black broke apart and laughed at his freaked-out expression.

"Okay, you two," Claire said. "Better not get in trouble up in New York without me there to keep you in line."

"Black's taking me with him to buy you a big present. It's a good one, too. You're gonna love it."

"Really? Do tell." Claire looked at Black. "The big one? So, Rico, what is it?"

"I'm not telling you because I promised Nick. But we can only get it in New York City."

"That's boils down to pretty much anything and everything."

"All right, I guess we better get going before the snow starts up again," Black said. "The chopper's out there waiting to take us to the airstrip."

Claire kissed them both again, and then walked with them down the hall to Black's office. While his private elevator took them down to ground level, she stood at his office windows and watched them walk out of the building and toward the helipad on the point. Halfway, Black turned around and waved at her. Her heart reacted to the sight of them together, walking and talking. Like a father and his son. It really seemed as if they were a real family now, a happy one. She just hoped nothing happened to mess that up. In her life, something usually came along and threw a wrench in her happy times.

After the helicopter rose slowly and banked out over the lake, she turned around and headed back to the penthouse. Her day was already busy. First, she wanted to go to the hospital and make sure Bud was still doing all right. After that, she had to get to the office and do some paperwork on the case. The hit-and-run attack was being treated as the attempted murder of two police officers. Charlie was incensed at what had happened and said he was calling in help on the case. Before she got embroiled in the written reports, however, she needed to stop by and see Harve Lester.

Right after she graduated from the LAPD police academy, Harve Lester had been her partner, her first mentor, and probably the best friend she'd ever had in law enforcement. He had always been there for her, no matter what. She loved him like a father. He'd given her a cabin on his private cove, the same one that Black was rebuilding, and at a time when she'd been down on her luck and had nowhere else to go. Harve had been her partner the night he'd been cut down in the line of duty and lost the use of his legs. Even the fact that he was confined to a wheelchair had never taken away his spirit for living. He had accepted his fate, as bad as it was, and slowly built up an Internet research and headhunter firm that he operated out of his home. Lately, however, he had been much more interested in playing nanny to Rico than working at his computers. They were already best buddies. Harve adored Rico, almost as much as Black did. And that was saying a lot.

Claire made it out to Harve's place around ten o'clock. He saw her coming from the glassed-in porch he used as an office and was opening the door by the time she reached it. He had a big, welcoming grin on his face, and the most scrumptious smell of goodies hit her the moment she crossed his threshold. Sugar cookies, had to be, and did they ever smell great.

Claire blamed herself for Harve's disability, because her ex-husband had gone crazy and opened fire on them both. Her ex had died that night, and so had poor little Zack. She quickly blocked out those thoughts. Harve was happy to see her so she had to be, too. She needed to concentrate on that. Right now, both their cups runneth over with good things.

The first words that came out of Harve's mouth were his concern for Bud. "How's he doing today, Claire? I drove over to the hospital last night but he was still sedated. The doctor told me the surgery was a success, but that he'd be laid up a while. Have you seen him?"

"He's conscious now, not in too much pain. Still pretty woozy from all the drugs. He wants to go home, and he's worrying about Brianna getting here because of the weather. Black's going to send his helicopter over there to pick her up. He and Rico took the jet to New York early this morning."

Harve nodded. "Good. That boy's got it bad for that girl. She'll get here and start babying him, and he'll like that well enough. You can quote me on that."

"Do I ever know it. He's so nuts about her." They shared a smile, both envisioning Bud's face with the beauteous and leggy Brianna hovering over him night and day. He'd be in hog heaven, all right.

"What about the hit-and-run driver, Claire? You ID him yet? Any sign of him?"

"Assuming it's a him. No, but we've got a BOLO out statewide, and law enforcement personnel at the airports and train stations watching for the Mustang. We found out that it's not a rental, so he's probably hiding it in a garage somewhere. He might have tried to get out of state, but if he goes that route he'll be picked up by the Missouri Highway Patrol. Same thing with Oliver Wood. Can't be too upset with him, though, since he saved my life. Shoved me clear of that car, or I would've been in that hospital alongside Bud. That takes the edge off him fleeing the scene, but I'm going to find him, trust me. He knows more about this case than he's letting on."

"I saw him shove you out of the way on TV. He saved your bacon, all right."

"Yeah, Black and I watched that again. And I have a giant purple bruise to prove it."

"Looks like you're still up on your feet and working, despite that limp. That's an encouraging sign. Sometimes it doesn't happen this fast."

"I'm pretty sore, and I've got a fierce headache that comes and goes. But nothing serious. Hey, how about giving me one of those cookies that smell so good. Can't stay long, though. Charlie wants me down at the office to fill him in. Apparently, he's back at work, flu be damned."

"Well, first you gotta see the tree that Rico helped me decorate. Actually, he did most of it."

Smiling at his indulgent doting, Claire trailed him into the living room. Rico had a tendency to cheer people up. He was just a little piece of sunshine, that's all there was to it. And Harve was right about the tree. "That looks fantastic, Harve. I haven't seen strings of popcorn and cranberries since I was a kid."

"Rico wanted to string that stuff. Said his grandparents out in California always did that when he was a little fella and let him help." He looked at her. "Guess you haven't found them yet, huh?"

"No luck so far. They don't appear to be in California anymore. At least, not at their prior address. Black's trying everything in the book to locate them. He's got John Booker on the case, too, and he's trying to run them down. Nothing so far. Looks like they just pulled up stakes, never to be heard from again. Have you found anything on them?"

"No. You're right, it's as if they never existed. It's really peculiar. Rico insists they do, of course. He's not saying much lately. He's a pretty happy kid now, here with you guys."

"Did he say that?"

"No, he didn't have to. He changes the subject when I mention his grandparents. But he's worried about them, I can tell. I told him that we'd find them." Harve's serious expression changed to a smile. "How about some hot chocolate with those sugar cookies? Got time for that?"

"You bet. I skipped breakfast."

Harve motored his wheelchair into the kitchen and then showed up a few minutes later with a tray of cookies and two mugs of steaming cocoa. He sat the tray down on the table and Claire grabbed a cookie as big as a saucer.

Harve handed her a mug. "That's hot, so watch it. What about the case? Anything helpful turn up yet?"

"We were making some progress until that car tried to run us down. We had Oliver Wood with us and were headed in for interrogation. He could very well be the killer—I'm just not sure what to think about him yet."

"I've been researching murders associated with games, like you asked, and trying to pinpoint anything remotely connected to game tokens left behind at murder scenes."

"Any luck?"

"Actually, I have uncovered a couple of interesting things."

"Great, we need the help. Tell me."

"I can't say whether they'll apply to your case. They seem a bit far flung to be connected. One is a murder that happened down in Mexico. Some guy was hung by a rope in his home. They found a small metal piece stuck up into the roof of his mouth. It was one of those coiled rope weapons out of a Detection game."

Claire shot him an interested look. "Sounds like it might be the same guy. Maybe he leaves the tokens in different parts of his victims' bodies. When did that murder happen?"

"About eight or nine years ago. And there were a few more similar murders. One happened out in Aspen. Police records show that they also found a game piece. The knife this time. Cause of death was a slashed throat. Victim was cut up pretty bad, too. Game piece was in her mouth, as well. A lawyer in Santa Clarita, California, was murdered with a Beretta, and the game token of a pistol was forced down his throat."

"Man, that's brutal, but not as brutal as what he did with our victim. This guy has to be a serial. I've thought that since we found the girl's body posed up on that balcony bannister." Claire cringed inside as she thought about it. Here it was, Christmastime. Having a brutal serial killer running around the lake was not going to be conducive to peace and goodwill and belting out Christmas carols. They already had one dead angel on their hands.

"All three of these cases I dug up? Police said the bodies looked posed. Some more than others."

"It keeps getting worse, I guess."

"You and Bud turn up anything down at that game store?"

"Still looking for something that'll help us. Mainly just the Jonesy Jax connection so far, like I was telling you on the phone last night. The victim is his long-lost daughter, and that can't just be some strange coincidence, not in my book. With the murder going down inside his house? Huh uh. But it's Oliver Wood who's bugging me, big time. He sought me out. And I can't figure out for the life of me why he'd come to Cedar Bend and put on that weird show for Black and me the way he did. It's strange. He's strange. The whole damn case is strange."

"What's Jonesy Jax say about it?"

"Bud and I hadn't interviewed him yet. We were planning to head back to Cedar Bend to talk to him after we finished interrogating Wood, but the car got us first. Guess I'll go interview him by myself after Charlie gets done with me. See if he wants me to go it alone or assigns me a new partner. I don't see how there's anybody left at the office to help me. Everybody's out sick."

"I'll keep searching."

"Sounds good to me. We need to get the killer off the streets."

"I'll keep looking for relevant cases. I'm like you, though: I think it's safe to say this perp is a serial murderer who's been doing this for a long time. He's made it into some kind of game that gives him a thrill. Or, he could be throwing in those game tokens as misdirection."

"Yeah, I thought of that. If he's smart he'd do that, but this guy seems to get off on leaving a real dramatic production behind. Like he's some kind of movie director or something—which also fits with Jax. Talk about a publicity hog." Claire sighed and took a sip of the chocolate. "Okay, I guess I better get going. I can't be late or Charlie'll hit the roof. He's already pissed off that he got sick. He thinks he's above illness."

Harve laughed. "I know the feeling. I was down with the flu last year. It ain't exactly fun."

Thirty minutes after bidding Harve adieu, Claire pulled her new dark blue Range Rover into Bud's parking space in the lot behind the sheriff's office. She turned off the ignition, climbed out, and headed with a pronounced limp for Charlie's office. When she got there, she nixed the limp and took on the pain, for fear he'd take her off the case and put her on sick leave.

After one look at the sheriff, she was glad Black had talked her into getting a flu shot right after they'd returned from Kauai. Charlie looked awful. In fact, he looked like death warmed over. He should not have come in. He should not have gotten out of bed. Last time he called Bud, he'd sounded horrible and hacked a rumbling cough all through their conversation. He should've let her run the case and keep in touch by telephone. But nobody on staff ever argued with Charlie about anything— not if they were smart. She sure wasn't going to jump his case. He didn't look as if he was in a stellar mood.

Charlie Ramsay's bark was always worse than his bite, but he had been known to take a chunk out of somebody's hide a time or two. Especially if they'd done something stupid or reckless. Claire had been on the receiving end herself and had not enjoyed the reaming out. The sheriff was a stocky man, usually flushed in the face, with his trusty black pipe stuck in one corner of his mouth. He wasn't always in a good mood. He usually wasn't, in fact. He wasn't now, either. His door stood wide open. Madge, his tiny, efficient, birdlike secretary, had taken the day off, also sick with the flu. It was like an infirmary around the building. Claire hoped to hell her shot kept working. Charlie motioned her inside with a sharp jerk of his hand. He did not look happy, but he rarely did, so she was not alarmed. Yet.

Once inside, the alarm hit real quick—at warp speed, in fact. There was a second man sitting in front of Charlie's desk. He had a big grin on his face that had no legit cause to be there, not that Claire could ascertain. She had never seen the guy before. Dressed in an expensive black suit with a black-and-white-striped tie, he appeared composed and fully at ease. Happy, considering his no-good-reason smile. He looked tall, with long legs that were crossed and short blond hair gelled up by some fine barber and what looked like a lot of muscles underneath his sharp clothes. He was pretty good-looking, and seemed to know and like that about himself. He kept up with the good cheer, his dark eyes lingering way too long on her face.

Claire broke eye contact. She was pretty sure she was going to despise him. More problematic, she was afraid to consider what he was there for. A bad feeling seeped into her mind. Charlie was quick to make the introduction. "Okay, Claire, thank you for coming in. Please sit down. This is Special Agent Bob Brady. Brady, this is Detective Claire Morgan." He paused. "Should I put Black on the end of that? Or are you being modern with that hyphenated thing?"

Claire looked at Charlie. "I've been using my maiden name professionally, sir." He already knew that, she was pretty sure. More of interest to her was why there was an FBI agent sitting there and what it had to do with her. And what it had to do with Oliver Wood. She was pretty damn sure he was there to horn in on her case. She did not want that to happen. No way, and never ever in one million years.

"Special Agent Brady is here to help us out. I suspect you can use him, what with Bud in the hospital and the fact that this case appears to be going nowhere fast."

Claire just stared back at him with earnest and pleading eyes. She did not want some egotistical Fed trying to take over her case.

"He's been working other cases that seem to be associated with this one. He would like to join your investigation and help you solve this mess, and I told him that would be very helpful since we're short-handed." He stopped breathlessly and then succumbed to a horrible fit of hacking that sounded downright painful to what was left of his lungs.

Claire turned to the new self-satisfied guy. "You're the second FBI agent who wants to be involved with this case. You have a partner here at the lake that you're working with?"

"No, I'm assigned down here solo. Nobody else came with me."

"I thought you Feds always traveled around in twosomes."

His smile widened. "Not always. Not today. Not this case. We have flu in Kansas City, too."

Claire frowned. "Aren't you interested in the other guy's name? You know, in case he's an impersonator?"

"I have to say that's a rare occurrence in my experience. But okay. What's his name?"

"He said he was Special Agent Oliver Wood, but I'm not sure I believe that. He's showing up at a lot of places where I happen to be, including yesterday when my partner was run down."

The man looked interested, but his reply didn't verify it. "Right. The sheriff told me about what happened to your partner. I'm sorry to hear it. Glad neither of you were killed."

"Yeah, me too." Then he smiled again. Claire was not quite sure if he was mocking her or not. She had a feeling he was. "Have you ever heard that name before?"

"Oliver Wood? Yes, I know who he is, and I'll be happy to fill you in on him when we discuss the case. He's not from our office, I can assure you of that."

"How about filling me in now?"

"Better to wait until we have time to discuss him in detail."

Apparently, Claire was going to have to be patient. "And you hail from K.C.?"

"Yes, I do. As far as I know, he's not affiliated with the FBI at all."

"My FBI contact said he's been lying to me about being an agent."

"I agree. That's a federal offense. Maybe we can team up and go after him together and find out what he's up to. We don't like people impersonating our agents."

"I should think not." Claire did not want to work with this guy, or any other FBI agent. Somebody like this Brady guy would be pompous and annoying. Heck, he already was. Self-confidence and bureau superiority oozed out his pores. She wished Charlie could see that. But at the moment, he was noticing her lengthy hesitation and frowning about it. Then he had another coughing spasm. Thank God, he coughed into his shoulder.

She decided to make a valiant effort to send the unwanted FBI interloper back along his way. "Well, I know your office is probably really busy and shorthanded, too. I think I can handle this case just fine on my own until Bud gets out of the hospital. But I'd like permission to call you if I should need your assistance. Would that be okay with you?" She smiled to show that it wasn't personal.

Bob Brady's mouth curved up into a slow smile. "I've heard all about you, Detective. You are well-known in our office. However, we were under the impression that you went into private work not so long ago."

Claire didn't trust him. She wasn't sure why yet, other than the fact that she never trusted anybody she hadn't known for more than five years—

especially Feds that showed up out of nowhere and uninvited. "How did you happen to get wind of our case, by the way? Just curious about that knowledge, you understand."

"We follow the news statewide, like you no doubt do, and we try to keep up and coordinate with all state law enforcement agencies. I was tagged to be informed if anything dealing with board games or game tokens came across the wire."

Claire perked up at that, and Charlie joined the conversation. "Special Agent Brady has been working down in Mexico. He's been down there under deep cover for over a year after he infiltrated the Ruiz cartel. While he was there, he stumbled onto a murder that sounds a hell of a lot like our case. He's willing to share information and work alongside you to help you solve this thing. I figured that would appeal to you." Right after he wheezed that out, he started in with some super-strength barking that ended up with breathless gagging noises. He was as sick as a dog, for God's sake. He needed to go home and stay there for three months. Besides, he was spewing germs all over the place. With Claire's luck, she'd end up on oxygen in the bed next to Bud's.

Claire glanced back at Brady. She knew all about the Ruiz cartel from something Will Novak had been working on a few months ago. Not a plum assignment Brady had been given, not if he infiltrated that cartel. Must have had an American either killed or kidnapped by them for him to get involved. That organization was made up of a bevy of stone-cold killers and drug smugglers. Maybe Brady could be of some help, if she listened to him. Still, something about him just seemed off to Claire, just as it had seemed off with Oliver Wood. Something similar about their attitudes. Something that made her reluctant to spend time alone with Brady, and even less keen about sharing her information with him. What little she had. She wasn't going to trust him or work with him, if she could find a way to finagle her way out of it.

Claire turned back to Charlie. "Sheriff, if you don't mind, I really do prefer to work alone right now. It's not that I don't appreciate the special agent's help, but I'm perfectly capable of solving this case without the Feds involved."

Charlie sneezed, then jerked a tissue out of the box on his desk. He wiped his nose thoroughly while they watched and waited, totally grossed out. "I do mind, so get used to the idea. If the FBI can help us get this guy and get him quickly, then I'm all in. Take the help and be gracious about it, damn it."

"Yes, sir." Claire couldn't argue with him any more than she already had, but she sure had a lot she wished she could say. She turned back to Brady. She tried to be gracious, but didn't pull it off all that well. "Tell me, Special Agent Brady, if you are really in that deep undercover with Ruiz, how did you manage to make it back to the States and find time to invite yourself into my case?"

"Ruiz trusts me. I told him my mother was ill and I had to come see about her. I told him I could take care of some of his business while I'm up here. Supposed to be in Kansas City, but I've been looking for this game token killer for a long time now. I want to know what you know."

Of course you do, thought Claire. That's what she was afraid of. Something was mighty off with this fellow, she could feel it in her bones. It was her highly suspicious nature springing up in her defense.

"I've got a whole briefcase here full of my investigatory notes. My SAC's okay with me sharing it with you guys at Canton County. They're just not sanctioning this case at this point. I have some vacation time saved up, and I'm taking it."

Ah ha, he had not been assigned anything. He was doing this on his own. Claire gave Charlie another significant look. She hoped he recognized it as such. Everything Brady had just let out of the bag sounded highly irregular and like a pack of damn lies. "Is that the same story you got from Quantico, Sheriff? You did check this guy's credentials, right?"

Charlie heaved a deep sigh, bone tired of her already. "Yes, of course I did, Detective. Don't look a gift horse in the mouth. Now get back to work and fill him in. I've got to go home. I feel like crap."

Brady just smiled at her. So pleasant and ingratiating, he was.

"Yes, sir," she said.

Charlie's eyes were watering and his nose was as red as Santa's. He appeared ready to pass out. "Keep me posted, Claire, both on this case and Bud's condition. I'll be at home. Good luck, Special Agent Brady. Thank you in advance for your help. We do appreciate it, despite the detective's surly attitude."

Well, that was unnecessary, Claire thought. Or maybe it wasn't. She had never been one to hide her true feelings.

Play Time

By the time Junior and Lucky were in their early thirties, they had already killed a boatload of innocent people. At times when they were overcome with unrelenting bloodlust and boredom, they would play their game once a week for a month or more. They were so adept at their game by then that they felt impervious to danger, much less the possibility of getting caught by law enforcement. Except there was one big problem plaguing them both: There was this guy who seemed to be on to them. He had FBI credentials and even showed up at Junior's Beverly Hills mansion once, asking a bunch of questions about the day his mother died. Worse, he asked Junior some specific questions about Lucky being their pool boy at the time of his mother's drowning.

Junior was a good liar, though, and slathered on the falsehoods as fast and thick as icing on a birthday cake. He related how Lucky had left his job a couple of months after his mother had died. As usual, Junior did a great job with all his lies and subterfuge, but somehow he felt as if the agent suspected him but didn't have enough proof to nail him. On the other hand, there was no way the investigator could know squat. Lucky said to ignore him, and the guy never showed up on their radar again, so Junior began to breathe easier. Still, both of them tripled their guard and tightened their security, just to be cautious. The FBI was not something to mess around with.

In other years, both young men would wait for longer periods, busy with other things or special girlfriends or studying crime and attending forensic seminars. They became very good at their art of killing, and Junior gradually lost his aversion to ending the life of someone innocent. In his brilliant but sociopathic mind, victims became just a means to a satisfying end. He rarely had residual remnants of remorse.

They didn't always resort to Live or Die to choose victims anymore. Didn't really need it.

Mostly, the manner in which they planned the murders simply depended on their moods. Sometimes they didn't have time or want to exert the effort expended to play games with their intended victim. Sometimes they were in a hurry and just ran down somebody walking alone on the street with the old and nondescript killing van that they'd bought for that specific purpose. He and Lucky had designated it The Murder Machine, and used it with great gusto. Lucky had always liked that MO the most, and from his early teenage years. He considered it a smooth, hands-clean approach to murder one. Junior had to agree. "Run 'em down and drive like hell" was one of Lucky's mottos, and it certainly got the job done, as clean as a whistle, too. Lucky liked to see the horrified expressions on the victims' faces when they realized he wasn't going to stop, and he liked the big bump and lurch as his tires ran over the bodies. At other times, they craved action that was up close and personal so they could enjoy the terror of somebody's last moment alive and listen for his very last breath.

When they weren't flying off to murder in beautiful resorts around the world, in Monte Carlo or Miami or Rio de Janeiro or Bali, which was their penchant, they sometimes sickened of each other's company and just wanted to get away and pursue their own interests. With Lucky that usually meant finding a good-looking woman and flying off to a tropical clime and getting it on. Sometimes his trysts lasted only a week; sometimes less than that. Sometimes a whole month or more. When he tired of the girl, or she didn't care for his sadistic sexual proclivities, he just killed her off and disposed of her body. He was good at such things, so nothing ever went wrong. He was indeed the better killer by far if he was in a contest with Junior, no doubt at all about that, and he loved to regale Junior with the details and photos of his lovely corpses.

Although still highly competitive, Junior didn't mind Lucky holding that particular crown. He was now pretty damn good at ending people's lives, too, but he didn't get the same kind of prurient pleasure, unless, of course, he held a personal grudge against them. He liked those victims the best, the ones that had pissed him off somehow, so Junior sometimes just chose people he didn't take to for some reason: for their political views, perhaps, or their unpleasant looks, or their very stupid mistake of being rude to him at a checkout counter. The last one he offed on his own was a sullen clerk at a McDonald's who left out his order of French fries. He usually performed those kinds of personal vendettas in The Murder Machine.

There were other times, months on end, even years, when they didn't play Live or Die. Instead, they honed its rules further, until the game of death met their criteria for absolute perfection. They employed the knowledge learned from auditing university courses to ensure they did not leave clues behind for the usually clueless detectives that investigated their murder sprees. They took courses together, under assumed names with forged driver's licenses that Junior had become quite good at counterfeiting using his superior computer skills. They learned about blood spatter and DNA testing and fingerprinting and ballistics.

Other times, they were successful at attaining jobs as assistants, associates, and apprentices in forensics departments of colleges and police departments. Junior once even got on staff temporarily at an FBI office. He was especially good at putting on the mask of a legitimate student eager to learn about forensic science. It was good for them, and the knowledge they acquired became invaluable to their fun and games.

Now the time had rolled around for them to kill again. Since it had been a while, two whole months, they were both excited about choosing the perfect victim. Lucky had just come back from his jaunt to the Great Barrier Reef in Australia. He'd had a fabulous time there with some Aussie girl that he'd liked a lot, and she'd been accommodating enough that he decided to leave her alive and well when he returned to the States. She had been one of the lucky ones. He really hadn't left all that many girls alive after they'd slept with him. All of them unaware he was a coldblooded, evil—but charming—murderer.

Tonight, they sat again at the game table, their old homemade board of Live or Die spread between them. It looked very amateur to them now that they were such competent and experienced killers. Junior was so much better now with graphics and laser printing; he really should make them a new board. He would if they continued to use it, as well as various decks of death cards. There was also the usual stack of magazines and newspapers from which to choose the type of victim they would put down.

"Okay, Junior, first off, let's pick out who we're gonna go after. Here are some magazines to look through. Take this half. I'll take the others."

Junior sifted through the half dozen or so lying in front of him, wanting to get a good feel for what was happening around the world and where the hotspots were. They needed to avoid anywhere that the paparazzi were congregating and snapping pictures of some exciting current event. They definitely did not want to be seen and remembered. Nothing much appeared to be happening anywhere, which gave him an open field from which to choose. He picked up a copy of *Star*, one of those pathetic tabloids with lots of wild stories that targeted flamboyant celebrities and slandered them with lies and distortions and doctored photos. But this time, the cover brought him up short and snatched his breath away.

Right there, in black and white, was Junior's very own detestable, disgusting dad. He hadn't seen or heard anything about the aging rock star for a long time now, hadn't sought out news of him, hadn't really even thought about him much. He looked a lot older than Junior remembered him, but still had the stupid white braids and tattoos. He didn't need the guy anymore, not as long as his mom's money came rolling in hand over foot the way it had for so many years. Because of that, he hoped his dear old dad wasn't thinking of retiring anytime soon. But this article didn't turn out to be about his drug-fueled antics on stage or his young and sexy girlfriends. This time the media was covering a whole different story. There was one photograph that showed his father on the stage at his latest Chicago concert. Junior was more interested in the girl standing beside him. His father was hugging her tight against him with one arm and holding a mic in his other hand. They both were smiling and hugging and acting as if they were simply ecstatic with each other. At first, Junior thought it was his newest slutty lover, but then he read the headline. Across the top of the page, in big red caps: *Rock Star Reunited with Long-Lost Daughter.*

"Long-lost daughter! What the hell?"

Lucky jerked his head up. "What?"

Junior quickly skimmed the article. "My dad's got a daughter, and he's acting like she's his only kid. Fuck him, he's invited her to live with him. He bought her a goddamn house already."

"You didn't tell me you had a sister."

"I don't have a sister, damn it. She's some kid from one of his one-night stands. He probably doesn't even remember who her mother is. But it says here that he's already done a paternity test and she's his biological child. He's gonna adopt her, the bastard." Junior was so enraged that he couldn't speak for a moment. "He can't do that. I'm not going to let him do that. That bitch is trying to cut into my inheritance."

That caused Lucky some concern. "That mean he's gonna split our bank account with some girl?"

"Over my dead body. Mom's lawyers wrote in the amount, and it's concrete for life. But he might write that little bitch into his will, and she'd get half of my inheritance. Maybe, I don't know all the legal stipulations Mom got put in the divorce settlement. But that's not the point, Lucky. He acts like he loves her, says they've been together for a while now. Look at him, look at the way he's beaming down at her. It says here that he's buying her a house on this big lake that he grew up on somewhere in Missouri. He's doing all this for her, and he's never given me a fucking thought, not since I was six years old. Damn him, damn him!"

"That sucks, man, but quit freakin' out about it. You get big bucks, anyway. It ain't that bad. Plenty enough comes in for both of us to get anything we want. Don't get greedy on me and screw things up."

"It *is* that bad, you moron. He loves her, and he never loved me. It says he just met that little shit a year ago and he already loves her. Don't you get what an insult that is to me? I'm his real son, his firstborn child. I'm his legal issue."

"Hey, don't call me names because your dad's a jerk."

Junior ignored Lucky, still intently poring over the article. "She just went to see him at one of his concerts and somehow got backstage and told him that he was her father, just like that. Says he got a paternity test and a DNA analysis. It says here that she already took his name legally!"

Junior was so furious that he could barely breathe. This was a slap in his face. His face got hot and his skin flushed dark with the kind of rage that he could not contain. "Lucky, he's treating her better than he ever treated me!" He stood up and walked jerkily around the room, trying to get a hold on himself. Lucky just watched him pace without comment.

"You know what I'm gonna do? I'm gonna kill that little bitch," Junior spit out through his clamped jaw.

Lucky shrugged. "Fine with me, bro. I got no problem with that. End her. I'm game. Let's do her good."

"Well, fine, but I don't give a crap what you think."

"Ditto, asshole."

Junior came down a bit. This development was not Lucky's fault. "And I want her to suffer. I want to hurt her so bad I can taste it. I want to watch her face when I do it. Because that's gonna hurt him. I want him to suffer like he's never suffered before."

"Like I said, I'm all in. Kill your whole family. Fine by me. More money for us."

Something about that idea struck Junior as the funniest thing he'd ever heard. He couldn't help but laugh, which brought down his temper a bit. His buddy joined in. "We gotta be careful when we kill her. They might suspect me. That's a connection the cops can figure out. We've gotten away with all this so far because our victims were totally random, except for Mom."

"We can counteract that, no problem. Hey, I'm all for you stickin' a big old butcher knife in your stupid little sis. Let me see that picture. How old is she?"

"Just turned eighteen, it says."

"We kill young girls all the time. Quit worrying. She's a little thing. It's gonna be a breeze."

"You will help me do it, right? Or do you want your own victim?"

"Nah, I'll help you do her. Keep it in the family. Sounds like my financial survival depends on putting her to sleep."

Junior was already thinking the murder through. "We need to go there now, pick a place where we can make our plans in complete privacy. I want a house of my own, under an assumed name, of course. That way we can hole up and case things out and won't be noticed as transients passing through the area."

"You been there before?"

"No, but I've Googled it, because that's where my dad grew up. I know where it is and what it's like."

"What's the name of the place?"

"Lake of the Ozarks. It's way out in the sticks in the middle of Missouri. Rural place. Big lake, though, about halfway between Kansas City and St. Louis. Lots of tourists go there."

"Good, rural towns like that have Podunk, dumbass cops. Sounds good, like it's destiny, my friend. A celestial sign from heaven above. Or more likely from hell. Maybe the devil's gonna help us right some wrongs with your daddy. This is meant to be, my brother. I can feel it in my bones."

"I don't give a flyin' fuck if it's meant to be. It's a way to screw my dad. He's gonna be sorry that he abandoned me and took up with her."

Then they settled down and got serious about their plans. They pulled up info on the lake where Junior's half-sister was gonna get herself a great big, new house. But hell was gonna rain down on her as soon as Junior got there and found the little bitch. Oh yeah, he was going to make her pay.

Chapter 16

Trying not to gnash her teeth but highly exasperated, Claire walked alongside FBI Special Agent Bob Brady all the way down a completely deserted corridor to the conference room. Neither of them spoke a word. They sat down at the head of the long table facing each other. Claire studied his face intently, trying to see something amiss. He did the same to her, openly but less antagonistically.

Claire sucked it up. "Mind if I take a look at your badge, Special Agent? I'm getting a mite wary of FBI impersonators showing up so willy-nilly in my sphere of operations."

Face impassive, Brady simply gazed at her for a moment and then reached into his inside jacket pocket and pulled out a badge folder. That's when she saw that he carried a Glock 23 9mm in a leather shoulder holster. Well, at least he had good taste in weapons, though she preferred her own Glock 19. He handed over his credentials. Claire examined the badge at some length and found nothing wrong that she could ascertain, so she handed it back without comment. Then they sat there, staring silently at each other.

Claire bit first. "Okay, FBI Special Agent Brady, go ahead: Tell me what you've got on this game killer. Maybe his name and social security number, by any chance? That would give you a really pertinent reason to jump aboard on my case."

Unperturbed, he smiled, giving her the impression he thought her silly, and maybe stupid as hell, but also of a cautious bent. Oliver Wood came to mind. "Actually, Detective, I do happen to know his name. His birth name, anyhow. He could be operating under a false identity now, of course. Probably is, in fact. And please, call me Bob, if that's not a problem. No need for such formality. We're all on the same side here, now aren't we?"

"Okay. Special Agent Bob. Please, hit me with his birth name."

Brady smiled some, but not much. "You're everything I've heard and more. The more is the problem right now, I suppose, and that would be your apparent distrust of everyone, no matter if they're on your side or not. I understand that you've been betrayed a number of times, but I assure you right here and now: I am legitimate. Background check me, do whatever you like, but we need to trust each other and work together or we're not going to get anywhere on this case."

Well, slap me down and make me cry, why don't you? Claire thought. But he was probably right. No, he *was* right. She didn't trust him. He was going to have to earn that, just like everybody else in her life. She didn't deign to comment.

"Okay then, let's get back to the case. I've got the medical records right here of whom I believe to be your perp. I think you're going to want to see them."

Okay, now he was talking. She decided to stop with the accusatory attitude, accept what she couldn't change, and let him share his information. Maybe he did have something important that she and Bud could use. "Yes, by all means. I would love to see your documentation."

Claire watched as he retrieved a black leather briefcase off the floor beside him. He put it down on top of the table facing him and clicked open both latches. Then he lifted the lid and pulled out a thick manila folder held together by a heavy-duty red rubber band. His gaze met hers. "I've been looking for this guy for over a decade. Ever since he left home around the age of thirteen."

"That's a long time to tail somebody. He must be clever at evasion. What's his name?"

Brady held her regard for a few extra seconds. His eyes were unusual, a dark green color, like swamp water. He had long black eyelashes, looked almost as if he wore mascara. She was pretty sure he didn't. Still, those lashes were downright girlish. She wouldn't mind having them. "My suspect's name is Troy Edward Wood. He's from around here. Born in Columbia, Missouri, in fact, just right up the road from your lake. He's been in and out of psychiatric hospitals since he was around eight years old."

Okay, now that was a mouthful of info, and she needed a minute to digest it. She took several seconds to absorb the ramifications; the most striking was the fact that that name was more than familiar. "And his diagnosis is?"

"Schizophrenia with homicidal tendencies. He's been designated a sociopath—batshit crazy, using layman's terminology."

Since hooking up with a one Dr. Nicholas Black, and after incarcerating several off-the-charts-nuts serial killers, Claire had, unsurprisingly, become adept with such psycho talk. She and Bud preferred the layman's speak, of course, but she didn't use it in front of Black for fear of offending his shrink sensibilities. "Sounds like the crazy I'm looking for, all right."

"I think he's still somewhere nearby. Somewhere out around the lake. I've studied his movements a long time, Detective. I can feel it in my bones. I'm close now, and I want to get him."

"Well, I can ditto that. Would you happen to have a photograph of him, so I can spot him if I should happen to run into him in the grocery store?"

Brady stared at her, a serious sort, it seemed. "Actually, I do. Several, as a matter of fact." He shuffled through a pile of eight-by-ten photographs and slid one across to her. "Here, this is a family picture of Troy Wood and his brother. I got it when I visited his father's assisted living facility in Columbia. He gave me permission to take it out of its frame for ID purposes. He still lives there, and is totally blind now, I'm afraid. He's afraid of his son, worried he'll come back and kill him, too."

"Too?"

"Troy Wood murdered his mother when he was still in his teens."

"Well then, I can see his daddy's concern."

The photo depicted two young boys. Scrawny teenagers, by the look of them. One was taller and staring straight into the camera lens—oh, yeah, and he looked a hell of a lot like Oliver Wood, aka Superman Eyes. Exactly like him, in fact.

It was Wood, all right. He was years younger, not as tall, and not as broad-shouldered or muscular. The other kid was a bit shorter and had his face averted, looked like he'd rather be anywhere but where he was. He was scared out of his wits by his insane big brother. The kid's body language revealed that in no uncertain terms. She suspected that Troy Edward Wood had already started to display his mental deficiencies by that time and his poor little brother had been the beneficiary of his growing insanity. Having your brother kill your mother did that to a person, she suspected.

Claire reversed the photo on the tabletop and put her finger on the tall guy. "This is our suspect. He said his name was Oliver Wood."

The FBI agent kept his eyes riveted on the photo a moment and then looked up at her. "Yes, and he lied to you. The taller one is Troy Edward Wood. The little guy is his brother, Oliver, who joined the Marines as soon as he reached legal age. He's deployed in Iraq, I believe, on his second tour of duty. I spoke to him once by satellite, and he told me that he lost touch with his older brother years ago. He calls their dad regularly but hasn't been able visit him much. Their last visit in person was about three years ago."

"So you're telling me that your suspect, Troy Wood, is going by his kid brother's name when he's out murdering people? That's not very brotherly. He's been here at the lake for a while. I had a one-on-one with him a couple of nights ago, in fact. We had him at the game store and were taking him down to the sheriff's office when that car tried to run us down. He took advantage of the situation and promptly disappeared."

"Maybe he's running with an accomplice who was driving that Mustang."

"Maybe."

"Here's a picture of him at a mental institution when he was just a kid."

Claire looked at it closely but couldn't tell much. It was black and white and depicted a young boy sitting at a table, but it was too grainy to see his features all that well. Brady slid another picture across the table with his right forefinger. "This one was taken out of a yearbook from Hickman High School in Columbia. He dropped out before he graduated."

Claire pulled the picture up close and stared down at the face of a teenage boy. This one looked a lot like Oliver Wood, too. But it appeared to be a photo taken of a photo and wasn't all that clear, either. He looked very young. She looked up at Brady. "Yeah, I'm pretty sure this is the guy who came to the hotel to see me. Not exactly—he's a lot younger and less developed in these photos—but his eyes look sort of the same. The guy we met kept staring at me, very intensely, to an unsettling degree. He seemed to look right through me, and he made a point to pull Black's chain."

"Black?"

"My husband, Nicholas Black."

"You call him by his last name?"

"Long story."

Their gazes held for a brief moment. "Yes, I did happen to notice your wedding ring. Quite the diamond you've got there. You and Black must do very well."

Claire resisted rolling her eyes. This guy was quite the nosy nelly. Not one iota of her personal life was any of his business, so she pretended he hadn't said anything. "The guy said his name was Oliver Wood. And he's going by his brother's name? If he was a man on the run, a psycho as you said, why would he do that, Special Agent? Why wouldn't he opt for a totally fake identity?"

Brady shrugged. "Please, call me Bob."

"Why do you think he'd do that? Stick with his family's last name? That doesn't make sense. Not very bright of him, either, and I think this killer is very bright." Claire kept the conversation on point, because she did not know this guy yet and did not want to get chummy; all she wanted was to solve this case, sooner rather than later.

Brady grinned a little. "Nothing he does makes a whole lot of sense. That's because he's crazy, which also makes it hard for me to catch him. He's inconsistent in his actions, and that makes it difficult to pin down his motivations or his next move. But he's clever, as you've already recognized. I think he lives inside some kind of fantasy world of his own making, at least that's what all the psychiatrists' reports say. Read some of his hospital interviews and your hair just might stand up on end. He particularly gets his jollies killing animals. Started with his own Golden Retriever puppy when he was six."

Brady watched for Claire's reaction to that distasteful image, but she'd dealt with insane serials plenty of times, so she just stared at him until he continued.

"After that, he quickly graduated up to harming people. I can't prove it yet, but I know he's perpetrated multiple crimes all over the world. All random, all miles apart, with little evidence left behind. I think he killed your victim, the young girl you found dressed up as an angel, and this time, I think he might have chosen her for a specific reason."

"What reason?"

"If only I knew."

"How did you know our victim was left looking like an angel?"

"Sheriff Ramsay mentioned it."

Again, Claire contemplated the agent. "If he's so sick in the head, why was he released from the hospitals?"

"His family committed him for observation and psychological treatment several times when he was young, but he always managed to either con his way out or escape. He's got a brilliant mind, albeit a criminal one. They say he's easily able to manipulate others. Hospital employees always talked about how charming he could be. It's all down there in that folder for you to read through." He stopped, found another piece of paper and brought it out. "Here, take a look at this. After he got out of the psych ward the last time he was committed by family members, he went straight home and ran down his mother with her own car. It says he lay in wait until she was crossing the street from her workplace and then just plowed right over her. Then he actually put the car into reverse, backed up, and ran over her two more times. Then he took off, never been seen again. Not that I know about, anyway. Until you met up with him."

Claire pulled the report closer and skimmed through the first page. "So you're saying it's his M.O. to use a car as a weapon? And you're sayin' he's the one who tried to kill me and Bud? That's funny, because he wasn't driving the car that hit us, he was walking across the street with us. And he pushed me out of the way and saved my life. How do you explain that?"

"I'm not saying that I can explain anything for certain about your case. I am saying that vehicular hit-and-run is one of his known methods of murder. It's happened before, and more than once. I believe he could now have an accomplice working with him. Could be a woman he's taken up with, a wife or a lover, somebody like that. She could have been in that car that plowed into you in order to keep him from going to jail. Also, he knows you are now in the process of looking for him, intent on bringing him to justice. He's already made face-to-face contact with you. I think he must've decided you and your partner were getting too close and needed to go." Brady's serious stare held her full attention, nice and steady and quite intense. "You're lucky to be alive, that's what I'm trying to tell you. So is your partner. I think he's committed a long and bloody string of homicides by vehicle, starting with his mother. And even more kills that have something to do with those game pieces we've found at some of the murder scenes. He likes to leave them in his victims' mouths, or forced halfway down their throats. Like your Christmas angel. Your sheriff said you found a game piece and also a dog tag shoved down into her stomach. That's new, and even more violent."

"Yes, it is." She nixed a rising vision of green goo. But all this wasn't quite adding up in Claire's mind. "Why would he come see me in person like that and use his brother's name? Why take that kind of chance? Doesn't make any sense."

"Because you're investigating his case, I would think. Maybe he was playing around with you. Baiting you. Evidently, he likes to do that. Did he spar verbally with you? According to the shrinks, that's one of Troy's trademarks. Clever repartee, I guess you'd call it."

"Yes, he did that. Not all that clever, just stupid stuff. But then he was out in public the next day, and stuck around after that car hit us until I called 911. That doesn't sound like the man you've been describing."

Brady shook his head. "He's demented. Who knows how his brain works? Again, maybe he's got a partner or some kind of apprentice he's training. I'm telling you, the hospital reports tell me he edges right up there at the genius-level IQ. Problem that faces us right now, though, is that he descended into madness at an extremely young age. I feel like he now thinks, after all these years of murdering people and getting away with it, that he's invincible and unstoppable by anyone. I think he toys with police and investigators now. I also think he enjoys killing people for whatever kind of sick pleasure it gives him. His dad told me that he loves to play games and that he excelled at them. Raged around and tore up the house when he didn't win, punched holes through the walls and destroyed furniture."

"You really think he's still here at the lake?"

"I only know that he's been known to hang around and taunt investigators with false clues until they get too close. You know, tantalize the cops and try to lead them down the wrong roads—and he's smart enough to do it."

"Nobody's ever caught him?"

"No. We've got some hits of him on security cameras in various towns, but he usually wears a hoodie that hides his features. He is highly intelligent, I'm telling you, and that's how he evades capture. Some of his shrinks think he believes everything in life is just a game to be played and won."

"If he is Troy Edward Wood instead of Oliver Wood, and he wants me dead, why would he push me out of the way yesterday? Why did the driver almost hit him, too, if the driver was working with him?"

"Good questions that I'm afraid I can't answer yet. Hopefully, if we work together amicably, we just might catch him this time. Especially if he's hanging around here because of some kind of fascination with you."

Claire jerked her face up. "Why would you say that?"

"Because he approached you and talked face to face. I've never known him to do that before." He paused. "Did you happen to do or say anything that he might have taken as a come-on when he met you and your husband?"

That felt insulting. "You think I came on to some stranger in front of my husband?"

"Well, I don't know you very well yet."

"Obviously."

"If you did not encourage him, I might have a working theory as to why he targeted you."

"Let's hear it, by all means."

"Please don't be offended by what I'm about to bring up."

Claire knew immediately that she was definitely going to be offended. Talk about a loaded comment. And she was fairly certain about what he was going to say, so she beat him to the punch: "I take it you're referring to that write-up in the *National Enquirer*?"

"Well, I've got to say, Detective, those photos of you were highly provocative. To a mentally deficient man like Troy Edward Wood, you might personify something he craves. I think any guy who saw you in that picture would want you carnally. No doubt about it. Maybe that's why he chose you. Those pictures probably appealed to him, along with the fact that you're the detective in charge of this murder case."

Claire became incensed and in less than half a nanosecond. What the hell was with this guy? "Sorry, Special Agent, I must disagree. I think most decent men who looked at that picture, which was taken without my knowledge or permission, would think that some jerk paparazzi idiot had invaded my privacy while I was trying to enjoy my honeymoon."

Brady lifted a shoulder, gave a half-hearted, abbreviated shrug. "I realize it's a problem for you to have suggestive photographs floating around, but don't kid yourself: Complete strangers are probably fantasizing about you as we speak. Not that I'm saying you wanted any of this to happen, or that you actually posed for those pictures, nothing like that, I assure you. No insult meant. But the truth's the truth, and we both need to face it. You now have guys lusting after you, through no fault of your own. And that fits nicely into Troy Edward Wood's sexual fantasies, I would say."

Claire's jaw clamped. She would just love to send her doubled fist into his serious face. But he could be right. That was exactly what Black had feared. Still, she didn't like Brady laying his conjecture out there on the table. Now it was even more embarrassing. "Okay. So enough about me, Special Agent Brady."

"Please, I don't want to insult you. I'm just a direct person. I want you to know that you need to be on the lookout for this guy. Watch your back. He's approached you twice already, luckily in public places. Next time, he might make a move on you."

"I'm heavily armed. And we found him when we went to Games Galore—he wasn't looking for me."

"You sure about that? Did you see him inside that store when you first got there? Or was it after you'd been there awhile that you noticed him? If that was the case, he could have been following you and your partner."

Claire didn't answer.

"C'mon, Claire, let me investigate alongside you, tag along, be there to help if anything goes wrong. What could that hurt? Interoffice cooperation at its finest. This guy is extremely dangerous. We believe he goes for thrill kills—fun and games. Your partner's out of the picture right now. You need backup with this guy, and I think you're a good enough cop to know that."

Of course she knew that. Didn't like it much, but she wasn't an idiot. If Oliver Wood, aka Troy Edward Wood, or whatever the hell his name was, had begun to stalk her as Brady suspected, a trained and armed FBI agent might be useful to have on her six. He certainly looked as if he could hold his own in any altercation, maybe in his trademark suave and debonair manner, but she did need his help. Bud was out, Black and Will Novak were gone, and no more choices were available. "Well, all that goes without saying. I've been ordered to work with you, so I guess I will have to."

"So how about running your case for me? I'm sure the sheriff didn't know the whole story." He leaned back in his chair and clasped some very large hands atop the table, ready to listen and learn.

Claire hated that she had to tell him she didn't have much to share. "We're at the beginning of the investigation. The victim is the daughter of a hard rocker who recently bought property here at Lake of the Ozarks."

Brady contemplated her. "What hard rocker is that?"

"Jonesy Jax."

"Really? Jonesy Jax. Hmm, now that is very interesting. Sheriff didn't mention that. Tell me everything you know so far. But first, which game token did you find on the body?"

Claire was reluctant to tell him anything, not that she didn't trust him— well, maybe it was because she didn't trust him. It took her time to warm up to people. Learned that the hard way. But she really had no choice. "The victim was bludgeoned with a heavy marble trophy, one that the perpetrator left behind, tucked under the Christmas tree with the presents. The game piece was coordinated: the little metal token shaped like a trophy that comes in Detection games. So it does appear as if we're looking for the same guy. Except this time, the token wasn't in her mouth—it was wrapped up in a little box as a gift to us."

"I thought the sheriff said it was in her stomach."

Claire watched his eyes as she told him. "No. The killer took time to whittle a hole through her abdomen wall, then he forced a dog tag down into her stomach. An engraved dog tag that read: Love, Dad."

Brady's eyes didn't react. "That sounds exactly like something Troy Wood would do. He's gradually getting more extreme when he plays his murder games. And now he's added the dog tag, for some perverted reason. We need to catch this guy, Claire."

"I'd say so."

"What's next up in your investigation?"

"I've got to go back and interview Jonesy Jax about his daughter. She has a strange background. He pretty much went to pieces when I notified him of her death. Although he hadn't known her very long, he loved her dearly, I have no doubt in my mind."

"What's strange about her background?"

"Apparently her mother was one of Jax's one-night stands, a woman he didn't remember, one of thousands, evidently. When she died, her daughter found out that her father was Jonesy Jax and showed up at one of his concerts about a year ago and found a way to meet him."

"And she turned out to be his biological daughter?"

"He did the tests. She looked a bit like him, too, I guess."

Brady nodded and sat thinking for a moment. "Okay, why don't we do that interview together? I can't this afternoon; I've got some calls to make concerning the Ruiz cartel. Can't put them off. How about tomorrow morning for the ID? I'd like to ask Jonesy Jax a few questions."

"All right. How about letting me take your file home with me tonight so I can study it?"

"I'm not supposed to give access to FBI files without SAC approval, but I will bend the rules this time, because I'm butting into your case and I want to show you my confidence in your professionalism. We need to find this man before he takes off again. I'm afraid you're going to end up as bait. That's something we'll have to deal with. So, partners?"

"Bud's my partner. But you and I can work together temporarily until he feels up to getting back on his feet."

"According to Sheriff Ramsay, Bud's femur has a compound fracture. That tells me he's not coming back anytime soon. But I'll take whatever cooperation I can get. I've tracked Troy Wood too long to miss this opportunity to put him down for good."

"Put him down?"

"Put him back into an asylum for the criminally insane. So, I guess that about does it for now."

Brady gathered the file and handed it over. Then they both stood up and walked out into the hall. Claire felt her phone vibrate inside her coat pocket. She pulled it out. It was Black.

"You'll have to excuse me, Special Agent Brady. I need to take this."

"One more time: please, call me Bob."

Claire nodded and moved around the corner into the adjacent hallway before she picked up. "Hey, Black. You make it to the big city safe and sound?"

"Sure did. We're in our suite at the Ritz-Carlton. Rico's eating everything in the mini fridge."

"That'll cost you a bundle. So you're just slummin' it up at the Ritz again, huh? You rich guys, my, my. You really know how to live the good life."

"I share it all with you, sweetheart. Everything I have is now yours, too, in writing and legally. Wish you were here. There's a hot tub that is calling our names."

"Yeah, the three of us could really get some romance going in that tub. But hey, don't tempt me. I just got stuck with working with a Fed that's big-time sniffing around my case."

"Please tell me it's not that jerk Oliver Wood."

"It's not him. It's another guy. A one Special Agent Bob Brady. Not quite as abrasive as our first agent-wannabe, but this one seems on the level. Ever hear of him? Says he works out of the K.C. office."

"Name doesn't ring a bell. He's working with you now?"

"Yeah. Charlie put him on with me since Bud got hurt. Brady thinks he's after the same perpetrator we are. He showed me his guy's psych files, and it's not pretty. He also showed me a picture of our friend Oliver. It's him, all right."

"Maybe he can help you catch him."

"I don't know yet. He's says that Oliver's real name is Troy Edward Wood, Oliver Wood's brother, and Brady says he's been after him for years."

"Why did he approach us in the lobby?"

"Good question. Brady says Troy Wood ran over his mother in a car, and also says he's pretty much the biggest freak this side of Tokyo. I've got his file in my hand as we speak. Want to read through it when you get home and give me your professional opinion on whether any of his shrinks know what they're talking about?"

"I'd love to. Thanks for asking."

Claire smiled. Black did so like his forensic psychiatry. "So, when are you getting back? Why don't you finish up your shopping today and get yourselves back home, because I'm already as lonely as hell."

"Maybe we will."

"Maybe I hope so. But right now, I gotta go. The Fed is waiting. Again, wish you were here to talk this out with me. You know what I've discovered, Black? I don't trust anybody anymore. It's a little worrisome. I always expect everybody to stab me in the back."

"Me too. Must be catching. But that can be a good thing. Keeps you wary and alive."

"Bought me my extravagant present yet?"

"About to. Hope you like it."

"Well, let me tell you, I have one super-duper, fantastic present for you. One you've never had before and that you couldn't guess in five million years. And that's hard to do, since you have everything ever made on planet Earth."

"I've got you, that's everything I want."

Wow, he was a smooth talker, all right, and a real catch, if she said so herself. And he loved her a lot and showed it all the time. Who could ask for anything more? Marriage had not turned out to be the bear trap she had feared for so many years—lucky for them both.

"All right. We're getting ready to hit the stores," Black was telling her now. "Toy and electronics stores first. Rico's going crazy with excitement. He loves New York already. Likes the taxi cabs and skyscrapers."

"Guess you'll have to buy yourself a giant penthouse there so he can have his fun whenever he wants."

"Maybe that's what I'm getting you for Christmas. Did Rico spill the beans?"

Claire blinked. It could happen. "No, but I don't really need a New York penthouse, Black. I hate New York. I'd rather have a new rifle with one of those super good night scopes like Will Novak's got. Okay, I've got to go, too, so give Rico a hug and hurry back home. I'm lost without you two, and I haven't even made it back home yet."

"We may very well cut this trip short. I don't like being away anymore, either. It hurts my heart when you're not in arm's reach."

Claire laughed at that. "Oh, yeah, sure. I imagine you'll live. Just be careful. Don't get lost or pick up any loose women in Times Square. New York's known for that kind of thing, you know. And avoid your ex-wife like the plague, or Jude will probably force the two of you to have dinner with her. Just like always."

"You sound jealous, but I like that in you. It's so rare. Don't see it nearly enough. But don't worry: We aren't going to see her. You be careful. This Brady guy going to be okay to work with, you think?"

"Don't know yet. He seems pretty serious. Thinks I looked sexy in those *National Enquirer* photos. Wants me to call him by his first name."

"Claire..."

"Just teasing. Lighten up and have some fun."

"Is he really coming on to you?"

"Oh yeah. I figure he's going to jump all over me as soon as we hang up."

"After hearing about Oliver Wood, or Troy Wood, or whatever that sociopath's name is, I'd be careful about who I trusted, especially FBI agents who show up out of the blue. Did he have legitimate credentials?"

"Charlie said he's already checked him out. I think this one is for real. He's got that innate Fed arrogance."

"How's Bud?"

"The physical therapists were trying to get him up on crutches last time I called. He didn't like it much. He's so looking forward to seeing Brianna."

"Guess I better let you go. Rico's raring at the bit. Take care, for God's sake. Don't let any more cars run you over. How's your hip today?"

"It's sore, but doable. I'm fine."

"Sounds like you were saved from a psychopath driver by a psychopath. That kind of thing can only happen to you, Claire. I think I'm glad you've got that special agent working with you. Wish Novak would get back up here and help you out. I trust him."

"I'm good. Really."

"I love you."

"Yeah, right back at you. That's a given: I signed the papers."

They hung up, and Claire walked back around the corner and found Brady down at the coffee station at the far end of the hall. He was getting two cups of coffee. It smelled good. She met him halfway down the corridor. "Thought you might like something to keep you warm on the way home."

"Thanks. I take mine black."

"I figured that."

"How about ten o'clock tomorrow morning for Jonesy's interview?" Claire asked him, sipping her coffee. It tasted pretty good for a change. Police departments weren't especially known for the excellence of their coffee. Must have been freshly brewed.

"Sounds good."

"We also have to take Jonesy down to the morgue for the official identification. You want to go with me?"

"Of course. Thank you for the opportunity."

Outside in the parking lot, she watched him get into some kind of dark SUV, a Ford Fusion, maybe. He drove off without looking at her again. Good, she was glad to get rid of him, too.

Play Time

Junior and Lucky's carefully laid plans about visiting Missouri in the dead of winter seemed blessed from day one. Everything fell into place as if ordained by Harry Potter's magic wand. It was as though their new mission had been charmed from the beginning and all would be well with all their intended spilling of familial blood. They traveled across the country in Junior's hot red Mercedes with plenty of cold cash in hand, mainly because they enjoyed road trips together, but also because they didn't want to leave a paper trail with plane tickets and credit cards and nary a way to transport their favored murder weapons created out of their improved but warped version of Detection. They had already become joint owners of a lovely lake property, the house key already mailed to them and tucked safely inside Junior's jeans pocket.

The property they had chosen had been purchased over the Internet, with a nondescript St. Louis realtor handling the negotiations. Junior had used a fictitious name, of course, but one with which he'd already built up a good credit rating, so there was no problem whatsoever. After the great state of California's real estate prices, the old mill, with its attached log cabin, was the damn steal of the century. The previous owner had already set up residence in Fairbanks, Alaska, and had left both the house and the mill fully furnished and ready for immediate occupancy. He'd also left an old brown Chevrolet pickup truck and a beat-to-hell white 2008 Concorde, both thrown into the deal for some extra cash. The deed was done and signed and notarized—they were definitely good to go.

Junior and Lucky were now proud residents of the Show-Me State and ready to show off their considerable murder skills. They were eager to set up operations at their very own distinctly private killing lair on the shores of Lake of the Ozarks. They'd always wanted a place where they were isolated enough to butcher a person to their heart's delight. Neither had ever done that before—but it was a definite challenge that was now in the cards.

It might take a lot of time to set up those kinds of intricate torture chambers, but they would have all the time in the world after they finished killing Junior's little sis. She would have to die the old-fashioned way, but that was how Junior wanted it to go down—inside her new house that his daddy had bought her. He wanted his daddy to find her dead and bloody and violated in extreme ways.

They drove into a cold and snowy Camdenton on Highway 5 and found the road out to their new property. The old mill lay at the end of a narrow, weed-choked gravel road. Neither of them had ever lived out in the woods, and they liked the idea of being conveniently cloaked from neighbors by stands of towering trees and underbrush. It felt unsettling at first—way out there in the middle of the nowhere, it was bizarrely quiet and as dark as pitch at night, but pretty nice, too. No traffic or nosy neighbors, no police sirens, no police presence, period. Yes, that was indeed a plus.

The millhouse had this great big gristwheel that turned slowly on the current of their very own personal stream that rushed through their property before gurgling itself down a hill into an inlet of the lake. It creaked round and round with a horror-movie clunk and groan. They decided they could put it to good use as a water torture device once they got settled and got their games going. That idea particularly appealed to Junior. This could be their secret hidey-hole out in the woods where all sorts of macabre fantasies could rise to fruition. But first things first: they had to find Junior's dear little soon-to-be-deceased sissy and put the newfound heiress out of her misery.

And find her they did. In record time, too. It didn't take them long at all once they ferreted out the location of the house that Junior's father had bought for her. The rustic mansion was being used for a Christmas tour, of all the stupidest things in the world. So they dressed up in nondescript jeans, sweatshirts, and winter jackets, bought a couple of tickets, and waltzed their way innocently through the house where they intended to commit the most horrific of murders.

Since all was meant to be, their luck held, and as the tour wound up, who should show up in a late-model black Mustang but his soon-to-be-dead half-sister. Junior recognized her right away as he was getting into the old brown truck after the tour had finished. He watched her park the Mustang, get out, and wait for the other people to clear out of the driveway. After most of them were gone, she stood in front of the house, holding a pizza box in her hand and chatting with some lady as it gradually got dark outside and at least fifty million strings of lights blinked on.

"Let's go meet that little bitch," Junior said to Lucky, starting up the truck. He rolled his vehicle slowly over to where she was now standing alone and slid down his window. "Excuse me, miss, but the tour's already over. Sorry you missed it."

The girl turned around and presented him with a friendly smile, then she walked up to the driver's window. "Oh, I know. I've been waiting for everyone to clear out." She glanced up at the big house. "This is my new house, but I can barely believe it. It's so beautiful."

"It sure is," Lucky told her, grinning real friendly-like. "Awfully big for little old you, isn't it?"

She giggled. "Yeah, it's way too big for me. But my daddy's gonna live here with me for part of the year. When he can get away."

Junior felt his muscles tensing up. "That's nice. I don't think he's here, though. We didn't see him. Are you waiting for him?"

"No, no, I sneaked in a day early so I could surprise him. He's staying at Cedar Bend Lodge. Can you tell me where that is?"

"Afraid not. We're new in town."

"Well, I'm Heather Jax. It's very nice to meet you."

They both smiled and related their false identities. Junior's expression was more of a grimace.

"Man, does that pizza ever smell good," Lucky said with a big, fake grin.

"It's my favorite: pineapple papaya. It's hard to find, but it's yummy."

"Sounds good."

Heather Jax smiled at them some more. "Did you enjoy the Christmas tour?"

"Yes, ma'am, we sure did. You have got yourself one gorgeous house."

"Thank you. My daddy's very generous with his gifts. He calls me his little angel."

Yeah, and she's gonna be a dead little angel real soon, Junior thought. His teeth came together hard enough to crack, but he kept up the smiling. "Okay then, if you're okay out here alone, we're gonna take off. We just wanted to make sure you were going to be all right."

"Thank you. That's so considerate. I've found that the people I've met around here are just really as nice as can be."

"We have, too. How about we wait here until you get inside?" offered Lucky from the passenger seat.

"I appreciate that. But I'll be fine out here until tomorrow morning. Then my daddy's coming out here to be with me."

Huh uh, thought Junior. *You won't be fine ever again, not after tonight.* The thought got him all excited. The two coldblooded murderers sat there and watched her, their truck idling, their bloodlust rising, as she climbed up the steps and opened the front door with her own damn key. She turned and smiled and waved before she went inside and shut the door. She was in there all by her lonesome now, ripe for the taking. Junior and Lucky looked at each other and started laughing their heads off. She was just so friendly and naïve. They were casing her murder scene, and she didn't have a clue. Sweet. They drove off, highly pleased. Now they knew where

Junior's daddy was, too, and they decided to check that out. Make sure he was in town so he could find his angel's body.

As it turned out, the first thing they caught sight of at the big, fancy hotel was a large crowd of paparazzi around the front portico. Not so good, that. They parked and hung around the edges of the throng, eavesdropping on what they were saying to each other and pretending they were press, too. Most of the guys seemed to be waiting around to shoot pictures of some semi-famous couple who owned the hotel, but the reporters were also getting excited about rumors that a rock star had checked in recently. One had even caught a glimpse of the guy standing out on a balcony and pointed out the exact room for them. They decided to check it out. Lucky went inside and reserved them a fancy suite right down the hall from daddy dearest. Junior pulled his hood up and hung back out of sight, even though he figured his dad wouldn't recognize him in a million years. He'd changed a lot since he was six, after all.

Lucky, on the other hand, was not as restricted. Nobody knew him, so he was free to reconnoiter the lay of the land. Lucky had always been a friendly sort, when he wasn't offing people, a downright sociable homeboy, a real chameleon who could change his mien depending on who he was talking to. Quite an actor, he was. He joked around with the security guards and shutterbugs and didn't cause one iota of suspicion, especially from the big black guy who stood guard outside Junior's daddy's suite. He stood there and talked basketball and Beyoncé with the guy, and it didn't take Lucky long to catch a glimpse of the notorious rock star and some sexpot who was his latest squeeze. She looked good, too, and gave Lucky a flirty glance as she walked past him and down to the ice machine.

Junior was elated to hear that he now had a front row seat to his father's grief and suffering once he found his very dead little daughter inside her new house. Watching him cry would make the trip totally worthwhile. Junior wasted no time putting his plan into action. Murdering a young, defenseless girl in an empty house out in the middle of nowhere wouldn't exactly comport with brain surgery—not for them, anyway. The silly girl was all alone and just asking for it. How damned convenient.

It would have to be that night—his daddy might come the next day, and their window of opportunity would be lost. The next tour wasn't scheduled until the following afternoon—it was now or never. No problem; they had already planned the whole thing out on the long and boring drive east from Los Angeles to Missouri.

So, later that night, when it was dark and quiet in those remote woods around little sissy's house, they hunkered down inside a thicket of tall trees out back. Despite the snow and inclement weather, they had hiked in so as to avoid the electronic gate at the entrance to the exclusive subdivision. They weren't in California anymore, or there would've been a security guard manning that ornate bricked entrance. The tons of falling snow boded well for them as well, because it was covering up their footprints. So far, everything was going well with their detailed game plan. They were at the scene, jacked up to kill a young girl who needed to die. It was so late at night that all the exterior Christmas lights were off, and sissy was in bed. There was just one small light burning on the second floor. It was the master bathroom—they'd seen it on the tour. The master suite also had a nice screened-in balcony, with log walls that had footholds which were a cinch to climb.

They made it to their entry point easily enough, and Lucky slit the screen with his switchblade. No problems whatsoever. Not a sound. Dead silence. They waited a few minutes and listened for movement inside, but heard nothing. Man, it was just eerily quiet. Dear Heather had to be asleep; it was three o'clock in the morning. Lucky hunched over and moved to the French door. The handle turned easily—unlocked. Easy, peasy. This murder was meant to be, all right. It was so effortless that it was almost a let-down. No challenge whatsoever. Then, there she was: their precious little victim, lying on her side, sound asleep in bed. Easy pickings, you bet your life.

They tiptoed across the room and made it to the large sleigh bed before she roused. Heather quickly sat up in bed, but Junior was already on one side and Lucky on the other. She let out the shrillest shriek Junior had ever heard, high-pitched enough to vibrate his eardrums, but he didn't bother to shut her up. Nobody was anywhere near the place—all the other houses were at least a half mile away, certainly not within hearing distance. He liked to hear women scream in terror. It had become music to his ears.

His sweet little sister was nothing but a sitting duck, all right. They grabbed her and pulled her out of the bed, then they shoved her back and forth between them for a while to scare the absolute crap out of her. After that, they dragged her down the hall to the second-floor balcony of the big library, which was full to the brim with more Christmas lights. They turned them all on. She had on a long, flowing white nightgown; it made her look like her daddy's little angel, all right—albeit a terrified one. So Hark! the Herald Angels Sing, and they'd get her to heaven so she could join with the heavenly host.

"Who are you? What do you want?" she kept screaming at the top of her voice.

"I'm your big bro, kiddo," Junior told her calmly, pushing her down onto her knees beside the upstairs bannister. "Didn't know you had a brother, now did you? Well, guess what? You do. And it's me. And guess what else? You are gonna die tonight—right now, in fact."

That's when she really started putting up a life-and-death, scratching, kicking fight for survival. She was small and light, but she struggled and screamed and jerked with all her scrawny might. But her might didn't amount to all that much. She was too little-bitty. She never had a chance in hell. They slapped her around some, and then they forced her to sit on the floor and play Live or Die with them. Aw, she proved to be such an unlucky soul: She drew the Dead card right off the bat, poor kid. Then she drew the Get-Clobbered-in-the-Head card, so that's exactly what Junior would do—with the utmost pleasure.

"Wait a sec," Lucky told him, grabbing his arm. "She looks like an angel. Let's put her on top of the tree first." He laughed at the idea. "That ought to shock your daddy."

Junior held her up onto her tiptoes by her throat and glanced down at the big Christmas tree on the other side of the bannister. He laughed, too, thinking Lucky's idea was way cool. Lucky picked her up and put her atop the rail, and then took out the nails and hammer he'd brought along. Heather screamed and struggled as he put a nail in each hand, and then she gave up the struggle and just slumped there, moaning and groaning. Junior pulled out the big trophy he'd gotten at a flea market in Arizona and decided to use as the murder weapon. Lucky stepped back out of the way, and Junior swung the heavy black trophy hard. Poor kid was dead and gone the second the blow shattered the back of her skull. Blood flew about everywhere, just the way Junior liked it, all over the hardwood floor and the timber wall behind them. Their little angel slumped down and was never heard from again. Junior felt nothing. Daddy's poor little daughter. Gone, baby, gone.

Then they leaned her back, and Lucky held her steady while Junior whittled out a hole in her stomach with a switchblade and stuffed the little dog tag way down into her body. Now she really was a true trophy daughter. After that, Junior stood back and was satisfied. He had never hated anybody the way he hated her. He watched Lucky wrap a halo of lights around her head for effect; Lucky always had to be theatrical. He should've been a movie actor. But that was okay—Junior's daddy deserved to find her posed that way. Right above the Christmas tree that he had no doubt bought for her. Lucky situated the hem of her gown to hang over the edge and cover the star. Nothing beat a life-size bloody angel on the top of a beautiful Christmas tree, now did it?

After that, they descended a wide spiral staircase and stood at the base of the tree. Lucky took the murder weapon in his gloved hands and tucked it, blood and all, among the wrapped presents. Then they placed the little gaily wrapped box with the dog tag out in front of the other gifts for the detectives to ponder over and get all confused. For a time, Junior and Lucky just stood there at the bottom of the tree and gazed up at their dead little angel. Then they looked at each other, more than pleased by their artful handiwork. Now, *this* was a murder scene that the hick local police would never be able to forget, not in a million years. Neither would a certain aging rock star, who now had only one surviving son to inherit every cent of his money.

"Okay, there you go, she's dead as a doornail and on her way to heaven," Lucky told Junior. "You happy now?"

"You bet I am. I haven't felt this good about anything in a long time."

"Then let's get the hell out of here and watch the fun over at Cedar Bend when your daddy gets the bad news. I bet we can hear him howling all the way down the hall."

"I hope so," said Junior. "It serves him right for cutting me out of his life the way he did."

They made sure everything was wiped clean and left the place in pristine order as they always did. After they were satisfied that there were no clues left behind, they took little Heather's driver's license and car keys and headed out into that beautiful, soft snowfall coming down all around. They let themselves out the front door and hurried down the sidewalk to her black Mustang. They drove down the long drive to the main road, and then through the front gates that they opened wide with a touch to his dead sister's remote control. Heather's car would make one hell of a good killing machine to stash at the mill and use around the lake. Oh yeah, before they left, they were going to enjoy a real hot-damn thrill killing spree in the tangled wilds of rural Missouri.

Chapter 17

Vaguely, somewhere in the groggy depths of her mind, Claire could hear faint strains of music. It took a moment to realize it was her cell phone playing "Turn the Lights Down Low," Bud's favorite Josh Turner ringtone, his tribute to Brianna. She roused up on one elbow, fighting her way out of deep slumber and fumbling blindly around for her cell. She finally got a hold on it and pushed up to sitting.

She had not slept particularly well; she never got restful sleep when her bed was empty. There was always a pleasurable sense of security when Black's long, hard body was pressed up close against her—not to mention the other enjoyable aspects of sharing a bed with him. They hadn't been apart much since their honeymoon. She had better get re-used to his jet-setting away to far flung clinics around the world. Her guy was a busy man.

Claire cleared her throat and answered the phone, her voice gravelly and thick with sleep. "Yeah, Bud? You okay?"

"I'm fine, except I'm going nuts confined to this freakin' bed. Charlie said he hooked you up with some Fed. Bet you just love that."

Pushing her hair out of her eyes, Claire had to smile. "He's your typical Fed, and you know what that means. I want you back, please, even over the phone or on crutches."

"I don't blame you. I am awesome."

"Is Brianna here yet?"

"Nope. Black's helicopter's picking her up later today, though. Tell him thank you very much, and I owe him one."

"He's not here to tell. But it was his pleasure, believe me."

"The Fed and I are pretty sure that Oliver Wood is our culprit. But his real name is Troy Edward Wood. All this is according to my new buttoned-up, stuffy, pretend partner. Says he thinks this guy has done these nasty kinds of killings here and all over the world."

"You just don't like the guy 'cause he's not me."

"That's very true. I'll take you on a walker any day, so get goin' with that rehab. We're planning to interview Jonesy Jax later today. I've already put out a BOLO on Oliver, aka Troy Wood."

"Sounds like you're about to wrap this one up in a big, tidy red Christmas bow."

"I hope so. You just worry about getting back up on your feet. My invitation for you and Brianna to stay here at Cedar Bend is still on the table. Black will comp you with a suite overlooking the water. Room service is what you need right now. And lots of people to wait on you and Bri both."

"Nah, Bri'll probably want to be alone with me and make up for lost time. You know how appealing I am. She really digs me. She tells me that a lot."

Claire laughed. "So things are lookin' up for you guys, I take it."

"Oh yeah. She's been gone from me for three weeks. What do you think she's gonna want to do now that I'm all helpless and pitiful?"

"You just relax and take care of that leg. I'll keep you posted on what's going down with the case. I could use your input with this guy, Bob Brady."

"You really don't like him?"

"Hard to say right now. If forced to take a stand, I'd say maybe. Don't have an extremely good reason for going either way right now. He's fairly professional, but he brought up those *National Enquirer* pictures, which irked me. Other than that, he's polite enough, I guess. Has a slightly arrogant bent to him, and he's a know-it-all but he attempts to hide it from me. He did provide me with a lot of info on our perp."

"Hang in there. You'll get this guy. We always do. Just be careful. Avoid speeding cars."

"Yeah, right back at you."

They hung up. Claire felt better now that she'd heard Bud's voice and he sounded halfway upbeat and happy. Brianna's presence had always been the key to cheering him up.

As agreed upon, Special Agent Bob Brady showed up at ten o'clock, right on the minute. He was in for a treat meeting up with Jonesy Jax and his suite mate. Not a run-of-the-mill duo. But Claire had seen the other side of Jonesy when she'd given him the worst news that could ever be given to a loving parent. She had a feeling she would see that somber, grieving guy again today. This time, she gave him the courtesy of calling his suite for permission to visit before they showed up and started asking difficult questions. Jonesy answered the telephone himself, not the prickly

Ms. Kisses. With utmost civility, Claire asked him if they might come down and talk to him. He said he'd been waiting for her to call and set up an interview.

Fifteen minutes later, Claire and Special Agent Brady were granted entry into the rocker's suite by the same giant bodyguard. This time, his living room looked spotless. Pristine, in fact. No empty booze bottles sitting around, no overflowing ashtrays, and no choke-provoking pall of gray smoke clinging to the ceiling. Best of all, no Candi Kisses. Claire might have actually gagged if she had to suffer the sight of another black teddy and those ridiculous fishnets.

Jonesy was sitting by himself on a long tan-and-black-striped sofa. A pot of coffee and a silver tray of flaky croissants and mini-donuts were sitting on the marble coffee table in front of him. He looked haggard and pale and dull-eyed, as if he were coming down hard off drugs and booze, but almost sober again.

"Thank you for seeing us, Mr. Jax."

Jonesy looked up at them out of the most bloodshot eyes that Claire had ever seen. "I wasn't born Jonesy Jax. Did you know that? My real name is James Swan." He gave a small self-deprecatory chuckle, but one devoid of humor. "I was born in a little Arkansas town on the Rolling Fork River, believe it or not. But I grew up here at the lake." Then he abruptly stopped talking and looked horribly sad.

"I'm very sorry for your loss," said Brady in a suitably somber tone.

Claire didn't think that Jonesy's birth name fit the morose, heavily tattooed guy sitting alone on the couch. Brady was giving him his due respect. That was something she could admire about the Fed.

"Thank you. All this is just really hard for me to believe. You know, I'd just found Heather after so damn long. Years and years. I didn't know I had any children, other than my son. Now she's gone, just like that. And my son, I don't even know him. I haven't seen Junior in years. Probably never will."

Interested, Brady leaned forward. "He is a child from your first marriage, I believe; is that correct?"

Claire glanced from one man to the other. She had not heard any mention of a son. Brady hadn't mentioned it, and she hadn't seen that in the file she'd read on Troy Wood. That meant Brady hadn't filled her in completely. He'd left that little tidbit out of his briefing. Why would he do that? She placed her full attention on Jonesy and waited for his answer.

"Yes, he was a child from my first marriage, when I was still young. I lost custody of him the day his mother and I signed divorce papers. I agreed to give him up so I could get rid of that gold-digging slut I was stupid and naïve enough to elope with. I didn't want to leave him, but I couldn't stand to be around her anymore. Hell, I guess I wouldn't know him if I saw him today. I suspect he's turned out to be a rotten person. His mother's influence was insidious. I regret not seeing him for all these years."

Claire frowned. Brady just stared at the rock star and didn't reply, so Claire took up the conversation.

"We think a man by the name of Troy Edward Wood may have killed your daughter. Have you ever heard that name?"

"No." He thought about her question. "I don't remember ever hearing that name. Are you sure that it was him?"

"Not completely certain, but the facts are pointing to him. We're still investigating and looking into everything we can find. Right now, we want to locate Wood so we can ask him some questions. He's been hanging around the lake for a few weeks, we think, but we can't find him. We're beginning to think he could be working with an accomplice. Once we locate him and get a chance to interrogate him, we can tell you more."

"There were two of them? Two guys hurt her like that?" Jonesy's jaw clamped shut, his face flushing dark with anger. When he spoke, his words came harshly between clenched teeth, but he remained calm. "I hope you just put that Glock of yours on his forehead and pull the trigger. Take off his head. Like he did to my poor baby."

"I understand how you feel, sir, but that's not going happen. We will get him and put him in jail. After that, it's up to the jury."

"Yeah, unless I find him first. I've already put out a half-a-million-dollar reward on him, dead or alive."

Oh my God, Claire thought. *That's the worst thing that he could ever do.* She glanced at Brady. To her shock, his lips were curved in a slight smile, one that faded fast, but not before she'd glimpsed it. What the hell? No way could Brady think that a family member offering a dead-or-alive reward was a good thing. She quickly jumped on that in the negative. "You need to rescind that reward, Jonesy. Right now. Believe me, we both understand how you feel. We've all suffered personal losses in our lives. We know you're in a place where you feel hopeless and only want revenge. But this isn't the way to do it. You need to pull that offer off the board. Right now."

Oh yeah, Claire knew how he felt, all right. There had been people in her past that she'd wanted to gun down so badly that she had trembled all over with the need to exact revenge. She had killed a few them when she'd had no choice; she had never regretted it. Right now? She was a sworn law enforcement officer, and so was Brady. He needed to wipe that smirk off his face. What the hell was he thinking?

"If you put out that reward, innocent people are going to get hurt. You have to know that. We are handling this case, and we are making progress. It's just been a matter of days. Please stay calm and don't do anything stupid that will create havoc. Like I told you, we'll keep you posted every step of the way, I can promise you that."

"I've already done it. I contacted all the networks and news channels. The phone interviews aired on all the morning news shows fifteen minutes ago. It's too late to stop anything now."

Claire wanted to grab Jonesy by his throat and throttle some sense into him. Brady was looking a tad more on the serious side now, too. Claire tried again. "You don't know what you've done, sir. There's gonna be a feeding frenzy around here from the minute those interviews go on the air, both from the media and from do-gooders and bounty hunters trying to get that money."

"I want everyone out looking for those fuckin' animals. I want them both dead. I want to see their cold, lifeless bodies on a slab, like my daughter's is."

Brady nodded. "Maybe you're right. Maybe the reward will knock something loose for our investigation and help us get the killers."

Claire turned and stared at him. "Are you out of your mind, Brady?"

His shrug was careless, indifferent. "No, it's just the truth. I want him, too. Now everyone in this state will be on the lookout for him."

"Seriously? You're okay with vigilantes out combing the woods? You have any idea what this will do to the tip lines down at the sheriff's office?"

Suddenly Jonesy Jax stood up. "Sorry you don't like this, Mrs. Black, but it's already done. I just hope it works. I want them dead. I don't care how they do it, I just hope they suffer. The bloodier, the better. Until then, I'm not sure I can step foot in her house right now, maybe I never can. Maybe I'll sell it. I'm gonna stay here at Cedar Bend. Tell Nick I'm sorry for all the publicity blowback he's probably gonna get about this. I can't help that, but I am going to do everything in my power to get those two murdering sons of bitches put down." His voice broke, and he hung his head and stifled a groan. "All I see, night and day, is what they did to my girl. My God, I called the morgue and they told me that he nailed her hands to a bannister. That he pushed something down into her body. Oh God, I can't bear to think about it." After that, Jonesy's entire body shuddered.

Claire truly felt sympathy for him—she would for any father going through something like this. After her baby died in Los Angeles, she never wanted to go back there. She had only returned once, when a case had made it necessary. All she had left in southern California were nightmare memories. She doubted if Jonesy would ever step foot in Missouri again.

"I do understand how upset you are, believe me, but could we ask you a few more questions?"

"Yes. I'm sorry—I'm just havin' a hard time dealing with all this."

"Of course you are. Anybody would be. We're sorry we have to bother you when you're going through this terrible thing."

They all sat down. Jonesy managed to pour them all cups of coffee. Brady took a croissant on a napkin, but food was the last thing on Claire's mind. "Tell us more about this son of yours. Where does he live at present?"

"To be honest, I'm not sure. His mother died years ago, I guess. After the divorce was final, I never saw her again. I wasn't allowed to see my son at all. She told the judge that I was a drug addict and unfit parent. He agreed with her. And I guess I was, back then."

Evidently he had accepted who he had been. "Has your son ever tried to contact you?"

"A few times, I think. But he was just a little kid, and I was always out on tour. I made sure that he was well taken care of in the divorce settlement. And his bitch of a mom didn't give him any of the birthday or Christmas presents I sent to him. She sent me videos showing her burning them. So I eventually just stopped trying. I guess he did, too."

"Do you think your son could be doing this to you out of his sense of being abandoned? Killing the daughter that you'd recently taken in his rightful place?" Brady asked him.

Claire waited. It was a damn good question. And a damn good motive. In fact, she'd been thinking along those same lines.

After a long pause, Jonesy finally answered. "I don't know. I don't know him from Adam. He inherited her money, and there was a lot of it to inherit, believe me. All I know is that he hasn't tried to contact me, before or after she died. I suspect he hates me and is happy enough never to see me again. I can't see why he'd object to Heather coming into my life. Why he would even care? Not after all this time."

If that were true, Jonesy was being a bit obtuse. A son who thought he had been abandoned without a second thought could definitely resent a new kid showing up and receiving the royal treatment. Jealousy and resentment were both extremely strong motives for murder. "Do you happen to have a picture of him?"

"No, not a recent one. I used to have some baby pictures, you know, from when I was still with them. Others I got when he was six or seven and the paparazzi caught him out shopping with his mom in Beverly Hills, you know, that kind of thing. But years have gone by now." He sighed, inhaled deeply, looked troubled. "You know how that is. I don't know what happened to him. I'm afraid to know."

And he obviously didn't give enough of a rip to find out. They sat there a bit longer, asked him several more questions that he couldn't answer. Claire finally gave up and reminded him not to leave the area. She also suggested again, in strong words, that he rescind the reward notices.

"What about my baby's body? I want to give her a decent burial out in California near my estate."

"I don't think the medical examiner is ready to release her remains yet. I'm sorry, but I'll let you know as soon as possible." Claire hesitated. "We still need her official identification. Are you up to going down to the medical examiner's office with us?"

Jonesy looked sick to his stomach. He stared down at his lap. "Yes, but can it wait until tomorrow? I'm just not ready to face that yet."

"Of course. Would tomorrow afternoon be okay? Say around three o'clock?"

"I'll be here waiting, don't worry. I have nowhere else to go. I canceled the rest of my tour. I just dread seeing her, you know, like that."

"We understand, of course. We'll see you then. Again, we're both very sorry for your loss. We do appreciate your cooperation at this terrible time."

Jonesy Jax just nodded and watched them walk to the door.

The minute she and Brady stepped outside of Jonesy's suite, the Fed once again suddenly decided he had somewhere to go in a hurry. "Sorry, Detective, but I've got to meet somebody. I almost forgot. I'll call you as soon as I finish talking to him."

"Hey, maybe I should tag along. Make sure you're doing things on the up and up and not praising victims who offer big rewards that could end up getting innocent people killed."

Brady didn't react to her jibe. "No need. This is a personal matter. Nothing at all to do with the case, but something I do have to take care of today."

"Okay, I guess." Hell, she didn't care where he was going if it wasn't about the case. She needed time alone. Time to think everything through. Nothing was making much sense to her. Something about the whole thing bothered her big time, including Bob Brady showing up the way he had. Things were beginning to stick in her craw, and she could not get a hold on what was what. A son suddenly cropping up out of the blue was highly suspicious and a damn good lead. She would check into that without delay.

She expected the proverbial boom to drop down on her head at any given moment. Something bad was going to happen—maybe even something terrible. It very well could be another torture-murder of another unaware victim wandering innocently around their heretofore peaceful lake. Seemed like serials always liked to strike at least twice before they crept away. And the damn reward was going to complicate everything. Maybe she needed to ask Charlie if she could call a press conference and downplay the reward somehow. Put the brakes on it. No telling what kind of crazies half a million dollars would bring bopping into town. And the paparazzi— oh God, she'd forgotten about them already being on scene. They would have a heyday with this sordid tale. And now, this guy, this Troy Edward Wood, aka Oliver Wood, was in her sights, front and center. Brady's file on him was a portrait of criminal insanity. He would be the kind of whacko who would do the kinds of cruel things that had been done to Heather Jax. If it was him, she wanted to bring him down in the worst way—and she was going to.

Claire and Brady rode downstairs together in the elevator, and she watched him head out the front doors as if on a mission of dire importance, one that didn't include her but maybe should have. Maybe he wanted to go lone wolf on the case now. Maybe he wanted all the glory for the Bureau. Maybe he and his team already knew where the bad guy was and they were going to get him right now and cut the local cops out. Who knew what that guy was up to? In that instant, she realized that she really didn't trust him, not one iota. She didn't trust anybody she'd met while investigating this case. She needed to talk it over with Bud and Harve and Black, but especially Black. She wished to hell he hadn't gone to New York.

She pulled out her phone to call him but it rang before she could. It was him. They were psychically connected, it seemed. Smiling, she picked up quickly. "Well, speak of the devil."

Momentary silence. "Can't say I like the sound of that. Am I in trouble?"

Claire only smiled. "Where are you? I need your advice on this case in the worst way. I need lots of things from you in the worst way."

"Yeah, I know that feeling. Well, you're in luck, darlin'. We're in the helicopter and almost back to Cedar Bend. Ten more minutes, say, and you can give me the welcome I deserve. Miss us much?"

"What? Are you kidding me? I thought you were staying another night."

"I wanted to get back home. I've grown accustomed to having you at my side. And I don't have a good feeling about that case you're working on. In fact, I've got a hell of a bad feeling about it. Especially after I saw Jonesy on the air this morning, offering that damn reward. You know what that means, right?"

"It means trouble. Coming in droves."

"So I want to help you solve this thing, if I can, and you'll let me. And I want to talk Jonesy out of that reward. It was a stupid decision that he made out of anger and grief. He's going to regret it. But maybe I can make him listen to reason. He usually hears me out."

"I need your input. There have been some new developments."

"Good stuff? Helpful stuff?"

"Not good enough. It just increased the mystery, as per usual in my homicides."

"Well, Rico's eager to get back and wrap the gift he bought you. You're going to like it, I believe. He picked it out himself. So where are you? Home at Cedar Bend, I hope. And I really mean that."

"I'm standing right here in the lobby. I'll meet you upstairs."

"Good. Love you. See you in a few minutes."

"Love you, too."

The line went dead and Claire clicked off. She was smiling. Couldn't help it. They were the only two good things going on in her world at the moment. Now that Bud was injured, she didn't like anybody or anything remotely connected with this damn case. She felt like she'd been winging it on her own, but now she was about to get some good backup. Black was a formidable forensic psychiatrist. He would get off big time reading Brady's file and giving her his take on it. He just loved head-examining psychotic maniacs.

Play Time

After the murder of Junior's little sissy, Junior and Lucky took time to enjoy their stay at the ultra-luxurious and comfortable Cedar Bend Lodge, where they waited for the grief show to begin. That's where they started hearing rumors about the hot detective that the hotel's owner had recently married. The security guards with whom Lucky had struck up some casual friendships informed him that she was also tough, a real super-cop, of sorts. The more they heard about her, the more Lucky thought she might turn out to be an interesting possibility for some additional fun and games. Lucky also discovered that she had been featured on the cover of the latest *National Enquirer*. Double intriguing, oh yes, sir, it sure was. Junior waited at the hotel while Lucky went out to the nearest Quick Stop and bought a copy. Once Lucky saw her wearing the yellow string bikini, he decided that all those rumors were right on target. She was as sexy as hell, and he decided he was interested in getting to know her in an anxious, erotic, and murderous sort of way.

Lucky showed the pictures to Junior. "Know what, Junior? I want me some of that. But she's gonna be all mine—hands off for you. You got to kill your dad's brat, that was your perk. She's my treat."

Junior shrugged. He was only interested in his father, and the fact that Lucky's sexy lady was the detective investigating his sister's murder. So the detective was their enemy, and she needed to be taken out of the picture without delay. Lucky, however, wasn't immediately amendable to Junior's suggestion to off her ASAP.

"No, just hold your horses, Junior. You are not to touch a hair on that pretty head of hers until I'm finished with her. I want her, and I want her under my control. You got that, bud? I want time to enjoy tying her up and subjugating her to all manner of painful stuff. I got tabs on that cop, understand? I put dibs on her right now as my next game player, and you are going to go along with me on this. You chose your sister, and I'm choosing this Claire Morgan chick. I already know exactly how I can get her: She's got this little kid living with her. I've seen him down in the lobby and in the snack bar. It appears to me he's the apple of her eye, so all we have to do is grab him first, and then bingo! She'll be putty in my hot little hands."

"Nope, way too dangerous, Lucky. She's a freakin' cop, for God's sake. She's investigating us."

"I don't care. She's got guts, from what I've heard, a real fighter. I wouldn't mind putting the screws to that husband of hers, either. As if *he's* the sexiest man alive. Give me a break. She'll find out what sexy is when I get her alone and bound up nice and tight."

Junior eventually had to agree. There was no changing Lucky's mind this time. He didn't like the idea much at all, but he had gotten the kill he wanted, and it had been an important kill for his future livelihood. Fair was fair; it was Lucky's turn. And killing the cop who was investigating them would be the same as killing two birds with one stone. He did like the sound of that.

Chapter 18

"Excuse me, Mrs. Black?"

From where she stood, awaiting the penthouse elevator, Claire spun quickly toward the voice behind her. Nobody called her that except Black and a few of his hotel employees. She figured his staff did it out of respect for him and his wishes, and she rather liked the sound of it at times, now that she had gotten used to being married. Black liked the hell out of it and didn't mind saying so.

It was the desk clerk, standing right behind her, appearing a trifle flustered. The young man's name was Jimmy Stovall. His face looked worried, and he was twisting a senior class ring on his finger, antsy as hell. Oh no, she wasn't sure she wanted to face another crisis.

"What's the matter, Jimmy?" She glanced over at the media pool, still bunched up outside the dark glass of the portico windows where Black had relegated them once they'd pushed him past his indulgent limit. Their numbers appeared larger now, probably due to Jonesy's posted reward and the newly circulated rumors that he was a guest at Cedar Bend. They were snapping pictures galore, finding her interesting while she was simply standing there minding her own business. She turned her face away, always willing and eager to ruin their shots. "Are the paparazzi giving you trouble again?"

"No, ma'am. It's just that you've got some guests out there waiting for you. They don't seem to be scheduled, and I didn't know exactly what to tell them. Dr. Black warned me that people were gonna try to get in here for unauthorized interviews, you know, and that kind of sneaky stuff. He said I was not to let anybody get anywhere near you. He said that specifically."

"Yes, and you've been doing a great job. We both appreciate it, Jimmy."

"Thank you. But those people waiting now out there seem different, you know, respectable and everything. I don't know why, but I just felt I shouldn't tell them they had to leave. I asked them to sit down by the big fireplace and I would try to get hold of you and see if you had time to speak with them."

Claire nodded. "Well, okay, that sounds good. Do you know who they are?"

"No, they didn't seem to want to give me their names. They just said it was a personal matter between you and them. They've been waiting out there for almost three hours now."

Claire peered around the lobby. "Okay. Which ones are they? It must be important if they've been waiting that long."

"They're sitting right over there. See them? The couple on the black leather sofa facing the small fireplace."

Claire found the couple quickly enough. Looked like senior citizens. Both had on matching red and green plaid sweaters and jeans and snow boots. They had short white hair but looked relatively young for the ages she suspected they actually were. She couldn't imagine who they were or what they wanted with her. Surely they weren't reporters or photographers in disguises; they definitely did not look as if they were up to chasing celebrities and notorious detectives or psychiatrists around town in order to sell embarrassing photos to tabloids. On the other hand, stranger things had happened. It was a crazy world. Claire knew that only too well.

"And they didn't say what they wanted? No hint at all?"

"Well, first they wanted to speak to Dr. Black, if and when he was available. When I told them he was out of town, they asked to speak to you."

Claire decided the couple had gotten lucky. Black would show up at the hotel any minute now. She had a feeling they might be outpatients still under his care, or at the lodge to visit one of his in-house patients down in the bungalows. "Okay, they look harmless enough. I'll go talk to them. Black's coming in early on the chopper. Right now, as a matter of fact."

"I'm sorry, ma'am. I didn't know if it was my place to ask them questions. You know, I felt like it might not be any of my business, but they were very nice and polite so I thought I should ask you what to do about them."

"It's okay. Don't worry about it."

On the other hand, Claire became a tad concerned as she made her way across the busy lobby. Christmas music was playing, and people were there for the free cookies and hot apple cider. She glanced again at the media hounds. They were crowded around the big, jewel-beveled front door now, trying their best to get good photos of her. Every camera was focused solely on her movements. It was unnerving. What the devil was the matter with those people? She wasn't even that famous. They were like leeches hanging on to her skin. She really did hate them, each and every one. But at least they couldn't get to her, not without getting thrown back out for their efforts.

"Hello," she said, stopping in front of the elderly couple. "I'm Claire Morgan Black. May I help you with something? My husband's out of town but he's returning shortly. If there's a problem with your accommodations or you need an appointment to see him, I can make sure that someone helps you with that."

The two guests practically jumped to their feet. They appeared to be overjoyed. At least, that's what Claire took from their delighted faces. Maybe they were paparazzi in disguise, after all. The man held out his hand, and Claire took it. He squeezed her fingers, gave her a firm shake and a warm smile. He looked even more ecstatic, which made Claire über-wary. He cut right to the chase, not one to twiddle his thumbs, it seemed. "We're Rico's grandparents, Mrs. Black. Mr. and Mrs. Warren Hammons. We've come to take him back home with us."

Claire's entire body went to stone in a matter of seconds. Her heart felt as if it had turned to granite and then spiraled right down to slam on the floor. She tried her best to muster a smile, but couldn't quite bring it all the way off. Down deep inside, she felt a curious streak of fear, or maybe it was devastation. Secretly, she had been hoping all along that Black wouldn't turn up Rico's relatives. She suddenly realized that she wanted that boy to stay and live with them in the worst way imaginable. Black wanted it even more than she did. But now that dream was dead and swept away. Here they were in the flesh, come to get him back, looking like a perfectly acceptable pair of guardians who loved him dearly and were so excited that they'd found him.

They were looking at her eagerly now. Oh God, it was just going to kill Black. She forced a smile but felt sick to her stomach. "Very nice to meet you, Mr. and Mrs. Hammons. Please, won't you come upstairs to the penthouse? My husband and Rico happen to be on their way home right now. They should arrive here any moment."

That caused a new rush of glee, and happy chatter about all the Christmas gifts they'd brought along for Rico and how much they'd missed him, all of which Claire barely listened to. All she could think about was the awful look Black was going to get on his face when he realized who they were and what they wanted.

Claire attempted small talk in the elevator but didn't pull it off so hot. Neither of them seemed to notice. She made them comfortable in the living room and ordered up a tray of coffee and Christmas cookies and pumpkin bread from the restaurant.

Black and Rico arrived about fifteen minutes later. She heard the roar of the helicopter and mentally braced herself. She had been trying to call and text Black, but he hadn't picked up. Probably could not hear over the noise of the rotors. She sat back and smiled as the Hammonses happily chatted her up, all the while waiting with a knot of dread building up inside her chest.

* * * *

Nicholas Black rode up to the penthouse by way of his office elevator. Rico was carrying shopping bags in both hands, more than eager to see Claire and regale her with all the fun they'd had in New York. Black was anxious to see her, too—that was never going to change. He simply hated being away from her, even overnight. Always had, always would. Rico ran ahead of him down the hallway of the office wing and veered right into the doorway of their private living quarters. Black followed, pulling out his phone to check his messages. Before he could read them, he heard unfamiliar voices from down the hall somewhere. He stopped in his tracks at the living room archway, surprised to find Claire sitting inside and entertaining guests. Claire often had her friends up, but these two were complete strangers.

They were older, neatly dressed, and both were smiling as if they'd just heard the most fantastic news in the world. The minute Rico saw them, he skidded to an abrupt stop, looked momentarily shocked, and then dropped all the bags and ran straight into their arms. They gathered him up between them, all three crying and laughing at the same time. In that instant, Black knew exactly who they were and why they were there. His regard moved over to Claire, who looked absolutely sick at heart. She shook her head, and Black just stood there in the doorway watching their happy reunion. They were members of Rico's family. They had to be. And they had to have come there to take him away, take him home with them—which was where he probably belonged. Black forced down a hard swallow and tried to hide his disappointment. It wasn't easy. Claire wasn't even trying to hide her feelings.

Moving over to where she sat on the couch, he put his hand on her shoulder and squeezed. She looked as if she was about to cry but was trying hard to hold it back. Black felt like that's what he needed to do. Rico was bawling and hiding his face in the woman's shoulder as he clutched them both around their necks. They were sobbing, too. It was damn hard to watch, as Rico suddenly started blurting out all the terrible things that had happened to him the summer before, including how he'd witnessed his parents murdered in cold blood on that veritable stronghold on that godforsaken Sicilian cliff. He hadn't said much about it of late, had finally stopped waking up with nightmares about the evil that had invaded his home, taken his parents, and put him through his own kind of hell on earth.

But his terror was back now, ratcheted up into high gear and coming out in a trembling voice and shaky tears. His grandmother pulled him onto her lap, patting his back and consoling him and doing a damn good job of it. Black watched her rocking the boy and whispering how much they both loved him and how happy they were to find him at last. Black felt his chest begin to constrict, an overwhelming sadness that he hadn't experienced in a long time, because he knew what was coming next. He knew exactly what was going to happen. He felt a curious mix of misery for him and Claire, but happiness for the three people reuniting across the room.

After a moment of watching them, Black walked across the room. He smiled. "Hello. I'm Nicholas Black. I take it from all these happy tears that you are Rico's grandparents."

The man stood up. "Yes, I'm Warren Hammons, Rico's grandfather. His mother was our only daughter. This is my wife, Sally."

Black nodded politely at Sally Hammons. She smiled through her tears, but kept clutching Rico as if she'd never let go of him again. *Claire and I are going to have to give him up*, Black thought. The idea cut his heart like a switchblade. "I've been searching for you. I had no luck whatsoever," he told them.

"We live up in Canada now. Toronto suburbs. Our daughter warned us about the Soquets and what they were capable of, right before she went into hiding on that island. We've been trying our best to find out what happened to them. We assumed they were all dead, and pretty much mourned their deaths. Now we know." She hugged Rico tighter, tears filling her eyes.

"Please, sit down," Black said. "I think we've got a lot to talk about."

They sat down with Rico on his grandmother's lap, and silence dropped down around them. The atmosphere quickly became uncomfortable. Mrs. Hammons was the first one to speak. "We thought Rico was gone as well, but then we saw those photos of him. A few days ago, I was just standing in the checkout line at Loblaws market and caught sight of those pictures of you, Mrs. Black, you know, the ones on the cover of the *National Enquirer*. I don't know why I picked it up or why I thumbed through the pages the way I did—I usually hold those types of tabloids as trash. I guess my angels were guiding my hands, because I saw Rico standing on that beach with you in Hawaii. I knew it was him instantly. I knew he was still alive and well and being taken good care of. So we immediately made arrangements to fly here and see if it really could be him, and our prayers have been answered."

Rico's arms tightened around her neck. He had stopped crying but seemed unwilling to let go of her. Black sat down on the couch beside Claire and picked up her hand. She was trying her best to look happy for them but it wasn't coming off so well. His attempt probably wasn't either, truth be told.

"We want to thank you for taking such good care of him," Mr. Hammons was telling them now. "He looks so good and healthy and apparently he's very happy living here with the two of you."

"He is a pleasure to have around, that's for sure," Black told them. "Rico's a good boy. No one could ask for a better kid than Rico. Right, Claire?"

"Yes, he's really special."

At Claire's remark, Rico quickly sat up on his grandmother's lap and stared over at Claire and Black. His eyes were still wet from his happy tears, but they both saw the moment that his own realization struck him, about why his grandparents had come there. His glad expression faded quickly, and he looked as conflicted as they felt. He stood up and ran over and pressed himself into Black's embrace. He started crying again. Black tried to pull off a smile—didn't come off so well. "Hey now, it's okay, Rico. We're happy that your family's finally found you. You know that I've been searching for them. I told you that I was looking everywhere."

"I don't wanna go with them," he mumbled against Black's shoulder. "Except that I do, too."

"I know. Sure I do. I know how you love all of us. But don't worry about that right now. Let's just be glad they're here and you get to see them again."

Rico wept against Black's shoulder for a few moments. His grandparents had grown sober, their expressions worried. Everyone was realizing what was going to happen. Nobody wanted anything to ever be difficult for Rico again. But this decision was going to be awful for him to make, and they all knew it.

"Have you been here at the lake very long?" Claire asked the Hammons, trying to break the silence.

"No, we just arrived this afternoon. We landed in Kansas City and rented a car." They both were trying to smile, but their attention was riveted on Rico where he sat on Black's lap.

"Then you must stay here at Cedar Bend," Black told them. "Claire and I would love to provide you with a suite for as long as you'd like to stay. Let it be our Christmas present to you."

That perked up Rico a bit. He sat up and looked across the room. "Yes, Memo, you can stay here for Christmas! That would be awesome! I can show you around, Papa. There's lots for us to do here at the hotel."

Then he got up and walked back over to them, smiling, happy again.

Mr. Hammons looked at Black. "Well, actually, we were hoping we could take Rico out tonight for dinner and maybe a bit of Christmas shopping. You know, to get reacquainted, and such as that."

"Yeah, Papa, I can show you around the lake. This is a real neat place to live. I know how to fish for bass now, and I can catch them, too."

"We have several good restaurants here on the grounds, as well as some gift shops," Black suggested. "Our treat, if you should decide to visit them."

Mr. Hammons smiled. "Well, we sort of wanted some time alone with our grandson here. It's been such a long time since we've seen him."

"Of course," Claire said quickly. "We understand completely."

They chatted some more. The Hammonses had lots of baby pictures of Rico that they'd brought along, as well as some happy family portraits of him with his parents. They had a copy of his birth certificate and every other kind of document that Black would need to see as proof that Rico was truly their grandson. More than enough.

"Okay, if you're sure it's all right, we'd like to take him out."

"Of course. Rico, it's okay if you want to go shopping with them," Black told the boy. "Claire and I will be fine right here."

The child nodded and gave them a big, bright smile. "Okay, but we're coming back here tonight, aren't we?" he asked his grandparents. "They'll be missing me if we don't. And Harve will, too. He's my best friend now."

"We sure will, sweetie, we'll come right back here after we eat and do some shopping. We'll check in before we leave," his grandmother told him and then gave him another tight squeeze.

"Don't worry about that," Black said. "I'll arrange everything for you. Just go to the desk when you come back and ask for the key to your suite."

They left a few minutes later, holding hands in a swirl of excited talk and memories and easy laughter. Claire and Black sat silently together after the elevator doors had whispered closed down the hall. He looked at Claire. She was trying her level best to look positive, probably more for his benefit than anything else. That's what she usually did when she thought he was hurt or upset.

"C'mon, Black. You look as though you've lost your last friend."

"So do you. But that's how we feel. No use in denying it."

"I know."

"They're going to want him back."

"I know."

"I don't want to lose him."

"I don't either."

Black pulled her into his arms and held her close. He laid his cheek on top of her head, sighing. "He'll want to go home with them, you know. Once he gets used to the idea."

"He can come see us."

"Yeah."

But they were both sick with the kind of loss that penetrated their hearts. They sat there together, and Black hugged her closer. Neither of them cried, but both of them wanted to.

Chapter 19

Special Agent Brady arrived at Cedar Bend the next afternoon right before three o'clock, punctual as usual. Claire met him in the lobby, and they rode up to the rock star's suite and escorted a quiet and subdued Jonesy Jax down to the back lobby. He was dressed appropriately in a dark suit, white shirt, and gray and white tie, with a black winter raincoat. Showing respect for his daughter. Something Claire had not totally expected to see from him, but it was a nice thing. Maybe Black had been right about the guy. Maybe there was more to Jonesy Jax than she had figured. At the rear exterior door, Claire explained to him where the paparazzi were lurking and pulled up the hood on his coat to hide his identity, and then she did the same thing for herself. Jonesy pulled out a pair of expensive sunglasses and pushed them on as they made their way down the snowy sidewalk to Brady's Ford Fusion.

Photographers lined the barricade about forty yards across the lawn but didn't seem to recognize the famous rock star—and thank goodness for that. When they saw him and realized he was outside, absolute hell was going to break loose and send Cedar Bend Lodge, the lake, and all its inhabitants into a world of hurt. It was exactly the kind of thing that Claire and Brady did not need to deal with.

Once inside the car, Jonesy hunkered down in the back seat and tried to make himself invisible as they headed off to the morgue for one very unpleasant task. Fun, fun—not really. Zero, in fact. That's the only kind that Claire seemed to be having lately, anyway.

It was not a good time for her or anyone that she knew. Black was still acting like he was fine and happy the Hammonses had shown up, but he wasn't fooling her. He was down in the dumps right alongside her, a situation

Claire had rarely seen. Rico was now spending every waking moment with his beloved Memo and Papa. Black and Claire had seen very little of him since they'd arrived—he had even spent the night in their suite. But Black had always been the kind of guy who recognized the writing on the wall when he saw it. A man as emotional as Jonesy Jax, on the other hand, was going to have a hard time identifying his dead daughter's body without going to pieces—that was the understatement of the year.

They negotiated slick streets and light snowfall in hushed silence until they finally pulled into the medical examiner's parking lot. Brady chose a parking space at the end of the building, a good distance from the front door, for some reason that Claire couldn't fathom. Maybe he liked to slide around on slick sidewalks until he fell and broke his arm. Maybe he was prolonging Jonesy's emotional breakdown out of personal dread. As soon as Brady killed the motor, Claire turned around and looked at the heretofore crazy ass rock star. Now he looked absolutely as white as a brand-new percale sheet, fresh out of the package. His eyes were glazed over with either tranquilizers or fear, probably both. He looked as if he was going to keel over right there and sob his heart out. But then, as she nodded to him, he straightened his shoulders, took a deep breath, and said, "Okay, let's get this thing over with. Please. I have to do it. For her. But I'd rather jump into hell with both feet."

A good analogy, and pretty much what he was about to do. Claire felt for him, she really did. "Okay, Mr. Jax, but first, let me tell you how it's going to go down inside the office. That okay with you?"

"Yes," he answered, but his sick expression told her that he just might throw up whatever pills he'd swallowed that morning.

"You will view your daughter's remains through a screened window from an outside hallway. The morgue assistant, Johnny Becker, will fold back the sheet covering her head, only enough to allow you to identify her. You won't be able to see anything but her face. The process will only take a moment, and then it will be over. He will cover her again, and the blinds will be closed. Do you understand? Is that procedure all right with you?"

Jonesy just nodded. "I don't want to do this. I don't want to go in there and see her. I don't think I can." Claire and Brady looked at each other, then turned back to the grieving father, who continued in a shaky voice. "But I know I have to. I owe it to poor little Heather and to myself to do the right thing."

Claire really felt sorry for the guy. He was crushed, beaten down to a mere replica of his usual bold, abrasive self. "We do understand how hard this is, Mr. Jax. We do. I promise you that. You can take all the time you need with her, if you should choose to. Or you can just look, identify her, and we'll take you home. We are here to help you get through this."

Jonesy broke down and began sobbing again. Claire's heart clutched, because she knew exactly how he felt. Her low regard for the man in the back seat had certainly taken a one-eighty. He was okay under all that stupid showmanship, it appeared. He was suffering now, and suffering brutally, and it was difficult for her to watch. She'd be glad when it was over and she could concentrate her energy on finding that young woman's killer.

"Okay then, let's just do it," she said after a few minutes.

The three of them just sat there, unmoving. Claire was waiting for Jonesy to pull the back door handle and exit the car. Brady said nothing, but a glance told her that he was nervous. Jonesy looked at Claire and wiped away more tears with a clean white handkerchief. "I appreciate your kindness, Mrs. Black. So much. Believe me when I say that."

Claire nodded. "Fifteen minutes from now? It will all be over."

"Okay, Claire. Put your hands on the dash, and don't try anything stupid."

At first, Claire didn't gather what Brady was talking about. She looked at him, and then she looked at the small weapon he held in his right hand. It looked like a tranquilizer dart gun, the kind they used on wild animals. He was pointing it at her chest.

Jonesy sat up straighter. "Hey, what the hell—"

Brady turned quickly and shot a dart into Jonesy's chest, then quickly swiveled back to Claire. He hastily inserted another dart. That's when Claire reacted, trying to knock his gun hand aside with her left hand as she scratched inside her coat for her Glock, but she wasn't quite fast enough. The dart hit her in the side of her neck. She jerked it out about the same time she got her weapon out, but not fast enough to pull the trigger. Brady grabbed her gun arm, and the drug hit her hard and fast. All she saw was a flash of white light and a blur of reality—then there was nothing.

Play Time

Lucky backed his newly purchased Ford out of the parking space at the front of the Canton County morgue, maneuvered his way out to the street, and then turned left and headed toward the millhouse. Claire Morgan was slumped unconscious in the passenger's seat beside him, and Junior's soon-to-be-dead daddy was sprawled across the back seat. The animal tranquilizer had acted fast, but that's why they'd chosen it. He really hadn't meant to shoot them until after Jonesy identified his daughter's body, but he could not resist the temptation. It had been the perfect time and place. Nobody around. No cars on the street. No witnesses, whatsoever. Nobody knew what time they'd arrived, or if they had arrived at all. There were no windows at the front of the morgue, just the front door, which had no windows. No traffic passing by on such a cold and snowy afternoon, and it was soon to be dark. Anything could have gone wrong inside with the medical examiner and his staff, so he had acted on impulse. But he had always been good at choosing the right move at the right time. Yep, good timing was everything, and he had developed a real knack for it. Always had it, really. Rarely had it turned out to be an ill-conceived action for him.

Reaching over, he pulled the tough and suspicious detective over toward him and down below the window where nobody would spot her. He reached over again and got the Glock still in her hand. She had gotten to it fast, but not fast enough. She had not come out the winner this time around, but he had no doubt she'd shoot him point-blank if she came to with a weapon in her hand. She was a worthy adversary, and he had better remember that.

Lucky drove until he reached the gravel road that led out into the woods. He laughed softly when he took the turn. "Man alive, this is just going great. Junior is going to be pleased as punch, all right. His daddy and the detective, both in one fell swoop." Awesome, man, he was awesome.

He couldn't blame Claire for being so gullible. It wasn't her fault. It was Sheriff Charles Ramsay's fault. Everything Lucky had given him had looked legitimate, but was only an illusion. Special Agent Bob Brady was a real FBI agent, oh yeah, he sure was, one that had been hot on their trail. That is, until about a week ago when they'd caught him sneaking around the mill. They had captured him easily enough, then they'd put him through their own special kind of ringer until he spilled his guts and told them everything they needed to know about his case against them.

Lucky smiled to himself. Brady had been investigating them for years, alerted to Heather Jax's death by the dog tag found inside her. He had been suspicious of Junior and Lucky both, but Lucky had been his main target. He'd left his thick FBI file on Lucky's homicidal childhood inside the trunk of his car, labeled with his real name, Troy Edward Wood. It had been a godsend for their plans, and Lucky had jumped at the chance to impersonate him.

All Lucky had to do was don the badge and show up at Ramsay's office with that extremely incriminating file. Lucky chose only the photographs that did not look like him and destroyed the others. He didn't look the same anymore, anyway: he was bigger and buffer and his hair was dark, but he still didn't take that chance. He told the sheriff the truth, albeit Bob Brady's story of chasing two murderers across the country. Lucky was in on the case against him and Junior. It was the most delicious ruse that he'd ever played, and he'd played a lot. He was a good actor and a good liar and could fool the best of them.

Claire Morgan had been suspicious at first, more so than most of his rubes had been in the past, he'd give her that, but she'd had no recourse but to work with him. She'd been ordered to. When he'd run down her partner in front of Games Galore, he hadn't realized what a serendipitous snap decision it would turn out to be. He had wanted to kill his big brother, Oliver, who was also out to get him for killing their mother. Oliver got away; he hadn't seen him since. It worried him, but not too much. They wouldn't hang around long after they killed Jonesy and the detective.

Best of all? He now had Claire Morgan at his disposal, to do with whatever he wanted. She was going to be a fun captive. She would not bend easily, and those were the kinds of victims he liked best. In just a little while, she was going to be very sorry she'd gone after Junior and him so hard. Sorry she'd trusted a false Bob Brady, too. He had looked forward to having her under his control since the first minute he'd seen her photograph in that tabloid.

And Lucky was going to have her to himself, because Junior would only have eyes for his daddy. Both of them were in for a special treat today. Claire Morgan and Jonesy Jax. Two prime catches, both well-known and notorious. Real notches on his belt. He was still grinning when he turned and drove up the deserted gravel road that led to their millhouse lair. He could barely wait for the moment their two newest victims would wake up and find out what hot water they were in. Wow, the things they were going to do with these two poor souls. Lucky got shivers all over, just thinking about the hours of fun he was about to enjoy.

Chapter 20

Smiling, about as happy as he'd ever been, Rico strolled along between his Memo and Papa on the sidewalk of a big outdoor mall. They were all holding hands, both of his grandparents, one on each side of him. He was a little old for them to be hanging on to him like he was a little kid or something, but he didn't say anything. He still couldn't believe they had showed up, just like that. When Nick and Claire couldn't find them no matter how hard they looked—and they were really good at finding people—Rico had given up on ever seeing his grandparents again. He'd got to thinking that they'd been murdered like his mom and dad.

But here they were, and just because they'd seen those pictures of Claire that Black didn't like so much. They were right here with him and he was so excited about it that it was hard to stop grinning. Sometimes, though, he'd think about it and feel sort of bad, too, especially if he had to leave the lake and all his friends. The more he thought about leaving Cedar Bend, the more upset he became. He didn't know what to do about it, either.

Memo and Papa were just so happy to see him. He could see that, for sure, how pleased they were. They looked older than they had before, but it had been a long time since Rico and his parents left California to go hide in that witness protection program on that island. Memo told him that her hair turned white when they thought Rico was lost somewhere and they would never find him. He wasn't so sure about that, though. It wasn't all the way white, anyway. It still had lots of brown in it.

So far tonight they'd gone into lots of different stores, especially toy stores and department stores, anywhere that he wanted to go, really. All he had to do was ask, and they'd do it. That's how glad they were to see him. They'd bought him lots of stuff, too, just about anything he said he liked. That was awesome, and then they'd taken him to eat at McDonald's when he'd wanted a Big Mac meal. Memo sat close beside him in the booth, and Papa sat across from them, smiling the entire time. They just kept up that smiling and smiling, and laughing some, and Rico did, too, but now, inside his head, he was feeling awfully worried about things. Now he didn't know what to do or what he really wanted.

If he left the lake to live with his grandparents, which is pretty much what they wanted him to do, then they were going to take him back to Canada and live in some big city called Toronto. But what about Claire and Nick? He'd never get to see them. Canada was up north, a whole different country. Thinking about that made him feel pretty bad. He loved Claire and Nick. He loved living with them. But he loved his Memo and Papa, too. He loved them all the same: a lot.

After they left McDonald's, Memo decided they should stop one last time at a different mall and buy Claire and Nick a gift for taking such good care of him all this time. Rico had been telling them how good they'd treated him since they'd been together, but he couldn't really think of anything to buy them because Claire and Black already had a whole lot of neat stuff. Just about everything anybody could want, really. Especially Nick. They were pretty darn rich, he guessed.

"They like pictures," he finally suggested as they browsed around Macy's. "You know, pictures of me, and of them, and of the places we go together. When we lived out there on that island called Kauai for a while, Nick took lots of pictures of us. Even Harve got to go with us. He's real nice. I helped him decorate his tree."

"Really? Tell us about Harve," said Papa.

"He's lots of fun. He's got to sit in a wheelchair all the time, you know, to get around and stuff. He used to be a policeman in Los Angeles with Claire. He takes me fishing all the time. That's his favorite thing to do. He taught me how to use a spinner bait and purple plastic worms when we want to catch bass, and all kinds of stuff like that. It's always fun when I get to be with him."

"Well, that's good. I'm glad you have such a good friend here."

Rico smiled at his Papa.

"Yes, we saw those pictures of you out in Hawaii in the magazines," Memo was telling him. "That's how we found out where you were. We were just so thrilled to see that you were safe and sound. It's a miracle, isn't it, sweetheart?"

Rico nodded and followed her down the aisle while she kept looking for more things to buy. She finally decided to get Claire and Black some pretty silver picture frames, and she asked Rico to help her choose which ones they'd like the best. Rico told her it would be good if she added a big package of Snickers to put with those frames because Claire liked those candy bars a lot, and maybe then she could get some yellow legal pads because Nick was always writing stuff down on them. They said of course they would. It was fun, really, being with them again, at least until he remembered that he'd probably have to leave Cedar Bend and the special bedroom that Nick had fixed up with all the Star Wars wallpaper and posters and stuff. He was going to get his own room at Claire's new cabin, too, as soon as the carpenters were completely done with it. But when he left, he wouldn't even see them anymore. Not very often, anyway. He felt the burn of tears for a second time that night, but he turned his head away and didn't let his grandparents see that he was real sad, too, even when he was so happy.

When they were finished shopping in the mall, they stopped outside on the parking lot, where a big winter carnival was in full swing. There were lots of booths with sparkling Christmas lights and people all bundled up in parkas and caps and carolers strolling around and singing to everybody. There was a big Ferris wheel, and a Tilt-a-Whirl, and all kinds of other rides. It was really crowded, lots of shoppers bundled up in the cold, eating at picnic tables. They mingled awhile and watched the rides. It was fun. Papa rode on the swings with him, and Memo rode on the Ferris wheel with him but she said she didn't like it much. They gave Rico some money to buy cotton candy for all of them, and he ran up to the booth and stood in line for a long time. There were people everywhere.

Once he finally got the cotton candy and had Papa's change in his hand, he started back toward the table. Halfway there, he stopped in his tracks when a big guy suddenly stepped out from the shadows and grabbed his arm. Rico was shocked; then the man jerked him back into the dark and pressed a big gun against his neck. Then Rico reacted as he'd learned to do when he'd been held captive on the island. He lurched away as hard as he could and let out a yell for help, but then he felt something sharp jab into his neck and everything started getting all woozy and dizzy and he stumbled and fell on his knees. The man caught him before he hit the concrete, and then he only knew that somebody was carrying him through the dark, away from the carnival and his grandparents, and there was nothing he could do about it. Then he fell asleep and couldn't even worry about it anymore.

When Rico came to later, he couldn't think straight at first. He was lying on his back in a truck or a van. They were moving fast, and the vehicle was shimmying around and rocking back and forth as it barreled its way down some kind of rocky road. He could hear the gravel crunching and flying up under the wheels and hitting the fenders. There were lots of odors around him, too, motor oil for one thing, and some kind of paint maybe, and some really strong cigarette smoke all mingled together. He lay still once he was able to think straight, and then he slowly tested his arms and legs and found that he wasn't bound with ropes or tape or anything. That's when he took a couple of deep breaths and played like he was asleep. Rico had learned to do that the hard way when those mean people had him. The redheaded woman had tied him up and treated him like her pet dog. He wasn't going to let them tie him up. He was going to get away.

After Claire and Black had rescued him and brought him back to America, Nick spent lots of time talking to him about what he'd gone through, and he always told Rico that he should stay calm and think things through if anything like that ever happened to him again. Nick told him that he was a real smart kid, and very brave, that he had proved it. He said that Rico could deal with anything bad that ever happened to him, because he'd already survived the worst thing anyone could live through.

So Rico pushed away some of the scary feelings ballooning up inside him and moved his hand slowly down to his coat pocket where he kept his cell phone. It was gone. They already took it. That made him panic some, and his heart sped up but he forced himself to lie still. He thought about what he should do next. He tried to figure out what Claire and Black would do, because they were both really brave people and they'd been through a lot of bad stuff, just like him. Then he went over a plan in his head a bunch of times before he worked up the courage to even move an inch. Once he was ready, he opened his eyes just a little bit and tried to see the man who'd grabbed him.

It looked as if they were riding in a van without windows. He could see the front seat and the windshield and the guy driving. Rico could see the man's face reflected in the rearview mirror. He had on black glasses and had really short dark hair. Rico had never seen him before; he wasn't the one who kidnapped him.

He was driving hard and fast and causing all the jouncing and bouncing. He had a cigarette hanging out of the corner of his mouth. The guy who'd caught him at the carnival was in the back of the van, sitting on the floor right across from him. His back was leaning against the opposite wall and he was looking down at the cell phone in his hand, the pale glow of the screen lighting up his face. Maybe that was Rico's phone. Maybe he could get it back and then he could call Nick. The guy who'd grabbed him was a big guy, sort of, but not near as big and strong as Nick. Not as tall, either. The black ski cap he'd worn at the carnival was now pushed up on top of his head. He wasn't paying a bit of attention to Rico. Maybe he thought Rico was gonna be asleep for a long time and scared to death when he woke up. But Nick had been right. After those bad people last summer, this didn't seem as awful as all that. Not yet, anyway. He wasn't even tied up, and nobody had put a shock collar on him the way the mean lady had done. He hated her so much. Even now that she was dead, he couldn't stop hating her. He knew it was wrong to hate her so much, but he did. He hated her brother and her father, too, even if they were all dead and could never hurt him again, like Claire always said.

So Rico lay real still and quiet and didn't move a single muscle, but his mind was busy figuring stuff out. He turned his head a little and searched the back of the van, looking for something he could use as a weapon. Then he saw a heavy tire iron that was rolling back and forth with the sway of the van. If he could reach it—and he was pretty sure he could—he could hit the man with the phone, slide back the door, and get away. Nick had been teaching him how to box and where to hit a bad guy if anybody ever attacked him again. Nick said it was important to be able to defend yourself, no matter how young or small you were. He said that even if Rico was just a little kid, he could take care of himself, that he'd already proved that. He taught him some karate stuff, too, but Rico wasn't good at that yet. He sure couldn't take down some big guy. But he could hit him in the head with that tire iron, all right. It looked heavy enough to knock him out. He had to knock him out, too, or he'd just catch him again and be mad about getting hit in the head. So that's what he had to do: get that tire iron and knock that guy out with it. Then maybe the driver would throw on the brakes and Rico could get out the door before they could stop him. It was a pretty good plan, he had to admit.

Still, he was a little bit afraid to try it, so he lay there some more, trembling with nerves. He was scared to hit the man really hard, but knew he had to. Nick would want him to do that and try to get away, he was pretty sure. Outside the front windshield, he could see that it was dark, so it was still night outside. Snow was coming down and slanting straight into the windshield and making the wipers slap back and forth real hard. He was pretty sure they were out in the country somewhere, still traveling fast down a dark road. There were no streetlights or buildings or houses or anything lit up that would mean that other people were around. His neck stung pretty badly where the needle had gone in, but he tried to ignore all that.

Rico waited some more, wishing he didn't have to hit anybody with that tire iron, but he couldn't just lie there and do nothing. He didn't know where the men were taking him, but he knew they probably were going to hurt him when they got there, so he had to do something. He had to get away right now, and then call Claire and Nick so they could help him. He had to get that phone back. Claire was going to be so mad at these guys. She was going to find them and put them in jail, but he had to get away from them first and let her know where he was so she could come pick him up, and fast.

The van hit a pothole and the whole vehicle lurched violently to one side. That's when Rico sucked it up and made his move. He rolled over onto his stomach as if he'd been flung there by the swerving van and got hold of the tire iron in his right fist. Grabbing a good, firm grip on it, he looked at the guy in the back with him. He was sitting very close now, telling the driver to quit sliding around and drive slower. Rico jumped up onto his knees, lunged toward his captor, and swung the heavy bar with both hands as hard as he could. It struck the left side of the guy's head, but the man had seen it coming and managed to lunge sideways enough to fend off the force of the blow. But Rico had managed to get him good enough in the temple to knock him sideways onto his back.

When the driver heard the scuffle going on in back, he stomped the brakes, and Rico and his captor got slammed hard into the back of the front seat. The man groaned, holding his injured head with one hand, but he managed to grab hold of the back of Rico's parka with his other one. Rico jerked away from him and scrambled to find the phone on the floor. He found it by the glow on the screen, grabbed it, and lunged toward the door.

Rico knew what he had to do, and he didn't hesitate for one second. He grabbed the door handle and slid the door all the way open. It hit the end of the track with a loud bang, and the driver lurched to a skidding stop. Rico held on for dear life as the van slid on the ice for a few seconds, and then he leaped out into the darkness. He landed in a big snowbank that the snowplows must have left on the side of the road, then he scrambled up over it and down into a ditch on the other side. It was covered with ice and he felt the breath knocked out of him when he hit the hard surface on his stomach. He rolled over onto his back and gasped for air. He'd hurt his knee on the snowbank. The van was still running; he could hear the motor idling. Then he heard the driver yelling—it sounded like he was coming after Rico.

Really scared now, Rico pushed himself onto his belly and scrambled up the other side of the ditch until he could duck under some snowy bushes.

An avalanche of icy snow poured down on top of him and got into the neck of his coat and into his mouth and eyes. He was so cold now that he was shivering and shaking all over. He was way out in the middle of nowhere. It was pitch black outside and super cold and deep snow covered everything around him. He could hear the little ice pellets popping on the back of his parka so he knew the snow had turned into sleet. He crawled deeper under the thick brush on his hands and knees.

Breathless and terrified that the men would catch him, he kept stopping and looking behind him. The driver had a flashlight out now. He was shining it under the trees where Rico was, so Rico hit the ground and lay down flat and kept a death grip on the cell phone. The trees around him were close together, with lots of saplings and bushes and rocks and boulders around them, all of it icy and frozen, but there were some patches underneath the bushes where the snow hadn't fallen through the tangled, dead vegetation. It looked like a deep, dark tunnel that he could maybe crawl through, one that might hide him and his footprints from the bad guys. He could hear them shouting back and forth to each other now. They sounded mad at each other—really mad. They were coming after him now, and moving faster than he was. He had to hurry up and get going!

Panting, his breath pluming out in the frigid air, Rico forced himself to remain calm, just like Nick had taught him. *Take a deep breath, calm down, and think about what you have to do.* He halted every few minutes and took some more of those deep breaths. He was pretty sure he could hide from the two men if his tracks didn't give him away, for a little while anyway. He had done that plenty of times on the island when he got loose and hid in the underground tunnels. And he had a phone this time. He could call Nick and Claire and they'd grab their guns and come right out there and get him. And they'd get those bad guys chasing him, too, just like last time.

After a few minutes of rapid combat crawling, he stopped moving and listened. That's when he heard the van start up out on the road. That shocked him a little bit. Had they given up already? Were they just leaving him out there? He smiled a little, hopeful, but scared, too. Maybe they were afraid and wanted to get away before they got caught. One of them could still be coming after him, right behind him, getting closer and closer in the cold darkness.

Still shivering, he opened the phone. He pulled off his gloves and punched in Claire's number. Nothing happened. His heart fell—there was no service out this far in the woods. There were no bars at the top of the screen. He started moving along again, keeping under the bushes and trying to call home every few minutes. Nothing happened. He finally stopped, sat up on his knees, and tried to think what he should do next. He had to find somewhere to get warm. He was really, really cold now, and kinda wet. Maybe he could find a house nearby. Maybe there would be people who lived there who might help him and let him use their phone. He had to keep going until he found a house; he'd just have to help himself get there until Claire and Nick could find him. And they would. He knew they would. They were like that. They always knew what to do. Both of them.

Chapter 21

"So how's Claire taking all this?"

Nick Black looked across his desk at John Booker. Booker was Black's best friend, and his private investigator when he needed somebody he could trust. Right now, he was filling Booker in on the Hammons couple. Black wanted an in-depth background check on both husband and wife before he would even consider turning Rico over into their care. He thought they were okay, but he was going to make damn sure.

"You know Claire, Book. She's not saying much yet, but she doesn't want to lose Rico any more than I do."

"You think these people have ulterior motives for coming for the boy?"

"No, not really. I just want to make sure they are legitimate relatives and good people who'll love him the way we do. I've got money, and some people will do lots of things to get hold of some of it. They could be here to make a deal. Like I said, I don't think that's the case, but we'll have to wait and see. What I want you to find out is if they're really who they say they are, if their story stacks up the way they laid it out for us. You need to make sure they aren't involved in any illegal dealings or drugs or criminal activities, either now or in their past. You find anything like that, it's a deal-breaker and they'll never get their hands on Rico. Like I said, my gut's telling me they're perfectly clean. But Rico is not going off with complete strangers that I know nothing about. You need to get up to Toronto now and check out everything about them. If they're on the up and up, then I'll probably have no choice but to let him go back to Canada with them."

Booker gazed at him a moment. "Does he even want to?"

"We haven't really had time to discuss that with him yet. He's been with the Hammonses most of the time since they arrived here. He ought to be home soon. Then Claire and I have got to sit down and talk to him about what is coming up the pike, what his choices are and what's the best thing for him."

"You don't look so thrilled about any of this, my friend."

"I'm not happy about it, but how I feel doesn't matter in the long term. It's what's in Rico's best interest that counts. It's about what's going to make him happy."

"Personally, I don't see him wanting to ever leave here. Not with them, or anybody else. I've seen how much he loves you two. He's happy with you."

"I hope to hell you're right. But he loves them, too. They are his Memo and Papa, and that's something we can't take away from them, or him."

When Black's cell vibrated, he quickly picked it up. Caller ID told him it was Buckeye Boyd, Canton County's medical examiner. Whatever he wanted, it couldn't be good. He was Claire's colleague, and he'd never once called Black, not that he could remember.

"This is Nick Black."

"Is Claire there with you?"

The shaky tone rattling Buck's voice alerted Black instantly to trouble. He'd gotten similar calls about Claire in the past, from other friends of hers, more times than he liked to remember. "No, she's not home yet. What's wrong?"

"I don't know if anything's wrong, but she was supposed to show up here to ID the victim's body, along with Jonesy Jax and some FBI fella she's working with. The appointment was at three o'clock this afternoon, and there's no sign of them yet. She's not picking up her cell, either. Nobody answered in Jonesy's suite, I just tried, so I need to know if I should keep waiting or postpone the viewing. I'm a little worried about her, to tell you the truth. This is not like her, at all."

Before he even finished, Black's instinct told him something awful had happened. Claire did not miss appointments, especially official ones that entailed a victim's positive ID. His gut clenched, and he jerked his attention to Booker.

"What happened?" Book asked, sitting up straighter and looking concerned.

"I'll find her and have her call you back, Buck," Black said. Then he clicked off. "Claire missed an appointment at the morgue hours ago. Something's wrong. She's in trouble. I can feel it."

"Maybe not. Maybe she's just late. You know, could be she got caught up with some police emergency, something like that. Don't buy trouble, Nick."

"I've found that it's expedient to buy trouble where she's concerned. Claire would never be late for something like this, not without calling Buck and cancelling it."

Quickly punching in Claire's cell number, Black sat and listened to it ring. No answer for him, either, and Claire always picked up for him. It was a promise she'd made a long time ago because he worried about her so much. And now he was worried, all right—more than worried. He clicked off and phoned down to Jonesy Jax's suite. No answer there, either.

"Something bad is going on. We need to—"

He stopped in mid-sentence and stood up quickly when his executive assistant, Miki Tudor, tapped on the open door, looking highly apologetic. "Mr. and Mrs. Hammons are out here, Nick. They say it's urgent. They're really upset. You better see them."

Mr. Hammons didn't wait for Miki to usher him inside. He pushed past her. "Rico's gone! Somebody took him!"

Black's muscles went to rock, but then he knew—he knew in his heart. Claire and Rico both disappearing at the same time was no coincidence; they were both in trouble. Maybe together. Probably together. Probably connected to Claire's homicide case. Which involved a psychopathic murderer. His heartbeat went into overdrive.

Across from him, Booker was on his feet, too, and he looked every bit as worried as Black did. Trying to remain calm, Black was more concerned with what had gone down. "Tell me what happened. What do you mean, he's gone?"

"We were down at that winter festival out at the mall, you know, the one with the Ferris wheel. He went to buy us some cotton candy and didn't come back. We were just yards away from that booth, Dr. Black, holding our spots at a picnic table. He was standing there in line at the booth one minute, and we glanced away to watch the carolers, and then when I looked back he was simply gone. We found three cones of cotton candy on sidewalk. He's in trouble. I know it. I don't know what to do!" His voice had grown increasingly panicky. He looked about ready to have a heart attack.

Black's heart was knocking against his chest, too, but he forced it down. He had to find Rico and Claire, and he had to find them now. "Okay, calm down. I'm going to find him. Try not to worry. This is my friend, John Booker. He and I will handle this. You need to get down to your suite and stay there until I bring him back."

"How are you going to find him? Who would take him? He's such a sweet boy," Mrs. Hammons said, now in the office with them, too. She was crying and distraught. When her husband put his arms around her and held her close, she buried her face in his coat.

"Rico's got a GPS chip in his arm, just in case anything like this ever happened. It's going to give off a signal, and we can track him, wherever he is."

They both looked immediately relieved. "Did somebody take him? Is that what you think?"

"Has he been kidnapped?" Sally's voice was verging close to hysteria.

"I don't know what happened. But it's possible. Try not to think the worst. I'm not going to stop until I find him and bring him back here, don't worry about that."

"We tried and tried to call Claire's number, but she's not answering. Is she all right?"

"How long ago did you try to call her?"

"On the way over here, when we couldn't find him. The phone just rang and then went to voicemail."

"Okay, listen closely: I need you to go down to your suite and sit tight until you hear from me. There's not a thing you can do until we get him back. Maybe he just got lost somehow. Carnivals are crowded. Or maybe he just got distracted by something he saw in a store window." None of that was remotely possible, of course, and Black knew it. Rico was a very smart little kid. He acted twice his age most of the time. He had guts and resiliency like no other child that Black had ever seen. Rico didn't know about the GPS chip, but Black had made the kid promise to always keep his phone with him. Rico would've called Black immediately if he had gotten lost or needed help of any kind—unless he was restrained or prevented from calling, and that's what Black was afraid of. It was the only thing that made sense. Same with Claire.

Black hastily ushered the Hammonses out of his office, still trying to calm their worries as best he could, but without much avail, not with his own nerves jumping around and threatening to flame up out of control. This was not good. He and Booker had to get on the road, right now.

Minutes later, they were inside his weapons room, arming themselves. Then, not long after that, they were in the back parking lot, inside Booker's Jeep. Black was in the passenger's seat, staring down at Rico's GPS blinking on his phone.

"He's been abducted, goddamn it to hell," he muttered softly, so angry he could barely speak. "I promised him he'd be safe here with us at the lake, Booker. I thought he was. I thought it was okay for him to go out with the Hammonses. I can't think who's got him. Who'd want him enough to do this kind of thing?"

"Maybe the grandparents are in on it. They have to know how wealthy you are. Maybe all this is a grab for the ransom. Maybe their accomplice is holding him."

"No way. You saw their faces. They're terrified that he's in danger. Somebody else took him. We've got to get to him quick."

"Where is he?"

"GPS puts him about ten miles north of the lake. It's mainly just woods out there, I think. I'm not all that familiar with the area. We need to get there fast, and I need to find Claire. She's still not picking up."

"You think the same people have her, too, don't you?"

"Yeah, I do. And I'm pretty sure whoever killed that girl in Claire's homicide case is the one who has them. They may have Jonesy Jax, too. He was with Claire, and there was an FBI guy working with her, too. Claire wasn't sure she could trust him, so maybe he's in on the whole thing, as well. Oh God, I can't believe this is happening again."

Within minutes, they were off the hotel grounds and on their way. Black kept calling Claire but got no answer. He called the sheriff's office and was told they were getting no response, either. Black told them to put out a BOLO on her and Rico, stat. When he called Jonesy's suite again, he finally got an answer: Candi picked up. She sounded as if she was stoned out of her mind, but managed to tell him that Jax had left with Claire and the Fed about three or four hours ago. He hung up and tried to figure out what the hell was going on. A lot of terrible things could be happening to her. Three hours spent in the company of a homicidal maniac who nailed his victim to a wood bannister. God help him, it was happening again.

Chapter 22

Claire came back to awareness slowly, feeling extremely weak and nauseous. Her mind was fuzzy, but her first realization was that she was shivering with cold. Then she realized that her wrists were bound together and her arms were stretched up over her head. That's the moment when she remembered Jonesy Jax—right after that, she recalled Bob Brady.

Oh God, Brady was the killer and he'd drugged them both with some kind of dart. She could still feel the drug, clouding her mind and warping her thoughts, making her feel woozy and strange and as if she was going to throw up. But she knew she had to shake that fog off, and shake it off fast. She had to think straight, because she was in a world of hurt. She didn't know how much yet, but she was going to find out as soon as she forced open her bleary eyes and looked the devil in the face.

For the first few moments after regaining her faculties, she did not want to do it. Couldn't make herself face what had to be some extremely bad odds. She didn't want to see what was happening around her, either. She did not want to face Brady or know what he was doing. But she could hear voices, and it sounded like two men talking to each other. They were not far away from her.

"Okay, Claire, man up, pull it together before it's too late," she told herself firmly, it came out weak and muddled up. Brady had taken her Glock; she couldn't feel the weight of it under her arm. She shifted her right foot enough to realize with a sinking heart that he'd also found the .38 snub nose in her ankle holster. She was completely unarmed. Not good. She sucked in a deep breath, held it inside a second to calm her racing pulse, and told herself firmly that she could do this, that she'd gotten herself out of plenty of tight scrapes before. With monsters just as bad as the one who she feared had her in their control right now. *Just do it, do something. Just get yourself free. You have to do it, so go ahead and do it now.*

It still took a few minutes to garner the courage. When Claire forced herself to open her eyes, she wished she hadn't. She was in some kind of big, open room, but her vision was a little off—everything still looked blurry. The voices were still there. Somewhere nearby. There was a different sound, too, in the background but also close. It sounded like a repetitive sloshing of water—*swish, thud, swish, thud*, over and over, with spattering and splashing, as if water was raining forcefully down into a pool.

She struggled desperately to clear the cobwebs in her head. Once she did that, she realized that she was in some kind of gristmill, the old-fashioned kind with the big waterwheel. That's what she'd been hearing. It was directly in front of her, and very big, maybe twelve feet high and three feet wide, turning very slowly, with lots of creaking and grinding and groaning of ancient wood. There were steps leading down to a lower floor on the right side of the wheel. Okay, there was a way out, right there in front of her. No door, no lock. And there was a big pool of water around the wheel, it looked like. If she recalled, wheels like that had to roll down into a river where the current pushed it around and up again. Another escape hatch, maybe. She shut her eyes again and tried to force herself calm.

A moment later, Claire blinked away the drug daze impeding her vision and tried to focus on the gristwheel again. It was chugging away, the top rolling forward and down like a Ferris wheel and plunging back into the pool below, or stream, or whatever it was. Then she blinked some more and caught her breath in horror as a body suddenly appeared out of the water, slowly coming up, lashed to the wheel. The head appeared first, and oh God, it was a woman. She was bound to the wheel with ropes. Her body looked frozen solid from the frigid water, her skin white and limbs rigid, but her eyes were open and staring straight at Claire. Then the woman's body rolled up over the top with the turning wheel, her feet disappearing down the back. Then it rolled on, and to Claire's horror, a second body appeared tied to the other side. This time it was a man, dressed in a dark suit and tie, a huge red wound on his forehead, the blood frozen in streaming icicles down over his face. His body was frozen, too, eyes hidden under the red ice as he rolled upward and disappeared. Claire stifled a groan, not wanting to see those bodies when they came around again. That was probably what Brady was going to do to her: strap her on a wooden wheel and roll her down into icy water, over and over until she either drowned or froze to death. It was a cruel and medieval method of torture, and she was going to die on that thing, if she didn't do something about it.

That's when Claire's heartbeat jump-started and sped into overdrive, beating so hard and fast against her breastbone that her body actually moved with it. She had to get loose before somebody strapped her to that wheel! She pulled at the bindings above her head. Her arms were attached to an open ceiling beam. The ropes held tight. Her feet were barely touching the ground but her captor had left them unbound. Okay, that was a good thing, maybe. That gave her the opportunity to kick.

At that point, Claire made herself suck it up big time, and she inhaled a deep, cleansing lungful of air and tried hard to tamp down her quick-rising panic. *Okay, think, Claire.* Bob Brady had her. She had to be smart. She had to look around and gauge the situation. She had to see if he was acting alone, find where he was and how she could escape him. So she forced herself to do that. Didn't like what she faced.

Off to her right, she could see three other people inside the big room. They were sitting several yards away at a big, round table. There were four chairs, and some kind of game board sitting in the middle of the table. One place left. Her place, she feared. They were waiting for her to wake up and then she was going to have to sit in that empty chair. The game board could only mean small Detection tokens jammed down into body orifices.

Claire squeezed her eyes shut, and let herself be scared to death for a few seconds. Then she pulled it back under control again and tried to figure out what to do. She opened her eyes but only to a mere slit. She did not want them to know she was awake, because right now they weren't paying any attention to her. She turned her head slightly and scanned the other side of the room. Over to her left, there was a table sitting against the back wall near a window. She could see her holsters and weapons lying on top of it, both the Glock and the .38. If she could get loose somehow and make it to them, she might have a chance. She chanced a glance back at the two psychopaths, but they hadn't been watching her. They were too busy torturing their captured rock star.

Jonesy Jax was sitting in the chair facing her. It looked as if his wrists were tied down onto the table somehow. He was groaning out loud, as if in awful pain, and rolling his head around on his shoulders, maybe fighting to stay conscious. The other two guys were sitting close on either side of him. Neither was bound. They were the nightmare duo, she guessed. She recognized the man on Jonesy's left right away: that was Bob Brady. The other guy had on glasses—he was the one she'd seen playing chess that day in Games Galore. They were the killers, some kind of tag team from hell. They were smiling at each other, talking, laughing, having a good old time as Jonesy suffered terrible fear and groaned with pain.

Okay, Claire thought, squeezing her eyes shut again. *You cannot panic. You cannot go to pieces. Okay, okay, hold it together.* Black was going to miss her and track her with GPS. Unless the killers had disabled her phone, or thrown it away on their way back to this hellhole. They probably had done that. They had showed exemplary skills at the game of murder so far. She knew that, if only from the modicum of clues left behind at the Heather Jax homicide scene. Practiced and proficient killers, for sure, both of them. Who they really were didn't much matter anymore.

Buckeye and Shaggy would surely report her missing when she didn't show up at the morgue. Or at least call her to find out why. She never missed appointments without calling them first. That would alert them, and they would contact Black and he would come and try to find her. But she couldn't count on help arriving in time to save her life, or Jonesy's— no way could she just hang there and wait. She had to use her head to get herself out of this godawful mess, and she had to save Jonesy, too. In no way was he capable of getting free on his own. He was already injured and moaning with pain. Claire only hoped he had some residual courage somewhere inside that he could summon up when he needed to. She was going to need his help to get them both out of this hellhole.

Subtly, she exerted more pressure on the ropes, testing their strength further. They still held fast. Apparently her movements hadn't been subtle enough—Bob Brady had seen her moving.

"Well, well, now, look who's awake, and just in time for game night," he said in a loud, sarcastic voice. Brady scooted back his folding chair and swaggered over to her while his partner sat watching. He was grinning at her, real friendly-like. He stood right in front of Claire for a moment or two, just staring into her eyes. "Hey there, good lookin'. Bet you're not feeling so hot right now, are you? That dart had some potent drugs in it. Our own special recipe, made just for victims like you."

"Who are you? Why are you doing this?"

Brady only smiled. "Ah, don't you worry. You'll know all our secrets soon enough, I promise. You're not gonna like them, though. I suppose you noticed our frozen FBI agent over there on the wheel? He'll come up again in a second, if you missed the show. There's a lady, too, that we grabbed the other day, just for practice with the tranquilizer gun, you understand. Didn't want to get it too strong for you to survive. Both of them are losers. They didn't take to Live or Die well at all. In fact, they were downright terrible at it. Maybe you'll do better. Hope so, for your sake. I'd like to keep you around for a while, if that's okay. I've got some fun plans for me and you. You shouldn't've treated me so badly, my love. It's gonna cause some blow back on you in the next few days, you know."

After that, Claire kept her mouth shut. Right now, she had to be careful. These guys were lunatics, and she had faced off with these kinds of sicko freaks before. She did not want to get him rattled too soon, so she just stared back at him and attempted to look unafraid. He chuckled softly, and then he pulled a twelve-inch butcher knife off a sheath strapped to his thigh. "Okay, game time, sweetheart. Come along now. I've got a feeling you're gonna give us a run for our money, more than most of the idiots we've invited to play with us." He leaned in close and put his tongue in her ear. She jerked her head away, and then he whispered softly in a rasping voice meant to frighten her. "I wanna play a game. And I wanna do things to you that you just won't believe. You see, Detective, I saw those pictures of you. That's why I chose you."

Claire set her jaw. "Untie me, you creep. If you want me to play games with you, get ready. I'm good at games. I'll give you a beatdown at anything you want me to try."

Brady looked surprised, and then laughed. "Oh goody, we got us some fire in our girl. I do so like that about you, Claire. I saw it from the beginning. Guts and gumption and always on full display. Better not push your luck, though. Junior over there, he is definitely not as into you as I am. Push the wrong buttons on him, and you'll end up tied to that wheel before Jonesy even gets his turn."

Then he raised the knife. Claire tried not to cringe as he swiped the sharp blade through the taut rope holding her arms aloft. She sagged, but her wrists were still bound together as he jerked her up by one arm and shoved her roughly toward the card table. He slammed her bodily into the empty chair and sat down beside her.

"Hello, Detective," said the man he'd called Junior. He was staring intently into her face, a slight smile curving his lips. "You already know Lucky here, so I guess I ought to introduce myself, too, before the games begin."

Claire watched warily, but she was also appraising the situation. Nothing about it was good. Not in any way.

"My name is John Scott Jax II, legally, but everybody calls me Junior. You see, Jonesy here is my daddy dearest. Of course, he abandoned me when I was just a little kid. Didn't give a fuckin' thought to me after that. He just left me alone in the hands of my crazy mother, to suffer her abuse all the days of my life." Then he moved so fast that Claire jumped, doubling his right fist and slamming it into the side of Jonesy's head. Jonesy jerked sideways with the violent impact and slumped to one side, only half conscious. "That's how my mom liked to punish me when I was in elementary school. Hit me in the head, just like that. Maybe not *that* hard, but that's not the point, now is it? That's why I drowned her in our swimming pool." He grabbed up Jonesy by one braid and sneered viciously down into his face through gritted teeth. "I'm going to drown you, too, Daddy, over there in that pool of ice water. Then I'll just let your body float down our stream, into the lake. They won't find you until spring, and we'll be long gone by then."

Jonesy only moaned. Frowning at his lack of response, Junior slapped his face a few times, hard enough to draw blood from the side of Jonesy's mouth. Then he continued speaking to Claire as if nothing had happened. "It takes a long time for a person to drown on that wheel, you know. I just want to give you some warning before it's your turn. It all depends on how fast the wheel moves, you understand. Sometimes it just stops on its own, you know, down there under the water, when some poor soul is holding his breath. It's kinda old and cantankerous that way. That's when you drown quickly, and then your body freezes nice and hard. Other times, you freeze first, from hypothermia and frozen skin and tissue. That's not a fun way to die, either. The body simply turns to ice. Like the real Special Agent Bob Brady over there on that wheel. First things first, though: We like to play a game with our selected victim. Remember how we used to play games before you walked out on us, Daddy?"

Jonesy tried to lift his head. He'd been beaten, mostly around the head and face, it looked like. He spoke through swollen lips and bloodied teeth. "She kicked me out. Wouldn't let me see you."

"Oh, nice try, but I don't believe that, not for one second. I watched your sweet little parting scene from upstairs on the night you left. That was the last time I ever saw you. And this is the last time you're ever gonna see me. Then we'll be even. But I do want to show you this game that I invented. Lucky helped me, too. You remember Lucky, he's sitting right over there. See him? He's my best bud ever. This game? It's been just hours of fun for us. Victim after victim has just died to play. You'll see. You and Lucky's pretty little detective here."

"I like to play games," Claire told them. She had to buy herself some time, all right. She sure as hell didn't have much left. These guys were stone cold killers. Maybe they were sociopaths, but she had a feeling they were out more to get their jollies. It was the process, maybe, for them, the learning how to end lives without being caught and then using creative methods to keep killing. They were partners in multiple murders, and they'd already told them they were both going to die strapped to that wheel.

"I knew you would like to play," Lucky told her. "I just felt it in my bones. But are you good at it? That's the question. I still can't believe you fell for my FBI impersonation. It was pretty lame, but easy for me, you know? I had his name, and his badge, and that thick file he'd compiled on my life's work. You understand now."

"So you are Troy Edward Wood?"

"That's right. Killed my traitor mom and haven't stopped since."

"Then who is Oliver Wood?"

"My big brother, who hates my guts. He's been trying to catch me for that mom thing. He just can't seem to get over me running her down. He's been in the military, but apparently he's out now and trying to track me. Not gonna catch me, because I'm smarter than he is. You really fell for all that crap I fed you. Not feeling so smart anymore, now are you?"

Claire ignored that last crack, but it brought things into a clear focus. She wanted to play their game, all right. And make it last as long as she could. "Boo-hoo, Lucky. You think you're the only one who had a tough childhood? Get real. I'll tell you one thing: I've always been damn good at games. Any kind you want to play. Just name it. Try me. I'm lucky as hell, even luckier than you are, I'll wager. Untie my hands and let's get started. I bet you that I can beat you both on the first try."

Lucky looked shocked. "Yeah, right. Please allow me to point out your stupidity: You were partnered up with the guy you were hunting down. Now that's not so intelligent on your part, is it? But in all fairness, your sheriff didn't blink an eye, either. The whole lot of you were pretty easy to play, especially after Junior ran down your dopey partner."

"So you killed an FBI agent and took his identity. How did you manage that?"

"We got the jump on him first. Then we gave him a bit of the water torture treatment, as you can see. Wait a second, and Agent Bob will come right up out of the water again. It's just like clockwork, you see. Well, what do you know? There he is again, right on time. Special Agent Bob Brady, in the frozen flesh. Yep, he made the mistake of sniffing around out here at our new lair, but we happened to see him first. Not sure how he found us, but he's been on our case for years. Not anymore. He's gone to his heavenly reward, and you just might get to meet him up there. When we are ready to clear out of here, we'll be ending a lot of our past problems and tying up all our loose ends."

"Meaning your brother?"

"Yes, ma'am. My brother. You don't know how much I want to finish him. He's the one who convinced my parents to put me in that first looney bin. He despised me from the day I killed his stupid favorite dog. My parents thought he hung the moon in the sky. It was always all about my brother. You know him. I saw you with him down in the lobby one night before you sent him packing. Yep, old Ollie, he's the hero of our family. Did it all. Mr. Wunderkind. Basketball star. Honored Marine. The whole nine yards of glory and flag waving. I'm gonna hunt him down and kill him, too, one of these days, when I've got the time."

Claire had heard enough. What she wanted to talk about right now was playing the game. She wanted him to untie her. "Blah, blah, blah. Seems to me that you're putting me off. What? Too chicken to play your own game? Afraid I'll beat you? That why you're boring us with all this family history?"

Lucky and Junior glanced at each other. They looked surprised, and then they looked angry. "You want to play, huh? Well, okay, miss hot shot detective, let's see what you've got."

"Game on," she said tightly, challenging him with her eyes. These guys wanted to win, had to win. Maybe if they got enthralled in the game they'd make a mistake.

"You just might regret being in such a hurry, once you know what you're getting into."

"Well, Lucky, like I told you: I'm a lucky kind of gal. No reason to think I won't be this time, too."

"You better hope so," Junior said in his quiet voice. When Claire looked at him, his eyes were scary cold. Not like the intensity of Oliver Wood's, or the cruelty in Lucky's gaze. Junior's eyes were dark and masochistically excited. He loved having them as captives at his mercy, that was abundantly clear. So did Troy Wood, but he seemed to have a soft spot for Claire, one she hated to consider very long, but she was going to have to use that to her advantage. Right up until she took that knife out of his belt and plunged it into his jugular vein.

"You'll see how good I am." Claire looked down at the board. "So what's this game called?"

"It's called Live or Die. And you are gonna love it. We'll just watch you and Daddy play," said Junior.

"He's not going to be much competition for me, not if you keep hitting him in the head. That can't be good for his concentration."

"I'll help him out. You know, sort of a silent mentor, like he never was for me."

"That's why you killed Heather? You were jealous of her and Jonesy's relationship?"

"Nothing to be jealous about anymore, now is there, Detective?"

Apparently halfway alert, Jonesy raised severely swollen eyes to Junior's face. Maybe he'd been faking some of his stupor; maybe he wasn't as out of his mind as he wanted them all to believe. Claire hoped to hell he wasn't and could help her when the chips were down. "You killed your own sister," he muttered to Junior. "How could you do something like that? You didn't even know her."

"She wasn't my sister. She wasn't anything to me." Junior was really angry now. "She was just a little bitch from some one-night stand whore after your money. Like Momma, like daughter, I always say. But your money will be all ours very soon."

"Half-sister," Jonesy managed through cracked lips.

Junior leaned back. "You loved her. You never loved me. So I made her pay the price and play by my rules. She wasn't nearly as brave as you are, let me tell you. She was way too scared, so we didn't even waste time. We just put her out of her misery so we wouldn't have to listen to her screaming anymore."

"Enough bellyaching and crying about how daddy doesn't love you," Claire said to Junior. She sensed some tension between the two killers— maybe she could exploit it, unless she went too far. She braced for the blow she had a feeling was coming, and coming fast.

Troy Wood, aka Lucky, laughed softly. Junior leaned over and slapped her across the face. Her head slung to the side and her cheek stung like fire, but she clamped her jaw and did not react, just kept her eyes leveled on Junior's flushed face.

"Don't mess up her face, Junior. That's the best thing about her. That and her guts. It'll be fun to break her down, just like that wild filly I once had to work with in Oklahoma. And I got dibs on her, remember?"

"Do you want to play this game or not? Looks to me like you're both stalling because you're scared to death I'll beat you. After all this big talk, you don't even want to play me."

"Nobody survives this game. You won't, either."

"You survived it," Claire said.

"Yeah, that's true. But we cheat. We cheat at just about everything we do. It suits our purposes." Then he smiled and kissed her on the cheek.

Fear started rising up inside Claire again, a towering wave of dread that threatened her false bravado. Jonesy groaned some more. His face was so cut up and bruised that he was having trouble breathing. His nose was bleeding again, running down the front of his white dress shirt.

Lucky grabbed her chin and forced her to look up at him. "Okay, Claire, since you're such an eager beaver. You go first."

"Untie me. I won't try to escape. I want to beat you in the worst way."

"Yeah, sure. What do you take us for? Idiots? Just for your information: we both register at the genius level. IQs over 160."

"Yeah, I'll bet. Keep telling yourself that, while I kill you at your own game."

"Go ahead, draw your first card, big mouth," Junior said to her. He was getting angrier. Good. Angry people made stupid mistakes. "Right here. From the Live or Die pile."

"What's that supposed to mean?"

"You draw the die card. One of us gets to kill you. Easy as can be. Go ahead. Game on, as you taunted us a moment ago. What color do you want to be? You know, which token do you choose?"

Claire only stared at him. These two guys really were crazy as loons. Evil as hell, but they meant business. She looked down at the game board. It appeared professionally made, as if they'd had somebody make it by hand to their specifications. All business. Four game pieces were sitting at the start square. "Okay, I'll take yellow. It's so sunshiny."

"Go ahead, draw. Let's see if you get to live another minute."

"Thought you said you wanted to keep me around, for entertainment. What? Don't like my personality so much, after all? Am I too tough for you, Lucky?"

Lucky was not taking the bait, damn it. "No, I like everything about you. Especially that tough girl thing you got going on at the moment. So go ahead, draw your card, before Junior goes berserk and puts a blade in you. He's such a loose cannon at times like this."

Claire glanced across the table at Jonesy. He looked more alert now. His injured eyes were latched onto her face, and she had a feeling he was warning her not to draw the card. He knew something she didn't know, all right.

Lucky noticed her hesitation. "What's the problem, sweetie? You gettin' cold feet already?"

Heart escalating, Claire moved her bound hands up to the pile of small white cards. She got hold of the top one. She turned it over. The word ALIVE was printed on the other side. She laid it down on the table. Her heart slowed down again.

"Oh, oh, oh, my new girlfriend's as lucky as she claims." Lucky threw back his head and enjoyed a good laugh. Nobody joined him in his good cheer. "Know what that means, Claire? That means you aren't slated to die this time around, but you're slated to kill somebody else. Lucky you. And it won't be me or Junior. So guess who you get as a victim?"

"I'm not gonna kill anybody."

"Think again," said Lucky. This time his voice was deep and harsh.

"My turn now." Junior appeared eager to take his turn. That couldn't be a good sign. "I get to draw a token out of this little bag. Watch and learn, Daddy."

His hatred for Jonesy was so deep and palpable that it almost oozed from his pores. He opened the drawstring bag and reached inside. He pulled out a weapon and held it up. It was a small metal revolver, like the one in the Detection game she'd bought.

"Well now, girl, you just got lucky again. This is gonna give old Jonesy Jax here a quick death, depending how good a shot you are. We'll probably back you off so you'll have to shoot him multiple times.

"All right, your turn now, Dad. You get to draw from the Live or Die pile. Good luck to you. Hope like hell it's the dead card."

Jonesy looked at Claire again, both of them trying to figure out a way to make the game work to their advantage. The game made little sense. No sense, actually. It was just a means to find a unique way to murder someone. Jonesy drew off the top. His card read ALIVE.

"Well, you two are damn lucky, I've got to hand it to you." Lucky shook his head. "Almost as lucky as I am. Not quite. That's why my friends call me Lucky. You can call me that, Claire. Until you lose the game, and then I'll call you 'Unlucky.'" He and Junior seemed to enjoy his joke. "But now it's my turn to draw a weapon for Mr. Rock Star over there to use on you."

They watched Lucky open the bag. Claire didn't recognize the weapon he chose at first, but then he smiled and held it up in front of her eyes. "Oh boy, Jonesy Boy gets to kill Claire with a nail gun! We had this one specially made for our game. Uh oh, Claire, not so lucky anymore. That's gonna hurt, all those nails going in that sweet little bod of yours. You know how long it takes to die from nails being shot into your body? It takes a long time, and lots of nails and lots of blood. Hope we've got enough to do the job. We'll nail you up on that wheel afterwards. Let you get nice and frozen for us."

Claire tried not to react, but terror was slowly creeping up and threatening her willpower. These guys were as serious as sin, and this game had only one outcome. The two people drawing the cards were both going to die—and at each other's hands.

"Okay, Claire, it's your turn to draw again. Now we'll see just how lucky you really are. Wouldn't want to be you. Nail gun deaths are awful things to behold. Well, in our case, we like to watch, but you and Jonesy won't."

Claire stared at the pile of cards. She was going to have to make a move. She could not draw a die card or it would be over. Hesitating, she tried to think what she could do to distract them. Problem was, she couldn't think of anything. She was out of ideas and out of hope. She stared across the table at Jonesy. He was crying now, silently, tears running down his cheeks and smearing the blood. He knew it was just a matter of time before they killed him. Junior and Lucky just sat there, smiling in anticipation.

Chapter 23

After Rico decided the guys in the van were really gone and not coming back, he fought his way out of the snowy bushes and climbed back over the snow drift onto the road. It was really dark out there, but using the light from his phone he could see the van's tire tracks. Maybe if he followed them he'd find a house. Shivering, he realized that he was awfully cold, and more than anything needed to find a warm place to hide out. Zipping his parka all the way up to his neck, he flipped the hood back up and pulled the drawstring tight under his chin. Then he tried to get hold of Claire again. Still no signal.

So, okay: He was standing all alone on a dark road, about to freeze to death. He didn't know what else to do, so he just started trudging up the road in the direction the van drove, but he kept listening and watching both sides of the road, not wanting somebody to jump out and get him. He was not so much afraid of the dark; he'd been alone in the dark lots of times. What really scared him was being all alone in the cold and not knowing where he was. But he was going to try to be brave like Claire always told him he was. It was a pretty hard thing to do, though, when he was shivering and snow was coming down.

After about thirty minutes spent trudging through the snow hugging the side of the road, he found that the van's tracks turned off the gravel road and headed up a narrow dirt road. Way off, up at the top of the hill, he could see the glow of a dusk-to-dawn light. It looked pretty far up there, though. He stopped and stamped his feet and tried to figure out if he should walk all the way up there or not. Maybe his phone would catch a signal up higher, way up that hill at the end of the road. Maybe those guys had a satellite or a ground line he could use without them catching him. He was pretty good at sneaking around without anybody seeing him.

Rico took one last glance up and down the gravel road and didn't see anything. Nothing. No lights. No cars. Just pitch black and gently blowing snow and a soft pale glow where the snow was covering the ground. It felt as if he were the only person on earth. But his toes and his nose felt like they were already frozen solid. What he had to do was find a warm place, so there wasn't anything else he could do but climb up to where the bad guys were. Still, he hesitated, pretty sure that wasn't a good idea. He did not want them to catch him again.

But after a few more minutes of cold contemplation and worry, he finally turned and started walking up to that light. Each footstep crunched through a thin layer of ice on the road where the ruts weren't worn down. Halfway up, snow turned into sleet again and blew straight at him, so he hurried faster. He was so cold now—he just wanted to find a warm place. Anywhere at all where he could get inside some shelter. A shed, maybe, or a garage, or even a doghouse. He had to find a phone up there, too, without the bad guys seeing him, and then he had to hurry up and call Black and Claire. They'd come get him. He knew they would. So he just kept on walking up the long rise and trying not to shiver too hard.

When the house with the light post finally came into sight, he stepped off to the side of the road and walked in the snow so he wouldn't make that crackling sound, just the quiet little squeaks of his boots. The light was situated at the corner of the front yard. There was a log house attached to what looked like a big mill. He'd seen pictures of mills in his history books, the ones that had big turning wheels to grind up wheat and other kinds of stuff. This wheel was huge and rolled down into a swift stream, and it was moving slowly. He couldn't see very well because of the gusting sleet peppering his face, but he could hear that old wheel making lots of creaking and thumping noises.

Nobody was around anywhere, but the panel van that he'd jumped out of was parked right out in front of the log house. There were lights on inside, and that probably meant the heat was on in there, too. Man, he sure would like to be inside, but he couldn't just go and knock on the door, because those two bad guys were sitting around in there. He could see their footprints on the snowy front steps. And there might even be more than two bad guys inside—maybe they had a whole gang in there. Like the outlaw gangs he'd read about. Rico swallowed hard. He sure couldn't let them find out that he was out there in the front yard snooping around, but he had to find a way to stay warm until Black came and got him.

Rico just stood there in the shadows and tried to figure out what he should do. Back on the island, he knew how to sneak around and evade capture. He knew who the bad people were and where they were, and there had been secret tunnels under his house that he could creep through quietly without being seen. But right now, the deep snow on the ground was up to his knees, and it crunched when he walked through it, but he probably wouldn't be heard because the night was loud with wind and the racket of that wheel. Still, it was pretty eerie and dark, and he was afraid of what those guys would do to him if they caught him. Still, he knew he had to do something.

He jumped down off the road and headed at an angle around the house. Maybe there was a garden shed or a barn that he could hide in for a while. So he trudged on, stopping often to listen. About the time he got to the back part of the house, he saw the dogs. It looked like three or four big ones, and they were inside a chicken wire pen. He swallowed hard, because they looked like German shepherds and rottweilers. He loved dogs, especially Claire's little poodle Jules Verne, but these dogs looked like they could tear a kid like him to pieces.

Moving more cautiously and trying not to disturb the dogs, he headed for a structure behind the house that looked a whole lot like a small barn. Halfway there, the dogs started yapping like crazy. Rico froze in his tracks and didn't move for a second, but then he took off running for that barn as fast as he could. He burst through the front doors and ran straight into a great big man squatting down. The man grabbed him from the back and slapped a hand over his mouth, then dragged him backward into the shadows.

"Don't make a sound, Rico, you hear me?" The man's voice was deep and gruff and sounded familiar.

Rico didn't make a sound. He stood rigid, held up on his toes by the big guy's arms, one around his neck and one around his chest. He didn't like to be held like that. The tight grip was cutting off his air. The mean people on the island did that to him all the time. So he rammed his elbow into the man's side and tried to jerk loose at the same time. His captor grunted out a bunch of air, but he caught Rico by the back of his jacket and jerked him around.

"Stop fighting, Rico. It's me, Oliver."

Rico went still with relief. Oliver Wood was his new friend. They had played video games together at Cedar Bend. Oh, he was so glad to see somebody he knew that he just sagged down to his knees. Oliver hunkered down beside him.

"What the hell are you doing out here?" Oliver whispered in a low voice, glancing outside. "The guys inside this house are bad news. How did you get here?"

Rico started trembling all over, really scared now. Oliver was a big, strong guy and he sounded afraid, too. "Those guys inside? They tried to kidnap me from the mall but I got away. I've been trying to call Claire and Black on this phone but it won't work."

"Listen to me. Claire's inside that house, too. I tracked them out here and was hiding when they took her and some other guy inside. I've got to get her out safely. I can't take time to worry about you, too. Understand me, Rico? You're safe out here, unless you do something stupid. You've got to hide and stay quiet. Understand?"

"No, no, I need to help Claire, too, if she's in there with them. They're mean."

"You are staying out here, damn it. I will get her out of there if you don't interfere. I know what I'm doing. I've been following them."

"Is Nick in there, too? With Claire? Did they get him, too?"

"No, I don't know where he is."

"You got yourself a gun?" Rico asked. "You're gonna need a gun to get her out. They've got guns, I saw them."

Oliver shushed him again. "Yes, I've got a gun. Look, I don't have time for this. I'm going in. Just stay out of my way and hide back there in the dark. I can't worry about you. I'll get Claire out, just don't mess it up."

"Who are those bad people? Why do they want Claire and me?"

"We'll talk about that later. Just hide out here. I'll come get you when I've got her."

"But what about those guns?"

"Just stay here, or the dogs will bark and alert them. Don't you dare move out of this barn, you got that, Rico?"

"Yes, sir."

Then his friend was just gone, slipping out into windblown snow and disappearing around the side of the barn. Rico moved to the door and watched him move stealthily through the trees, just like somebody's shadow. He made no sounds that Rico could hear, not with the wind blowing so hard. Nothing made any sound except for the thump and swish and gurgle of that waterwheel. He watched until Oliver got to the back of the house and then swung up onto a tree limb and climbed quickly onto the roof. Wow, he was doing stuff just like a superhero would, like Spiderman or the Green Arrow. Rico could do that, too, he bet. He was good at climbing trees and stuff.

Claire was in there. That really scared Rico. How did they get her? She had all those guns, the one in her shoulder holster and the one in her ankle holster. How could they have gotten her? He just didn't understand it. The thought of her being inside that house with those two bad guys made him feel sick to his stomach. Maybe he ought to go and help Oliver get her out. Rico had gotten Claire out of trouble before; she had been glad he came around that time. Yeah, maybe he should go inside, too, and help her. There were too many of them for Oliver to handle all by himself anyway.

Still undecided and afraid, he waited awhile like Oliver had told him, and then he decided Oliver and Claire were going to need his help, whether they knew it or not. Rico had helped Claire and Black escape off the island. He could help again. He knew what it felt like to be held captive by mean people, and it wasn't good. He just wished Black were there, too. He was really good at that stuff. And he always carried a gun. Black was going to be so mad when he found out that those guys had taken him and Claire. Rico wished he had a gun. Maybe Nick would get him one for Christmas when he got back home. Maybe he'd see now that Rico really needed it for protection. He took a deep breath, and then he moved outside into the snow and crept his way toward that tree.

About a mile from the old mill, Black and Booker were following Rico's GPS signal. Booker was driving the Jeep, and Black was riding shotgun, about as anxious as he'd ever been in his life. Both Claire and Rico had gone missing, and he knew it had everything to do with this stretch of back road. The phone's GPS was getting harder to read because of the snow and the leaden clouds hanging low overhead. The road was deserted and out in the middle of nowhere. No houses, no businesses, no farms. Just dark and trees and one narrow, crooked gravel road. Where the hell was Rico?

"Wait a sec, Book," he said, spotting something. "I see some footprints at the side of the road. Small ones, small enough to be Rico's. Hold up a second."

Book stopped the vehicle and let the motor idle, and Black got out and squatted down beside the tracks. They were a kid's, all right, and the treads looked like the ones on the new snow boots Black had bought Rico in New York. It had to be Rico. He had gotten away from the kidnappers somehow, because there was just one set of tracks and they appeared to be walking, not running. That didn't really surprise Black. Not with that kid. At only ten years old, Rico was about as resourceful as anybody Black had ever met. He'd had to be.

Climbing back into the jeep, he pointed ahead. "I think he's been walking along here. I hope to God we're getting close now."

Booker drove on slowly, and Black kept his eyes sweeping the side of the road, where he held his flashlight beam. They reached a private drive heading up a hill off to his right, and it looked like Rico's tracks had stopped and then turned up the hill. "Okay, he's got to be up that road somewhere. Let's go in quiet."

They turned and drove slowly, snow pelting the windshield, barely able to get traction on the icy road. When they caught sight of a light burning in the yard, Booker braked and turned off both lights and the ignition. "Okay, we better go in on foot from here, Nick, until we find out what we're dealing with."

They got out quietly, and Black racked his .45 and gripped it in his right hand. Booker did the same with a shotgun. If anybody had hurt a hair on Rico's head—or Claire's, because Black hoped to God she was up there, too—he was going to make them pay. If they weren't too late. He increased his pace, knowing he probably didn't have much time left to find them. They'd both been gone a long time now. He set his jaw and kept going, the wind whipping icy sleet straight at him.

Chapter 24

Still sitting at the game table with the three men, Claire reached out and slowly turned over the top card in the Live or Die pile. She blew out a relieved breath. ALIVE. Okay, so far, so good, but this kind of luck was not going to last much longer. She felt a shiver start up her spine and tried to stop it.

Lucky hooted and clapped his hands. "Well shit, woman, you are as lucky as Satan himself. But this time you gotta draw from our bag of tricks. We need to get this show on the road. We get bored if things don't move faster than this."

"What bag of tricks?"

"Just watch and learn, my love. I can't believe there's been no blood spilled yet. Damn, you two are really beginning to grate on my nerves."

Claire realized that Junior was not laughing with Lucky, also known in police precincts as the psychopath Troy Edward Wood. Junior was not enjoying the game as much as his partner in crime. This game was serious business for him: the business of murdering his father, something he had no doubt looked forward to for years. To him, Claire was just icing on the cake, somebody Lucky could play with. She watched Junior take hold of the bag and pull out a card. He read it silently, and then he grinned evilly at his father. "Now we are talking, Dad."

Junior turned the card around so Claire and Lucky could see it: FINGER FUN WITH JUNIOR.

Lucky laughed out loud. He reached down and cupped his hand over Claire's breast. She slapped it away with her bound hands. "Touchy, touchy, but you'll get used to me touching you, Claire. You'll end up begging me to do that instead of hurting you. And now you're going to see something you don't see every day. Finally, some blood's gonna get spilled on this nice clean table."

Claire felt herself tense up. She had been sitting still since they'd brought her to the table; her whole body felt as rigid as a board. She wasn't sure what they were going to do next. She was afraid to think. They were sadists. They loved to hurt people and inflict as much pain as they could. She watched Junior pull out a large switchblade knife. He slung it out hard so that the blade flipped open. Claire could see that the edge had been honed until it was razor sharp. Oh God, what was he going to do?

"Put your hand down on the table, daddy dearest," Junior was telling Jonesy. His face had grown hard now, unrelenting, and something else glowed inside his eyes, behind those black glasses: pleasure. "And spread out those talented guitar-pickin' fingers of yours."

"No." Jonesy's voice came out very low. Claire froze up even more, afraid for what was going to happen to him.

Junior smiled. It was one of the most evil expressions that Claire had ever seen on a human being. "Do it, or I will cut off your ears one at a time. Then your nose, then other parts I'm sure you don't want to lose, not with that sexy girlfriend waiting for you back at the hotel."

"No." Jonesy managed to draw himself up a little, displaying a belated burst of courage. He balled both hands into fists and held them down on his lap. Claire was glad to see him resisting a little. These guys were not men who admired cowardice, no matter what terrible deed they were perpetrating on their victim.

Junior did not hesitate. He gripped the knife by the hilt with the blade pointed down, and then swiped down through Jonesy Jax's ear. Part of it came off in Junior's hand, and Jonesy's scream was so shrill and awful that Claire's blood ran cold.

"Stop!" Claire tried to grab Junior's hand with the knife but he shook her off. Then Lucky stood behind Claire and held her down in her chair with a tight, two-fisted grip on her shoulders. Jonesy was breathing hard, holding his bleeding wound, sucking air in and blowing it out. He was staring down at his partially severed ear lying on the table in front of him.

"Okay, Dad, you want your other ear down there on the table, too? Quit playing around and put your hand on the table and spread out your fingers."

Jonesy was pressing his bound hands tight over the bleeding. Junior held the dripping blade aloft, more than eager to take off the other ear. Claire struggled to get free as Jonesy slowly placed his hands down on the table. He spread his fingers wide and shut his eyes. That's when Claire realized what Junior was going to do. She'd seen it done before, in films.

"Now you hold real still," Junior told Jonesy, "and maybe I won't cut off your fingers by mistake."

Jonesy did not move. What was left of his ear was bleeding down the side of his neck. Claire held her breath. Junior started his game by placing the sharp tip of the blade down between Jonesy's spread fingers, very slowly at first, just tapping the table, and then he started doing it faster and faster until he finally missed, and the blade sliced deeply into Jonesy's ring finger. Jonesy screamed in agony, and Claire squeezed her eyes shut. These guys loved inflicting pain. They were laughing together now, and Jonesy was hugging his injured hand up tight against his chest. He was losing a lot of blood and gasping for breath.

"Stop it, stop it!" Claire was angry now, angry that they were just sitting there laughing and torturing him. She made a grab for the knife at Lucky's waist, but he was faster. He got hold of her arm and twisted it until she was forced down in her chair.

"The fun is just getting started, love o' mine. You still have your own torture to look forward to. Be patient. It's just his finger. He's gonna miss that ear more. But he'll die soon, so no real harm done."

Outside, the strident barking of dogs interrupted their grisly game. Junior and Lucky darted looks at each other, then they jumped up and took off down the steps beside the big waterwheel. Claire jumped to her feet. In his panic, Junior had left the switchblade stuck point down in the tabletop. She grabbed it and turned it around, awkwardly trying to saw through the ropes binding her hands together. She could hear shouting now, and then the rope snapped apart and she was free! She cut Jonesy's hands free, too, and then she got an arm around his waist and tried to help him stand up. When she got him to the top of the steps, she could see the room right below: They weren't down there. She wasn't sure where they were, but this was her only chance to get away.

"C'mon, Jonesy, I've got to get my guns and then we can get out of here," she whispered to the moaning man. He was holding the side of his head, and blood was oozing through his fingers. Before she could turn back, a big hand closed over her shoulder and jerked her back away from Jonesy. Another arm snaked around her waist and a hand clamped down over her mouth. Jonesy fell weakly to his knees at the top of the steps.

"Don't fight, Claire, it's me!"

Then he let her go, and Claire spun around to face him, shocked when she saw Oliver Wood. "You've got to help us! They're trying to kill us."

"They're downstairs. C'mon, we got to get him out the back. Help me get him up." Oliver was already half-dragging Jonesy back into the shadows at the far end of the room. Still holding the knife in one fist, Claire turned to follow, but she heard somebody coming hard up the steps right behind her. She spun just as Lucky reached her. Claire slashed at him with the knife, but he was too quick. He tackled her low around the knees and took her down hard on the floor. She twisted desperately to free herself, but he sent his fist hard against her face. She evaded the blow but it landed on her shoulder, numbing one arm. She screamed in pain and started stabbing hysterically at his body, driving the sharp knife down hard into his back. He yelled and let her go, trying to twist away from the knife, but now Junior was right behind him on the steps. He got hold of Claire's foot as she scooted back away from him and lunged out to stab Junior. She got him once in the arm, but he jumped down on top of her and started twisting the weapon out of her hands.

Behind her, Oliver had dropped Jonesy and run back to help her. He stopped in his tracks, his gun pointed at Junior, but Junior now had the barrel of his gun pressed up against Claire's head. Nobody said anything for a moment, panting and groaning, but then a small voice came from right behind Oliver.

"Let her go, or I'll shoot that guy down on the floor."

That's when Claire saw Rico. She couldn't believe her eyes for a minute, but it was him. He stood about five feet away from them, her Glock 19 held in both hands and pointed straight at Lucky's chest. "I'll shoot him if you don't let her go. I will. I promise I will."

Before anyone else could move, Oliver opened up on Lucky where he lay on the floor, and Junior staggered toward the steps, his gun still hard against Claire's head. "Die, you bitch!" he yelled, backing down the steps. That's when Rico pulled the trigger. The retort was so loud, and the bullet went wide. Claire ducked down away from Junior and grabbed his arm before he could shoot Rico, but then more shots rang out from the room below. Junior fell forward hard, dropping his gun. It skittered across the floor, and Claire scrabbled on her hands and knees after it, but Junior was already down on the ground and not moving. Claire crawled toward Rico, and the boy dropped the gun and ran into her arms. She grabbed him and held on tightly as somebody downstairs cried out her name. It was Black. Then his footsteps were thundering up the steps, and she went limp with relief, with Rico still clutched in her arms. He was clasping his arms around her neck in a stranglehold.

"Okay, Rico, you're okay now, don't cry."

But Rico was crying, and Claire felt like it, too, from the fear and the relief and the overwhelming rush of adrenaline. Black was at the top of the steps, his .45 in his hand. He pointed his weapon at Oliver Wood, who was back with Jonesy and trying to wrap up his wounds. Then Black headed straight for Claire and Rico. He dropped down on his haunches beside them. "Are you okay? Did they hurt you?"

"We're okay," Claire got out somehow, just relieved they were all still alive. It had been way too close this time. "Call an ambulance, Black. They cut up Jonesy pretty bad."

"Booker's already called 911 on the landline downstairs. What the hell happened here? How did they get you? You sure you're all right?"

Claire nodded, but Rico couldn't seem to stop crying so Black picked him up and held him tight, and then reached down and helped Claire to stand up. It was over, but it didn't seem over to Claire. She was shaking like an oak leaf because she knew how close she'd come this time. They would have killed her. They would have put her on that waterwheel. And Rico, too. How did he even get there? He was so little, and he'd seen so much violence, violence from which she and Black had sworn to shield him. But he was okay, all of them were okay. That had to be enough right now. She couldn't deal with anything else. She just wanted to go home and let somebody else handle it for a while. Booker and Oliver tried to take care of Jonesy, and Black kept one arm around her as he carried Rico outside. He wrapped them both in blankets, settled Rico on Claire's lap inside the Jeep, and got the heater going. Then they all just sat there and waited for the cops to show up. They were all alive, that's all that Claire could think about. They were still breathing. Maybe later, she'd figure out the rest, but right now, all she wanted to do was hold Rico close and make him feel safe.

Epilogue

On Christmas Eve, Claire was surrounded by all her family and friends. Even Bud had made it, limping around on crutches, with Brianna hovering at his elbow every minute. Black had planned the holiday party out in detail, and it was being held in the ballroom at Cedar Bend Lodge, in the same room where they'd been wed, with all his staff invited, along with their families. There were Christmas trees hugging the walls, all decorated and blinking with white lights. Claire took it all in, relaxed and happy again, but it was a sedate and thankful sort of happy this time.

The events of the past week weighed heavily on her heart. Both of the psychotic killers were dead, thank God, but they had left behind a long line of victims through many years of killing rampages, people who suffered horribly and would never take a breath again. The real Special Agent Bob Brady had paid with his life for his long quest to hunt them down and kill them, and the Bureau had opened an investigation into his death. Jonesy was in the hospital, but he was in pretty bad shape. Still, the prognosis was good. Oliver Wood was there in the ballroom with them, but not smiling so much. He had cut down his own brother for killing his mother after many years searching for him. After the holidays, he was going to visit his father just down the road in Columbia and then start another deployment in Afghanistan. But he was a new and dear friend to Claire, one who had helped save Rico's life, and she would always be thankful to him for that.

The newspapers were going absolutely berserk with what they knew about the story so far, Black and Claire and Jonesy prominent in their lurid headlines, and the photographers were still out in force. Half of them were staked out down at the hospital now, so the crowd outside the hotel wasn't quite as bad.

Rico was okay, at least she hoped he was, and that was the most important thing to her. Black had talked with him at length about everything that had gone down, and the sad truth was, that terrible night in the mill wasn't half as bad as what that poor child had faced on the island. Black promised Claire that Rico's kidnapping had not affected Rico psychologically as much as he'd first feared. The boy had just suffered through so much, though, that he now considered this just another awful thing he'd had to endure. Black told her that Rico's experiences on the island had prepared him for the darkness in the world, and that they just needed to make sure he had more love and light and laughter to make up for the things he'd seen. That's why the festive party around her had not been cancelled.

Black had gifted all their friends in attendance free vacations to any of his luxury hotels, transportation included. Everyone was more than happy with that, to be sure, and people all around her were laughing and thanking each other after the gift exchange. Claire was trying her best to put the darkness behind her as Rico seemed to have done so easily. She wasn't having as much luck. Of course, Black had noticed her mood, because he always noticed everything about her.

"You okay?" he asked once more, coming up and kissing the top of her head.

"Yes, I do believe I'm getting there."

"Good."

"Have you talked to the Hammonses yet, about taking Rico back home with them?"

"They want to, and I think it might be best. Maybe they can protect him better than we can. I let him down this time; I'll never forgive myself for that."

Claire glanced over at Warren and Sally Hammons, where they were laughing with Rico beside one of the Christmas trees. "No, you didn't. How could you have known? How could either of us had known? He doesn't want to leave us. He told me."

"I know. He told me the same thing. His grandparents said he could make the decision, and they'd abide by it."

Claire took a deep breath. "Has he?"

"Not yet. But here he comes. Probably to tell us what he wants to do. You ready to hear it?"

"I don't think so."

Rico came bounding up and grabbed Claire around the waist. "You gotta come and open your presents from me and Nick, Claire. You're going to like what he bought you. It's a big apartment in New York City so we can go ride in the taxis and go to the big toy stores anytime I want to."

Claire hugged him. "Well, that sounds good. Maybe a trifle extravagant, Black. I mean, seriously? But maybe we can go there for New Year's Eve and watch the ball drop in Times Square. Would you like that, Rico?"

Rico simply beamed. "That'd be awesome, but Disney World would be even better. I do get to stay here with you, don't I? Memo and Papa said it's up to me, and I want to be with you. I'll go see them and stuff in the summer, but I want to live here. That's okay, isn't it?" He looked up at her with his big, dark, questioning eyes. "Is that okay? You still want me to stay here, don't you? I'll be good, I promise."

Claire just looked up at Black and laughed. "Oh yeah, yes, sir, Rico, we want you with us, all right. More than just about anything I can think of."

"Then come on and open your presents. I got you a necklace with the Statue of Liberty thingy hanging off the chain. I got it in New York, too."

Claire laughed again, and Black heaved a huge sigh of relief as the boy ran back to the tree to get Claire's present. "Well, thank God," he breathed out.

"That's the understatement of the year," Claire said. She couldn't stop smiling.

Black took her hand and kissed the back of it, then turned it over and pressed his mouth into her palm. Claire smiled up at him and let him lead her back across the room to the heart of the festivities. It was going to be a very good year, after all. Thank God they'd all made it out alive and well, because she had a fabulous one-of-a-kind present for Black this year, too. Something he'd never had before, and he was going to love it. Oh, was he ever. It was something she knew he had wanted all his life, more than just about anything in the world, and now she could give it to him. She allowed herself a secret little smile, watching him presenting a New Year's toast to all their friends. He was just going to die of happiness when he found out.

Truth be told, so was she.

If you enjoyed *Fatal Game*, be sure not to miss Linda Ladd's

SAY YOUR GOODBYES

SAY YOU'RE DREAMING

When a scream wakes Will Novak in the middle of the night, at first he puts it down to the nightmares. He's alone on a sailboat in the Caribbean, miles from land. And his demons never leave him.

SAY YOUR PRAYERS

The screams are real, though, coming from another boat just a rifle's night scope away. It only takes seconds for Novak to witness one murder and stop another. But with the killer on the run and a beautiful stranger dripping on his deck, Novak has gotten himself into a new kind of deep water.

BUT DON'T SAY YOUR NAME

The young woman he saved says she doesn't know who she is. But someone does, and they're burning fuel and cash to chase Novak and his new acquaintance from one island to the next, across dangerous seas and right into the wilds of the Yucatan jungle. If either of them is going to live, Novak is going to need answers, fast—and he's guessing he won't like what he finds out . . .

A Lyrical Underground e-book on sale now.

Meet the Author

LINDA LADD is the bestselling author of over a dozen novels, including the Claire Morgan thrillers and the Will Novak thrillers. Linda makes her home in Missouri, where she lives with her husband and beloved beagle named Banjo. She loves traveling and spending time with her two adult children, their spouses, and her two grandsons. In addition to writing, Linda enjoys target shooting and is a good markswoman with a Glock 19 similar to Claire Morgan's. She loves to read good books, play tennis and board games, and watch fast-paced action movies. She is currently at work on her next novel featuring Claire Morgan. Learn more at lindaladd.com.

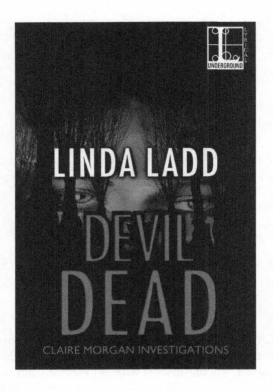

LOST GIRL

She was last seen in New Orleans. Her father, a rich, powerful arms dealer, believes she was abducted. For ransom. For revenge. For reasons too horrible to imagine.

LOST INNOCENCE

Claire Morgan, recent former cop turned private investigator, and her new partner begin their search at the girl's school, where a violent junkie attacks Claire with scissors, raves of "demons and devils," and then takes her own life.

LAST RITES

Sinister clues lead Claire on a twisted trail through the bars and bayous of New Orleans to a bloodstained altar in Paris. Vast, secret, and powerful, it is a world that few enter or escape. And Claire is going in—the devil be damned . . .

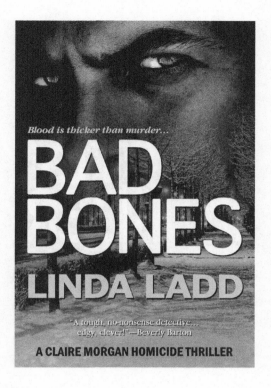

Blood is thicker than murder...

BAD BONES

LINDA LADD

"A tough, no-nonsense detective... edgy, clever!"—Beverly Barton

A CLAIRE MORGAN HOMICIDE THRILLER

BAD OMEN

Homicide detective Claire Morgan has a bad feeling when a man's body is found in a Missouri state park. The crime scene is buried in snow. The corpse is frozen in ice. And nearly every bone has been broken, shattered, or crushed . . .

BAD BLOOD

Claire's suspicions only get worse when the body is thawed and identified. The victim was an ultimate fighter on the cage-match circuit. His wife blames her ex-husband, a Russian mafioso. But Claire knows this is no mob-style execution. This is something worse. Something evil . . .

BAD BONES

Raised from childhood to inflict pain, the killer uses rage as a weapon. Punishing without mercy. Killing without conscience. Upholding a dark family tradition that is so twisted, so powerful, it destroys everything in its path. And Claire is about to meet the family . . .

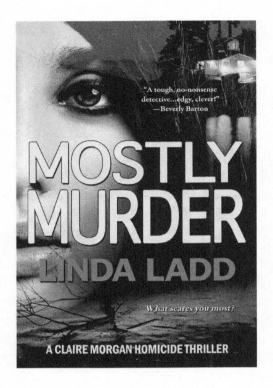

MOSTLY MURDER

LINDA LADD

What scares you most?

A CLAIRE MORGAN HOMICIDE THRILLER

MOSTLY FEAR

She suffered a terrifying coma. She survived a serial killer's obsession. Now homicide detective Claire Morgan hopes to forget the nightmare of her Missouri past in the city of New Orleans. But when a body is discovered near her home, her darkest fears come rushing back . . .

MOSTLY SUPERSTITION

Surrounded by candles and skulls, the victim is bound to an altar like a human sacrifice. More disturbing to Claire is the voodoo doll in the woman's hands. A doll pierced with pins and wearing a picture on its face. A picture of Claire Morgan . . .

MOSTLY MURDER

Claire doesn't believe in voodoo. But she does believe in the power of superstition to warp a person's mind and feed a killer's madness. It is here, in the muddy bayous where it festers, that Claire must face her fear head on—and meet the man who's marked her for death . . .